LENINGRAD DECEPTION

★ BOOK 3 IN THE DECEPTION SERIES ★

RICHARD LYNTTON

MALCHIK
MEDIA

www.richardlynttonbooks.com

Published by Malchik Media

ISBNs: 979-8-9860794-1-7 (eBook)
       979-8-9860794-2-4 (paperback)
       978-1-959755-01-2 (hardback)
       978-1-959755-02-9 (audiobook)

Library of Congress Control Number: 2022908433

First publication/printing.

Cover and map design by Jae Song
Interior design by Gary A. Rosenberg • thebookcouple.com
Editing by Candace Johnson • Change It Up Editing, Inc.

Thank you in advance for reading

LENINGRAD DECEPTION

Look for the audio book — available soon.

✪   ✪   ✪

Enjoy *North Korea Deception* and *Hyde Park Deception*
available now in The Deception Series:
https://www.amazon.com/gp/product/B08LDR8RW2

Follow this link for THE DECEPTION SERIES book trailer:
https://www.youtube.com/watch?v=OUnIz_M63Nk

Visit https://richardlynttonbooks.com/contact
for more information and to join our
FREE Reader Regiment newsletter
(click the black *JOIN NOW* button).

As always, for my wife, Michelle Wenitsky,
and my sons, Stefan and Blake

"General Secretary Gorbachev, if you seek peace,
if you seek prosperity for the Soviet Union
and Eastern Europe, if you seek liberalization:
Come here to this gate! Mr. Gorbachev, open this
gate! Mr. Gorbachev, tear down this wall!"

—RONALD REAGAN, BERLIN, JUNE 12, 1987

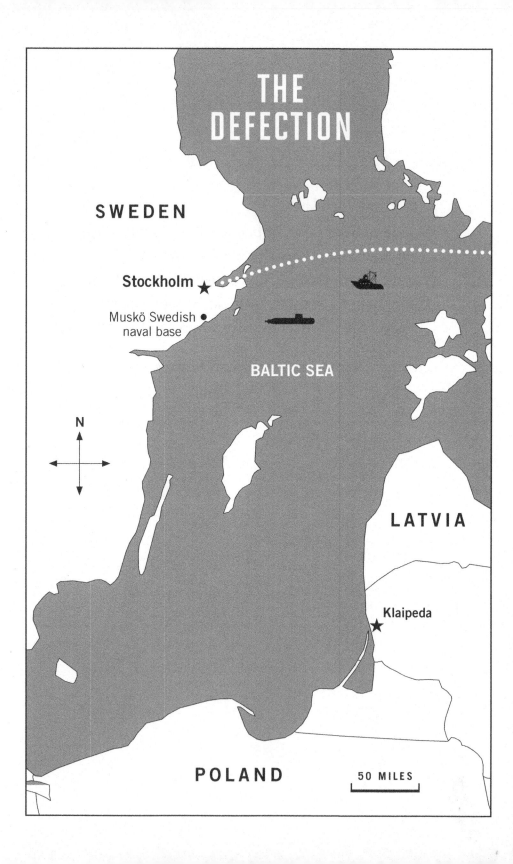

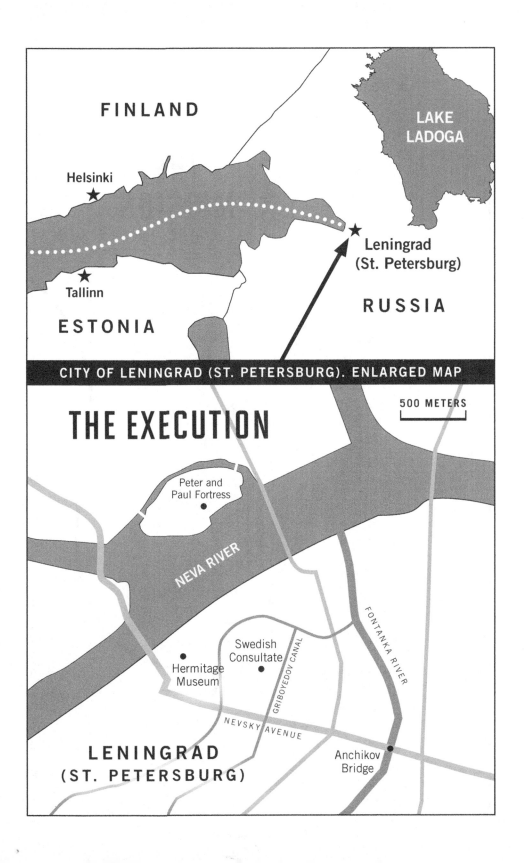

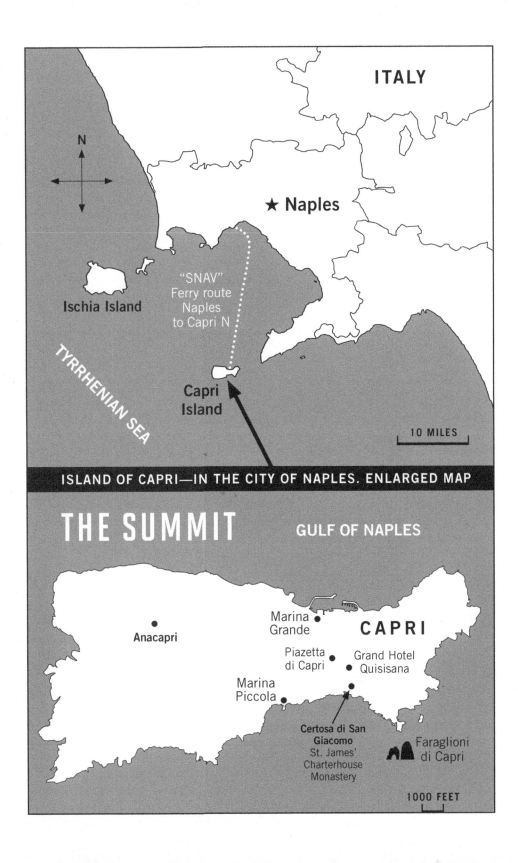

ITALY

N

★ Naples

Ischia Island

"SNAV"
Ferry route
Naples
to Capri N

TYRRHENIAN SEA

Capri
Island

10 MILES

ISLAND OF CAPRI—IN THE CITY OF NAPLES. ENLARGED MAP

THE SUMMIT   GULF OF NAPLES

Marina
Grande   CAPRI

Anacapri

Piazetta
di Capri   Grand Hotel
Quisisana

Marina
Piccola

Certosa di San
Giacomo
St. James'
Charterhouse
Monastery

Faraglioni
di Capri

1000 FEET

FOREWORD

The Berlin Wall was built by the Communist government in East Germany in August 1961 to keep Germans from escaping from Communist-dominated East Berlin into Democratic West Berlin. The twelve-foot concrete wall extended for a hundred miles, surrounding West Berlin, and included electrified fences and guard posts. The wall stood as a stark symbol of the decades-old Cold War between the United States and Soviet Russia, in which the two politically opposed super-powers wrestled for omniscient supremacy, stopping just short of actual warfare. In the author's opinion, it marks the beginning and sews the proverbial seeds for the invasion of Ukraine by Russia on February 24, 2022.

This speech by President Ronald Reagan to the people of West Berlin contains one of the most memorable lines of his presidency. (Abridged).

"Chancellor Kohl, Governing Mayor Diepgen, ladies and gentlemen: Twenty-four years ago, President John F. Kennedy visited Berlin, speaking to the people of this city and the world at the City Hall. Well, since then two other presidents have come, each in his turn, to Berlin. And today I, myself, make my second visit to your city.

"Behind me stands a wall that encircles the free sectors of this city, part of a vast system of barriers that divides the entire continent of Europe. From the Baltic, south, those barriers cut across Germany in a gash of barbed wire, concrete, dog runs, and guard towers. Farther south, there may be no visible, no obvious wall. But there remain armed guards and checkpoints all the same—still a restriction on the right to travel, still an instrument to impose upon ordinary men and women the will of a totalitarian state. Yet it is here in Berlin where the wall emerges most clearly; here, cutting across your city, where the news photo and the television screen have imprinted this brutal division of a continent upon the mind of the world. Standing before the Brandenburg Gate, every man is a German, separated from his fellow men. Every man is a Berliner, forced to look upon a scar.

"President von Weizsäcker has said, 'The German question is open as long as the Brandenburg Gate is closed.' Today I say: As long as the gate is closed, as long as this scar of a wall is permitted to stand, it is not the German question alone that remains open, but the question of freedom for all mankind. From devastation, from utter ruin, you Berliners have, in freedom, rebuilt a city that once again ranks as one of the greatest on earth.

"In the 1950s, Khrushchev predicted: 'We will bury you.' But in the West today, we see a free world that has achieved a level of prosperity and well-being unprecedented in all human history. In the Communist world, we see failure, technological backwardness, declining standards of health, even want of the most basic kind—too little food. Even today, the Soviet Union still cannot feed itself. After these four decades, then, there stands before the entire world one great and inescapable conclusion: Freedom leads to prosperity. Freedom replaces the ancient hatreds among the nations with comity and peace. Freedom is the victor.

"And now the Soviets themselves may, in a limited way, be coming to understand the importance of freedom. We hear much from Moscow about a new policy of reform and openness. Some political prisoners have been released. Certain foreign news broadcasts are no longer being jammed. Some economic enterprises have been permitted to operate with greater freedom from state control.

"Are these the beginnings of profound changes in the Soviet state? Or are they token gestures, intended to raise false hopes in the West, or to strengthen the Soviet system without changing it? We welcome change and openness; for we believe that freedom and security go together, that the advance of human liberty can only strengthen the cause of world peace. There is one sign the Soviets can make that would be unmistakable, that would advance dramatically the cause of freedom and peace.

"General Secretary Gorbachev, if you seek peace, if you seek prosperity for the Soviet Union and Eastern Europe, if you seek liberalization: Come here to this gate! Mr. Gorbachev, open this gate! Mr. Gorbachev, tear down this wall!

Beginning ten years ago, the Soviets challenged the Western alliance with a grave new threat, hundreds of new and more deadly SS-20 nuclear missiles, capable of striking every capital in Europe. The Western alliance responded by committing itself to a counter-deployment unless the Soviets agreed to negotiate a better solution; namely, the elimination of such weapons on both sides. For many months, the Soviets refused to bargain in earnestness. As the alliance, in turn, prepared to go forward with its counter-deployment, there were difficult days—days of protests like those during my 1982 visit to this city—and the Soviets later walked away from the table.

"While we pursue these arms reductions, I pledge to you that we will maintain the capacity to deter Soviet aggression at any level at which it might occur. And in cooperation with many of our allies, the United States is pursuing the Strategic Defense Initiative—research to base deterrence not on the threat of offensive retaliation, but on defenses that truly defend; on systems, in short, that will not target populations, but shield them. By these means we seek to increase the safety of Europe and all the world. But we must remember a crucial fact: East and West do not mistrust each other because we are armed; we are armed because we mistrust each other. And our differences are not about weapons but about liberty. When President Kennedy spoke at the City Hall those twenty-four years ago, freedom was encircled, Berlin was under siege. And today, despite all the pressures upon this city, Berlin stands secure in its liberty. And freedom itself is transforming the globe.

"In Europe, only one nation and those it controls refuse to join the community of freedom. Yet in this age of redoubled economic growth, of information and innovation, the Soviet Union faces a choice: It must make fundamental changes, or it will become obsolete.

"And I invite Mr. Gorbachev: Let us work to bring the eastern and western parts of the city closer together, so that all the inhabitants of all Berlin can enjoy the benefits that come with life in one of the great cities of the world.

"Thank you and God bless you all."
President Ronald Reagan—June 12, 1987

Postscript

Two years later, in November 1989, East Germans opened the wall, allowing East Germans to travel freely to West Berlin. Families that had been separated for decades were finally reunited again. The wall was completely torn down by the end of 1990 upon the collapse of Communism in Eastern Europe and in Soviet Russia itself, marking the end of the Cold War era. Or so we thought ... until February 24, 2022.

PROLOGUE

August 26, 1989 ~ Island of Capri, Italy

It was a beautiful day on the island of Capri ... wasn't it always? He might have thought otherwise had he known about the murder about to take place a few hundred yards away up the stone steps on Via Mulo (pedestrians only) that crisscrossed the steep, hairpin-bend road, Via Marina Piccola. Both streets lead up to Capri town center.

The sun did its very best, and he couldn't imagine Capri without it. Perhaps it was because Vincenzo Alfonso had never set foot on the luxury island during winter months when even the ferries and island-hopping boats were sometimes unable to make the short journey from Naples to Marina Grande because of treacherous waters and winter storms. Vincenzo Alfonso wasn't one to sunbathe, but that didn't mean he couldn't enjoy God's heat on his widow's peak forehead and the warm, salt-scented air wafting off the Tyrrhenian Sea in the Campanian Archipelago.

He reached the bottom of the never-ending steps that he had attempted to count—for fun—but gave up halfway down. The descent on foot to Marina Piccola was easy—but he decided to take the local Capri transport authority bus, or even treat himself to an open-top taxi to get back up to Capri town that sat majestically—almost medieval-looking—atop the island.

His cassock was a problem ... his pet peeve. He couldn't exactly strip off and reveal his puny chest—covered with only a smattering of curly black hairs—and his white T-shirt and lavender-colored boxer briefs. On reflection, none of the day-trippers and families, local and tourist alike, would give two chalices if he stripped down to his underwear. Most of them, apart from the waiters and bar staff on the beach, were wearing far less for all the world to see. The tourists—just like in "Mad Dogs and Englishmen," his favorite Noel Coward song—were busy soaking up rays in the midday sun, determined to get their money's worth.

Vincenzo sat on the wall outside the small, white Chiesa di Sant'Andrea—*Saint Andrew's Church*—built for local fishermen in 1900. He was disappointed he did not have time to enter for spiritual nourishment, not to mention a cooldown. In the high heat of summer, one of his secret habits during official Vatican trips was to dip into a quiet local church, enter the confessional, take off his cassock, and sit in peace and tranquility. Not only was it a chance to sit and pray, but he considered this his way of getting his own back on the archaic dress code he found profoundly unfair, given that nearly every other profession in the modern world—except the military, perhaps—seemed to have adapted to contemporary fashion and today's more frequent European heat waves.

"Buongiorno," said a young boy who flip-flopped past him with a large yellow Lilo—inflatable mattress—that was so tightly inflated it looked set to burst. The boy's parents were close behind and smiled, seemingly thankful their ten-year-old had shown respect for one of God's servants.

"Buongiorno," replied Vincenzo with one of his best godly smiles, perfected in the mirror over the years. That was one of the perks of his trade, so to speak. People he had never seen or known before, people he would probably never see or hear of again, nearly always smiled ... *at him.* Ever since he had joined the priesthood—first as a Jesuit priest and then more recently as one of the most senior advisers to Pope Karl himself—humanity at large smiled at him every day.

Vincenzo eyed the orange and white awning of Ristorante Marina Piccola and wondered if the carbonara was good. It was an Italian cliché, but it was still his favorite dish. He might stop at the restaurant after his mysterious meeting, which was about to take place on a luxury yacht anchored close to shore. But then again, he was sure the Russians would offer him a bite to eat. He might even allow himself a shot of vodka, although that was strictly against Vatican rules. But if he couldn't break the rules on a boat in the Tyrrhenian Sea, when could he? *Second thoughts … Forgive me, father. You are always looking out for me.*

The priest leaned back slightly, straightened his legs and crossed them, folded his arms, lowered his eyelids, and allowed the gentle sea breeze to stroke his face. God's hand, he thought. The waves in the near distance crashed at the shore and muffled the jovial shrieks and cries that might otherwise have spoiled the moment. Vincenzo was good at being in the moment. That, he had learned, was another perk of his spiritual vocation.

Oleg Stepanovich Pugachev had spent two days casing the joint, as the Americans would say. Most of his KGB colleagues and brethren would never have chosen this location for an execution, but Oleg was no ordinary field officer. He was determined—literally—to rewrite the KGB playbook one day. And in some ways, he had already begun the first draft. Some of their Soviet espionage methods and practices were so absurdly antiquated and impractical, he lamented often. It was as if Lenin himself was still in charge. *This* operation was a simple delete-and-insert, he called it, almost as simple as if he was tapping away on his clunky computer keyboard in his soulless KGB office back home in Moscow and had misspelled a word. *Tap-delete-insert.*

Shoot the target, throw him over the wall into the undergrowth, and insert myself into the operation.

The operation that, at least for Oleg, meant the start of Cold

War 2.0, when so many others had their disloyal and despicable hearts already set on the end of Cold War 1.0. This would be an utter travesty of geopolitics and modern history. His loyalty to the motherland and depth of Soviet philosophical and intellectual belief in his country was unquestionable. Oleg was clear about where he stood on these matters. But many of his Soviet comrades seemed ambivalent.

I have work to do.

Oleg had chosen this section of the steps because of its scenic beauty—he wanted his target to be off guard, never dreaming—as the man took in the Campanian Archipelago's sparkling, turquoise canvas—that this would be his final moment. During the day, the chances of passersby on this section of the steps were minuscule. Oleg had surveilled and observed over the past two days. Even if someone were to stumble across him as he pulled the trigger on his target, one more hit would be a blip in the big-picture future and well-being of the motherland he dreamed of.

It was true, he conceded, Capri was an exquisitely beautiful island. The sea's velvet hue of deep blue-green reminded him of Yalta on the Black Sea, where he promised himself he would one day build his own luxury villa when (not if) all went according to life's plan. But this business trip was no sightseeing tour, and he would command life to pan out as he saw fit. For Oleg, there was no God's plan. Life was what *he* would make of it.

At 2:21 pm, the local Capri-Marina Piccola bus stopped at the bus stop above his location on the stone steps. The Russian diplomat got off and descended the last section of steps before reaching Marina Piccola as per Oleg's instructions. Oleg hated to liquidate one of his own—such a waste—but some things were more important than others in this world. Oleg had chosen this section of the twisting, winding steps because it provided

a good line of sight in both directions, and the wall on the west side was less than six feet high. He had researched the Russian diplomat's weight and height and was confident that, using his judo-like strength, he would be able to shoot Arkady Gregorovich, pick him up, and manhandle him over the wall into the undergrowth of this local Marina Piccola vineyard.

Oleg stood under a lemon tree whose branches dipped over the wall of the garden it belonged to. Arkady's guard would be down. He was a harmless Soviet embassy cultural diplomat and had no connection to the security services, and this was a mid-level "cultural exchange" meeting with the Vatican representative, no less. The weather was perfect, and Arkady was sure to have helped himself to a hearty breakfast he knew the Russian embassy's expense account could handle.

"Hello, comrade," Oleg said in Russian. "Thank you for coming and for following my instructions. You will go far in our Communist universe of brotherhood and unity." He smiled his best weasel smile—teeth visible, corners of his mouth turned upward—but Oleg's eyes were blank. He showed zero emotion, so much so that no one, not even his masters at the Lubyanka, was able to assess what he was really thinking most of the time. Many of his superior officers, he had been told, thought this was a good thing.

Arkady's eyes widened. "Oleg Stepanovich?" he said, nearly choking with surprise. "What are you doing here?"

Arkady did not smile, and he registered instantly that Oleg's presence was not part of the plan. "I don't understand, Oleg Stepanovich. I saw you in Leningrad."

"Change of plan. Didn't they tell you?" As he drew his Makarov with a silencer, Oleg said, "I promise to file a report."

One shot to the forehead was all he needed. After Oleg pulled the trigger, Arkady's straw hat blew off and tumbled down the steps as he crumpled to the ground. The Ray-Bans he'd spent a month's salary on at Rome airport crunched as his head hit the ground. As though part of his daily exercise routine, Oleg squatted and lifted Arkady in one slick motion like a world-champion weightlifter. He pushed Arkady Gregorovich up the wall scraping the man's face and torso against the mottled texture of the cement. There was a tiny trail of blood, but not enough that anyone would notice. Arkady's head, the heaviest part of his body, dipped over the top of the wall and, as planned, made it easy for Oleg to push the Russian diplomat's legs and feet up and over. Oleg heard a thud as the body landed in the undergrowth on the other side.

Done.

The location of the vineyard meant that there were no houses close by that might contain witnesses. No one had seen anything. It would take at least a few days for anyone to discover the body. It would probably be the smell of a rotting corpse in the summer heat that would attract attention first, he thought.

He was wrong.

"Buongiorno!" said a child's voice.

The voice came from the lower side of the steps. What had the boy seen? Oleg had not expected any foot traffic from the lower direction that led up from the sea. No one was leaving the beach at this time except—

He saw a ten-year-old boy with a large yellow Lilo coming up from the beach—probably heading back to a vacation apartment. "Yop tvayou matz—" *Fuck it.*

"Buongiorno," said the boy.

"Buongiorno," replied Oleg in Italian. "How are you, young man?"

"I'm good." The boy squinted as he looked up toward Oleg, blinded by the piercingly blue sky above him.

"That's good to hear." Pointing at the yellow inflatable, he said in Italian, "That's my favorite color."

The boy glanced down, proud of his swimming aid. Oleg pointed the Makarov at the boy's head and pulled the trigger.

PART 1

CHAPTER ONE

Same day ~ Friedrichstraße, Berlin

Jack Steele was on leave, making the most of his freedom. Rude not to. He was about to finish his six-month officer training course at the Royal Military Academy, Sandhurst, in Camberley, Surrey. He had studied Russian at the Maurice Thorez Institute of Foreign Languages in Moscow and was looking forward to using his languages—Russian, German, and French—in the British army. They had told him his languages would be useful. But for now, he was a bog-standard young Cavalry officer. He would graduate Sandhurst, spend some time at his regiment, and then return to the Royal Armored Corps training center in Bovington, Dorset. There, he would learn to become a tank commander—tactics, maintenance, ammunitions, including armored piercing and high explosives, gunnery school, history of warfare, and more. They would even teach him how to change a tank track and fix the engine. Then he would spend a few years in Germany and perhaps later be chosen for ceremonial mounted duties in London, one of the best "jollies" in the British army. He might even get to the bottom of the amusing rumor that some of the cavalrymen—soldiers, not officers—preferred to get their hair cut in the Harrods hair salon rather than waste time sitting in the queue of the regimental barbershop at Knightsbridge Barracks.

But for now, he was not yet a fully fledged commissioned officer in the British army, and he would enjoy the last few days on leave before he returned to the academy for the final exercise on the Sandhurst training area, followed by the passing-out parade attended by family and friends that even the prime minister herself would take the salute for.

Steele stared out of the window as his train trundled through East and West Berlin. The U-Bahn lines passed in and out of both sectors, clinically separated by the wall. It was night and day. Whatever the weather, East Berlin and East Germany looked drab and gray and contrasted sharply with the razzmatazz of commercial West Berlin. He had always wanted to see the wall, "die Mauer," for himself and visit the Checkpoint Charlie Museum.

He had spent a few days relaxing in the South of France with Simone, his French girlfriend, whom he'd met in London. Steele knew deep down that it was time to end their relationship, especially as he would be spending the next few years in BAOR (British Army of the Rhine) in Germany. If he was honest, he liked the idea of having a *German* girlfriend. The best way to learn a language is "horizontally," a visiting BBC producer to Exeter University had once said during a lecture on his Russian documentary series called *Comrades.*

This trip to Berlin would be fleeting. And technically, he would have to report it to British security services. Any travel behind the Iron Curtain had to be reported, even though he would probably not encounter any East German nationals in West Berlin. The Iron Curtain? The phrase itself was intriguing—there was an entire world behind this "Iron Curtain." And Steele had been privileged to experience it during his year of study abroad in Russia.

He exited the U-Bahn at Friedrichstraße and made the short walk to the Checkpoint Charlie Museum. Even though he had spent a year in Moscow, Jack Steele had never seen "die Mauer"—the physical and symbolic barrier between East and West. Checkpoint Charlie (or "Checkpoint C") was named after the letter "C" in the British army phonetic alphabet—Alpha,

Bravo, Charlie, Delta, and so on. As Steele made his way to Haus am Checkpoint Charlie, he caught sight of the large concrete wall that meandered in both directions.

An old man was shuffling along, leading his dog who didn't want to be led. "Which way to the museum, please?" Steele asked in German.

"Straight on," replied the man. "Just keep going, unless they shoot you first."

"Danke schön," he replied. *Thank you.* He wasn't sure if the man was joking.

It wasn't just the wall that intrigued Steele. Minefields, watchtowers with mirrored glass, and an electric fence also seemed unfathomable in this urban setting. *How could it be? thought Steele. How could the Russians construct these monstrous barriers and use such barbaric methods to punish those who fled?* He knew and loved the Russians—he had spent a year studying the language in Moscow. He went to concerts, sang folk songs, and recited Pushkin and Dostoevsky with friends. But this wall was a vicious symbol of inhumanity.

Steele approached the museum cashier. "How long are you open for?" he asked in German. It was already late afternoon.

"We close in one hour," the old lady replied. "You have time. Enjoy the museum."

"Great. Thank you," he said.

Steele took his ticket and entered the museum. At first, there didn't seem to be much there. He had traveled across Europe to visit this place and was initially disappointed. There were giant black-and-white photographs and posters, lists of people and their stories about daring escapes and attempted escapes over the wall. Within minutes, he became engrossed in those stories. People had hidden in cars, made hot-air balloon flights, and dug tunnels between 1961 and present-day, just to make their escape from Moscow's tentacles and all that she stood for. There was even an exhibit of an old pale-blue VW Beatle, inside of which someone had hidden under a fake engine to make their escape.

Then he saw her behind the gift counter. Tall, with long, dark hair that was almost black, a thin body, small breasts, and long legs. She wore minimal makeup, perhaps a dash of rouge. She looked like an Olympic 400M hurdler.

There was an instant attraction on his part. *Forget it,* he told himself. *You haven't traveled all this way to seduce a museum worker you've never met. And you haven't split up with Simone yet. Have some scruples, man.*

The woman behind the counter glanced in his direction, and they locked eyes for a moment. He might have been wrong, but he thought he caught a glimpse of a smile. Then she continued serving museum customers.

Again he told himself he had better things to do than to flirt with a West German older woman—she was definitely ten to fifteen years older than him. He estimated around thirty-five. He continued to walk around the museum and read more history about the wall and was amazed by more daring escapes and methods people had used to penetrate the Iron Curtain. But on the other hand, this woman was certainly attractive, and he had no plans for the evening.

Steele approached the gift counter, determined not to make it too obvious that he was looking for more than a Berlin postcard. He had studied German as well as Russian and French and reasoned it might be nice to spend the evening with an attractive German local.

"Do you have maps of the wall?" he asked.

"Of course," replied the woman. "Falk Plan Berlin has a special section. I have this one myself."

"I have Falk Plan Paris. I love it."

The handful of customers dissipated, and without looking at the clock, Steele reckoned there were only now a few minutes left until closing time.

"What's your name," the woman asked in German.

"Jack Steele," he replied. "Yours?"

"Claudia Rohweder." She smiled. "You are from England?"

"Is my accent so terrible?"

"No. Your German is excellent. But I work at this museum—I get a lot of practice, and I have a good ear for accents." Steele nodded. He sifted through some postcards and sensed her looking at him longer than normal. *I'm only in Berlin for twenty-four hours,* he thought. *Have I struck gold already?*

He handed her the Berlin Falk Plan special edition and some postcards. "How long have you worked at the museum?"

"I'm originally from East Berlin. I have one parent on each side."

"Divorced?"

"Technically, no. My mother was able to escape, but my father changed his name and disappeared into the priesthood many years ago. I have no contact with him."

"I'm sorry."

"No need. They are happy like this. If they had stayed together, I think they would have been divorced by now."

"Interesting."

"That will be seven Mark."

Steele reminded himself that he would have to report any contact with this woman to the British Army Intelligence Corps. *Can I be bothered? What if I don't report it?* Then he thought, *You're way ahead of yourself—it's not like she's going to say yes.*

"Are you doing anything after work?" he asked.

Claudia smiled. "Not tonight."

"I'm only here for one night. It would be great to have a drink with a real Berliner."

"It would be great to have a drink with a charming Englishman."

Steele smiled. "Any suggestions?"

"Give me thirty minutes. Meet me at the Charlie Stube two blocks that way." She pointed toward the exit.

"Charlie Stube?"

"Yes, it's a cheap and cheerful local bar—echt berlinerisch." *Typical Berlin.*

Steele nodded and gave his most charming smile. "Great. See you in a bit," he said, pocketing his change and putting away his purchases.

He exited the museum and turned right toward the Charlie Stube as directed. Steele felt awkward and a little guilty that he would have to give this woman's name to British intelligence, but those were the rules. During his year in Moscow, he had been allowed to have friends and even girlfriends—"fraternize with the locals," the army would say—as long as he reported all contacts.

Now, with two days left on leave and less than two weeks before he was commissioned into the British army proper, he decided he would let things roll tonight. Claudia was much older than him, but that excited him just as much as her slender figure. He might just "forget" to report whatever happened or didn't happen tonight.

Claudia grabbed her black leather jacket, but it was still too warm to wear it even at six o'clock in the evening. She turned left outside the museum and walked three blocks south down Friedrichstraße. "Naïve," she said to herself in German. "He's so naïve." Reaching the third floor of her apartment building, she entered her flat and walked straight to her bedroom. She picked up the telephone and dialed a local number in East Berlin.

"Hallo?" she began in Russian.

"Hello, Sunshine," the voice replied in a mix of Russian and German. "How's work? How is your mother?"

"Work is great," she replied. "Mutter is good too."

"When are you coming to visit?" the man asked.

"Soon."

"Will you keep the job?"

"Yes, it's *perfect*."

"I am happy to hear this. Keep me posted." The man ended the call.

Claudia smiled and quickly changed from her museum clothes into something more comfortable … and revealing. Her plan was on track. She would make Oleg Stepanovich Pugachev proud of her.

CHAPTER TWO

Capri, Italy

S o far, so good. Vincenzo was delighted that his Russian diplomat rendezvous had arrived on time at the agreed meeting point in front of the church. Oleg Stepanovich, the man had called himself. He had proffered regrets from Arkady Gregorovich, the original Russian embassy liaison officer and cultural attaché. No matter. Oleg spoke good English. They would use English as their lingua franca.

They walked past the public beach area and made their way through a private beach club to a docking point for launches and shuttles to private yachts. It took ten minutes to reach the vessel, and Vincenzo enjoyed the short ride with the gentle *bump-bump-bump* of the bow hitting the waves—the breeze mixed with spray keeping him cool. Oleg made minimal conversation and eye contact.

The young captain of the boat was Italian (not Russian) and offered them a warm greeting when they came aboard. Vincenzo admired the young man's good looks and deep, dark tan. *If only I could stay awhile,* he mused. "I am Vincenzo," he shouted in Italian above the waves and noise of the motor.

"I am Ricardo," replied the captain. "Nice to meet you. Where are you from?"

"Vatican City." Vincenzo liked to play the Vatican card occasionally, just to get a reaction—or, at least, a nonplussed reaction. Not everyone was impressed to meet a priest from the Vatican.

"It's my lucky day," said Ricardo. "I like to know our good Lord is keeping an eye on me."

If the good Lord's not keeping an eye, I am certainly happy to, Vincenzo thought. Instead, he said, "God bless you."

Vincenzo held the handrail as the motor launch pulled up alongside a large modern yacht. *The Russians are richer than I imagined,* Vincenzo thought.

"Please," said Oleg, gesturing for the Italian to climb aboard.

Vincenzo heard movement in the bowels of the boat, but no one came up to introduce themselves. A fine spread of food and drink had been left for them—orange juice, salami and prosciutto, cheese, sparkling wine and vodka in separate ice buckets, and, of course, there was red and black caviar.

"Please ..." Oleg began. "Have a seat."

Vincenzo lifted his cassock a few inches and sat down on the white leather seats under a turquoise awning. "Thank you."

Oleg said, "You are probably wondering why we have invited you here."

"I am curious. But I allow my masters to guide me. Both of them."

"Both of them?"

"Pope Karl and the good Lord himself." Vincenzo pointed northward toward Rome and then to the sky.

"I understand. Of course." Oleg poured himself some Pellegrino sparkling water and placed his index finger on the bottle of sparkling wine for Vincenzo.

Vincenzo said, "Water, please."

Oleg nodded toward the hors d'oeuvres and poured. "Please help yourself. Your journey has given you an appetite, I am certain."

Vincenzo made himself a prosciutto ciabatta slice.

Oleg waited for his guest to finish a couple of mouthfuls. Then he said, "We understand your ... master is willing to help us bring peace to the world?"

"Pope Karl wishes to facilitate the best possible atmosphere so that we can bring an end to the Cold War. He senses the time is right."

"Let me ask you something," continued Oleg.

"Prego." *Please.*

"Do you trust Pope Karl?"

"Of course. Why would I not trust His Holiness?"

"Rumors."

"What rumors?"

"Never mind."

Oleg guzzled half a glass of freshly squeezed lemon juice. "We appreciate you contacting us. And the reason we invited you here is important for all our sakes. We must learn to trust each other and begin … shall we say … a dialogue. I like to meet my friends face-to-face."

"Please, ask whatever you need. Pope Karl is ready to help his flock on both sides of the Iron Curtain."

Vincenzo had been given clear instructions. Pope Karl, born in Leipzig, had grown up within the Communist system—he had dreamed of this moment when perhaps, just perhaps, the world could find a way to finally tear down the Iron Curtain, just as the American president had demanded two years ago. Ever since he had heard those words—"Mr. Leontev, open this gate! Mr. Leontev, tear down this wall!"—Pope Karl had prayed for guidance and inspiration to find a way to bring the two sides together and bring an end to the Cold War. He had lobbied clergy, academics, politicians, union leaders, and journalists in his homeland. He had exerted pressure on the Communist Party and its apparatchiks to make the world ready for a new era of détente, peace, and harmony between East and West. This all made perfect sense to Vincenzo. And now, finally, he was here to give credence to his master's plan—in complete secrecy, of course. The pope could not be seen to be meddling in geopolitical matters and world politics. That wasn't their purpose or holy remit.

"Can you be more specific?" Oleg smiled—mouth, no eyes.

"We are at your service."

"What does this mean?"

"It means that His Holiness will use his influence with Western powers to bring about a new era."

Oleg nodded. "This is wonderful news. I express eternal gratitude on behalf of the Soviet leadership."

"Pope Karl wishes to help his people, his children, from all countries, cultures, and political persuasions."

"What does he suggest?"

Vincenzo replied eagerly, "We think a peace summit with the American president is the next step."

"And how do we persuade His Highness, Mr. Kuvboy?"

"*Kuvboy?*"

Oleg said, "I am sorry for my English. *Cow*-boy."

"The beloved American movie-star president."

"Do you have new information about his intentions?"

Vincenzo replied, "Let me say that we sincerely believe he will be open to a new world order if you agree to certain levels of global security. In your own interests, of course."

"He is a bellicose man. He shows great bravado and much aggression toward the Soviet Union. Passivno-agressivni. How do you say it in English? *Passive-aggressive?* It is hard for us to believe he truly wants peace."

Vincenzo smiled. "I think we all agree that peace is better than war. Pope Karl will do his best—his very best—to make this peace summit as long as you are serious. Pope Karl is proud of his Germanic and Eastern European roots."

Oleg stared at Vincenzo for a few moments. Then he said, "I am pleased we had a chance to meet in person. *Trust* is probably the most important consideration between us, you understand? It is not just Russia but the future of the entire Soviet Union that is at stake. It is imperative that this process is genuine for Mr. Kuvboy."

Vincenzo smiled. "Yes, he is a good actor. I have enjoyed many of his movies. But we believe this initiative is possible."

Oleg said, "I do not care about his movies. I only care about his political intentions. That is why we wanted to meet you in person. There can be no mistakes. No misunderstandings."

"Mistakes?"

"If you are going to help us, there can be no mistakes. Vatican or no Vatican, I will defend my country to the end. If you betray us, I will hold you personally responsible."

Vincenzo had just guzzled a glass of San Pellegrino, but now he coughed, almost spluttered, at Oleg's unexpected aggression. Vincenzo said, "Please do not worry. His Holiness understands this is not a game."

They sat for a few moments in silence. Vincenzo always found silence to be the answer to many problems—large and small.

"Do you believe in our Lord?"

"Do I believe in *your* Lord? Or *a* Lord?"

Vincenzo waited for a smile that did not come. He wasn't sure if this was Oleg's attempt at levity. Vincenzo said, "Personally, I do not make a distinction."

"Why do you ask?"

Vincenzo said, "We would *also* like to trust our partners in peace."

"And if I am not a 'believer,' you do not trust me?"

"Shall we say it would make things run more smoothly upstairs?" Vincenzo gestured skyward.

Oleg nodded slowly. "Can I persuade you to try some?" He leaned forward and picked up a bottle of Stolichnaya vodka from the ice bucket. "Tradition. *When in Capri …*"

Vincenzo smiled and said, "I thought you would never ask."

Oleg poured the syrupy vodka. Vincenzo wasn't one to break the rules—often—but as Oleg had said, When in Capri …

"A toast to our dear leaders—Mikhail Pavlovich and Pope Karl …"

Both men emptied their glasses, and Vincenzo helped himself to some caviar—he preferred black to red—that served as a welcome chaser to the ice-cold vodka.

Oleg concluded the meeting. "I thank you for coming all this way. You understand why I prefer to meet in person?"

"Of course. It was His Holiness's wish also."

"I want you to know that our leader, Mikhail Pavlovich Leontev, is a great man. A true visionary. You will not be disappointed."

"God bless Mikhail Pavolich."

"Spaciba." *Thank you.*

On the return ride back to Marina Piccola, Vincenzo greeted Ricardo but this time did not feel the need to flirt with the handsome boat captain. He had more important matters to reflect upon. He felt as though he had done God's work today. Pope Karl would be proud. It was an audacious plan—so many pieces to fit together and so many ways to fail. But wasn't that the very essence of God's work at any given moment?

He slid along the bench that ran along the side of the motor launch toward the bow, again allowing the water's fine spray to refresh him. It was a sensation he had enjoyed ever since he could remember. He thought about his dear mother, but there was no time to visit her in Sorrento on this visit. He would call her from the railway station in Naples. Perhaps there would be more visits to meet the Russians in Capri? He said a prayer and asked for guidance from the good Lord.

Pope Karl was a great man, an exceptional human being, and he would do everything in his power to fulfill Pope Karl's mission, even if—a powerful thought suddenly crossed his mind—it meant giving up his own life.

Over the sound of the waves and the motor launch engine's purr, Vincenzo realized Ricardo was singing Renato Carosone's famous song "Tu Vuò Fa L'Americano"—*"You Want to*

Be American"—which he found ironic. *There are signs everywhere. Today's meeting was meant to be, and it will lead to great things.*

Vincenzo began humming along to the upbeat, timeless melody ...

Tu vuò fa l'americano!
'mmericano, 'mmericano ...

CHAPTER THREE

Somewhere in East Germany

Night and day. Black and white. Chalk and cheese. The platitudes were insufficient to describe what Steele saw out of the train window as he traveled through the train corridor from Berlin, through the East German countryside—part of the Soviet bloc—to West Germany. Safety, peace ... harmony? *Is the West really so great?* he reflected. In spite of the drab sights and sounds of Moscow and the Russian countryside during his student days, there was a simplicity and uniformity of life behind the Iron Curtain that was comforting in a strange way, harmonious, even.

Last night, Steele had 'gone rogue,' as the British army would say. And he didn't care. Claudia was an amazing woman to encounter in West Berlin. The spontaneous evening of engaging conversation and spectacular sex was unforgettable. *She's probably a spy*, he mused. *Claudia is an East German spy deep undercover and operating out of the Checkpoint Charlie Museum in West Berlin.* That info would keep the Intelligence Corps boys in Bulford Camp, Salisbury, busy for a few days.

Steele smiled. Claudia had explained that her father lived in East Berlin, and her mother had moved to West Berlin many years ago. Steele had found Claudia's story entirely plausible, and he had no reason to suspect any foul play on her part. *We had a harmless encounter,* he concluded.

The door slid open. A young East German border guard with

black hair and a fresh face gave Steele the once-over and seemed to know by osmosis that Steele was a foreigner. "Passport?" she said in English.

"Bitte sehr," Steele replied in German. *Here you go.* He handed his passport over and wondered if the East German authorities had any way of knowing he was about to be a commissioned officer in the British army ... *the enemy?* The guard stamped his passport with a metal stamp that looked much bigger and was certainly much louder than seemed necessary to complete the simple task. She returned Steele's passport, and the door slammed shut as she moved to the next compartment.

As he stared out the window, even the grass looked gray, not to mention every building in every town and hamlet as far as the eye could see. He also missed Russia already. His year abroad spent in Moscow had been the most exhilarating and exciting of his entire life. He had relished the foreigner's freedom, the low cost of living, the beautiful language, the folk music, the parties, and the simple quality of life Russians enjoyed and appreciated with very little in terms of wealth, money, homes, and possessions. Yes, they were ruled with an iron—sometimes ruthless— fist, but it seemed to work.

Now he was returning to Sandhurst—the Royal Military Academy Sandhurst, Camberley. Pastures really were green and pleasant, even in the military training area. One day, he hoped to use his languages—Russian, French, and German. The only problem was that even if he became a military attaché in Moscow, he could never go back to the apartments, dachas, and kitchens of Russian friends where he had enjoyed many hours and days of fun. The next time he returned to Moscow, he would probably be a serving officer in Her Majesty's armed forces, and no ordinary Russian would want to fraternize with him for fear of being reported to the KGB—the Committee for State Security. And for their part, British intelligence would not allow him or any other diplomat or military attaché that level of freedom with the natives.

He began to consider what and how much to tell British security services about this visit to Berlin. Telling them about the trip to his French girlfriend and her parents' house in the ski resort town of Grenoble wasn't a problem. But did he really want to divulge the private details of last night's sensual encounter with a West German woman who might conceivably be an East German spy? Yes, it was in the realm of 007 possibilities, but not inconceivable. Reporting it would be the right thing to do.

Steele observed the layers of barbed wire fencing outside that ran alongside the train tracks. Then the barricades suddenly disappeared like magic. One hour later, he was back in West Germany, and there was color once more. Yes, that was it. The main difference between East and West Germany—the Soviet Union and the West—was simply a matter of color. But perversely, life behind the Iron Curtain was in some ways richer and more colorful.

Then he thought, *Fuck 'em!* Fuck the security services on both sides of the Iron Curtain—the KGB, the GRU, MI6, MI5, SB, HVA, and the CIA, to name but a few. He would keep Claudia to himself—an exciting memory, a jaunt into another world. Unlike his time in Russia, on this occasion, he would respect the intimacy he had shared. *It's not like it's a matter of national security.*

Bulford Camp, Wiltshire, England

Staff Sergeant Jed Wilson stubbed out his twentieth cigarette of the day and whipped off his black-rimmed readers; British army standard issue, he liked to joke. He picked up the receiver and dialed the Ministry of Defense operator. Phillis, his wife, wanted him home for Sunday lunch, but he knew the general also worked on Sundays.

"Sandhurst, please. Commandant's office," he said in his London brogue.

"Connecting you now," the MOD operator replied with a Yorkshire accent.

Major General James Boswell picked up immediately. "Boswell," he said.

"Good afternoon, General," Wilson began. "Staff Sergeant Wilson, Bulford, here."

"Hello, Staff Sergeant. How the devil are you?"

"Never better, General."

"How's the wife?"

"Phillis is chipper, thank you, General. How's your lovely lady?"

"Lovely, just lovely," replied General Boswell. "How can we help today?"

"Yes, General. You have a cadet about to pass out. Lt. Jack Steele?"

"Doesn't ring a bell … let me check."

Seconds later, he said, "Yes, found him. Passing out next week."

"Apparently, he's a Russian speaker. He went to Exeter and spent a year in Moscow before Sandhurst."

"Roger that. I'm listening."

Wilson stubbed out another cigarette. "What's he like?"

"Give me a moment, I'll check his reports and comments. Wait one …"

"Thank you, General."

Wilson lit another cigarette. *Lucky I have my own office,* he thought. He leaned back in his chair and pushed open the window whose frame needed a lick of paint.

"In a word," continued General Boswell. "Average."

"Average?"

"Yes, decidedly average. Nothing stands out. No black marks. Lacking a bit fitness-wise, but otherwise looks like he's stayed gray throughout the course."

"If I may, General, …" Wilson said with hesitation.

"Please, whatever you need."

"He needs to be above 'average' … by next week."

"May I ask why?"

"Sorry, sir. No, you can't."

"Understood, Sergeant. Leave it with me. Anything else?"

"That's all for now, General. See what you can do with Steele. It's important. He needs to raise his game a notch or three. Shall we say 'silver' rather than 'gray'."

"Roger that. Give my best to her indoors."

"Will do, sir. Same to you."

Wilson hung up and took a long drag on his Silk Cut. MI6 must be desperate to want Jack Steele, he thought. "Oh well," he thought. "Ours is not to reason why …"

CHAPTER FOUR

New College, Royal Military Academy Sandhurst

Ten days later, sweat dripping down his face, Jack Steele lunged for the finish line in front of New College Building clocktower.

One of the Sandhurst PTIs held his stopwatch in front of him and shouted, "5.5, 5.6, 5.7, ..." as the cadets crossed the line. They were responsible for giving their own individual battle-fitness test times to the PT staff. It had been two weeks since his final leave in France and Germany, and 2LT Steele soon-to-be was already thinking about his next leave. *Perhaps I'll go back to the Checkpoint Charlie Museum.*

Fitness, small-arms instruction, and military history final tests and exams had all been completed, but there was still the final military exercise. It would be virtually impossible to fail the course at this stage, but Jack Steele's regiment—The Life Guards—would receive an overall mark out of one hundred for the entire course, and Steele wanted it to be good.

To avoid the queue of red-faced, red T-shirted cadets next to the boot scrapers and brushes, Steele kicked his combat boots against the wall to get rid of excess mud before he entered New College. He unbuckled his army-issue webbing filled with green army towels and socks to make it look full. His T-shirt was dark red with sweat, and he was looking forward to his hot shower.

Steele went to his bunk on the first floor, undressed, and

wrapped his green army towel around his waist. As he walked down the corridor, the Amiens Company NCO instructor belted from the end of the corridor, "Don't kick that towel, there's somebody in it!"

Guffaws and chuckles filled the corridor from inside the various bunks as cadets got undressed to take showers.

"Mr. Steele!" the Amiens Company NCO belted.

Steele turned. "Yes, Color Sergeant?" *What now?* he thought. Never a moment's peace in this place.

"Commandant wants to see you, Mr. Steele. ASAP."

"You mean the company commander?" asked Steele.

"No, sir, I mean the commandant. General Boswell wants to see you. Get a move on, sir."

"What's it about, Colour Sergeant?"

"Above my pay grade, Mr. Steele. Just get your fuckin' arse over there."

"Can I take a shower first?"

"No, you fuckin' can't, sir. Now!"

"Yes, Colour Sergeant. On my way."

Steele avoided the puddles of water from other cadets who had already showered and ran back to his room to change back into his PT kit.

★　　★　　★

Five minutes later, Steele jogged up the steps of Old College, entered the majestic building, and turned right toward the Royal Military Academy Sandhurst commandant's office.

The commandant's ADC was expecting him. "Jack Steele?" he asked.

"Yes, sir." Steele was still a few days away from becoming a commissioned officer, so the custom was to address the ADC captain as 'sir'.

"Boss is expecting you."

Steele pulled his feet in, which meant he made a one-two

stamp, then stood to attention. Steele wasn't wearing a beret, so he did not need to salute.

The ADC opened the door and allowed Steele to enter. Steele marched a few steps into the office and, again, pulled his feet in. "At ease, Jack," said General Boswell.

"Thank you, General."

"How's the fitness?" asked General Boswell.

"Err … fine, thank you, General."

"No bullshite, young Steele. From what I see, your fitness is a bag of bollocks."

"Doing my best, sir."

"Do better. Is that understood?"

"Roger that, sir." General Boswell chewed the inside of his bottom lip and stared at Jack. "Frankly, Jack, your best isn't good enough right now."

"Understood, sir."

"And your marksmanship could do with a boost also."

"Understood, sir." *Jesus, I'm a tank commander,* Steele thought. *I have plenty of time to practice marksmanship during tank commander's training at Bovington Camp.*

"I'll say this once," said General Boswell. "You've got your final exercise coming up. Sort it out. Raise your game. Do I make myself clear?"

"Yes, sir. Crystal clear, sir."

"If you don't raise your game, I'll fail you. Is that understood?"

Steele nodded.

"Carry on."

Steele took one step back, pulled his feet in, and made a sharp about-turn.

He sprinted back to New College and chastised himself for his lackluster performance. He vowed to crush his final exercise and pass with flying colors if it killed him. Only one thing puzzled him. *I've managed to stay 'gray' for the entire course. Why the sudden interest in yours truly?*

CHAPTER FIVE

Leningrad, USSR

The next day, Maria Ivanovich Pushkin, known to her family and friends as Masha, was running late. As usual, she had spent too much time staring out the window eastward toward the Neva River that led to the Gulf of Finland and, if she allowed her mind's eye to keep going, to Stockholm. From what she could see from picture books of other countries, Leningrad was one of the most beautiful cities in the world. But it was a prison. At least for her. Many would consider Masha's position in Soviet society that of a spoiled brat; she had everything most young Soviet teenagers could only dream about—a Sony Walkman, a desktop computer, access to black-market Western music and artists through her father's contacts with other Communist Party apparatchiks and foreign diplomats. Astrid, her Swedish pen pal, also sent her the latest Western music CDs in padded envelopes.

She was about to start her diploma course in linguistics at the Leningrad Linguistic Institute but still had not forgiven her father—and mother, for that matter—for missing her high school graduation from Leningrad School No. 207. Her father was an important man, but that was no excuse. Her mother was also a highly accomplished professor in her zoological field. She worked at the famous Zoological Institute of the Soviet Academy of Sciences. Her office overlooked the Neva River, too, but in the direction of Leningrad's world-renown Hermitage Museum.

At 7:45 am, Masha left the apartment, but before she could close the door, her father said, "Wait a minute, I'll walk downstairs with you. I can drop you at the institute."

"No. I'm late, Papa, and besides, I am not talking to you. Nothing has changed. I still hate you."

"This is ridiculous," said Masha's mother, Tatyana Borisovich Pushkin, exiting the kitchen and untying her apron. She was also about to leave for her short walk to work. "How long can you hold a grudge? You are immature. You're a college student now, for heaven's sake."

"Graduating high school was the most important day of my life, and *neither* of you was there to share it. It was embarrassing. You *both* broke your promise, and I will never forgive you. Your jobs, your *'professions,'* have always been more important than me." She glared at her parents one after the other. "I don't need your transport, and I don't need your privileges. I wish I could leave this disgusting country. I am going to live in Sweden as soon as I am old enough to get a job abroad. Astrid is going to help me. Her father is an important man."

Tatyana scoffed. "You'll be lucky to graduate from the institute if you keep this up. And it will be impossible to leave the motherland because of your father's position."

"I don't care about his *position*. And I *will* graduate. But I am not working in your stupid institute full of stuffed animals. I have my own life and my own dreams."

"But your father and I have discussed—"

"I don't care what you discussed!" Masha slammed the door and skipped down the stairs to the vestibule. As soon as she exited her building and saw the River Neva at the end of her street, her mood lifted. She would write a letter to Astrid as soon as she got to the institute cafeteria and tell her about her latest hopes, dreams, and family conflict. Astrid would write back within the week. Their letters came via the Swedish embassy diplomatic pouch and were much quicker than regular post from Russia to Sweden.

"Masha!" She heard her father's voice two floors above her as she descended the four flights of stairs. She ignored her father's call, slammed the front door, slung her bag across her, and was about to set off before she stopped in her tracks.

"Good morning, Masha," said a man in naval uniform sitting in a black Lada Zhiguli estate car in front of their building. Not the most prestigious military transport, but it was still considered an honor to be driven in the larger version rather than the regular saloon. "How's life, young woman?"

"Good morning, Sergei Mikhailovich," replied Masha, not wishing to engage further. She had no argument with her father's driver, but she certainly didn't want to allow her father to catch up and insist on giving her a ride to the institute a few streets away.

Masha took off on foot. *I hate my father and I hate his job and I hate his privileges. One day, I will leave the motherland and never come back.* Her parents honestly believed Masha had no idea what her father did. It was supposed to be a secret. She wasn't stupid, and she knew exactly what he did. Let him and his driver go straight to their destination at the regional Main Intelligence Directorate (GRU). Chort s'nimi. *The devil take him.* I want nothing to do with him or his state security job.

Sandhurst Training Area, Surrey

"Take cover!" Steele heard someone in his platoon shouting in the distance.

But it was too late. Steele had not seen them coming. Two Gurkha soldiers had swooped out of nowhere, placed a hood over Steele's head, tied his hands behind his back, and taken his weapon. Ten minutes later, he was standing on tiptoes, stark naked, with a bungee cord stretching from his right nostril to a branch in the tree a few feet above him. Apart from the humiliation and the fact that he was literally freezing his bollocks off, all he could think about was the F-word.

Fail? The commandant had given him a personal warning. He could not fail—he could not let himself down nor his mother and brother—not that his brother would care. Peter Steele, Jack's twin brother, had already made himself perfectly clear about his feelings toward the British army. He disapproved.

The section of "enemy" Gurkhas had left Steele in the middle of the woods and hightailed it to the next ambush position.

This platoon attack had failed because the platoon had allowed one of their unit to be captured—Mr. Steele. The platoon commander approached and cut Steele down from the tree. Steele got dressed and wiped the blood from his bleeding nostril—the end of the bungee hook was metal. *Gotta keep going,* he told himself.

Steele got dressed in one minute flat. The demo team had left all his equipment next to him.

"Put down that fucker, and get on with that cunt!" screamed CSGT Mulberry in a heavy Yorkshire accent. He pointed to the light machine gun—LMG—and the belt of 7.62mm ammunition lying next to it.

It was Steele's turn to be fire support on the right flank for the next platoon attack. Sandhurst's "enemy"—the Gurkha regiment demonstration unit—would be lying in wait. Steele passed his SLR rifle to Mark Lacy, a fellow Sandhurst cadet, and picked up the LMG. Lacy was in a similar situation to Steele in that he had also studied a (Communist) foreign language and hoped to use his linguistic talent. Lacy spoke Chinese, and Steele spoke Russian.

Steele folded the LMG bipod away and stowed the belts of ammunition. It was nighttime, and there were flares going up in every direction as the mock attack started. Andy Simpson, another Sandhurst cadet from New College, shouted, "Right behind you, Steele!"

"Roger that." Steele was relieved. Simpson was a competent soldier and a decent map reader ... there was no danger of them ending up in the middle of nowhere, or, as their CSGT often said when cadets got lost, "Congratulations, gentlemen, on your induction into the *wherethefugawee tribe*."

Steele reminded himself to save some energy and aggression for his command appointment. Cadets were appointed one by one to a command appointment—IC or 2IC—for each platoon attack. The more confidence the Sandhurst instructors had in any particular individual, the fewer appointments he was assigned. Steele had stayed gray most of the course, but he knew his appointment would be up soon. He had a plan. This would and must be his chance to shine.

The platoon regrouped after the attack, and CSGT Mulberry checked the direction and coordinates of the next assault. "Mr. Steele," said CSGT Mulberry. "You're next, sir." Only in the British army did the NCOs train their future military leaders and call them 'sir.' Apparently, it was to get the Sandhurst cadets used to being called 'sir' before they arrived at their regiments. Many of the cadets were from public schools like Harrow, Eton, and Marlborough. At these prestigious schools, or colleges as some of them were known, British hierarchy, rank, and class consciousness were instilled in their students from birth … or as soon as possible thereafter.

"I'm ready, Colour Sergeant."

This was his chance. This was what the commandant had been talking about. He had warned Steele to pull his finger out, knuckle down, produce the goods—or whatever metaphor General Boswell had used as Steele marched out of his office the day before.

CSGT Mulberry said, "Mr. Steele, you are platoon commander for this attack." He turned and answered his clansman radio as it crackled incomprehensibly. "Delta Sierra One, roger that, we will commence in zero one minute, over."

Steele heard the reply. "Delta Sierra Two, roger. Who is India Charlie on this one?"

CSGT Mulberry said, "Mr. Steele. And Two India Charlie is Mr. Simpson. Nothing further, out."

CSGT Mulberry gave the nod, and Steele let rip. He immediately yelled, "Spread out along the ridge!"

The cadets moved slowly and lethargically. After twelve hours on exercise, they were tired, but that wasn't Steele's problem right now.

"What the fuck!" Steele changed gears. This was a performance, and his every word, action, thought, and deed was being meticulously monitored and observed by Sandhurst directing staff.

He sprinted across to Tom Boyd, who was lethargically crawling across the ground to an untactical fire position. Steele crouched as he approached Boyd and screamed: "YOU FUCKING IDIOT! WHAT THE FUCK DO YOU THINK YOU'RE DOING? MOVE! WE ARE UNDER FIRE, YOU FUCKING WANKER!"

Boyd and Steele knew each other well. They drank beer in the mess together. But as Steele picked up Boyd's entire body off the ground using his webbing straps like a carrier bag, the terrified look on Boyd's face made Steele laugh out loud when he thought about it later. Boyd's expression gave the impression he thought Steele had gone berserk. Instead, Steele was giving the instructors exactly what they wanted. He was acting the part, and he was very good at it. *I should be an actor ... or a spy,* he thought.

Once Boyd was in position—pre-assault fire position—Steele ran along the rest of his platoon to instill discipline and make everyone pay attention using good old fashion aggression—a kick, a punch, and lots of expletives.

It worked.

Every member of the thirty-man platoon was suddenly "switched on to fuck" as the Sandhurst instructors demanded. Steele sent his LMG fire support off to the left flank and launched his very own Sandhurst Charge of the Light Brigade. Flares, thunder flashes, and thousands of rounds of blank ammunition ignited into the Sandhurst training area night sky. Even the Gurkhas retreated from their trench quicker than expected.

Amid the pretend sights and sounds of battle, Steele doubted the effectiveness of the training. *This is a fiasco. How can anyone assess me, my 2IC, or my platoon from this? What would we really do in a real battle using real ammunition against a real enemy?* It was a joke. *On the other hand*, he thought, *I think I just passed with flying colors.*

"Regroup!" shouted CSGT Mulberry.

The attack was over.

CSGT Mulberry said, "I think everyone's awake now." He looked at Steele. "Not bad, sir. Not bad at all...."

The sergeant turned away and spoke into his radio. More crackling and electronic mush no one except a seasoned British army NCO could understand. "I'll send him back."

Steele wiped away the sweat that dripped down from under his helmet.

CSGT Mulberry said, "Head back to New College, sir. Commandant's waiting."

Steele could not believe his ears. *Commandant's waiting? Now what?*

"Colour Sergeant—"

"Mr. Steele, go back to New College, get changed, and report to the commandant."

"But—"

"Mr. Steele, that's a direct order. Move it. Now!"

"Roger that, Colour Sergeant."

Steele snatched a map from the nearest cadet and ran off into the darkness.

CHAPTER SIX

Sandhurst Village, Camberley

Steele had no idea what was going on, but something out of the ordinary was happening. After weeks of shining shoes and boots; oiling, cleaning, and zeroing rifles, machine guns, and magazines; scrubbing bathrooms and latrines; marching in quick time, slow time, and double time; and becoming sick of the smell of spray starch used to iron uniforms—both combat and dress—Steele was ready for some excitement and adventure. General Boswell himself had been waiting for Steele at New College and had told him—no, *ordered* him—to change into civies immediately and report to said pub as soon as possible.

Steele had not even showered. Thirty minutes later, he had signed out of the RMAS Guard Room, made the short drive westward, and pulled into the car park of the Lamb and Flag pub near the village of Sandhurst. It was 9:10 pm.

The door creaked as only English pub doors can creak, and Steele entered the low-beamed inn looking for his rendezvous and looking forward to the pint of London Pride he was about to order at the bar—lukewarm, no head. The smell of warm beer was a welcome change from the smell of starch and Kiwi boot polish.

Steele looked around for anyone who looked out of place. It was Sunday night, so there weren't many locals to filter. It was between two men, both in their thirties—but before Steele had time to choose, the one wearing a black turtleneck and ubiquitous (in these parts) Barbour jacket gave him a surreptitious nod.

Enough said.

Formalities swiftly exchanged, Nigel Rhodes Stampa—*not* hyphenated, he informed Steele on introduction—ordered two pints of London Pride, two packets of crisps—Cheese & Onion and Smoky Bacon—and a large packet of salted peanuts. He ushered Steele from the bar to a seat in the corner.

Nigel said, "Thought you might be peckish. Did you eat?"

"No. General Boswell said it was urgent."

"Bless him," Nigel continued. "He's a good man. He's sent us some good people in the past."

"Us?" Steele retorted.

"Boys from Vauxhall Bridge? He didn't mention it?"

"Security people, he said … more important than polishing brown shoes tonight."

"Sorry to drag you out at short notice."

"Don't apologize. This is the most interesting thing that's happened since I came back from leave."

"Yes, I've heard it can be a bit tedious."

Steele had hoped and dreamed of working for the security services one day—he had preferred the idea of MI6 rather than the domestic version, MI5—but he hadn't even passed out from Sandhurst yet. He tried to control his eagerness and didn't want to appear too excited. To be plucked from Sandhurst obscurity was a welcome respite from monotonous military training.

"Roger that." Nigel smiled, sipped his lukewarm beer, and tore open his crisps.

Steele did the same. He held back from asking questions to give the impression of being cool, calm, and collected.

Nigel said, "You're passing out next week?"

"Yes, that's right."

"Congratulations."

"Thank you."

"Heading to the regiment before Bovington, I understand?" Nigel was referring to the fact that Steele would spend some time at the regiment—The Life Guards, Household Cavalry based in BAOR Sennelager, Germany—before he returned to Dorset, on the south coast of England, for tank commander training at the Royal Armoured Corps in Bovington.

"Yep. That's the plan."

"You ready for action?"

Steele smiled. "Yes, sir."

"Nigel, please. You don't have to call me 'sir.' But I would stop jiggling your leg like that … makes you look nervous. Are you nervous?"

"Hmm, I suppose I am … sorry." Steele was embarrassed that his nervous twitching was so apparent.

"Nothing worse," Nigel continued.

"Sorry?"

"Nothing worse than talking to someone who can't keep still."

"Quite … " replied Steele. "I'll work on it."

"Anyway, Jack. Why am I here?"

"Yes, why are you here, Nigel?"

Nigel paused for dramatic effect. "Look, Sandhurst is great and all that. And you'll have fun at the regiment, no doubt in my mind—unless there's a war, of course. But what do you want to do long term?"

Steele delved into his crisp packet to give himself a moment to formulate a good answer.

"I mean, I'm looking forward to the regiment. I want to use my languages."

"What do you speak, again—Russian, German, and French?"

"Yes."

"Impressive. Maybe we can teach you Bosnian too. Situation in former Yugoslavia is looking decidedly dodgy. Between you and me, something's going to kick off there before long."

"I'd love to learn Bosnian."

"Good to know. Anyway, that's not why I'm here. I'm here because we need you *now*."

"Me?"

"Yes, we need someone in Leningrad. ASAP."

"Leningrad, *Russia?*"

"Is there another? Yes, Leningrad, USSR. You spent a year in Moscow, right?"

"Yes."

"Did you visit Leningrad? White nights and all that romantic stuff?"

"I did."

Steele recalled his visit to Leningrad as an undergraduate language student. During his visit, he had called a friend from the Ukraine out of the blue for a catch-up. It turned out that her husband had been murdered on an overnight train journey to Odesa. Police had concluded it was a robbery. Steele had wanted to jump straight on a train to Odesa to comfort his friend, but he couldn't get permission from the British embassy.

Steele said slowly, "It was a memorable visit. Leningrad is the most beautiful city I've been to, apart from Paris." He had never shared the details about the murder with British security services on the grounds that it had not seemed important or relevant. "Why do you ask?"

"Fancy going back?"

"To Leningrad?"

"Yes, I understand they are going to rename it St. Petersburg again."

"Yes, I heard that." Steele frowned. "Why Leningrad?"

"We think you're a good fit for the job."

"What job?"

"A very important mission. If I spoke Russian, I'd volunteer."

"What's the job?"

"We need you to go and rekindle that friendship of yours with Masha Pushkin."

Steele hesitated. "Masha Pushkin?" he said slowly. Then he remembered.

"Yes. You told us about her in your debrief."

"She was the friend of another friend in Moscow. I wouldn't say we were close."

"Katya."

"Yes. But—"

"But that's why we debrief, young whippersnapper. Never know when one apparently tiny detail might be useful. It's all about puzzles, you see."

"Puzzles?"

"Yes, every mission is a puzzle. And we need all the pieces to make it work—for our chaps, of course."

"What do you want me to do?"

"We want you to bump into your girlfriend, Masha, at the Leningrad Institute of Linguistics. Rekindle old ties. Get to know her again."

"I said she was a friend, not a girlfriend—there's a difference."

"We want you to befriend your girlfriend's friend, Masha. Make sense?"

"Yes. I don't know ... I mean—"

"Let's not get too precious, Jack. We're talking about national security. It's important. All you must do is spend some time in Leningrad ... study ... have fun ... and make contact with Masha."

"I'm confused ... What are we talking about? Spying?"

"You're getting ahead of yourself. No, you're not Roger Moore just yet. This is low-level intelligence gathering."

"You haven't got anyone else?"

"Frankly, no. That's the point, you see. For all intents and purposes, you are a simple student without a care in the world. Even if you got caught, and don't get me wrong, there's nothing there to get caught up in ... but no one can trace you back to us."

"Comforting."

"Nothing to worry about. You'll be safe."

"I'm about to graduate from Sandhurst."

"You will not officially pass out from Sandhurst for the time being. You'll attend the parade to avoid gossip, but your name will be left off the official MOD roster. Once you complete the mission, you'll return to your regiment for a bit, and we'll finish the Sandhurst paperwork when it's all over."

"When what's all over?"

"Your assignment. Your *secret* assignment, Jack."

Steele smiled nervously. "Do I have a choice?"

Nigel gulped at his beer. "Do you have a choice? Do any of us have a choice, Jack? Yes, you have a choice—but a word in your shell-like. Just do as you're told. If you want a career in the army and with the security services, just do as you are told. That would be my recommendation at this moment in time. But, of course, no pressure. It's up to you."

Steele sipped his warm beer. *Okay*, he thought. *Interesting, to say the least*. He took a deep breath and exhaled slowly. "I'm up for it," he said calmly.

"Great," Nigel said. "Glad to hear it. It's an excellent fit."

"Why do you say that?"

"You're a good man, Jack. And we need you because you're a good man and because you speak the lingo—*and* you already know Masha Pushkin. In our world, that's already a huge part of the puzzle."

Steele nodded. "Thanks for the vote of confidence."

"You're welcome."

They want me because I knew Masha from the Maurice Thorez Institute of Foreign Languages in Moscow ... fair enough. Makes sense. But then he thought, *Doesn't that make me a traitor? Katya was my girlfriend*.

Steele asked, "What about Masha? What's so important about her?"

"It's not about Masha, Jack. It's about her father. Her father's a very important fellow—a VIP, you might say. Our partners need to get close. We need info."

"Partners?"

"Yes ..." Nigel paused. "Our *American* partners."

Steele froze for a second. He couldn't believe his ears. This felt like a scene from a le Carré spy novel. He leaned closer to Nigel. *"CIA?"*

Nigel nodded and smiled. "Like I said, national security."

Steele stared out the window at the evening pub-goers who were enjoying a few pints before Sunday night telly and their Monday morning monotony began again.

"Wow," he said finally. "Okay, what do you need me to do?"

"That's the spirit. Glad to hear it," replied Nigel. "Here's the outline." He crushed his bag of crisps, funneled the opening, and poured the pieces into his mouth. "Listen carefully ..."

Once he saw Steele exiting the pub, Nigel walked to the pay-phone near the back door of the pub. He dialed his personal number to speak to his contact at the MOD in Whitehall. For the time being, there would be no updates to MI6 about Steele. For now, Steele would be under the watchful eye of MOD, even though they would be ignorant of the plan behind this Leningrad deception. Steele would remain anonymous at Vauxhall Bridge. Need-to-know basis.

"How'd it go?" asked Wing Commander Nick Jenkins.

"Fine. He seems up for it."

"Excellent. As long as you're happy."

"Yes, nice one on connecting the dots."

Nigel was genuinely impressed that the security services' meticulous reporting, briefing, and debriefing methods had found the absolute perfect man for the job. Even the CIA couldn't come up with a suitable candidate. "Green Slime has its uses," he said. Nigel was referring to the fact that the British Army Intelligence Corps was known as "Green Slime" due to the deep green color of the regiment's beret.

"How much did you tell him?" asked Jenkins.

"Bare minimum."

"CIA connection?"

"In passing … thought it best—"

"For now, at least."

"Quite."

Even Jenkins did not know all the details about this operation. He had commented to Nigel how unusual it was to pluck a man straight from Sandhurst before he'd even finished his training. Nigel had assured him that this wasn't the first time, it wouldn't be the last, and that Steele would pass out and would eventually become a fully fledged commissioned officer. He would get to join his regiment in Germany once it was all over.

"I hope we don't disappoint the Yanks," said Wing Commander Jenkins.

"We can't control everything. All we can do is brief, monitor, and manage him to the best of our ability."

"Roger that."

"See you next week. Thank you, Wing Commander."

"You're welcome, Nigel. Our pleasure."

Nigel placed his index finger in the payphone's return shoot to retrieve the 50p piece that had fallen through earlier. He exited the pub and glanced at the locals in their Barbour jackets and green Wellingtons. He pitied them … *Tomorrow morning, they'll be sitting at their desks, but I'll be saving the world*, he thought wryly. He also pitied Jack Steele. Being a Russian language student was one thing—but being an untrained spy in the middle of Cold War USSR was quite another. *Poor fucker. It'll be a small miracle if he makes it out alive or doesn't end up in a Siberian gulag. I wish him well.*

Nigel climbed into his navy Volvo Estate and set off for his short journey back to Chelsea. He mentally prepared himself for the "weekend warrior" Sunday night M4 traffic into London.

CHAPTER SEVEN

Old College, Royal Military Academy, Sandhurst.

General Boswell nudged his gray charger with his spurs and rode to the center of the parade square in front of Old College. This marked the beginning of the Sovereign's Parade. Margaret Thatcher, the British prime minister, had canceled at the last minute, and her husband, Denis Thatcher, had stepped in and agreed to inspect the sovereign's company and take the salute on behalf of Her Majesty Queen Elizabeth II. There was an expectant hum of excitement in the spectator crowd of families, friends, and low-level dignitaries as the parade commenced.

The Academy Sergeant Major—AcSM—bellowed: "Duft-dight-duft-dight-duft-dight DUFT!" Every NCO in the British army had their own custom version of the traditional marching cadence: *"left-right-left-right-left-right-left."*

Steele straightened his marching arm and hoped his pristine self-loading rifle—SLR—did not slip from his laundered white gloves. He tightened his grip.

Again the AcSM: "Get on the heel! Duft-dight-duft-dight-duft-dight DUFT!"

The parade square was packed with a company of cadets passing out from the Royal Military Academy Sandhurst. Colorful dresses, hats, and umbrellas of mothers, wives, and girlfriends dotted the spectator stand erected on one side of the square; less colorful were the navy and gray suits of fathers, husbands, and brothers of graduating sons *and* daughters.

Sandhurst was a co-ed institution. The sound of crunching boots on gravel reverberated around the Old College stone pillars and entrance portico.

Steele searched for his mother and brother. It was a surprise that Peter had accepted the invitation. He hated the British army and all that it represented—he was a liberal lefty, some might say. If Steele was honest, he knew Peter was more intelligent than him, and Steele wasn't surprised that Peter had been accepted to read journalism at the University of Bristol, one of the top five universities in the country.

Steele scanned the spectators. He thought he saw his mother in the crowd wearing a pink straw hat.

The red cap bands, belts whitened with Blanco, gloves, and navy tunics of the Sandhurst cadets complimented the light gray stone of Old College. The pomp and ceremony were underway.

The AcSM barked, "Eyes right!"

The cadets executed the order and saluted General Boswell.

Jesus, thought Steele. *I hope this is all worth it. I am doing this parade for nothing. All this ceremonial pomp and circumstance is part of the show I will not be part of after all the work. Why did I agree to this crazy 'mission'?*

Steele's peaked cap slipped down an inch and distorted his field of view. He saw the back of the cadets in front and their phalanx of legs and boots as they marched up and down the parade ground for the next hour. He might try and flip his peaked cap upward, but he risked it flying off his head and drawing unnecessary attention to himself—not to mention embarrassment.

At last, the ceremony and parade drew to a close. From the music being blasted by the Sandhurst military band, Steele knew from rehearsals it was almost over. Just a few more minutes and a couple more military tunes. Then he would adjust his cap, give his mother a hug, and deal with Peter's snide comments about Steele's military journey being a complete waste of time, money, and effort. *I'll show him. One day, I'll show Peter I'm just as capable as he is.*

The band played "Auld Lang Syne" as the sovereign's company slow-marched up the steps of Old College. His company entered the gargantuan doors of Old College, signifying the end of the parade. As was the tradition since 1947, the commandant and his trusty steed also climbed the steps and entered Old College. The cadets were no longer cadets except for Steele. At midnight, everyone else would adopt the rank of British army second lieutenant.

The young men and women dispersed from the inside of Old College and walked back out to waiting family and friends. For the first time since the cadets had arrived at Sandhurst, the AcSM seemed to let down his barking instructor façade. He spoke to the cadets in a softer voice without shouting and said, "Congratulations, ladies and gentlemen. Allow me to wish you all the best in your future career." Then he added with a cheeky smile, "You're going to need it."

Steele made his way back to the parade square to meet and greet. He was sure his mother would be enjoying every minute of the festivities in spite of Peter's inevitable sourness. No need to tell her the truth and ruin her day.

Steele found his mother among the throngs of several hundred family and friends. "Hello, Mum," he said. "How was it?"

"Oh, wonderful," she replied. "Yes, very good."

"Did you see me?"

"Yes, I *think* I saw you." She patted him on the arm. "But everyone looks the same."

"I think that's the idea, Mum," Steele said. "Did you introduce yourself to Denis Thatcher?"

"No, he left without saying 'hello.' Rude man," she quipped.

"Where's Peter?"

April Steele looked down for a moment. It was a look he recognized. One that showed the genuine pain she felt when her boys did not see eye to eye. "I'm sorry, Jack. He let me down at the last minute. I tried to—"

"No problem, Mum," he replied. "I was amazed he'd even accepted."

"I know." She smiled demurely and said, "Anyway, you were wonderful. You've done well."

"Thanks, Mum. I love ya."

A sudden gust of wind caught the female guests and their hats off guard, and April held onto her pink straw hat. "Oh, my word!" she said, grappling with the brim of her hat.

Then Steele glanced over the top of his mother and saw Claudia Rohweder on the far side of the crowd.

At least, he *thought* he saw Claudia. Steele adjusted his cap and leaned left and right as he searched the crowd.

Nothing.

He searched again. It couldn't be. It was impossible.

On the far side of the navy tunics and the guests' bright-colored outfits and attire, Claudia was standing alone, staring straight at him.

Impossible!

"What's the matter?" April asked.

Steele placed his hand on April's shoulder. "Err … nothing. Everything's fine. I'll be back in a minute."

Steele walked a few steps, then stopped in his tracks and looked around. *What am I doing? The last thing I need is contact with a random one-night stand from Berlin who might conceivably be some German spy and whose existence I chose not to report to my people.*

By the time Steele looked back, Claudia had disappeared.

Steele returned to April. He looked over his shoulder, still searching for Claudia. He put his hand on his mother's arm. "Sorry, Mum. I thought I saw someone."

"Someone?"

"Someone I know."

Steele stood on tiptoes; still nothing. His heart started racing—a voice inside told him to exhale. *I must be seeing things. Calm the bloody hell down, Jack …*

Then another inner voice said: *That was her, damn it. That was Claudia Rohweder. I'm sure of it.*

Lubyanka Square, Moscow

One week later, at 7:35 am, Oleg Stepanovich Pugachev walked along Teatral'nyy Proyezd—*Theater Boulevard*—with short, decisive steps and a slight swagger, as was his gait, as he passed the Bolshoi Ballet. "Homosexual deviants," he muttered to himself while eyeing the theater. As he reached the next crossing at Neglinnaya Street, he saw a stray black-and-white dog with a pointed nose sitting next to a pile of dog dirt. Oleg quickened his pace and, a moment later, kicked the dog in its ribs as hard as he could, as though he was kicking a football. The dog yelped as it took flight. Had the blow met the dog's skull, Oleg mused, it would have killed it outright. "Fucking dogs," he said aloud. "I'm sick of these fucking stray dogs. We never used to have mangy, stray dogs on the street."

A woman across the street, who had no idea that Oleg was a rising star in the KGB eager to make his mark on the world, shouted: "U vas net sovyesti, gospodine. Chort s'vami!" *You have no scruples, sir. The devil take you!"*

Oleg ignored the woman and continued to the main entrance of KGB headquarters on Lubyanka Square. He showed his ID and made his way to the sixth floor and his office overlooking the square. His mother—were she alive—would be proud. His father had beaten her to death, and Oleg, of course, would never forgive him. He would never visit his father in the desolate Arkhangelsk Penal Colony #56, a thousand miles to the north of Moscow, where Stepan Igorovich Pugachev would spend the rest of his life. In the Soviet Union, a life sentence meant a life sentence. *Perhaps*, Oleg debated, *I will order my father's release if I become president of the motherland one day. Men who kill without emotion are always useful and trustworthy.*

Oleg picked up the red telephone on his desk and asked the operator for Admiral Pushkin's 'Domashni'—*private number*—in Leningrad District.

"Sekundu, Oleg Stepanovich," the operator replied. *One moment.*

"Spaciba." *Thank you.*

Moments later, Admiral Pushkin answered, "Yes, I am listening."

"Dimitri Viktorovich, this is Oleg Stepanovich."

"How are you?"

"I am well, thank you, Dimitri Viktorovich. How is your beautiful daughter?"

"Masha is as beautiful as ever, but she is driving me to kingdom come."

Oleg replied, "Of course, that is her job. She is a young woman."

"In this case, I can't wait for her to become a babushka."

Oleg smiled a plastic smile.

Admiral Pushkin said, "How can we help today? I am about to leave for the office."

"I am waiting to hear from our Italian friend. But I wanted to give you the latest information."

"Your plan is ambitious. I commend you."

"Our plan is the only plan. It is the plan for the motherland. It is the only way forward."

"I understand, Oleg Stepanovich. I agree."

"How is our Swedish operation going?" Oleg knew better than to utter the word *submarine.*

"Everything is under control."

"That's what I like to hear," replied Oleg. "We are honored to have the finest navy in the world."

"Yes, indeed, Oleg Stepanovich. May God protect it."

"Please continue as planned. Trust me. It will reap unexpected rewards."

"Of course. It is my honor to serve the motherland. Will the Vatican help us, do you think?"

"I am sure of it. Give me a few more days."

"Very good. Keep matters simple."

Oleg said, "Simple is good. Together we will bring an end to this Cold War."

"I hope," said Admiral Pushkin. "World peace is not so bad. I retire to my dacha in five years. I will smoke a cigar every day in peace."

Oleg did not smile and stayed silent for a moment. "God bless the motherland."

"Thank you for the latest news. I am at your service whenever you need me."

Oleg hung up.

Too bad, he thought, Dimitri Viktorovich's dacha will *never* be filled with the aroma of his cigar.

CHAPTER EIGHT

Leningrad, USSR

The same day, four hundred and thirty miles from Moscow, Masha waited for her father to hang up. She listened for the sound of his chair scraping across the floor in his study, and then she replaced the receiver. Astrid, her pen pal from Stockholm, had told her how much fun it was to listen to her father's private conversations. Astrid had installed a simple listening device in her father's home office and was fascinated by all the important government conversations—domestic and international—she had eavesdropped upon. Sometimes she even heard her father talking to other European leaders and sometimes to Swedish military generals. The telephone line in the Aronsson household was secure—but no one had foreseen or thought about the possibility of the eighteen-year-old daughter bugging her father's office.

Masha was fascinated by Astrid's real-life stories, political debacles, and matters of national security. Growing up in the Aronsson household meant that Astrid had become a well-informed, political animal. Masha had also begun to listen to her father's conversations using less sophisticated methods. All she had to do was pick up the telephone a second *before* her father answered his and place her hand over the speaker. The caller and Admiral Pushkin were oblivious to her domestic spying.

Masha had never quite understood his precise role in the military hierarchy, but she knew he had something to do with naval intelligence and naval operations in the Baltic, Norwegian, and

Barents Seas. That much Masha had in common with her father. She too loved the sea. If she ever managed to escape to another country, she would miss Leningrad's wide rivers and canals.

Masha and Astrid corresponded at least once a week and began to exchange stories they had heard while eavesdropping. Because Masha and Astrid's letters went back and forth via the Swedish embassy's diplomatic pouch, the sensitive yet informal nature and subject matter of their letters stayed under the radar of Swedish and Soviet security services.

"Masha!" shouted Admiral Pushkin. "I am leaving now. I must go straight to the office for a meeting. I can't be late."

"I know, Papa. You don't have to treat me like a child. You know I prefer to walk."

"Your mother left for the institute already. But she promised to cook something tasty tonight. Blinis with meat!"

"Okay, Papa. I understand. You can go." *Blinis, blinis, always blinis*, Masha thought. *It's the only thing my mother can cook.*

Admiral Pushkin said, "Okay. I'm leaving."

Masha heard the door to the large three-bedroom apartment slam shut. She gathered her books for the institute. Classes began at 9:00 am.

I can't wait to tell Astrid. My father is going to end the Cold War.

Admiral Pushkin asked Sergei Mikhailovich, his driver, to let him out a few streets from the office. He needed fresh air. At least, that's what he told his driver. Whenever he needed to clear his head, Admiral Pushkin would walk a few blocks along Leningrad canals to his office. Just being close to the water was calming.

Admiral Pushkin was worried about his daughter. She seemed more troubled than usual. Why did Masha like to be in her room so much? It was as though she was someone else's daughter. Perhaps his wife had spent too much of their life working at the Zoological Institute? Yes, she was a scientist, and her work was important, but it was true they had not given Masha enough attention over the years.

But now I need to switch focus, he told himself. *I have an important call in less than one hour.*

Could this really be the end of the Cold War? Were the rumors true? The end of the Cold War? What did that even mean? He trusted Oleg Stepanovich, his KGB colleague, but he also needed to extract information from an old friend he had met on an exchange visit between military and naval academies. Strictly speaking, he wasn't supposed to liaise with General Urmancheva. The general was more senior and commanded a completely different division from the naval intelligence work Admiral Pushkin coordinated. No matter, he had to do his job and he was a conscientious man. He would use his contacts to find out the best version of the truth. *Truth is power*, he recited mentally. *Truth is power.* He also conceded that what powerful men chose to do with the truth in the USSR was an entirely different matter.

Today, it was more than fresh air Admiral Pushkin needed on the banks of the Griboyedov Canal and the Fontanka River. Another reason he sometimes walked the last few blocks to work was to hold surreptitious meetings that he knew could not be recorded. He never used the same location because he could not rule out the KGB planting a microphone or camera, even outdoors.

Admiral Pushkin arrived at the intersection of Nevsky Prospekt and Fontanka Embankment that ran along the Fontanka River. General Pyotr Alekseevich Urmancheva was already waiting in the middle of the bridge carrying his briefcase. A high-ranking naval officer and an army general crossing paths in the middle of the Anichkov Bridge did not look out of place in Leningrad. Leningrad was a naval city on the water, and there were as many military officers as there were babushkas and matryoshkas.

"Good morning, Pyotr Alekseevich," said Admiral Pushkin. "Thank you for coming at short notice."

"Of course. I wish we could keep in touch more often. Please be brief—you know my people might get suspicious."

"You are being watched?"

"No, I have no reason to think so. But our KGB brothers are like snakes in that water"—he pointed to the river—"or maybe they have cameras pointing at us from that dome right now." He pointed to one of the three golden domes visible from their location.

"Cameras? I think you mean microphones." Admiral Pushkin chuckled.

"You are correct. They would hide equipment in a pile of dog shit if it gave them an advantage. How can I help, Dimitri Viktorovich?"

Admiral Pushkin turned toward the river as he spoke, and said, "Do you support our leader?"

"Which leader? The president?"

"Yes."

"Do you want to get me shot asking such questions? Do I support President Leontev?" asked General Urmancheva.

"Yes."

"Why wouldn't I support him? Is there something I should know, comrade?"

Admiral Pushkin said, "Do you think it is possible that the Cold War will end soon?"

"Anything is possible. Do I think it will happen? No."

"Why not?"

"Mikhail Pavlovich is weak. I do not think our president knows how to achieve such a pipe dream."

Admiral Pushkin said, "Weak, you say?"

"Yes, *weak*. Consider our history, Dimitri Viktorovich. The Soviet Union must be ruled with an iron fist. Our people do not know any other way."

"I agree."

"If our masters decide to end the Cold War, this will require a powerful and talented leader to hold our country together. If not, the Union will crumble. It will be a disaster."

Admiral Pushkin smiled and nodded. They shook hands.

"Thank you, Pyotr Alekseevich. I am grateful. Please know that *I* will never allow the Union to crumble. I swear on my daughter's life."

"I have never doubted your loyalty to the motherland."

Admiral Pushkin saluted.

The general returned the salute and said, "My only advice … Be careful who or what you swear on. I don't even trust my own wife, let alone my sons. Soviet youth have a different philosophy nowadays."

A tram shook the bridge as it trundled past, and General Urmancheva continued his walk to work.

"Until next time, Pyotr Alekseevich. And thank you."

On the other side of the Fontanka River, Masha took two steps back to hide underneath one of the ornate archways next to the canal. The phone call twenty minutes earlier with someone called Oleg Stepanovich had piqued her interest. Now, coincidentally, on her way to the institute, she had seen her father standing in the middle of the Anichkov Bridge talking to a senior military officer—by her reckoning from his gray fur hat, a general. Not unusual, perhaps, except for the fact that her father had said he was going straight to the office and, unusually, had *not* offered to take her.

She hadn't thought anything of it. But now, after the phone call about the Cold War, the chance meeting on the bridge, and Astrid's lingering words in her last letter—*You cannot trust anyone, not even your own family*—Masha was exploding with curiosity and determined to find out what was going on. Perhaps this new interest would take her mind off her main obsession to escape this wretched Soviet society. No, "society" was far too generous—*the USSR is an authoritarian gulag, plain and simple.*

CHAPTER NINE

Whitehall, London

Steele stepped down off a red London bus that still had the open section at the back—and just missed a puddle after the recent downpour. It was still raining steadily. He opened his umbrella and glanced down at his black Brogues to make sure they were spotless. He had polished them himself with a damp yellow duster and a tin of Kiwi polish. It was open to debate whether the skill of polishing your shoes to shine like glass was useful to man or beast. *But for now*, he thought, *I'm pleased with my handiwork.*

So this was it. They had scooped him from his moment of glory—his Sandhurst glory—and God knows what the next few days and weeks held in store. He had even split up with his French girlfriend. She was gorgeous—and sexy—and had the look of a ballet dancer. Were he ten years older, he might well, he thought, have ended up with her. The M-word. But at the moment, marriage was not on the cards. They had enjoyed a trans-Channel relationship and had commuted between the South of France, Paris, and London. Stephanie—her name sounded so much better in French—had taught him how to make a French omelet and how to use a Bialetti coffeepot in her Paris atelier. He would miss her. But as selfish as it sounded, duty was calling. *But what kind of duty?*

The MOD security guards checked his passport—Wing Commander Nick Jenkins had told him to bring it because a driver's license wasn't sufficient for all the paperwork that needed to be completed for foreign travel. As he exited the lift on the ninth floor, he bumped into Nigel Rhodes Stampa, who greeted him like an old friend. They had last met at the Lamb & Flag pub.

"Hello, Jack, old boy," he boomed. "Great to have you onboard."

"Thanks, Nigel."

"Glad you had a day off, but we need to get this moving. All packed?"

Steele nodded. "Yes. Can't wait."

"And don't worry about the regiment. They'll see you when they see you. I'll keep them abreast … personally."

"Sounds good."

They walked down a long corridor. Halfway down, Nigel ushered Steele into an outer office that led to a smaller office and then to a much larger, brighter conference room with lots of windows and a row of wall clocks set at different time zones from around the world. Steele noted the "Moscow" clock that showed it was three hours ahead. Leningrad would be the same time, but he also knew there were six time zones in the Soviet Union. He had traveled across them on the train during his student days the year before.

Wing Commander Nick Jenkins said, "Hello, Jack. Welcome to our humble abode."

"Pleasure to meet you, sir."

"Call me Nick. I'm RAF, not your lot," he countered. By "your lot," Jenkins meant the Brigade of Guards.

Steele nodded.

"Here's the plan. I'll give you a quick briefing, not too much detail for now. And you can ask questions. But we won't keep you long. I'm sure we all have pints to sup and girlfriends to fuck." He grinned as though he had just created a line of poetry.

Nigel said, "We're at the MOD because you're under their wing for the time being, even though you're not technically a commissioned officer—"

"And not a spook," added Jenkins.

Steele said, "Makes sense."

"This room is secure. So, whatever we say, whatever you hear, and whatever you tell us will go no further. Mother, brother, girlfriends, chums from Sandhurst, and the regiment. Is that understood?"

"Absolutely."

"First of all, the least we tell you, the better it is … for you. We will give you the gist of your mission, but you will not be privy to the big picture. Understood? Nigel has an idea what's going on, but I don't … I'm just as much in the dark as you are. And by next week, you'll know ten times more than I do."

Steele nodded.

Nigel went on, "We owe the Yanks a favor—"

Steel frowned. "You mean, CIA?"

"Let's just leave it at Yanks."

Jenkins said, "Jack, trust me when I tell you, it's in your best interests to know as little as possible."

"I understand, sir … Nick."

"Your mission is very simple: You are going to the Leningrad Linguistic Institute. You plan to do an MA in interpreting at Bath University, but they have enrolled you in their three-month exchange program for foreign students hosted by the institute. You plan to join the Foreign Office and become a diplomat once you finish at Bath."

Steele's eyes widened. "Aren't they going to know I was at Sandhurst?"

"We have removed all official trace of you becoming an officer. If anyone mentions the military training, say you failed the course and plan to join the Foreign Office."

Steele looked skeptical.

Jenkins said, "I promise you, Jack. It's not an issue. You were a university cadet studying Russian, and you have zero service as an army officer to date, so you're on solid ground."

"If you say so. And what happens when I get to Leningrad?"

Nigel continued, "Your old friend Masha—"

"Masha Pushkin?"

"Yes, she's gone back home to Leningrad to study at the institute. She also gives conversation lessons to foreign students. But the key point is that she's living with her parents."

"Who are her parents?"

"Admiral Pushkin, and her mother is a scientist at the Leningrad Zoology Institute?"

"And ... " began Steele.

Nigel said, "And we want you to ... 'rekindle' your relationship."

"I already told you—she wasn't my girlfriend."

"Just do your best." Nigel was insistent.

"Why?" asked Steele.

Nigel said, "*How* would be a more appropriate question."

"I mean, how do I get to know her?"

"I'm sure you can use your imagination. Whatever it takes to get the intelligence we need."

"Are we doing this for the Americans?"

Nigel rocked his head from side to side, and the corners of his mouth turned down as if he was in pain and mulling over the question. He inhaled slowly, "Yes, Jack. The *Yank's* mission. We're allies remember?"

Steele nodded and thought back to numerous lectures at Exeter University and Sandhurst about the start of the Cold War after the allies liberated Berlin after World War II. "Yes, indeed. I'm aware."

"Good." Jenkins held up a jug of water. "Thirsty?"

"Yes, please."

Nigel said, "Me, too." He had moved to the window and was staring at the stunning panoramic view across the Thames toward the Royal Festival Hall. Steele had spent many nights there attending classical music concerts with friends, enjoying Elgar, Mozart, Handel, Lutosławski, and many others. Steele's best friend, Roberto Mangiamo, from his North London grammar school, had already taken a very different path from Steele and was attending the Royal Northern College of Music. One day, Roberto, would no doubt be playing his cello at the Royal Festival Hall.

"Perhaps I should have kept up with my violin," Steele said.

Nigel said, "Sorry?"

Steele gestured toward the South Bank and said, "I used to play the violin. I have friends who want to be orchestral players instead of spies."

Nigel said, "Steady, Jack. You're not quite *that* important."

"What would you call it? This 'mission'?"

"Observation. Pure and simple. Information gathering."

"Fair enough."

There was a moment of awkward silence.

Jenkins said, "So, that's it, really, Jack. I'll keep in touch with Nigel here, but because you will be returning to the regiment, I'll be your OIC."

"So… "—Steele bit the inside of his cheek—"head to Leningrad, rekindle my friendship with Masha, and then what?"

Nigel said, "Report back to Simon Bird. You'll check in with him at the British embassy in Moscow and then overnight to Leningrad on the train."

"Do I call him?"

"No, never. Simon will explain in person."

"Got it. And how long will this take?"

"The journey?" asked Nigel.

"No, the mission."

"Short answer? As long as it takes … The long answer? We have no idea. The Americans have something big in the pipeline, and they need whatever intel they can get on Masha's father. That's all you need to know."

"Why didn't they send an American?" asked Steele.

"Why send an American when we have you, a Jack Steele?" Nigel smiled. "You already have a connection with Masha Pushkin."

Steele thought back for a moment and then it all made sense. He had divulged everything about his year abroad in Moscow to the Intelligence Corps. He nodded, "Green Slime and puzzles. I get it."

"Got it in one, Jack," said Nigel. "Green slime has its uses after all, right?"

Five minutes later, Steele shook hands goodbye with Nigel, who set off northward up Whitehall toward Trafalgar Square. Steele decided to walk through Horse Guards, across Horse Guards Parade to St James's Park. He needed to clear his head. It was still drizzling. Steele frowned and opened his umbrella. He wondered if he had made a huge mistake. He also wondered if he should take the umbrella with him to Russia. Perhaps MI6 could build a poison dart in it, just in case.

It was nearly autumn, but by all accounts, it didn't rain much in Leningrad … snow was more likely. And who knows, he might be back in London before then.

Steele walked past the mounted Household Cavalry sentries and pictured himself inspecting the 4:00 pm guard inspection one day. Tanks, armored reconnaissance vehicles, and ceremonial mounted duties were his regiment's remit. One day, he would be a tank commander and lead ceremonial mounted units across London for Changing the Guard or the Queen's Birthday Parade, also known as Trooping the Colour.

Just inside the ornate gates of the royal park, Steele stopped at the ice cream cart. "Orange Maid," he said to the vendor with gray hair.

"There we go, young sir. Thirty pence."

"Thank you." Steele took his ice lolly, discarded the wrapper, and savored the orange tang. He couldn't be sure when his next Orange Maid would be.

★   ★   ★

She kept her distance like any trained operative, especially one from East Germany's HVA—East German Intelligence Service. It was a close call at Sandhurst, but she had achieved her goal—allowed herself to be sighted for a second and then disappear.

Steele had spent less than one hour inside the British Ministry of Defense. Her instincts were already telling her that Second Lieutenant Jack Steele had been an excellent choice. Normally, it would take years to "cook" the asset before you "ate" it. Most of the time, the vast majority of targets turned out to be a waste of time. But this case file had suddenly taken an unexpected and promising turn. Something was telling her that her move on Steele, with his linguistic talents, had been the best decision of her career.

As white and gray swans approached her, Claudia threw the last handful of stale bread into the St James's Park Lake. She turned and followed Steele across the park and up the Duke of York monument steps. There was no need to follow him any further today. She wrote a brief message in code and placed it inside a small white envelope. It was highly unusual for Sandhurst cadets to visit the MOD right out of Sandhurst. Her instincts told her that Jack Steele was not the average cadet.

Claudia placed the envelope under the solid wooden door adorned with large metal rivets at the foot of the Duke of York monument. She left just enough of the envelope showing that her Soviet embassy contact would be able to retrieve it and pass the message to Oleg. She smiled at the brazenness of this dead-drop location—within spitting distance of the Athenaeum Club, one of London's most popular spy haunts for British security services.

CHAPTER TEN

Literary Café, Leningrad

Admiral Pushkin poured two more vodkas and ordered another plate of blini with caviar.

The Literary Café was the perfect location for a discrete meeting. It was frequented by the local KGB elite and, therefore, unlike most hotels and restaurants in one of the Soviet Union's most militarily saturated cities, it was less likely to have microphones and listening devices. The Literary Café was also a favorite of the mayor of Leningrad, whose wife was always trying to convince local comrades that she was a woman who supported the arts.

Admiral Pushkin said, "Thank you for coming all this way, but I don't understand. What are you afraid of?"

Oleg replied, "Let me be clear, Dimitri Viktorovich. I am not afraid of anything. Fear is not in my heart, in my mind, in my soul, or in my DNA."

"I apologize. I did not mean—"

"We need your help."

"Please ... As I said to you last week, we are at your service."

"I want you to use your influence within our Soviet navy to intimidate the West."

"I thought Mikhail Leontev's goal is to make détente. With the Cowboy. End the Cold War?"

"Yes, yes, we are planning to make friends. But we do not want to put all our eggs in one basket. Before you know it, we will be back in Tzarist times."

"What is your plan?"

"We want you to send a submarine to Sweden ... to Stockholm."

Admiral Pushkin stopped eating his blini and frowned. "Stockholm?"

"Yes, send a submarine to waters off the city of Stockholm. No aggressive action is necessary, of course. Just enough for a sighting offshore." Oleg snapped his fingers at the sullen waitress. "Young woman. More caviar."

The waitress nodded obediently.

Oleg continued, "Americans are trying to befriend Mikhail Leontev, our esteemed leader. But the Swedish government is hindering the situation."

"How so?" asked Admiral Pushkin.

"Normally, it would be helpful to us that they organize anti-Western propaganda—marches, demonstrations, newspaper editorials. But this prime minister has gone too far."

"Too far?"

"Too far with leftist politics."

"I understand."

"There is a danger he will derail our master plan to end the Cold War, or at least delay it. This is unacceptable."

Admiral Pushkin drank another shot of vodka, then chased it down with a *zakuska* topped with red caviar. "Why would he do this?"

"Why does a politician do anything? Because it is in his interests. They have an election soon, and he wants to secure a second term."

Admiral Pushkin chuckled. "These foreigners—why do they make so much trouble for themselves? Authoritarianism is so much simpler."

Oleg continued, "You are held in high regard in the upper echelons of the KGB. We trust you. We want you to order this mission under the auspices of Northern Sector Naval Command GRU."

"Thank you, Oleg Stepanovich. It is my honor to serve our GRU and you. But why is Sweden so important?"

"The Swedish prime minister is a very liberal man. We understand he detests the Cowboy and all that his administration represents."

Admiral Pushkin frowned, trying to grasp what Oleg was telling him.

Oleg continued, "But there are also very conservative elements in Sweden—in the military, business world, and high society. How can I say? One pitepalt does not know what is inside the other."

"You have lost me completely, Oleg Stepanovich. What are you talking about? I drank half a bottle of vodka with you, and it is only two in the afternoon. What is *pitepalt?*"

"Pitepalt is a Swedish delicacy similar to our blini. The Swedes make it with delicious fillings." Oleg gave a sly smirk.

"You are saying Sweden is a divided nation? I thought the opposite was true."

"I am saying that it will be easy to create the kind of conflict we need in our neighbor's hearth."

"I still don't follow."

"That is all you need to know for now."

Admiral Pushkin nodded slowly. "My daughter has a pen pal in Sweden."

Now it was Oleg's turn to be confused. "A what?"

"A pen pal. They have known each other for some time. There was a school project. The children were invited to correspond with students at a school in Stockholm to practice their written English—lingua franca."

"And Masha still writes to this friend?"

"Yes."

"Did you report this, Dimitri Viktorovich?"

"Of course. It is standard procedure."

"Indeed."

"I have reported all foreign contacts since I left the naval academy."

"And Masha? Did she report specifics of every contact?"

"I am not sure. I didn't think to check ... I don't want our beloved KGB to open a file on her. You understand?"

"Then you *did* think about it. She has not reported contact with a foreigner?"

"Not in person. But I made a report on her behalf when the pen pal project began two years ago."

"Very good, Dimitri Viktorovich. What is the girl's name?"

"What girl?"

"Masha's pen pal? Are you drunk?"

"Yes, a little. And yes, it's a girl. Her name is Astrid ... Astrid Aronsson."

Oleg stared intently at Admiral Pushkin. "Aronsson? The name is familiar ..."

Admiral Pushkin smiled as he poured more vodka. "Of course it is, Oleg Stepanovich. Astrid Aronsson is the Swedish prime minister's daughter."

Outside the Swedish Parliament, Stockholm

The young crowd—younger than an equivalent rally for the opposition Conservative Party at least—cheered, shouted, and laughed. Some heckled, but the majority was here to support Anders Aronsson, Swedish prime minister and leader of the Social Democratic Party. Astrid stood on the podium with her father, not because she supported his politics but because she still loved him in spite of his politics. For the time being, she kept her personal conservative opinions and ideology to herself.

But there was another reason she was here ... Astrid *loved* the world of politics. The speeches, the debates, and the discussions, both public and private. She had dated the son of a prominent Swedish general, and although they had broken up, it was Björn—named after the famous Swedish tennis player—who had planted, nurtured, and influenced most of her conservative views. In fact, so successful was his charm and charisma that she still called him with her father's itinerary and diary entries that were not public knowledge. She did not and could not know (due to her inexperience and lack of understanding of these matters) what kind of harm she might cause her father and even herself by divulging this private information.

"Hurrah!" chimed the crowds rolling their 'R' sound.

Anders Aronsson continued, "We are a neutral country, and we will *remain* a neutral country. We don't need help from Mr. Brad Madison, and we are tired of his movies!"

The crowd cheered again.

Astrid showed little emotion as she stood among the prime minister's entourage of assistants and helpers. She disagreed with his sentiment. She wanted Sweden to be more like America. She did not like the Soviets, and she knew that this kind of anti-American rhetoric could only fuel speculation that her father was a latent Communist. Personally, she didn't think he would go that far ... ever ... but her personal—and, she conceded, youthful—opinion had zero importance in this big-picture political scene.

"Integrity ... honor ..."—Aronsson paused for effect—"peace and stability for Sweden, Scandinavia, and the Baltic states."

"All right, Papa," Astrid said under her voice so that no one could hear, "that's enough already."

Aronsson continued, "Mr. Madison, please listen to us when we say, 'We will make our own decisions, thank you very much.' We appreciate your friendship, Mr. Madison, and your support in times of trouble, but never take our friendship for granted!"

Astrid took a step back from the huddle behind her father, and her face reddened with embarrassment. *No, wait, it's not embarrassment; I'm angry.*

★   ★   ★

Dan Mascaro, the CIA station chief for Stockholm, stood with his arms folded, watching the Swedish television news live feed of Aronsson's rally.

"God *damn* it," he said, shaking his head. "Who the fuck does he think he is?"

"The Swedish prime minister?" replied Erin, his assistant.

Mascaro gave her a look that said, *Don't mess with me right now.*

"Sorry," she said, "not funny."

"POTUS is gonna go nuts. He already thinks we do too much for these guys."

Erin continued, "Yeah, our ambassador's blue and yellow cake was a bit much." She was referring to the Swedish flag birthday cake that the American ambassador had delivered to the prime minister's office on his birthday.

Erin apologized again for her untimely humor. "Sorry, is it really that serious? It's just a rally. Aronsson *loves* rallies. That's his thing."

"The president wants to rally the West against the Sovs. We need everyone on board, and we certainly don't need—or deserve, for that matter—this BS. POTUS won't stand for it."

"We're in Europe."

Mascaro frowned. "*We* dictate the agenda. You should know that by now."

"Understood."

"When the President sees this, he's gonna be pissed and tell us we're not doing our job."

"What are we supposed to do? It's called democracy." Erin lowered the volume of the TV now that the rally had concluded.

"There's always *something* we can do." Dan smiled, unfolded his arms, pushed back his thick head of salt and pepper hair, and picked up the satellite phone to Langley, Virginia.

CHAPTER ELEVEN

Sofiyskaya Embankment, Moscow

Steele entered the British embassy on Sofiyskaya Embankment by showing his passport to the militsiya—*policeman*. To his right at the other entrance, Soviet citizens from far and wide stood patiently in the queue to get inside. They were here to collect tourist and business visas that had probably taken months to process—and even then, *these* Soviets were the lucky ones. The average comrade did not stand a chance of getting a foreign visa. They were either too poor or too unimportant. Your ties to the Communist Party had to be watertight, or you had to be a citizen of exceptional talent—artist, musician, or sportsman. Steele loved the mystique, culture, and history of the Russian narod—*people*—but he was eternally grateful not to have been born in this *wonderland,* as the Russians euphemistically called it. Corruption was ubiquitous, and the standard of living was diabolical.

The traffic had been unusually light. Steele had been instructed to take a taxi or private car from the airport. Yes, private cars doubling as taxis were safer in some ways than official taxis. At least he wouldn't be ripped off. Try to pay in rubles, they had said. If not, use dollars, which should be a fraction of the price because of the black-market exchange rate. The official exchange rate at the airport was one to one—one dollar for one ruble. But everyone knew that the black-market exchange rate was more like fifty or one hundred rubles to one dollar.

In the Soviet Union, everyone exchanged money on the black market—even foreign diplomats.

Steele glanced at the Kremlin across the Moskva River and back to the prime real estate of the British embassy located on this side of the river. On its own, the building might have been a French or Austrian country villa and was certainly more ornate than most of the monstrous Moscow buildings that served as an eternal reminder of the Stalin and Soviet era and its architecture. Yes, it felt good to be a British citizen. His embassy boasted prime real estate opposite the ominous yet enchanting golden domes of the Kremlin and its surrounding red brick walls.

Simon Bird, a senior MI6 case officer, greeted Steele at the main entrance and, disappointingly, escorted Steele around the side of the building to a separate, more modern office location.

"Welcome, Jack," he said in Russian as they entered the building to the left of the Cultural Section. "You can leave your stuff over there."

Steele smiled, dropped his luggage, and returned Bird's greeting in Russian. Steele knew his own Russian was good, excellent even, but he was a perfectionist. He wanted to be able to pass as a native, or at least someone from the Baltic states— Latvia, Lithuania, or Estonia. *That* was his linguistic goal and benchmark. Even as a student in Moscow the year before, when chatting up pretty girls with his friend, Charlie, they would compete to see which of them would be discovered as a foreigner first—whose accent had betrayed them the quickest.

"Happy to be here. Happy to help," said Steele. He wasn't sure if *happy* was the right word. *Fucking terrified* might be more accurate, but he certainly wasn't going to show it. This was it. This was the start of his military career, and he was going to do his best for them—show them he had what it takes. If that meant spying—*let's call it what it is*—then so be it, even though he had been trained to kill as a soldier and had no idea how to spy. It certainly beats working in the City or even serving in the regiment, which he was not particularly looking forward to because, by all accounts, regimental life in Germany was mundane and monotonous. The good news, however, was that his regimental officers' mess Army Catering Corps chef was rumored to be Michelin standard.

"How was the flight?" asked Bird.

"Disappointing. No caviar." Steele raised an eyebrow.

Bird smiled, "Outrageous. I'll be sure to make a note in the daily sitrep. 'Aeroflot's flop.'"

He closed the door behind them and gestured to a leather sofa opposite his desk, and Steele took a seat.

Bird said, "Tea? Coffee?"

"I'm fine for now."

"Roger that." Bird poured himself some coffee into a standard government-issue white porcelain cup and added milk and sugar. "Down to business."

"Ready when you are."

"You are heading straight to Leningrad tonight on the train. Overnight. Trains are a bit hit-and-miss here. There's talk of a fast train, but it hasn't happened yet."

"No problem."

"We want you to check in at the Leningrad Linguistic Institute hall of residence—they're expecting you. Tomorrow, you'll meet the dean. He's also expecting you."

Steele said, "Then what?" He shifted uneasily on the sofa.

"Simple. Just be a student. You will find Masha Pushkin in due course … act surprised, of course. You are back in Russia on a scholarship for a one-year diploma in advanced interpretation and translation."

"I thought it was a three-month exchange program?"

"Good. I'm glad you were paying attention."

"Then back to Bath."

"Correct. MA in interpreting."

"That's it?"

"Yes. Just be a student."

"Just be a student? Sounds easy. Why don't you say, *spy*?"

"That's a big word, Jack. I'd be careful how and when you use it. Locals get nervous." Bird stroked his beard and whipped off his glasses, whose smeary lenses, Steele noticed, needed a good clean. "We are very grateful and appreciative, Jack. But don't be under any misconceptions. You are *not* a spy. You are a British student who is passionate about the Russian language and culture and one day hopes to be a British diplomat."

"No one in Russia knows I'm a Sandhurst cadet?"

Bird replaced his glasses and eyed Steele. "Fair question. Your military profile has been wiped from the system for now, just in case. You don't really have much of a paper trail now, anyway. There's no official record that you've been to Sandhurst or were about to join the army."

Steele felt momentarily light-headed. *This doesn't feel good.* "How long do you want me to stay here?" He suddenly wished they had not plucked him from obscurity and that he was going to his regiment like everyone else.

Bird pulled a face of mock discomfort. "Honestly, I don't know. It depends on our American brothers and how long they need you in situ."

"And why are we so interested in Masha and her father? No one has told me yet."

Bird paused as though he was genuinely surprised. "Err, sorry about that, Jack. Masha's father is the top-ranking GRU officer in Leningrad. We believe—or at least, the Yanks believe—he's doing something he shouldn't be, but we don't know for sure. Usual story in our merry world." Bird placed his empty cup on the table. "And *that*, as they say, is all you need to know."

"That's it?"

"That's it," Bird replied. "Best of British."

Washington D.C., USA

Brad Madison, president of the United States of America, threw the remote down on the sofa in the Oval Office.

"What in God's name is his problem?" he remonstrated. "I'm fed up with these anti-American interviews."

Kolby Webster, deputy director of CIA operations, said, "He's a Liberal, sir. Who can figure out a goddamn Liberal?"

"Damn right there, Kolby. Motherfucking Swedes. I have never been able to figure them out, either. They have the most beautiful women on earth, but they eat shit food and have no idea how fortunate they are to have us on their team."

"Aronsson seems to be an outlier, Mr. President." Webster frowned. "But I know you wanted them on board."

"He's screwing up the plan. It's Leontev and his cronies Aronsson should be worried about. Where are we with President Leontev and his shithole country?"

"Things not looking good. They're falling apart as we speak."

"Be more specific, Kolby. You sound like the Six Million Dollar Man."

"Yes, sir. I mean, all our readouts show that Leontev might not be able to hold the Soviet Union—as we know it—together. Their economy's in tatters, and we think they might be looking for an out. A big one."

"Good. That's perfect."

"Yes, sir. That's our reading."

"That's what I'm banking on." Madison walked to his desk, sat down, and leaned back. "I'm gonna end this goddamn Cold War if it kills me. Let's kick him while he's down, Kolby."

"The Deception Committee?"

"You better believe it." The president pointed to the remote lying on the sofa. "Turn up the volume. Let's see if he's still ranting and raving."

But CNN International's live election coverage from Stockholm had finished.

Webster continued, "Very good, sir. If you're sure."

"Sure? Why wouldn't I be sure? Did you see this guy?"

"Yes, sir. I saw him."

"Right. Let's teach the son of a bitch a lesson."

"But the Deception Committee is for the Soviets, sir."

"I want options to piss off Anders Aronsson till he's begging to climb back into bed with us. Do you understand me?"

Webster hesitated. "Err—"

President Madison raised his voice. "Do you understand me?"

"Yessir. Options."

"Better still, his opponent wins in the election."

"Understood."

"Whatever it takes, Kolby. Understand?"

Webster nodded. "Yessir, Mr. President."

CHAPTER TWELVE

Somewhere between Moscow and Leningrad, USSR

Steele stepped into the corridor to take in the view on the other side of the northbound train. He estimated that they were halfway to Leningrad and would arrive in three or four hours. In the darkness, Steele could make out occasional ink-black shapes of country dachas. *The Russians love their dachas*, Steele thought. He had visited several during his year in Moscow. Rich or poor, everyone, it seemed, had a dacha—or knew someone *with* a dacha. It made perfect sense. Everyone needed a place to unwind outside the city. For the working class, a dacha might be a shed next to a vegetable allotment. For the Communists, elites, or intelligentsia, it might be a small mansion in the middle of the Russian countryside.

"Tickets, please!" the conductor said in Russian. "Tickets, dear comrades."

Standing between Steele and the conductor was a tall blond man with a sharp-pointed nose. "You English?" he asked.

From his accent, the man was definitely a Brit.

"Yes," replied Steele. "How's it going?"

"Yes, good. Where you off to?"

"Leningrad," Steele replied.

The man smiled. "Obviously, but what's your business there?"

"I'm a student. Postgrad. I'm on an exchange for foreign students."

"LLI?"

"Yes."

"Quite prestigious."

Steele moved closer to the man so he could hear better over the noise of the train.

The babushka conductor in charge of their train car approached with a tray of tea. "Let's go, boys. Have some hot tea," she said in Russian.

"Service in the dead of night. I'm impressed," observed Steele. He reached out, picked up one of the glasses filled with hot, sweet tea served in an ornate silver holder, and took a sip. "Jack Steele."

"Ian Patterson. ITN Bureau chief, Moscow, and Leningrad. Mainly Moscow—there's not much news in Leningrad."

"Right. I think I've seen you."

"Yes, I do the occasional piece-to-camera if our correspondent is on assignment."

"What's the latest?"

"News?"

"Yes, anything I should know about?"

Patterson blew on his hot tea. "Between you and me, things aren't looking good."

"*Things?*"

"Things you won't see on the news."

"Why not?"

"The Ministry of Foreign affairs will kick us out if we get too close to the bone."

"Report the truth?"

"Yes. Mikhail Leontev has a lot on his plate. The economy's in bits. The war in Afghanistan is eating the Soviet army alive. Peasants are starving in the countryside, and Leontev needs friends in the West."

Steele said, "Isn't that good? Chance for peace?"

"Except that there are darker forces at play. The old cronies like things the way they are."

"Cream at the top? Everyone else is screwed."

"Very poetic. But yes …"

"Is the leadership in danger?"

"Maybe. No one knows exactly what's going on. But things aren't as rosy as they seem. Even if Leontev and the Cowboy become best mates, there's going to be serious resistance from the old and bold commie apparatchiks."

"Cowboy?"

"POTUS. Hollywood actor—retired."

"Brad Madison. Got it." Steele nodded, then hesitated for a moment before he said, "Have you heard of a man called Admiral Pushkin?"

"Yes, he's GRU. Big wig."

"Big wig?"

"Bloody big wig. Old-school, apparently. The kind of operator who'd slit your throat if you mess with him. But that's just a rumor. I can't speak from experience."

Steele swallowed hard. "So he might not be in favor of détente with the West?"

Patterson shrugged. "Great question. Wish I knew the answer. I bet our boys in London do too."

"Right." Steele had only just met Patterson and decided to stop asking questions.

"One thing's for sure," continued Patterson. He stared out the window for a moment and said, "the Soviet Union as we know it—love it *or* hate it—is up shit creek without a paddle."

"How do you know for sure?" asked Steele.

"I've been a journalist for fifteen years. Instincts, my friend. The domes are a-trembling."

A few hours later, Steele arrived in Leningrad and shared a taxi with Patterson, who dropped him at the Leningrad Linguistic Institute halls of residence.

This city was considerably more beautiful than Moscow. As they reached the center, canals and church domes became more prevalent. Steele recalled literary passages from books by Dostoevsky and Gogol he had studied at Exeter University. It was invigorating to see the real thing—locations and settings of works like *Crime and Punishment, The Nose, The Overcoat,* and *Diary of a Madman.* He had read them in Russian but also enjoyed his Russian professor's published translations.

"Pop by the bureau anytime," said Patterson. "We might get you some work as an interpreter." Steele liked the idea of working with newspeople. They seemed more independent and free-thinking than diplomats and army colleagues.

"Thank you. I'll do that."

"And keep an eye out for the Bond movie."

"James Bond?"

"Yes, they're filming in the city. Apparently, it took two years and some heavy backhanders to get permission. But you might see them. Some kind of chase sequence."

"Sounds interesting."

Steele said goodbye and entered the student residence building, where he was greeted by a babushka at the front desk. He introduced himself, and she showed him to his room. He hadn't slept much on the train, but he was running on adrenaline now. He had drunk several teas during the night.

Steele closed the door and wondered who his roommate would be and if he was a Russian spy. It was highly likely—even if his status as a Sandhurst cadet had not filtered down to the security services in Leningrad. Any new foreigner was a target and fair game for the ubiquitous KGB.

Nigel Rhodes Stampa had at first seemed pompous and rather arrogant. But he had also given Steele a thorough briefing on basic spy craft. Sandhurst had taught him how to be a trained killer on the battlefield, but that wasn't much use to a student in Leningrad.

Steele dropped his rucksack on the bed and headed down the corridor to the men's lavatories, not difficult to locate, thanks to the pungent smell of urine. Steele entered, eager to relieve himself. "Jesus," he said, trying not to breathe through his nostrils. Inside the stall, the lavatory had no seat and was leaking onto the red tile floor, forming a stream of urine that led to a central drain. *This place is literally leaking piss. What the hell have I got myself into?*

It was true. Soviet obshchezhitiye—*halls of residence*—were, literally, known shitholes. It was a common joke among foreign students who came to study in the Soviet Union. It was considered a badge of honor to reside in a Russian obshchezhitiye and do battle with ancient plumbing, cockroaches, and the stolovaya's—*cafeteria's*—most inedible food on earth.

Steele returned to his room and did a sweep for bugs—the electronic kind. He had not expected to find anything, but he was wrong. After only a cursory search, Steele found the first microphone in the electrical socket behind his bed. He unscrewed the panel with his Swiss army knife and found a tiny microphone inside. *Cheeky fuckers.* He was genuinely surprised. *These people don't mess around.* He wondered if Masha or Masha's father knew about him. *Have they turned the tables on me already? Or is this routine surveillance for a new foreign student?*

Steele exhaled. *Game on. I can use this. I can use this to my advantage.*

If there was an opportunity to lay a false trail about his mission or intentions, he would use the microphone. Steele had spent six months at Sandhurst learning how to engage the Soviet army on the battlefield. In some ways, he hated the idea of conflict with Russia. He loved the language, and he loved their people. But now, it hit him. He was working for his government against his friends, Katya and now Masha. His stomach tightened, and he suddenly felt sick. He wasn't sure if he could do this. *How long can I live this lie? How long before they catch me out?*

★   ★   ★

Ten minutes later, once Steele had exited the building for the short walk to the institute, the babushka dezhurnyy—*concierge*—picked up the telephone and made her report. The truth was, she didn't have much else to do. And this was her first foreign student to spy on for a while.

A voice said, "Yes, I'm listening."

"He just left for the institute."

"Anything to report?"

"He found the microphone already."

"Good. As we suspected."

The babushka glanced into the small makeup mirror on her otherwise empty desk to check her lipstick. "Anything else I can do?"

"No, Valya Borisovich. You have done well, comrade. We appreciate your service."

"Thank you. I'm proud to serve my country."

CHAPTER THIRTEEN

Castel Gandolfo, Rome

Vincenzo closed his eyes and said a short prayer as the helicopter descended and the Vatican pilot prepared to land at Castel Gandolfo. The prayer was one of thanks for his life, his calling, and a safe landing. He was sitting next to Pope Karl, the first German pope in a thousand years, and Vincenzo was honored and thankful for his own achievements and station in life.

Pope Karl glanced at Vincenzo and smiled. He raised his eyebrow and pointed down to the Apostolic Palace of Castel Gandolfo and the adjoining lake. The beauty of the summer residence with its manicured lawns and shrubs was celestial.

The helicopter—known affectionately among the clergy as the *pope-copter*—landed gently, and Vincenzo extended a hand to the elderly pope, who climbed out of the helicopter with God's grace.

As the two men made their way across the lawn, Vincenzo seized his opportunity before the pontiff retired for his afternoon nap. "Your Holiness, forgive me. Did you have time to think about our Russian friend? Next steps?"

Pope Karl watched the helicopter take off and then said, "Let's sit."

Vincenzo gestured to the attending staff to give them a moment, and they obediently retreated into the castle.

Vincenzo said, "Do you think we can help?"

"Peace, Vincenzo. I want peace."

"Of course, Your Holiness. Yes, I think we can shepherd them toward each other."

They reached a bench and sat down. This bench was Vincenzo's favorite. It was known as *the throne* because there was an unwritten rule that only the pontiff was allowed to use it. But Vincenzo would break the rule on occasion and sit on *the throne* in the early morning and late summer evenings when Pope Karl was safely tucked away in his quarters and no one else was looking.

"How was your trip to Capri?"

"Enchanting, Your Holiness. By God's grace."

Pope Karl said, "I have not been there for many years. I recall there is a beautiful monastery." He waved his hand, searching for the name but to no avail.

"Certosa San Giacomo," Vincenzo offered. *St. James's Charterhouse.*

"That's right. I spent a beautiful month on a silent retreat there when I first came to Rome." Pope Karl inhaled the warm breeze tripping off the lake. "Your Russian diplomat was genuine? Of good faith?"

Vincenzo smiled. "I think so. They see a chance for peace."

"Good. This must remain a secret, even among our own."

"Of course, Your Holiness. I understand."

"What does the Russian suggest?"

Vincenzo said, "It's very simple. He wants us to invite the Americans and host a summit. He has a message we must pass to the Americans."

"Why do they not reach out directly to the Americans?" asked Pope Karl.

"They have, but they also feel it will be taken more seriously if it comes from us, too—a Godly third party, so to speak. For so many years, there has been much mistrust between superpowers on both sides of the Iron Curtain."

Pope Karl, born and bred in Dresden, seemed only too aware

of the lies, propaganda, and mistrust that existed. He had shared as much with Vincenzo during their walks and conversations. "So we are the saintly go-between?"

Vincenzo nodded. "God willing."

"I want to be certain this does not become a political endeavor. It can *never* be political. It would be too damaging."

"I agree, Your Holiness. No one will ever know. As you say, *Not even our own.*"

Pope Karl looked into Vincenzo's eyes. "How can I trust a man who disrobes in the confessional?"

Vincenzo's eyes widened. He felt his face and neck flush with embarrassment. "Your Holiness, I—"

Pope Karl shook his head and tut-tutted. Then he laughed. "I am pulling your leg, my son." He gave Vincenzo's arm a comforting squeeze.

"But how—"

"Our confessionals have ears *and* tongues. They tell me all their secrets." He winked.

Vincenzo was confused. "Your Holiness, I am so sorry."

"Not at all. I don't blame you for cooling off in the confessional. I wish I had thought of it myself in my younger days. These vestments are not summer-friendly." Pope Karl looked away but continued, "Tell the Americans their president is 'on the money.' It is time to tear open the curtain."

Vincenzo felt exhilarated. An excited shiver ran down his spine. Perhaps it really *was* possible. Perhaps they could fulfill their religious and spiritual duty *and* help the politicians and world leaders make peace. When Vincenzo was a teenager, his father had often called him naïve. Vincenzo preferred to think of himself as spiritually enthusiastic.

He said, "Very good, Your Holiness. I will tell them. Our contact is in Venice. I will go there in person this weekend for the sake of secrecy."

"Very good." Pope Karl closed his eyes and said a prayer. "Heavenly Father, we thank you for this opportunity you have presented us today. Heavenly Father, know that we love you, and we pray for your guidance to bring peace and stability to our world as you see fit."

As they sat in silence, Pope Karl felt guilty, but he did not show it. He admired Vincenzo, one of God's true servants, but Pope Karl did not share the fact that he was praying more for the future of the Soviet Union and Bloc and less for world peace. In his heart, he suspected the Soviets might be plotting to assassinate the president of the United States. And in his heart, he knew he didn't want to intervene. Pope Karl's father had been deputy director of the HVA—East German Intelligence Service—and Pope Karl knew how best God could save the world.

Both men opened their eyes and unclasped their hands. Vincenzo helped Pope Karl to stand, and they set off toward the summer residence. Pope Karl said, "Time for some English tea. Cardinal Jeremy sent some from London. Fortnum's."

"What about your nap, Your Holiness?"

"Today, Fortnum's takes priority."

Leningrad Linguistic Institute

Steele loved the water. He took in the canals as he crossed a few bridges and ran his hand along the solid wrought iron balustrade that lined most of the embankments. There was a golden dome visible in every direction, and every one of them was unique and different. Leningrad really was an exquisitely beautiful city. As he walked past another artist painting the traditional canal-and-dome view, for a brief moment, he wished he was Russian and could stay here forever and become a painter or a poet.

Evidently, these kinds of paintings sold well. He saw one artist wearing a blue jacket and blue-and-white striped Russian navy T-shirt. These artists, he had read, were part of the *Mitki*, an art collective producing satirical poetry, prose, and artwork. He wanted to stop and buy the large painting of a tank and a giant Russian bear in the snow that he immediately fell in love with. But he had work to do. *I'm not a tourist, and I'm not here for souvenirs.*

Steele reached the Leningrad Linguistic Institute, entered, and asked for directions to the dean's office.

The babushka at the front desk said, "Go to the end, turn right into the alcove, and knock on the door. Welcome to our beautiful city."

Steele thanked the babushka, headed to the office, and knocked on the door.

"Yes, please!" shouted a Russian voice inside. "Enter!"

Steele entered and introduced himself to the thickset, surly-looking man with a bulbous nose, who seemed to be expecting him.

The dean spoke in Russian. "Please, *Jeck* Steele. Have a seat. Welcome to Leningrad Linguistic Institute." He smiled, but the man looked as though he was in pain, or even constipated.

"Thank you, Viktor Viktorovich," said Steele. "It's wonderful to be back in Russia."

"How was the journey?"

"It was good. I'm looking forward to Leningrad. Thank you for having me."

"No problem. It is our pleasure. The dean of the Maurice Thorez Institute of Foreign Languages is a personal friend. He spoke highly of your linguistic skills. It's a shame you will end up spying on us one day."

Steele's heart skipped a beat.

Viktor chuckled. "Just playing with you, *Jeck* Steele. Spying is not a worthwhile métier, in my humble opinion. Too much stress. Your application form said you plan to become a British diplomat?"

Steele wondered if the dean would use Steele's first and last name every time. "Yes, that's right. And yes, I agree with you about spying."

The dean picked up the phone. "Lenochka,"—he used the diminutive of his secretary's name, Lena—"Please can you find Masha Pushkin. Tell her to come to the office immediately."

Steele swallowed. *Masha Pushkin knows I'm here? Wasn't this supposed to be a secret?* He steadied his breathing. *How does she know I'm here?*

The dean shuffled some papers on his desk and placed them into plastic folders. Then he placed more papers into a desk drawer. "Masha will be here shortly. Your accommodation is good?" asked Viktor.

"It's …" Steele searched for the right words.

"I know." Viktor snorted. "There is room for improvement."

Steele knew most Soviet student halls of residence were dilapidated, and he couldn't resist asking, "Why are the bathrooms leaking? I mean the toilets themselves."

"*Jeck*, we had a very difficult war."

The only war Steele could think of in Leningrad was World War II against the Nazis. He said, "But that was fifty years ago."

"Yes, but it was a *very* difficult war. We lost many thousands of patriots in this city, but it was worth it for the motherland."

Steele nodded, confused.

There was a knock at the door.

"Please!" shouted Viktor. "Please, come in."

Lena opened the door, and Masha entered.

"I think you know each other," said Viktor.

Steele smiled, looking at Masha. "Yes," he said. "Great to see you again, Masha."

Masha looked different from when he had met her in Moscow. Her hair was longer and blonder. Her face was thinner, and she had blossomed into a beautiful young woman from the slightly rotund female student he had encountered briefly in Moscow through his friend, Katya.

"Hello, Jack," she said. "I am happy to see you again."

"Me too. How did you know I was here?"

"Viktor Viktorovich called me to the office."

Steele nodded, but her answer didn't make sense. "You …"—he hesitated—"you look great."

"You too," said Masha. "Come with me. We have a lot to catch up on. I will give you a tour of our institute."

Viktor Viktorovich said, "Thank you, Masha. Let me know if I can help you, *Jeck* Steele. I hope you will have successful studies with us."

"I appreciate that, sir," replied Steele. "Keep working on those bathrooms."

Viktor did not reply as Steele and Masha left his office. They walked back toward the main entrance vestibule.

Masha asked, "Are you hungry? Thirsty?"

"Um … yes, both."

"Let me show you the stolovaya."

Aware that the Russian word meant *cafeteria*, he said, "Perfect." Then he hesitated, not knowing quite where to start. "I appreciate you coming to welcome me."

"Of course. It's not a problem. I am happy to welcome you."

"You said the dean told you I was coming?"

"Yes, my father called him yesterday."

"Your father?" Steele's heart skipped another beat.

Masha smiled. "He just wants to make sure you are not a spy."

"That's the second time in ten minutes someone mentioned spies."

"This is Soviet Union. We have two masters—the Communist Party and the KGB."

"Are you saying your father is a spy?"

"He is an important admiral for Soviet navy. I am sure he is some kind of spy. And he also likes to monitor foreigners who come to our city. We have many military secrets in this city. Even we Russians have to be careful."

"Why?"

"We have spies watching spies in my country."

They descended a flight of stairs and reached the stolovaya.

Steele said, "Masha, why does your father want to meet me?"

"I don't know, but he said he wants to meet you."

"No one knows me here. I just arrived."

"He knows you are Katya's friend and we met in Moscow. It's his job to be suspicious."

"Your father wants to meet me in person?"

"Yes, you are invited to my home."

"When?"

"Tonight."

"Your home? Why?"

"*Why?* For dinner, of course. You are lucky. My mother is making meat blinis."

CHAPTER FOURTEEN

ITN Bureau, Leningrad

Steele hurried from the institute as fast as he could without running. He needed help or at least a helping hand. Events were unfolding too quickly, and part of him didn't like it. His stomach felt tight, and he could feel himself sweating without much physical exertion.

He glanced at his Leningrad Falk plan map and saw that the ITN Bureau was a ten-minute walk from the institute down Nevski Prospekt. A trolley bus going in the right direction stopped a few yards ahead of him. The doors clattered open, and he jumped aboard for two stops. He didn't need a ticket. He was a foreigner, and foreigners rode public transport in the Soviet Union as though they owned it because ticket inspectors were rare and never bothered penalizing foreigners who hadn't paid.

The ITN Bureau was in an old, dilapidated building right out of Dostoevsky's *Crime and Punishment*. But the office itself on the third floor was bright and clean (by Russian standards) and housed various computers, monitors, and mobile editing suites. The sinking feeling Steele felt when he left the institute was now turning to adrenaline, and he was excited to be in a British media hub that fed news stories via satellite back home to the UK.

Patterson stood up. "That was quick," he said. "You found us all right, then?"

They shook hands, and Steele said, "Yes, no problem. Took the trolley bus."

"Great. Let me show you around. There's not much to see."

Steele took in the office space. It was deserted. "Where is everyone?"

"I work mostly solo. London had to cut back. We used to have locals working for us full time, but now we hire as and when needed."

Steele nodded. "I have a problem."

"Already?"

"Yes." Steele made a circular motion to his ear. If his room in the *obshchezhitiye* was bugged, this office was sure to be too. Sotto voce, he mouthed, "Is there somewhere we can talk?"

Patterson understood and led the way to the french windows that led to an exterior balcony. They stepped onto the balcony overlooking a canal and more enchanting church domes left and right. "You're learning fast," said Patterson.

Steele bit the inside of his cheek. "I'm guessing you and Simon Bird know each other?"

"Yes, I know Simon. He's the cultural attaché at the British embassy."

"I know that. He's the one who sent me here. Look, I might be naïve, but I'm not stupid. If you're not a spook, I'm guessing you can get a secure message to Bird, or perhaps you can help me yourself?"

"My 'spidey' sense is tingling … but you've lost me."

"Are you saying it was just a coincidence we met on the train?"

"Yes, Jack. You've read too many spy novels. I'm a journo."

Steele stared at Patterson with a look that said, *I don't expect you to admit it, but I know you're lying.*

Patterson said, "Why don't you just call Bird at the embassy? There's a landline inside."

"We both know the phones are bugged. Foreign student 101."

"Is it urgent?"

"Yes, it's urgent. I wouldn't be here if it wasn't urgent."

"National security?"

"Yes."

"We have a SAT phone."

"Great." *Finally,* he thought. *An inkling of progress.*

"But there's a part missing … sorry, I forgot. We're stuck with the landline."

Steele frowned. "Something's happened, and I need to talk to Bird. Securely."

Patterson nodded. Then he said slowly, "Okay, Jack. *If* there was a way for me to contact Bird, what would you like me to tell him? What's the problem?"

"Admiral Pushkin."

Patterson eyed Jack for a moment. "Leningrad's finest."

"Quite," said Steele. "So everyone seems to think. Masha has invited me to dinner."

"Where?"

"To her flat. I thought Bird might like to know."

"And her father?"

"Yes, she said her father wanted to meet me."

Patterson raised an eyebrow. "She said that?"

"Yes."

"What were her precise words?"

"She said her father wants to meet me—he knows we know each other from Moscow—and it's his job to be suspicious."

"Did she say her father will be there?"

"Yes, of course."

"Are you sure? Tell me exactly what she said."

Steele sensed a shift in Patterson's tone. Gone was the nonchalant journo confidence; Patterson was shifting gears to interrogator.

"I mean, she said her father wanted to meet me, and that it was his job to be suspicious, and her mother would make meat blinis."

"So, she didn't actually say he would be there?"

"I mean, not those exact words. But from what she said, I'm ninety-five percent sure he's going to be there. What is this? Why is it so important?"

Patterson smiled. "Okay, Jack. You did the right thing ... coming here."

"You people didn't leave me much choice."

"I'll let Bird know."

"How?"

"Leave that to me."

"So, should I go?"

"Go where?"

"Should I go to Masha's flat?"

"Yes, you should go."

"This is why I'm here, right?"

"I don't follow."

"This is why they sent me ... to get to the admiral via Masha."

"I'm afraid you've lost me, Jack. Like I said, Admiral Pushkin is a tricky character. Just be polite, and be careful."

"Roger that." Steele turned to go inside.

"Jack, what time's the dinner?"

"Tonight at seven."

"Fuck," said Patterson very calmly. "I'll be in touch."

Once Steele had left the office, Patterson sat down at his desk and scraped both hands through his head of blond hair.

He leaned down to the right-hand side of his desk, picked up the large metal protective case with the state-of-the-art satellite telephone inside, stepped out onto the balcony again, and closed the door behind him. After punching in a security code and hearing dead silence on the first attempt, Patterson dialed again and got through to Simon Bird at the British embassy in Moscow.

"He's in."

Bird replied, "Come again?"

"He's bloody in. Already."

"He's made contact?"

"Yes."

"Jesus. That was fast. How?"

Patterson said, "As we planned. He met the daughter, and she invited him to dinner."

"But he's only been there a day."

"Maybe Rome *was* built in a day after all?"

"Funny. But seriously, it doesn't make sense."

"Too fast?"

"Yes. It's as though they knew he was coming."

"Well, we've done our part."

"We've only just started."

"What do you want me to do?"

"Nothing. For now. Just get ready in case things go tits up. It's not our show, remember."

"What's his extraction plan?"

"Extraction?"

"If things go tits up?"

"There isn't one. It's not our op."

"We're just going to leave him?" Patterson waited for an explanation that didn't come. Then he said, "Hello?"

"If the KGB doesn't arrest him, shoot him, or make him disappear, or shove him out a window, or whatever it is they do to spies, then you'll get him out."

"*What?*" Patterson steadied himself on the balustrade. "You're out of your mind. That's not what we agreed."

"Things change. First rule of spooking, my dear fellow."

"Seriously? I'm not fucking Harry Houdini."

"You were in the army, weren't you? We've given you the tools and resources to be used in extremis. So if I give you an order, you'll execute the order. Unless you want me to let ITN know what you've been up to. I am sure they would love to make *you* news of the day."

Patterson's chest tightened. "Fuck you, Bird."

"Thank you, Ian. I've always been mesmerized by your journalist charm and eloquence."

Patterson pressed the END CALL button and slammed the receiver back into the cradle.

CHAPTER FIFTEEN

Kremlin presidential apartments, Moscow

Soon it would be his favorite time of year. Mikhail Leon-tev—the president of not just Russia but of the entire mind-bending expanse of Soviet Socialist Republics covering eleven time zones—was looking forward to the first snowfall. It wouldn't be for six weeks or so, but as he looked out at the ornate, candy-like domes inside the Kremlin and at St. Basil's just a bit farther afield, he imagined them with a layer of snow. Certain parts of Moscow were stunning and magnificent, but they looked even better with snow.

Leontev turned up the volume on his twenty-eight-inch Sony television.

More inaccurate news.

The austere-looking female announcer was spouting the usual twaddle. *Why do these people never crack a smile?* Agricultural and industrial production was better than ever before, and the Soviet Union was experiencing a new lease of life thanks to perestroika—*restructuring*—and glasnost—*transparency*—the latest political jargon and propaganda designed to calm the masses and hold the fragile state of the union together.

"I am not sure how much longer we can last," he said to his wife, Irina Borisovich Leontev.

Irina set a tray of tea down on the table and poured two cups.

"Do you want honey, sugar, or preserves? You know sugar rots your teeth."

"Thank you, dearest. Always my best interests at heart."

"Of course. What other way is there? Till death do us part."

"No sugar. Give me preserves, my sweet one."

"Here you go." Irina served her husband of thirty-five years and poured her own cup. "Look, I am choosing honey today. Follow my example, husband, my not-so-sweet one."

He smiled. "Very well. Give me honey. And thank you."

They both sipped at the hot tea and watched the main Soviet news channel spewing propaganda. Leontev always marveled at how the television news stations were able to broadcast the news across multiple time zones and, at the same time, ensure the bulletin contained the very latest news and reportage. He said, "I have to go soon. I have to attend parliament. They want good news I don't have for them."

"What is happening?"

"I will tell you honestly, Irinichka. We need economic relief, and we need it now. If we don't find a way to feed our people, I fear the worst. We need a miracle."

"You are the president. You are our leader. Your job is to make the miracle."

"I understand, Irinichka. But unfortunately, I am not a magician. We will need help. Foreign help."

"Foreigners?"

"Yes, we need a new era of détente with the West."

"Is that so bad?"

"Of course not. But it is not so simple, my dearest." Leontev stood up with his cup of tea and walked to the window. Again, he marveled at the stunning view and thought back to his upbringing in a tiny village in the Russian Far East, his kolkhoz—*collective farm*—where he spent the first ten years of his life feeding pigs and wading through the mud on his parents' farm. It was indeed *a hard life*, as the Russians loved to lament, but it was somehow satisfying and even enjoyable. Yes, he even used to find joy in pig shit.

"Explain," Irina said. "Explain it to me as though we were

sitting together in our elementary school, wearing our pioneer uniforms like the old days."

The Russian president smiled and recalled the two of them sitting in the classroom together—she in her brown "pioneer" dress and white pinafore, he in his "pioneer" blue tunic—and both with the obligatory Communist Party red neckerchiefs. He said, "If only it were that simple."

"Make it simple, Misha. Remember how you got to where we are today."

Leontev nodded.

Irina continued, "Your gift is your eloquence—the reason why we are here is that you are able to explain important things like no other human I have met. That is why our people love you. That is why our wizened old apparatchiks accepted you, even though you were nothing like them. Part of you is more Western than you realize."

"I understand, Irinichka. But it is different this time." He did not look her in the eye as he spoke. "Our Union is too big to fail. But we are about to fail."

Irina slammed her cup down on the tray, walked over to her husband, placed both hands on his cheeks, and squeezed until it hurt him. "I won't hear of such things. Do you hear me? Do you understand?"

Leontev gently pulled away. He was not angry with Irina, but he *was* angry with himself—that he had allowed things to develop in this way after the debacle and coup attempt of his predecessor. The union had already come close to collapse, and he had not learned the lessons. He had let his guard down, and he wasn't sure if it was possible to raise it again. He had made the classic mistake when success comes—he had forgotten that failure is never far behind.

"The way I see it, there is only one solution."

"Well, good. Now we are talking. Let's hear it."

"We must befriend the West. We must eat humble pie."

Irina frowned. "Why do you say this?"

"Our union needs them. We have oil and gas, but we need their dollars, hard currency, and frankly, we need their ideology."

Irina shook her head with a double take. "What are you saying?"

"It's called democracy."

Irina laughed. "You're insane. You want democracy in the Soviet Union?"

"Of course not. Our people could never manage this. But we need to understand and accept theirs."

"America?"

"The West. They can no longer be our enemy."

Irina nodded and clasped her hands together in thought. "I understand. Yes, I understand what you are saying. Maybe it's not so bad?"

"It's not so bad, but I repeat, it's not so easy. Once we extend the olive branch, there are many here who will want to crush it."

"What does your heart tell you?"

Irina Borisovich, as usual, was on the mark. She had always made him realize what was important and how to address the root of any dilemma or problem. In his heart, he knew what the right thing to do was. He had always known when it was time to do the right thing. He recalled the image of his small terrier being eaten alive by his pig five decades ago. The class bully had trespassed onto his farm, untied the dog, broken one of its legs, and thrown the dog into the pigsty. Mikhail arrived to discover his best friend—Fritz the terrier—being eaten by his sow.

From that day, Mikhail had become almost superhuman. He wasn't a strong child in the physical sense, but on that day, he had beaten the bully to a pulp in the schoolyard. After explaining himself to his parents, his teachers, and even the local Communist Party, he had become a local hero, and it was the bully who was punished and chastised within the kolkhoz community.

On that day, Leontev learned that he would always stand up to bullies and always fight against injustice. It was also, he conceded, a small miracle that in this authoritarian empire he was now leading, his brand of leadership and justice had propelled him to the very top. He had always truly believed there was hope for the Soviet Union to be a great power militarily *and* economically.

Until now.

He said, "My heart, Irinichka, tells me to bow to Western superiority. If we don't, the USSR will implode within weeks."

"Then, I respect your decision. We will be victorious in whatever plan you make. We will make friends with President Madison."

"I don't trust him. He is all ego and no substance. And remember, he was an actor in Hollywood. He knows how to fool people with smiles and jokes. But Mr. Cowboy is not our biggest problem."

"Tell me."

"I am afraid our biggest enemy is among us."

Irina cocked her head. "Explain."

"There are those among us—dark, nefarious forces—who will see me dead rather than allow change. It is the curse of Mother Russia."

Near Stockholm, Sweden

Lars Endressen, aged ten, painted the finishing touches to the green and brown camouflage on his Saab 35 Draken fighter aircraft model. He would allow it to dry before placing the blue-and-yellow transfers on the wings. Then he would hang it from the wire that ran across his bedroom with the dozen or so British and German WWII model planes he had spent the summer holidays making, painting, and displaying. "It's not a bedroom," he'd curtly told his mother, Erika Endressen, "It's an aviation museum."

Lars glanced up at the window and heard the rain coming down harder now. He walked to the window and cracked it so he could hear the rain. He loved the sound of the rain, especially when it lashed against the window in waves as if someone was using a hose. He felt safe and secure.

Their red-painted house thirty miles from the Swedish naval base in Muskö was old but in reasonable condition. More importantly, it boasted a stunning view of the Baltic Sea within walking distance. If Lars had a speed boat like the ones in American action movies, he would head east and explore Russia—a country, he had learned at school, that was more secretive and mysterious than his own.

Then he saw it.

It was a sight he had never seen before. He was used to seeing and identifying Swedish naval ships and aircraft, but never—yes, he was sure—he had never seen a *submarine* half a mile away in the straits heading inland. He reached for his binoculars and confirmed his sighting.

"Mum!" he shouted. "Mum, come and see!"

He heard the sound of this mother rinsing a saucepan in the kitchen before she arrived a few moments later to investigate the commotion.

"Look, there's a submarine!"

"Nonsense," Erika replied. She took the binoculars and said, "It can't possibly—"

She stopped midsentence. "Wait." She refocused the binoculars just as Lars had done. Slowly, she said, "There's a submarine in the strait."

"I know, Mum. That's what I was trying to tell you."

"You're right, Lars. It's a submarine."

"I've never seen a submarine like that in the straits before," Lars said.

"You are right, my boy. I have never seen one like that either."

"What does it mean?"

"It means I need to make a phone call, Lars." She handed him the binoculars. "Keep an eye on it. Tell me if it changes direction."

"Or if it sinks, right, Mum?"

"Yes, tell me if it submerses."

★　　★　　★

Erika returned to the open-plan kitchen and dining room kitchen and picked up the cordless telephone. It crossed her mind to call her ex-husband, who was a journalist. He would devour this story. But her military instincts told her this was more sinister than a breaking-news photo op. An army and navy signals veteran, she now worked as a civil servant—the liaison and public relations officer for the Swedish naval base in Muskö.

Erika knew exactly who to call because her boss was the Swedish naval base chief of staff, and she was certain he would want to know that a submarine was in the middle of the strait a few miles from the base. She had been born and bred in Stockholm and was now thirty-eight years old. This was the first time she had seen a submarine so close to Stockholm and, for that matter, the mainland in general.

But that wasn't her most stunning observation.

"Hello?" said the chief of staff.

"Colonel, it's Erika Endressen."

"Good evening, Erika. I thought you were off work today."

"Yes, Colonel. I am at home with my son. He's sick."

"I'm sorry to hear that."

"Nothing serious, thank you. But that's not why I'm calling. Colonel, there's a submarine in the strait."

"A submarine, you say? That's impossible."

"That's why I'm calling. I've never seen a submarine this close to the mainland."

"Are you sure it's not a warship?"

"Sir, I know what a submarine looks like. I saw it with my own eyes, and I double-checked with binoculars."

"It can't be."

"I can assure you—"

"You are certain?"

"Yes, I'm certain."

"Thank you, Erika. I will look into it immediately."

"One more thing, Colonel."

"Please."

"If I am not mistaken, the submarine isn't ours."

"What are you talking about?"

"The shape. The submarine is not Swedish."

"You must be confused. What are you saying?"

"I don't know, sir. But I served in army and naval intelligence." Erika stopped short of saying *I was top of the class in aircraft and maritime recognition.*

"I am aware. That's one of the reasons I hired you."

"The submarine is not ours."

"I still don't follow."

"I am saying, sir, that the submarine I see less than a mile from my window is not Swedish."

"Then, who?"

"I have never seen one in person—but from where I'm standing, I see a Soviet vessel."

Stunned silence.

"Colonel?"

"Yes, I hear you. We will investigate immediately. You are to stay home and monitor. That's an order."

"I understand."

Erika hung up and returned to her son's bedroom. "Do you see it?"

"Yes, Mum, but it looks like it's diving."

Erika snatched the binoculars and watched.

Ten seconds later, there was no trace of a submarine in the Baltic Sea.

"Mum," said Lars.

"Yes, Lars?"

Lars held up his Saab 35 Draken. "Do you like it? I just have to stick the transfers on. Do you want to help me?"

Erika stared at the model aircraft. Then she caught herself. "Umm ... yes, I love it."

Lars walked back to the window. "Mum. Can you ask Dad to buy me a submarine for my birthday?"

Erika watched the rain sweeping across the strait and did not reply.

CHAPTER SIXTEEN

Stockholm, Sweden

Astrid Aronsson was drying her hair when the phone rang in her father's office. She had planned to go out to the local café to hang out with a classmate for an hour, but her father had stopped her before she had a chance to explain that she needed to work on a school project.

"But Papa, you don't understand—"

"It's a school night, end of story," replied the Swedish prime minister as he walked toward his office and closed the door.

He answered the telephone. "Aronsson."

Admiral Olof Bergman said, "Good evening, Prime Minister. Forgive the interruption, but an urgent matter has come to my attention."

"Of course. What is it?"

"We have unconfirmed reports of a Soviet naval vessel in our waters."

Aronsson sat down at his desk. "I beg your pardon."

"I know, Prime Minister. I was also shocked to hear this news."

"I don't understand. How can that be?"

"We don't understand either. The reports are unconfirmed, but the original source was reliable."

"Where exactly?"

"Near the naval base."

"Muskö?"

"Yes, Prime Minister."

"This must be a mistake. Why would the Soviets do this?" Aronsson began to sweat. He could feel his blood pulsing. If such a thing was true, this could mark the end of his entire neutral geopolitics agenda—everything he had worked his entire political career for. This would play right into American foreign policy talking points.

"Apparently, this is not the first time these sightings have been observed."

"What did you say?" Aronsson's voice was getting louder. "Why wasn't I informed?"

"I'm sorry, Prime Minister. It did not rise to the level—"

"Level?" Aronsson exhaled. *I need to stay calm. I need to get to the bottom of this.* "What 'level' are you talking about?"

"Your security level. What I mean, Prime Minister, is the security classification of the previous intelligence."

Aronsson said slowly, "Please explain what you are talking about."

"The intelligence wasn't deemed sufficiently reliable to alert you previously, Prime Minister."

"You said this was about security level classification. Which is it?"

"That's right. What I meant—"

"What's changed?"

Admiral Bergman said, "Sir, please understand. It was not my decision. This came from the highest level of our security service—"

"Admiral, I am the fucking prime minister. Give me one good reason why I shouldn't replace you immediately. What the fuck is going on?"

"That would not be wise, Prime Minister. I suspect anyone who replaces me would have done the same thing."

"I don't care what you suspect. I want you to tell me why I wasn't given this information sooner."

"Sir—"

"The truth."

"Sir, I understand. The truth is that it was considered an unconfirmed national security matter."

"How is not telling *me* about a Soviet submarine up our backside not a breach of national security in itself?"

"Might I suggest, Prime Minister—off the record—that your government has not been the most cooperative with the defense ministry and security services."

"Elaborate."

"Your 'neutral' stand toward the Soviet aggressor has shall we say, troubled some of my superiors."

"Our position of neutrality and what my elected government considers the best course of action with the Soviet Union has *nothing* to do with you or your secret circles! You work for me, understand?"

"Prime Minister, if I might—"

"You will report to my office first thing in the morning. In the meantime, what do your superiors, who know so much about keeping Sweden safe, suggest we do about the submarine?"

"Our American partners recommend a limited strike once we confirm the sighting."

"That's interesting. The Americans are telling us what to do before you even bother to tell me?"

"We weren't sure—"

"About the submarine?"

"Its identity."

"And now you are?"

"Yes, sir. As I mentioned, this is not the first incident. After consultation with the CIA Stockholm station, they recommend we engage."

Aronsson felt his blood boiling. "Listen to me, Admiral Bergman, and listen *very* carefully. You will do nothing of the kind. I am the prime minister, and, God willing, I will still be the prime minister after the election next week. You will send me every word, every detail of every sighting and report of these Soviet vessels *tonight*, and under no circumstances are you to 'engage.' Is that understood?

"Sir, I think—"

"*I* think I have made myself perfectly clear."

"Yes, Prime Minister."

"And call me during the night if you have any new information or updates."

"Very good, Prime Minister."

Aronsson slammed the phone down and shook his head in disbelief. "What the *fuck* is going on?" He reached for the telephone to call his deputy.

Swedish Defense Ministry, Stockholm

Admiral Bergman let his conversation with the prime minister sink in for a few moments. He looked up at the three uniformed senior staff officers standing in front of his desk.

Admiral Bergman sighed and said sarcastically, "As we thought … he took it well."

The first naval intelligence officer sneered and said, "As we thought."

"What's our next move?" asked the second officer, this one from army intelligence.

Admiral Bergman said, "Now that the government is aware of the situation, you have my permission to shoot on sight the next time the submarine appears."

The naval intelligence officer said, "But his orders were quite the opposite?"

Admiral Bergman replied, "Don't worry about what *he* said. Just follow *my* orders. I will take full responsibility."

The naval intelligence officer glanced at his colleagues and said, "Of course, Admiral. Received and understood. It's about time we taught those commie bastards a lesson."

All present nodded in agreement.

"Quite …" said Admiral Bergman. "There are commie bastards everywhere nowadays."

CHAPTER SEVENTEEN

Leningrad, USSR

The temperature had suddenly dropped, and it was raining hard, verging on sleet. Unusual for this time of year.

At 7:05 pm, Steele and Masha left the institute's stolovaya, where they had been drinking tea, for the short walk to the Pushkin family's flat. The wind slapped their faces as they turned the corner of Griboyedov Canal Embankment and headed toward the River Neva. The street was quiet. The occasional Lada spluttered by, but there were no other people out walking in the rain.

As they bowed their heads to shield themselves from the downpour, Steele stumbled. Masha's grip was stronger than he expected. She stopped him from falling flat on his face from an uneven, wet paving stone.

Steele pulled himself upright. "Thanks," he said in English. Masha had asked to practice her English.

"Don't mention it. Our municipal workers are behind on their repair list. That paving stone has been like that since last winter."

"Sounds like Camden Council."

"What is Camden Council? English political party?"

"Not quite. Just my local version of your municipal workers." They continued walking.

"Your father's at home?" asked Steele.

"Yes."

"Are you sure this is okay?"

"Of course. You are our guest. I told you—*meat blinis*. My mother's best dish."

"Great." Steele realized Masha was still holding his arm. This was the closest, physically, he had been to her. He pulled away, then regretted it. He was attracted to her. For a moment, he allowed himself to wonder if the feeling was mutual.

Steele continued, "I get that your father likes to keep an eye on foreigners, but I'm surprised he's invited me to his home."

"Foreigner is always exotic. You are like animals in a zoo for us. Understand?"

"Except that we're the ones who roam free."

"Maybe. But this is what we do in Russia. We invite friends to our homes—v gosti."

"I like that phrase. We don't really have an exact equivalent—*to be a guest* would be the literal translation."

"My father invited you *to be a guest*."

"What shall I call him? Admiral?"

"You are not in military, so you do not have to use his rank."

Steele acknowledged with an ironic—to him only—smile. "Right. Makes sense."

"His name is Dimitri Viktorovich Pushkin."

"Got it. *Dimitri Viktorovich*."

"And my mother is Tatyana Borisovich."

"Vsoh yasna," Steele replied. *Got it.*

Masha picked up the pace and linked arms, taking him by surprise.

"It's okay," Masha said, "I don't nibble."

Steele smiled and said, "You mean, you don't *bite*?"

"Sorry?"

"You mean you don't *bite*? That's how we say it. Mice and horses 'nibble.'" Steele exposed his front teeth and impersonated a small primate.

Masha laughed and said, "Thank you. This is good for my English." She mirrored his animal impersonation, and they shared the joke.

They passed a row of ornate residences on Shvedskiy Pereu-lok—*Swedish Lane*— including that of the Swedish Consulate. A fresh-faced militsiya stood outside with his collar up, smoking a cigarette. He eyed them suspiciously. *They must teach them that 'look' at the police academy,* Steele thought.

Masha said, "I will go to Sweden one day."

"Why Sweden?"

"I like the color of their flag—blue and yellow—like Ukraine. I have many friends in Ukraine also."

"You want to visit Sweden because it has a blue and yellow flag?"

"I am joking." Masha nudged him playfully. "One of my best friends lives there."

"Boy or girl?"

"Girl. Her name is Astrid."

"How did you meet?"

"We are pen pals since school days."

"That's nice."

Masha turned and looked Steele in the eye and said, "I am going to defect, Jack, and I want you to help me."

Steele stopped dead. He let go of Masha's arm. "What?"

"I want to defect. I want to leave my country. But I need your help."

"Hang on a minute ..." Steele felt his heart pounding. Thoughts flashed across his mind. *I am about to enter the home of a CIA target. And by the way, his daughter wants to defect. And by the way, she wants* me *to help her.*

Steele continued walking, but his steps were measured. "Masha, you can't be serious."

"I am very serious. Why do you think I invite you to my home."

"You said your father invited me."

"I lied."

"Does he know I'm coming?"

"Do not worry, Jack. Everything is organized."

"Masha, you don't understand."

"What I don't understand?"

Steele hesitated. "Never mind." *What am I supposed to tell her? Really sorry, but your father is under surveillance by Western spies. And I'm leading the operation. And I have no idea what I am doing.*

Masha turned to Steele. "Jack ..."

"I'm listening."

"All you have to do is have dinner with us. It is not complicated."

"Why did you invite me to dinner?"

"Why not? You are new student in Leningrad."

Steele nodded. *Hold it together, damn it. Nothing makes sense, but there's nothing I can do about it right now. I told Patterson that Admiral Pushkin will be at this location. I need to complete the mission. If I back out now, my future's screwed.* "Right. Fine. No problem. I'm really looking forward to it," he lied.

"And two more things."

Steele frowned. "I can't wait."

"I am going to introduce you to my parents as my boyfriend. Just—how do you say this?—go with flow."

More thoughts and images flashed across Steele's mind— *Sandhurst, Nigel Rhodes Stampa, Wing Commander Jenkins, Claudia, Simon Bird's 'orders,' Ian Patterson, and the microphone at the obshchezhitiye.* "No problem," Steele said unconvincingly. His chest tightened. "What's the second thing?"

Masha smiled. "Welcome! We are here. This is my house." She pointed to an imposing entrance and took out her key. She unlocked the pedestrian door within the large wooden door that in the old days would have serviced horses and carriages.

They reached the landing on the second floor, and Masha pressed the bell, presumably to warn her parents she was arriving. But she still used her key to enter.

Masha switched back to Russian. "Mama, Papa, we are here. We have a guest. A foreigner!"

Steele was pleased to get out of the rain and cold, and even more pleased to smell the homemade beef dish that wafted toward them. It made him feel even more hungry than before.

They kicked off their shoes and took off their wet coats at the entrance, and Masha used her foot to slide an old pair of slippers—probably her father's—to Steele for him to use.

"Mama ... I want you to meet someone. Where are you?" Masha glanced at Steele. "My father is probably in his office. Come and meet my mother. You will like her. She is a very intelligent woman."

Steele walked past the closed door he assumed was the office and followed Masha to an open door where the smell of cooking grew stronger. "I'm definitely hungry," he said in Russian.

"Good. You do not have to wait much longer. It will be better than stolovaya food, I promise."

The wooden parquet floor creaked as most do in old buildings. *Comforting,* he thought. *But still no answer from Masha's parents.* He said, "Maybe they left you dinner and went to the theater?"

"Mamochka? Why are you hiding? I have a guest with me. Come on now!"

They passed the dining room that Steele could see led to another room. The dining room table was laid for four, complete with a lit candle and what in England might be described as Sunday-best crockery.

They entered the kitchen, and there was still no sign of either parent.

"I don't understand," Masha said. "Where is my mother?"

Steele raised an eyebrow. "Bedroom?"

Masha was not amused. "Seriously, this doesn't make sense."

She turned and moved quickly to the dining room, but Steele did not follow. He eyed the kitchen table and picked up a slice of dried sausage that was neatly sliced on a large plate.

Then he heard a piercing scream followed immediately by "*Jack!*"

Steele gobbled down the mouthful he had started as he moved through the flat to reach Masha. He entered the dining room and crossed to the bedroom beyond, presumably belonging to Masha's parents. He heard a steady sobbing, then a kind of controlled high-pitched wailing. It reminded him of the sound mourners make at funerals. His instincts told him that whatever Masha had found in the bedroom was going to turn his world upside down.

Masha was in a ball on the floor, sobbing. As he entered the room and looked right, a man and a woman lay next to each other on the bed, each with a bullet hole in the forehead. The man was wearing a navy military uniform and the woman a floral dress. There was a pistol in the man's limp hand resting on his chest, and his eyes were open. Mrs. Pushkin's eyes were closed, and both parents were clearly deceased. Blood seeped into manila bedsheets and pillows surrounding them.

Masha sobbed as Steele knelt beside her. "I can't believe they did this?" she said.

"Who, Masha? Who did this? Let me call the police. Where's the telephone?"

Masha shook her head. It was almost as if she had expected this might happen.

"Masha, where is the telephone? We have to call the police."

Masha's voice trembled. "KGB did this. *Bastards.*" She tilted her head back, and her face became contorted as if her entire body was in excruciating pain. The sound caught up with what Steele saw at close quarters. Masha let out another blood-curdling scream that seemed to penetrate Steele's very heart and soul. "*Bastards!*" she screamed hysterically.

"Masha, I am so sorry. But I need to call the police."

"No. No police."

"Why not?"

"The police and KGB, they are all the same."

"But we have to call the authorities. They must investigate—"

"No police. It will ruin everything."

Masha rocked back and forth, and Steele tried to comfort her as she trembled and sobbed. Then she said, "There is nothing to investigate. I know who did this."

Steele's chest tightened, and he could hear himself breathing. "What exactly are you saying? *You know who did this?*"

"Yes, I know who did this. And I know why they did it."

Steele stared at Masha, stunned.

After a few seconds, he exhaled.

CHAPTER EIGHTEEN

"I need air," said Steele. "Let's go outside." He helped Masha to her feet and walked her to the french windows overlooking the River Neva embankment.

This is a nightmare, and I have no idea what to do next.

Steele opened the doors, and they stepped out onto the balcony.

Masha said, "Jack, you must leave. You don't understand. They will blame you."

"What are you talking about? I was with *you*. I had nothing to do with this."

Masha wiped her tears and nose with the back of her sleeve. "My country is not the same as yours. You don't understand. They can do anything they want."

The cool air and rain helped Steele to think clearly. "Masha. I'm sorry, but you need to help me understand. Your parents have been murdered. We have to call the police. You think you know who did this?"

"My father is a very important man. He has been working on a secret project for our government. For KGB."

"How do you know? You think that's why he was killed? Why would they murder your mother too?"

"Please, it's very complicated. You have to leave. They will blame you. You cannot be here when they come."

A voice shouted from street level. "Hey, comrades, everything okay?" It was the militsiya from the Swedish Consulate residence. He threw down his cigarette and started casually toward them.

Steele said quietly, "He must have heard you scream."

Masha gave the policeman a wave. "We are okay, comrade. Thank you. Everything's under control."

The policeman stopped and seemed to weigh whether to leave his post and investigate further. He said, "I heard someone scream."

Masha replied, "You are mistaken, comrade. Lover's quarrel. We are good." She placed her arms around Steele.

The policeman smiled. "Okay. No problem. Take care, you guys."

But he was still walking toward them, albeit at a slower pace.

Masha said, "We have to go."

"We?"

"Take me with you."

"What?" Steele's face twisted into utter confusion.

"There is nothing left for me here. Get me out of this country."

"You're insane. Your parents are dead, for God's sake."

"KGB murdered them, and they will blame you if you stay."

"How do you know? What are you saying?"

"I heard my father planning this whole thing. He made me invite you here for dinner. I thought they wanted to recruit you."

"Me? Recruit me for what?"

A Lada police car drew up alongside the policeman below, who leaned down to talk to the patrolmen inside the vehicle.

Masha looked back at Steele. "We don't have long. They will come up any moment. If you stay here, I promise they will arrest you, and you might never return to your country."

"But—"

"Interests. Politics. The truth does not matter in my country."

"I don't—"

"Trust me, Jack. This was planned. My father didn't know it, but now I understand."

"You just said he planned it."

"We don't have time now."

Steele swallowed hard and glanced down at the police car.

What in God's name? What if she's telling the truth? Why would she lie?

"Please," said Masha. "I'm coming with you. I promise you won't regret it. I know things."

Steele started for the door. Subconsciously, he had already made his decision. He knew what Rhodes Stampa and Patterson would want. They had made themselves perfectly clear. *If Masha knows things—secrets?—we need her on our side.*

Steele asked, "Is there another way out?"

"Yes, but you have to trust me."

"From what you're saying, I don't have a choice."

"Let's go."

"One thing," said Steele. "I can't guarantee anything for you. Okay? With my people, I mean. I don't have the authority."

Masha did not reply. She took the lead, headed to the flat entrance, and quickly put her boots on. Steele did likewise. Masha opened the door and then said, "Wait."

She ran back into the kitchen and grabbed a knife.

Steele said, "What's that for?"

"Just in case." Masha snatched the backpack she had left on the floor and put the knife away.

"Hey, young people!" It was the policeman again. He was now at the main entrance two floors below, calling up the stairs.

Masha put her finger to her lips. She whispered, "Come on."

They made their way along the landing to another set of stairs on the other side of the building. They descended two flights, and Masha opened a door that led down to some kind of cellar or storage space.

"This way," she said, flicking a light switch that did not work. "No light. Chort vazmi," she hissed. *Damn it.* "Wait, I have light in my bag." She fumbled around in her backpack as she walked and finally found a torch.

"Seems like you planned this escape."

"You are stupid, Jack. You think I would plan my parents' execution?"

Steele said nothing. He looked over his shoulder and listened. Then he heard footsteps. "How the bloody hell are we going to get out of here?"

"It's okay," she said. "This leads to the back entrance. I know a way into the next building."

"FUCK!" said Steele as his right knee struck a stack of wooden crates with sharp corners in the near darkness.

They kept moving.

"Where are we going, Masha? I can't see a thing."

Leading Steele by the hand, Masha reached a door. She pushed it open, and they were outside again.

Steele exhaled. "Thank God." He looked around, but there was nowhere to go. The yard in front of them had no doors or gates, and the wall was too high to scale. "Now where? It's a dead end."

"I went the wrong way. Can you climb?"

"Yes, I can climb. But where to?"

"Climb on my back and then pull me up."

"What?"

Masha knelt on all fours and made a platform with her back. "It's enough," she said. "You can reach now."

She was correct. Standing on Masha's back would give him just enough height to reach the top of the wall. *Insane. This is fucking insane*, he thought as he stood on Masha's back and scrambled up the face of the wall.

Somewhere above them, a woman's voice bellowed: "Who's there? Who's down there? I'm calling the police."

Masha replied, "It's okay, babushka. I am with my boyfriend." The babushka wasn't buying it. "Horse shit!" she replied. "You are thieves. Do you think I am stupid?"

Steele hoisted himself up and twisted around on the top of the wall facing Masha, his legs dangling down the other side.

"Let's go," he said, extending his arm toward her.

But something was wrong. Masha was still in the same spot,

still crouched down on her hands and knees. "Masha, let's go."
What now?

Then he saw it.

A dark, furry ball—a creature—was staring at Masha six feet
from her face. Steele looked again and saw that Masha was staring into the eyes of a large rat. He had never seen a rat this close
before, but by its stillness and the fact that it was staring directly
at Masha, this ugly vermin seemed poised to attack as it moved
slowly toward Masha.

Fuck! Steele shuddered involuntarily. "It's okay. It won't bite
you." Steele was guessing, but under the circumstances, it was a
vain attempt to get Masha moving again.

At Sandhurst, Steele had researched the story of a young
KGB officer who had been cornered by a rat—literally—and the
rat had attacked. This rat encounter had made the boy eternally
aware and conscious of getting caught in compromising positions as he became a rising star in the KGB. His name was Oleg
Pugachev.

"I promise," he said, "Get up slowly. It won't attack."

As he watched the situation unfold a few feet below him,
Steele couldn't believe his eyes. He saw that Masha was gnash-
ing her teeth and jaw, making a face like a rat. The rat stopped
moving.

Bang!

The sound of a gun in the confines of the small yard made
Steele's ears ring. Then Masha shouted, "Go, Jack! Please, go!"

Steele saw the militsiya raise his semiautomatic toward him.

"Don't move!" the policeman shouted.

Without thinking, Steele allowed himself to drop to the other
side of the wall.

A deafening volley of shots reverberated around the con-
fined space.

But it was too late. Steele was clear.

He landed firmly, turned, and ran to the corner of the next

yard, where he burst through a gate. He ran away from the immediate threat—the policeman—but had no idea where he was running to or to whom.

Part of him was relieved that Masha had failed to escape with him, but part of him regretted that he would not be bringing a Russian asset home for the boys at MI6. Not that he had the faintest clue how he would get Masha out of the country anyway. *I have more immediate concerns,* he told himself. *Masha was clear. I'm a fugitive behind the Iron Curtain—and the KGB is going to frame me for the murder of a Soviet admiral.*

Steele kept running, the wind and rain still falling. His mind raced. *Ian Patterson; I have to get to Ian Patterson. He can help me escape.* But Steele chastised himself for leaving Masha behind. *I know things, she said. And I want to know what she knows.*

PART 2

CHAPTER NINETEEN

Castel Gandolfo, Rome

E arly the next morning, Vincenzo knocked on the door of Pope Karl's office at Castel Gandolfo with a heavy heart.

He heard Pope Karl's muffled, "Enter."

Vincenzo bowed majestically. Until now, he had always greatly respected Pope Karl's iconic status both as a man and the pope. Even the treacle timbre of his voice was soothing and enigmatic. Usually, Vincenzo savored the gesture and imagined that he was in a medieval cathedral bowing to a king or queen. Stepping into the pope's office at Castel Gandolfo was like stepping back in time. "Your Holiness ..." he said, closing the door behind him.

"Please, sit," said Pope Karl. "I thought you had left for Venice already."

"I was about to leave, but ..."

"You heard the news?"

"Yes, more devasting news from Boston." Vincenzo had heard rumors about child abuse for many years, but no one in his circle seemed to take the matter seriously. This latest news could not be swept under the carpet. Arrests had been made, and the media was having a field day with victims finally willing to speak out publicly and on camera against Roman Catholic priests.

Pope Karl smiled warmly, but his gaze was distant. "I am listening."

"Your Holiness, I was hoping that I would listen to *you*. The accusations in Boston."

"We know each other well enough. You can say it—the child abuse in Boston."

"Yes, child abuse. I think we must do something finally. The monsignors are worried. Very worried. Apparently, there is even an American movie to be released. With actors—not a documentary."

Pope Karl's eyes watered. "I was not aware."

"The victims are speaking publicly."

"Victims?"

"A thirteen-year-old boy. And his father. They were both abused by the same priest."

Pope Karl nodded slowly. "And they want me to react?"

"Your Holiness, they want you to do more than 'react.' They want you to *do* something."

"I knew this time would come."

Vincenzo hesitated, then said, "Your Holiness was aware?"

"Yes, of course, I knew. *I know.* Just like every other member of our church around the world."

"But—"

"Vincenzo, you have much to learn. I am not God. I am just the pope."

"I understand, Your Holiness. But perhaps our Lord has chosen *you* … to do something?"

"I have asked myself for many years how long the lie can continue."

"What are you going to do?"

"You will be disappointed with me. There is nothing *I* can do. But I want you to be my eyes and ears in the coming turbulent days. You will finish what we started—our peace mission with America and Russia. But this homegrown scourge is beyond me."

Vincenzo's eyes widened, and he was at a loss for words.

Pope Karl's defeatist attitude was shocking. *How can Pope Karl let this happen?* Then, Vincenzo said, "Perhaps we should pray?"

"I have spent my whole life praying. Some things cannot be resolved with a prayer. Alas, it will take a stronger man than me to find the solution."

"Your Holiness?"

"Please know that I did not plan it this way. I wish it could be different."

"I don't understand."

"*You* must finish our peace efforts—*you* must succeed with the American and Russians. I have faith in you, Father Alfonso. But the Boston tragedy is beyond my capabilities."

Vincenzo shook his head. "What are you saying, Your Holiness?"

"It is time for me to hand over the papacy to my successor. I have failed you; I know."

"No pope has resigned in six hundred years. You don't have to resign. I can help you, Your Holiness. We have an army of God's servants to help us. We will make a plan. We can summon the Boston priest, and make an example of him. Summon every priest who had been accused. Excommunication? We can *act*, Your Holiness—"

"It is too late for me. It will all come out."

"What, exactly?" Vincenzo was close to tears. He had lived and worked with this holy man for five years. He had made many sacrifices for his priestly calling, and this one individual was almost like God to Vincenzo. *And now it's over? I will not allow it.* "What will come out?"

Pope Karl eyed Vincenzo. "My knowledge, Vincenzo. I knew *everything*."

"Please, Your Holiness. It can't be true. We all knew about the rumors. But there was never proof."

"People were fearful. Some are terrified of the scandal. The proof is and always has been available. But none of our brothers, including myself, wanted to be the first."

Vincenzo lowered his gaze. "I did not know."

"You are special, Vincenzo. You are truly God's servant. You believe the best in everyone, and that is why I chose you. Don't worry, you won't lose your job." He smiled.

"Please, Your Holiness. You are not making sense."

Pope Karl stood up from behind his fifteenth-century desk (complete with a more recently installed buzzer) and walked to the window. "I am making perfect sense. You just don't want to hear it. Now you know the truth, Vincenzo. You see, I am as guilty as the priest in Boston."

"No."

"Collective guilt, my son. I knew about the evil in our family."

"But—"

"But it is not too late for you to help our brothers and the Catholic Church?"

Pope Karl said, "You will stay and guide the next pontiff, Monsignor Francizek. He will be my successor. When you return from Venice, you will work with him and make a plan to clean up our church of this scourge."

Vincenzo was silent. He rubbed his face with both hands as if trying to stir himself from a nightmare. "And the Russians, Your Holiness? The Americans? Should we—"

"Yes, you should. I want you to go to Venice and host the meeting as agreed. This can only work if they have trust. Both sides must trust each other."

"I agree, Your Holiness. I will leave immediately."

"Very good."

Vincenzo stood up. He hesitated before asking, "You are really going to resign?"

"Your success will be my legacy. I have failed the hundreds— perhaps thousands—who have been abused, but you can still make our contribution to world peace. Monsignor Francizek is strong. He can resolve the scandal. I will retire and watch *you* succeed, Vincenzo. I have faith in you. God's work is never easy, and I am sorry … I apologize to you personally for my failure."

★   ★   ★

Vincenzo gathered his belongings from his transitory office and left the building to go and sit on the pope's bench near the lake. He couldn't believe what had happened. He was devasted and disappointed. He closed his eyes, lifted his head, and caught the breeze from the lake. He prayed for guidance. He prayed Pope Karl would come to his senses. But deep down, he knew it was futile, and he knew he could not change what had happened. Pope Karl's mind was made up. He had conceded defeat on the question of child abuse in the Catholic Church.

But it was true. Monsignor Francizek was, by all accounts, a good, holy, and devout man, much revered by all. There were already rumors that he might become the next pontiff in the event of an emergency or tragedy. Pope Karl's resignation would have to be officially sanctioned, of course, and there was no guarantee that it would happen as Pope Karl desired.

In the meantime, Vincenzo would obey his orders and continue God's work—the peace plan. If the Catholic Church could not solve their domestic sin, then he would at least do his best to end the Cold War and make world peace a reality.

You don't ask much of me, do you, Lord?

Vincenzo turned and gestured to one of the Vatican staff near Castel Gandolfo's rear entrance.

"Please," said Vincenzo, raising his finger. "Please order a car for me back to Rome."

The servant with gray hair said, "Of course, sir. We have one waiting for you at the front entrance."

As he crunched his way across the gravel path, Vincenzo glanced back at his favorite bench with its view of the lake and was filled with sadness and confusion. *How and why should anyone take us seriously now? Who will trust me now? The Catholic Church is a pariah.*

Vincenzo walked around the side of Castel Gandolfo and climbed into the black Mercedes. The car pulled away slowly down the driveway lined with cypress trees. Vincenzo looked out of the window and was awestruck by the emerald-green manicured lawns and the multitude of brightly colored flower-beds. *Nothing is ever what it seems,* he thought. *No one is ever who they appear to be. Pope Karl is the biggest disappointment of my life. But I will remain loyal.*

"Everything okay today, Father Alfonso, sir?" asked the driver.

"Everything is fine, thank you."

But things were not 'fine.' Vincenzo's world had been shattered, and his faith in God was on life support.

CHAPTER TWENTY

Leningrad, Russia

E arlier that morning, Patterson had arrived at the deserted Leningrad Linguistic Institute and located Steele in the stolovaya kitchen as per the message relayed to him by the British embassy. Steele had used some linen tablecloths and kitchen towels for a pillow and managed to doze for a couple of hours. He had tried to call Patterson at the ITN Bureau hours earlier but had reached the answerphone. Then he had left an urgent message for Patterson at the British embassy in Moscow and hoped for the best.

"Jesus Christ," said Steele. "I am pleased to see *you*."

Patterson said, "Sorry I'm late. Came as soon as I got the message."

"I called hours ago. A Russian stolovaya is not the best place to hide."

"We need to get you out of here."

"No shit, Sherlock."

"I said I'm sorry."

They left the stolovaya and made their way toward the institute's rear entrance.

"What the fuck is going on?" asked Steele. "Masha's parents were murdered last night."

"I know. It's a bloody shit show."

"It certainly was."

"I know this is a cliché, but I didn't sign up for this."

"What do you mean?" asked Steele as they left the institute.

"I have no idea who murdered them, but it wasn't part of the plan."

"What plan?"

"This way …"

They turned right into a side street that led to a canal. The street was deserted. The dawn sky was turning from pale yellow to pale blue.

"We can't go back to the office. Obviously. Police are already swarming the place. KGB is probably not far behind."

Steele glanced at the canal and saw the reflection of the church's golden domes they were passing. An old man—a fisherman—stood on the other side of the canal and paid no attention to them.

Steele continued, "They're after *me*?"

"Correct," said Patterson.

"Why me? I had nothing to do with it."

"And they know that. But they need someone to blame."

"Masha said the same thing."

"She's sharp. Everything was going according to plan. *Her* plan, I might add."

"I would love you to make some sense for a second or three."

Patterson kept walking. "Right. Yes, sorry. You deserve an explanation."

"Bloody right."

"Masha wants to defect. She knows *a lot.*"

"I can imagine. She told me that too."

"She told you she knows a lot?"

"Both of the above."

Patterson pulled out a map from his coat pocket and checked his route. "Her father … well, you know who her father is—"

"You told *me* who he is … *was.*"

"She's been 'listening in' to her father's conversations for months. She has some—"

"What do you mean, listening in?"

"She's been listening to his private telephone calls."

"How?"

"From her bedroom."

"What?"

"Yes, it's completely mad. So simple, but it worked for us. For months."

"No one knew?"

Patterson shook his head. "She literally picked up the telephone, covered the receiver, and listened to top-secret conversations her father was having with their security services and government officials."

"No way."

"Yes, way. Nuts."

"KGB?"

"Yes, KG fucking B. Of course, KGB."

"*Fuck.*"

"Precisely. It was too good to ignore. For us *and* the Yanks."

Patterson folded the map and slipped it back into his coat pocket. They turned another corner. Patterson said, "This way." Then he stopped. "Wait, wrong way. We have to get to the fortress."

"What fortress?"

"Peter and Paul Fortress."

"What's at Peter and Paul Fortress?"

Patterson grabbed Steele's arm, did a one-eighty, and headed in the opposite direction. "It's across the bridge. Someone's waiting for us."

"Who?"

"Let's get there. I told them not to involve you in Masha's extraction. They didn't listen."

"Why *am* I involved? Why am I even here, for God's sake?"

"Simple. They needed someone Masha would trust."

"Masha?"

"Yes, we promised her a way out. Once we got our boatload of intel."

"And did you?"

"Not exactly. But you were supposed to be here longer. I guess you could say things got 'fast-tracked.'"

"So that's it?"

"That's what?"

"I'm going home?"

"Yes, but it might take longer than expected. You can't leave the way you came. No hot tea on the train to Moscow."

"Why not?"

"They'll pin the murders on you."

"Why? Masha knows I had nothing to do with it."

"She's off the grid as of last night. Same as you."

"But we're both innocent."

"That's irrelevant. And Masha isn't exactly 'innocent.' We're talking KGB. They can do anything they want. And they report directly to the Kremlin. Russia's a beautiful country until it's not."

"But the police found Masha when I escaped."

"Yes, she lost them as soon as she had the opportunity. We had a plan—prearranged RV."

Steele exhaled as he walked, shook his head in disbelief, and jogged a couple of steps to catch up with Patterson's lean stride. "I think my head is exploding."

"Lots to take in, I know. Don't worry, we have a plan for you, too. You can thank *me* for that."

"Thank you."

"Bird said you didn't need one."

"A plan?"

"Yeah. He didn't plan for this to go tits up. But I insisted on a contingency for you, too."

"Thank you again. So ... what kind of intel did you get from Masha?"

"Let's just say there are a lot of moving parts—and right now, we need to keep moving."

"This is insane."

"KGB are good at what they do."

"I still don't understand. Why does the KGB want to pin this on me?

"They like to have a few chips in their shapkas."

"Chips in fur hats? What?" Steele frowned.

"Bartering chips. Leverage. Doesn't really matter who the chip is."

"As long as they're foreign? They just frame people?"

Patterson glanced at Steele and nodded. "Western is best. Brits and Americans seem to be flavor of the year."

"They have others?"

"Yes, they have an American businessman. He's screwed unless things change between the superpowers. There are rumors of a détente—even the Vatican might be involved—so the poor bastard might have a chance of being released before his hair turns gray." Patterson pulled a face as though he smelled something rotten. "But our people thought you wouldn't be of 'sufficient interest' to the Sovs."

"I won't take it personally."

"Foreign students usually get a pass."

"Not important enough?"

"Right. They want journalists, doctors, lawyers, or businessmen. Anyone who could conceivably carry out espionage."

"What about you?"

"I have a big enough profile—a public persona. Wouldn't work as well. Better if the person is unknown. That way, they can easily sew doubt in their propaganda machine when they label you as a spy."

"Propaganda? You mean barefaced lies."

"Nature of the beast. It's easy for us to forget that truth is a fickle commodity in many parts of the world. I'm not saying we're perfect—but we certainly don't spout as much propaganda, lies, and hogwash as they do on this side of the Iron

Curtain. They could invade Europe and still use their propaganda machine to gaslight their own people."

"Comforting. So basically, if they catch me, I'm screwed. I'll end up in a Russian gulag?"

"Have faith, my young friend. I might be a B-list reporter, but I take other people's lives seriously. Trust me, we'll get you out."

"I hate it when people ask me to trust them."

"If you're lucky, we might just stop you from being thrown in that gulag for the next five years."

Steele smiled. "Realism. That's more like it." Even though he had no idea what he had let himself in for and what might happen in the next hour, even the next day, Steele liked Patterson. *But how will he extricate me from behind the Iron Curtain when the KGB wants to frame me for murders—two murders?*

CHAPTER TWENTY-ONE

A s Steele tried to process all that he was hearing from Patterson, a deafening crash made them stop in their tracks. In fact, the noise was so loud they were half crouching. Both men looked across the canal and saw a military Jeep smashing through the embankment railing. As it headed for the water, there was another loud bang—an explosion. Steele felt the heat from an orange fireball on his face, even from the other side of the canal. He took two steps backward and shouted, *"What the fuck?"*

From the middle of the fireball, three soldiers were catapulted through the air and into the canal. The Jeep also plunged into the canal with a giant splash of spray followed by bubbles like a mechanical whale submerging from a great height—and the soldiers were its prey.

"CUT!" shouted a British man wearing a Barbour jacket who stood on Steele's side of the canal.

A round of applause followed.

Steele and Patterson stood upright from their crouched position.

"Wow," said Patterson, "it's the flippin' Bond movie."

"If that was a stunt, they had *me* fooled."

"Scared the shit out of me. *Jesus*. They're filming all over the city. Stunts—second unit stuff. Apparently, they have a tank chase sequence scheduled. I was supposed to do a story on them. The mayor of Leningrad's wife tried to shut the entire production down unless the production company paid her off. She supports the arts, and the arts 'support' her."

"Foreign currency rules?"

"Touché." Patterson picked up the pace again. "Keep up. And no, we can't stop for autographs."

They kept moving and reached the small huddle of the film crew mixed with local onlookers. From their brightly colored jackets and baseball caps, you could tell the difference between the international film crew and the locals. As Steele observed the scene more closely, he clocked the DOP—director of photography—a man with a gray beard and ponytail sitting behind a huge film camera mounted on a dolly that was now being moved along a track away from the canal.

The man wearing the Barbour jacket shouted, "Number ones!"

Steele and Patterson made their way through the film crew and onlookers who were standing behind the camera in the middle of the street. Steele sensed a wave of the excitement everyone was feeling after the spectacular stunt.

A woman wearing a baseball cap sitting on a director's chair took off her headphones and said, "No need to reset. We got it in one. Let's move on." She turned to high-five her assistant.

Another round of gentle applause and smiles from the film crew.

"Keep going," said Patterson. "We can't stop."

Steele said, "I wasn't planning to. But I think I want to make movies when I grow up—that was amazing."

As they moved past the film crew, Steele watched as the safety boat in the canal maneuvered to each stuntman to fish them out of the water.

Seconds later, once Steele and Patterson had cleared the crowd, Patterson stopped again.

Standing at the next corner, fifty feet ahead of them, were two policemen smoking and watching the filming.

The first policeman pointed at the stuntmen in the canal. "Yop tvoyou matz, bled!" he bellowed. *Fucking hell!* "Innostrantzi duraki." *Crazy foreigners.* Then he guffawed.

A moment later, Steele saw the second policeman look in *their* direction.

They locked eyes.

Steele wasn't sure if the policemen recognized him—*Is my KGB mugshot in circulation already?* Something about Steele's pace, his look—his clothes, perhaps?—made the policeman suspicious.

The policeman nudged his colleague, and now all four men squared up, facing each other like a gunfight on a Hollywood Western backlot. The only good news was that fifty feet still separated them, and there was the spectator crowd of about thirty people, which might give Steele and Patterson cover to make an escape.

Patterson whispered, "Fuck it. They've made us." He turned, and Steele followed.

"Now what?" asked Steele.

"Don't worry. Get ready to run."

"Stoi! Stoi na mestye, tovarischi!" the first policeman shouted, discarding his cigarette. *Stop! Stop where you are, comrades!*

Patterson pushed his way back through the film crew and started running. Steele accidentally bumped into the man with the Barbour jacket listening to his handheld radio. Steele heard a voice on the radio say, "Second Unit ready."

Steele caught up with Patterson and said, "Maybe these guys can help us?"

"Forget it. No time."

They ran to the next corner and turned right, taking them one block away from the Jeep stunt location.

"If the police catch us, you're screwed."

"Believe me, I get that," replied Steele.

They cut down an alleyway that led to a courtyard and through a passageway that led to the next street; they were now two blocks from the canal and the last contact with police. They made a left turn and stopped to get their bearings.

Steele couldn't believe his eyes. The street was empty ...

except that they were now standing in front of a main battle tank with its engine running.

Steele said, "*What the ...*"

"It's a stunt tank. Get in."

"What?"

Patterson placed both hands on his thighs to catch his breath. "I think we lost them. But get in the tank just in case."

Steele countered, "Let's keep going."

Patterson grabbed Steele's arm and said, "Trust me on this one. Get in the tank. Do it now."

Steele eyed Patterson, then he relented. He turned and climbed onto the tank.

Patterson said, "I'll circle round and see if we lost those goons. I'll be back soon. If I don't come back, you *must* get to the fortress."

Steele clambered up to the tank's turret. *If my Sandhurst mates could see me now.*

As he lowered himself down inside the loader's hatch, Steele saw Patterson reach the next corner and disappear. Steele squatted down next to the main armament inside the turret and looked up at the blue morning sky. *Please God ... please get me out of here in one piece.*

Moments later, once Steele had finally caught his breath, the tank began to move.

"*Shit ... no way.*" Then he shouted so that someone—the driver or a stuntman?—could hear him. "*Wait! Stop!*"

But it was too late. *If I jump, I'll bring even more attention to myself and probably break my neck.*

The tank was on the move and picking up speed. Except that it didn't feel like a tank. Steele had lived in a tank on pre-Sandhurst military exercises with his regiment—and this did not *feel* like a tank.

He heard the whirring of tires. Then he realized—this tank, complete with huge metal tank tracks, was … *on wheels.*

"*Wait, stop!*" he shouted again, this time in Russian. But the tank accelerated … still faster by the second. Steele saved his breath. He held on tight but was knocked backward as the tank changed gear with an unexpected jolt. This was immediately followed by a surge of acceleration that caused him to bang his head on the empty ammunition racks in the loader's bay where he was standing, or at least trying to stand.

"*Bloody hell—I'm screwed …*"

Steele picked himself up, standing taller so he could see out of the turret. Shouting was futile because the driver's compartment had been sealed off from the main body of the stunt tank.

Gripping the rim of the turret, Steele noticed the hatch was firmly locked open in position. *One small mercy.* Across the street and to his right, he saw a man standing next to a camera on a tripod frantically waving at him. There was nothing Steele could do except wave back. The man waved again, even more frantically.

Steele shrugged. Wherever this tank was going, he was going along for the ride.

The street was deserted—locked off and closed, presumably for another action stunt sequence.

Then Steele realized what was happening. The tank was picking up speed and being filmed from multiple angles. He was in the middle of a stunt scene, but he was no stuntman, and he had no clue how dangerous the stunt might get.

Jesus Christ. Steele looked ahead and saw a large open-backed truck filled with crates of something he couldn't yet identify at the end of the street. The tank was speeding toward the truck and showed no sign of slowing down.

Then it all made sense. The tank was going to crash into the truck—intentionally—another part of the action scene chase.

He could see a man—the truck driver, presumably another stunt man—waving at the tank. There was no way the tank-on-wheels could stop in time now, even if the driver wanted it to.

Steele noticed a film camera on top of a building to his left. There was another camera at the end of the street pointing directly at him. They were filming everything. He pictured a comic book strip of this tank crashing into what Steele could now see was a truck full of milk crates—the stick image flying through the air was *him*—just like the Jeep stunt he had seen minutes earlier.

Steele heard himself counting down—counting down *to impact.*

THREE ... TWO ... ONE ...

CRASH! The tank smashed into the truck.

He wasn't sure which was worse—the deafening crash of milk bottles ringing in his ears, the smell of rank, spoiled milk showering over him, or the sharp pain in his ribs as he was flung against the ammunition racks inside the turret.

The tank hissed, and the truck was smashed to pieces along with the crates of milk and flying glass that—it turned out—was not real glass. Steele realized now that the truck was fake and had been rigged up to shatter into thousands of pieces on impact with the tank.

"CUT!!" shouted a bald man with a megaphone.

Steele was front and center of the action scene with his head sticking out of the turret.

Bald head—presumably the first AD—came running to a mix of crushed lorry, shattered milk bottles, milk crates, and the stunt tank. He yelled in an American accent, "WHO THE *FUCK* ARE YOU, ASSHOLE?"

Disorientated, Steele rubbed his head and said, "I'm fine, thanks."

The first AD shook his head and shouted into his handheld radio, "Sergei, get the police here *now!*"

If the police stop us, you're screwed. Patterson's warning was fresh in his mind. "No, no," said Steele, holding up both hands. "You don't understand. No police. Please."

"Too late, buddy. I don't know who the fuck you are, but you're getting locked up for this." He spoke again into his radio. "Sergei? ETA police?"

Steele didn't wait to hear Sergei's reply. As he climbed out of the tank hatch covered in milk, Steele heard weapons being cocked.

Then he saw them—two policemen were standing next to the truck, their guns pointing directly at him.

CHAPTER TWENTY-TWO

Steele raised both hands. "I'm sorry."

He looked at the two policemen and realized they were not the duo who had been in hot pursuit minutes earlier. The two policemen laughed as though Steele had cracked a joke.

Then Steele realized from the policemen's relaxed demeanor that these were yet more stuntmen. They had assumed his climbing out of the tank was part of the scene.

"Relax, everyone," said the first AD. "Let's get this joker out of here and reset. Get the art department over here to rebuild." He turned to Steele. "The police will be right here, buddy. I hope they lock you up."

Steele wiped his face, still wet with rank milk. His hair was plastered to his head. He looked around—there were no real policemen anywhere. *I'm free to get the fuck out of here.*

Suddenly, a woman dressed in a raincoat and a mink fur hat arrived on the scene. She was flanked by two men wearing suits. "Is there a problem?" she asked in English but with a thick Russian accent.

The first AD replied, "Madame Mayor, yes, we have a problem. A big problem. This man destroyed the take. We need to reset and rebuild the truck."

She replied, "You have one hour left, as we agreed."

"But Madame Mayor—we didn't plan for this joker to crash our scene."

"That's not my problem," she said.

"Your policemen weren't doing their job. That's why we paid you, right?" countered the first AD.

"That is not my problem either, Mister Assistant Director. We cannot close this street any longer. People already complained to the mayor's office."

Steele retreated a few steps as the mayor's wife continued to give her orders. *Now's my chance.*

From the other side of the decimated truck, the two original policemen from the Jeep stunt arrived. Seeing the mayor's wife, they stood to attention and saluted.

"What are you doing?" she asked. "Why did you allow this foreigner to trespass onto the movie set? You had special orders to close the street."

"Comrade Madame Mayor, excuse us. But this was not our sector."

"We are looking for two foreigners—one is tall with blond hair, and the younger one has black hair ..."

Steele froze.

The mayor's wife said, "You are talking rubbish. These foreigners are making a movie. Can't you see that? Your comrades allowed this man to trespass. What are your names? I want to know why you allowed this to happen."

The first policeman said, "Madame Mayor, with the greatest respect, we don't have time for this. We are looking for dangerous fugitives on orders of the KGB."

"Look around, do you see dangerous fugitives? We are making a movie. Arrest this man." The mayor's wife pointed at Steele, who remained rooted to the spot.

It's over, he thought.

Both policemen eyed Steele suspiciously, but their gaze switched to the two stunt policemen in uniform carrying dummy AK-47s. They frowned dismissively and looked back at Steele.

Steele's heart stopped. But then ...

Both policemen looked straight through him. Apparently, they didn't recognize him without Patterson standing next to him.

The first AD said, "I want this man arrested." He pointed at milk-soaked Steele, who stood his ground.

Again, the policemen eyed Steele but did not make the connection.

"I am sorry, Madame Mayor, but this is not our priority. We have priority orders from our commander."

The duo departed in search of Steele and Patterson.

The mayor's wife continued to address them as they walked away. "Do what you must—but the next time, I am going to report you. I will not forget. I am very good with faces." She turned to the first AD and pointed at Steele. "Either you want to waste time with this 'milkman,' or you want to make your movie. You have less than one hour to finish your action."

"But Madame Mayor—"

Steele did not wait to hear the rest of the sentence. The policemen had not recognized him, and no one was about to arrest or restrain him. He moved toward the Winnebago as if he belonged on the movie set and intended to get changed. The milk stunt 'disguise' had saved him, but it wouldn't be long before the streets would be swarming with more police and KGB.

I must get to the fortress. Please, God, let Patterson be waiting.

Then he had an idea.

Castel Gandolfo, Rome

Monsignor Angelo Franciszek arrived on time. Pope Karl was a very old acquaintance; some might even say a friend. But Angelo would not have gone that far.

"Punctual as ever," said Pope Karl.

"Gott schuf die Zeit—von Eile hat er nichts gesagt," Angelo replied in perfect German. *God created time—but he said nothing about hurrying.*

"They taught you well in Argentina. You even have the accent down."

"One of God's many gifts we can be grateful for."

"It's a beautiful day," remarked Pope Karl.

"Not really, given the news from Boston. But yes, the weather is perfect. I recall a trip with you on the lake here many years ago when we visited the Vatican at the same time."

Pope Karl said, "I remember it well. There's something about being in a boat on the water with another person. The hours of conversation ..."

"Your Holiness has an excellent memory. But I also know you did not invite me here to talk about the weather."

Pope Karl sighed deeply. "If only ..." He stared out the window. "Please sit."

Monsignor Fran, as he was known in Vatican circles, chose to sit in the large gold lacquered armchair with red velvet upholstery.

"Is everything all right, Your Holiness?"

"Monsignor Fran," the pope began. "There will be a conclave soon."

"A conclave? Why?"

"To appoint my successor, of course."

"I don't understand. Are you sick? Are you dying?"

"That might be better for all of us. But no, I am not dying."

"Then what are you saying?"

"There will be a conclave in the coming weeks, and I want to be certain the best man will take my place."

"But that's not possible—"

"Anything is possible, my old friend. That is one thing I have learned. And *you* are the best. We both know you are more popular than I will ever be."

"I am honored that you hold me in such high regard, but our church rules will not allow—"

"They will allow it in exceptional circumstances. They will allow it for physical and mental ill-health of the pontiff."

Monsignor Fran extended his hands—palms up. "But forgive me, you do not look ill, and your marbles sparkle as ever."

"To you, perhaps. But I have already begun the process. I cannot go on like this. I am a coward, you see. I have betrayed my country, my church, and my soul. But most importantly, I have betrayed God."

"Perhaps you should let God decide if you betrayed him. Shall we pray?"

"You remind me of Father Alfonso. Ever the optimist … ever the unstirring belief in our Lord."

"What other path is there?"

Pope Karl gave an ironic smile. "There are many other paths. Consider yourself fortunate to know only one."

"By the way, where is Father Alfonso? How is he?"

"He is good. He is traveling to Venice for the night as we speak. On a top-secret errand—one that I will share with you shortly."

Monsignor Fran frowned. "Forgive me, Your Holiness. You are not making any sense."

Pope Karl nodded gently. "I understand, my friend. Let me explain. You will remember this day for the rest of your life. You deserve an explanation because your life will never be the same again."

CHAPTER TWENTY-THREE

Stockholm, Sweden

Prime Minister Anders Aronsson and his daughter, Astrid, climbed out of the black, bulletproof government car, complete with his security detail, and were greeted by the waiter at Den Gyldene Freden—*The Golden Peace*. Aronsson's favorite haunt, the restaurant was the second oldest in the world, more or less unchanged since 1722.

They were shown to their usual table outside on the terrace. It was still warm enough to sit outside before space heaters were needed. Even without space heaters, Astrid knew that her father would prefer to sit outside all through winter if he could. "Fresh air is crucial for an inquisitive mind," he had lectured her for as long as she could remember.

Aronsson smiled at the waiter and said, "The usual, please."

The waiter nodded. "Pitepalt?"

"Correct."

"Orange or grapefruit juice?"

"Orange."

Ever since she could remember, her father loved pitepalt for breakfast—the Swedish delicacy made with dumplings, mixed pork, and herbs.

Astrid said, "Orange juice also and a chocolate croissant, thank you."

The waiter nodded and walked away.

"What do you need?" Aronsson asked.

"I don't need anything."

"Liar."

Astrid smiled and touched her father's forearm. "What? Just because I invite you for breakfast, you think I need something?"

"Yes, that is precisely what I think. It's been six months since you invited me for breakfast, and that was because you wanted me to buy you a car."

"Do you have any rallies today?"

"I have three."

"Can I come and watch?"

"You hate my rallies, and you don't agree with my politics."

"Papa, this is old news. But it doesn't mean that I don't support you."

"Do you want me to win the election?"

Astrid hesitated—she was a good liar, but even this one might be a stretch. "Of course, I want you to win."

Aronsson smiled and said, "You are getting better. You will make a magnificent politician one day."

"No, I really do," she said, doubling down on the lie. Astrid hated his liberal politics and policies. "I respect your policies even if I don't agree with them. And I do think you are a great leader. Our country will be lucky to have you carry on."

"*Will?* Do you know something I don't? Do you have a crystal ball, my dear?"

"I have confidence in you, Papa. Yes, I think you *will* win next week. Does that make you happy?"

"Actually, it does. And the fact that we can agree to disagree would have made your mother proud too."

"Do you miss her? I mean, even with all your work and your success. Do you have time to miss her?"

"Of course, I think of her every day. I will never stop missing her."

"Do you want to get married again?"

"Maybe one day. But for now, I am too busy. Our country is more important. Now, tell me,"—he leaned toward Astrid with a twinkle in his eye—"what is it you need, daughter?"

The waiter arrived with the coffee, orange juice, and Astrid's croissant.

Astrid paused for the waiter to leave. "You promise not to get angry?"

"First things first. Eat something."

Astrid picked up her pain au chocolat and took a bite.

Aronsson continued, "Second, I don't make promises I can't keep."

"Seriously, you have to promise."

Aronsson playfully raised one eyebrow. "Very well, I promise. How many gray hairs is this going to cost me?"

Astrid took a few sips of orange juice and set her glass down on the white linen tablecloth.

"I know about the submarines."

"Sorry?"

"I know about the Soviet submarines."

Aronsson frowned but remained calm. "How do you know about the submarines, and who told you they are Soviet?"

"I mean, I don't *know* if they are Soviet, but Björn thinks they are."

Aronsson's eyes widened with incredulity. "Who is Björn?"

"Papa, you remember. He is Admiral Bergman's son. We were dating for a short time last year."

"Yes, I remember now. And what in God's name does Björn know about Soviet submarines?"

"His father is an admiral."

Aronsson nodded. "And ...?"

"And so, he hears things. And we share things. Secret things. We are still friends."

"Interesting. I'm expecting Admiral Bergman in my office this morning; I will be sure to mention it."

"Papa, please don't. You promised me." She gripped his forearm. "You *promised?*"

Aronsson pulled his arm away, starting to bristle. "Okay. But I don't understand why I am making all these promises?"

"Okay. Please listen carefully. And don't be angry."

Aronsson waited while Astrid used a yellow scrunchie to tie her hair into a ponytail. Then she said, "You remember my pen pal, Masha?"

"I do."

"She is coming to Stockholm."

"That's great. You will meet in person."

"Yes, I can't wait. But I was wondering if she could stay with us?"

"With *us*?"

"Yes, you like Russians, remember? That's part of your neutral geopolitical policy, right?"

Aronsson smiled. "Well … I mean …"

"You mean, yes? You spend your whole time talking about it. Sweden *must* remain a stable and neutral influence in Europe. Sweden must *not* rock the boat. Sweden will *never* bow to Bolshie American culture. You say this all the time."

"I am familiar with my talking points, Astrid. You don't need to remind me."

"So, she can stay with us, right?"

Aronsson sighed. "I suppose that would be okay. Is she coming by official invitation?" He sipped his coffee. "She was lucky to get clearance. Didn't you tell me her father is a Russian admiral?"

"Not exactly an invitation." Astrid straightened her posture and nonchalantly raised her eyebrows as if what she was about to say was nothing out of the ordinary. "She wants to defect."

Aronsson nearly choked on his coffee. "What did you say?" he spluttered. "Your friend wants to defect?"

Astrid nodded.

"And you want her to stay with us?"

"Yes, Papa. Look, she needs help. We are a neutral country, right? We are allowed to help friends."

"You don't know her."

"What are you talking about? She is my best friend. We have corresponded for two years. I know everything about her."

Aronsson frowned. "If she is coming to Sweden, but she doesn't have an official invitation, how will she get here?"

"We are helping her. Our government."

"How?"

"I don't know exactly. Björn told me this."

The waiter set down the plate of pitepalt, but Aronsson had clearly lost his appetite.

"I'm sorry, Papa. I didn't want to—"

"This is a very serious matter. I will need to investigate."

"Of course. But please don't mention Björn. We have an understanding."

"Tell me—explain one thing. Why does Masha want to defect? Why Sweden?"

"That's easy, Papa. It was my idea." Astrid waited for a reply that did not materialize.

Aronsson got up and left the café without saying a word.

CHAPTER TWENTY-FOUR

Leningrad, Russia

Steele entered Eon Production's wardrobe truck and helped himself to a Russian policeman's greatcoat, shapka, and black boots. He adjusted the holster and threaded it through his epaulet. The only problem was that there was no pistol inside the case, not even a prop gun. If he was stopped by the authorities, they would surely notice, and his cover—such that it was—would be blown. He smiled at the young wardrobe assistant as if he "belonged," and she was too busy adding finishing touches to other film extras' costumes to notice he did not.

Steele left the truck, walked a few blocks and canals, and then made his way across the vast expanse—breathtaking and historic—that was Leningrad's Dvortsovaya Ploshchad—*Palace Square*. There were groups of policemen at every intersection making cursory checks of any locals or tourists. The increasing police presence was undeniable. *The only question is whether my disguise will pass scrutiny*, he thought.

He crossed Dvortsovaya Naberezhnaya—*Palace Embankment*—and walked across Dvortsovaya Most—*Palace Bridge*. It was unusual for a Russian militsiya to be walking alone—they almost always walked in pairs or trios.

Where was Masha? Steele wondered. *Is she at the apartment? At the police station? Or at the mortuary?* He wished he could have got his people to help her—but thus far, this "operation" was way above his pay grade. People—important people, military people—were already dead. It was one thing to make friends with a would-be spy or defector, but it was another to be involved in the murder of Masha's parents. Not that he *was* involved in any way, shape, or form other than being invited to dinner. But apparently, *that* didn't matter to the KGB.

Was the whole thing a setup all along? Did Masha want me to be caught up in this mess? And why were there four places laid at the dinner table if Masha had lied about her father wanting to meet me?

He nodded to a trio of militsiya standing next to their Lada patrol car on the corner of the bridge as he passed by. He eyed his destination of the Petropavlovskaya Krepost—*Peter and Paul Fortress*—in the distance. The ornate gold spire and gold wedding cake domes of the Petropavlovskaya cathedral inside the fortress were five minutes away on foot.

"Comrade!" one of the policemen called from behind.

Steele's heart sank. *No point in running. Did they notice my holster is empty?*

Steele turned but told himself to keep his responses brief—one-word answers if possible. His Russian accent was very good to excellent, but even so, he wasn't sure he could fool a Russian militsiya at close quarters.

"Comrade … where are you going?" asked the militsiya in Russian.

"Foreigners." Steele pointed toward the fortress as he kept going—walking backward away from the militsiya trio but still facing them.

Then the second militsiya spoke into his radio. Steele could not hear the exchange, but it didn't seem to be related to him.

"I don't recognize you," said the first militsiya.

"Tenth district," Steele replied.

The man nodded and said, "You want a ride?"

"No need. Going to the fortress."

"I can take you."

"Not necessary, thank you."

"It's no problem. I'm bored shitless with these two apes."

He laughed and pointed his traffic baton at the two militsiya standing next to him.

"Okay." Steele was tempted to say: *It's okay, I'm fine, I don't need a ride.* But he decided to execute his deception head-on and not risk making them more suspicious. The last thing he wanted was for them to follow him to his meeting point, where he had no idea who or what he would find. "Thank you, comrade."

The first militsiya climbed into the driver's seat of his patrol car, and Steele nodded again to the two remaining policemen. Then he climbed in.

Steele continued in Russian. "Quickly, please. I'm in a hurry. And thanks again."

The militsiya, who seemed content to be in his warm car for a few minutes, replied, "No problem, comrade. We'll be there in one minute. Those foreigners won't get far. The whole of Leningrad is a fortress. What are they going to do, swim to Finland?"

They drove onto the small island that was home to the Petropavlovskaya Krepost.

"Where now?" asked the policeman.

Steele said, "Over there." He pointed to the top of the ramp that led to the quayside and the Neva River. He could already see the water.

The militsiya drove the Lada down the cobbled private road and turned a corner at the bottom that led to the quay. As they drew closer, the militsiya suddenly became suspicious. "What exactly are you doing here?"

Steele hesitated. He did not want to launch into a complicated explanation and risk having his accent and identity exposed. But as they turned another corner within sight of the landing stage, Ian Patterson was standing next to a tv camera and tripod, gesticulating to a small fishing boat.

Steele did not hesitate and pointed to Patterson. "I have to keep an eye on them."

"Making movies," the policeman said. "James Bond. *Boom, boom!*" He made a circling motion with his fist.

As the car stopped, Steele smiled and said, "Yes, that's right. Thanks again." Thankfully, this militsiya could not distinguish the difference between a tv news camera crew and a motion picture film crew. *Close call. Ignorance is bliss.*

The Lada drove away, and Steele walked toward Patterson, who did a double take.

"Jesus, I take it all back. You might make a good spy after all."

"Thanks. I do my best."

"Seriously. Good work. You had me fooled—shapka suits you."

"Thank the Bond costume department."

"You'll find a change of clothes on board."

Steele glanced at the fishing boat, and his eye lingered on a middle-aged woman at the helm with gray hair tied back in a ponytail at the helm. She wore fisherman's dungarees and an oilskin jacket.

"Don't worry," Patterson said. "She's one of ours—Oksana."

"Glad to hear it. No one stopped you?"

"The militsiya would never touch a man with a tv camera."

"Why?"

"It's instilled into them. Any foreign media with a video camera in public places has a special status as long as they have a permit. It's not worth their while to negotiate all the red tape if they get it wrong."

"But they're looking for *us?*"

Patterson pointed to the Lada driving away into the distance. "Those guys have no idea who they are looking for. Mother Russia doesn't pay them enough."

"What now?"

"Now, you get the hell out of here. As promised."

"Can't say I'm disappointed. On this old heap?" Steele pointed at the boat?"

"Don't knock it. This little baby is going to get you all the way to Stockholm."

"No customs?"

"It's been taken care of."

"I'm flattered. How much do we pay for something like this?"

"H. M. coffers. And we'll claim some back from POTUS."

"Americans *are* involved?"

"Americans are always involved."

"Of course."

"Honestly, I'm not quite sure anymore exactly who's involved. But we dodged a bullet last night—which is more than we can say for other people."

"Agreed. I don't get why they had to murder Masha's parents, even if she did want to defect." Steele glanced at the female skipper, who was already preparing to cast off. "Does Oksana speak English?"

"Yes, but I'd get your head down while you can. It's about thirty-six hours to Sweden."

"Stockholm's safe, right?"

"Yes, but the Yanks might want to debrief you there."

"Why?"

"Just a courtesy."

"Do I have to?"

"Let's see what Bird says. He's supposed to meet you there."

"Great. Whatever. I'm looking forward to going home. Shame about Masha."

"Why?"

"I mean, she's kind of screwed, right?"

"Not at all. She's kind of right here on the boat."

It was Steele's turn to do a double take. "What did you say?"

"That's the whole point, remember?"

"But—" Steele shook his head, befuddled.

"The reason you're here? To get Masha out."

"She's not being interrogated by the KGB?"

"No, she's a bit more switched on than that. This is what *she* wanted, remember."

"Masha's on the boat?"

"Yes, safe and sound, warming her hands on a cuppa."

"And no one is going to stop us?"

"It's a fishing boat. The people who need to be paid have been paid. Internal Security is searching on land. It will take a few more hours for the all-points bulletin to filter down to maritime. It was Masha's idea."

"To escape on a boat?"

"Yes, she even asked her father the best way for a fugitive to escape the country."

"I like her even more now. Is she okay?"

"Seems fine."

"I mean, about her parents?"

"I'll leave that to you. She certainly had to make some tough decisions in the last twelve hours. But this is what she wanted, and more importantly, this is what *we* wanted."

"Got it. I guess that makes sense—I mean if that's why they bothered to bring me here. For Masha."

"Like I told you already—attention to detail. Name of the spy game."

"What's she going to do when we get to Sweden?"

"Ask her yourself. I'm sure she's dying to catch up." Patterson smiled.

"I can't believe we just sail out of here."

"Never say never, but that's the gist."

"Okay … thanks."

"My pleasure. Your mum would be proud."

"My *mum?*"

"Figure of speech. Well done."

"Right." Steele eyed the boat and saw movement below deck. He wasn't sure if this filled him with excitement or terror. *If they catch me with Masha, I'm screwed.*

Claudia Rohweder, HVA—East German Intelligence Service—highflyer and, in her mind, rising star, stood at the base of Petropavlovskaya Krepost, watching the activity below on the quayside. She saw a man standing next to a television camera, a small boat, and her target, Jack Steele. She could have ended it all with one phone call. Jack Steele was a wanted man. But that was not part of *her* plan. She was in this for the long game—she even had the blessing of one of the KGB's most ambitious, prominent, and ruthless operatives—Oleg Stepanovich Pugachev. There was a reason she was following Jack Steele, and there was a reason Oleg wasn't using his own people to do the task that had started in Berlin a month earlier. She had no idea what the ultimate purpose of her mission was—but that was the way it was supposed to work. She recalled her father telling her as a child, *You will never beat the system. The system is there for a reason. It will keep us all safe and sound.* She would make her estranged father—wherever he was—and her country proud and do whatever it took to achieve her goal.

CHAPTER TWENTY-FIVE

Venice, Italy

Vincenzo traveled light. He carried a single black leather holdall that was part overnight bag and part briefcase. The journey from Rome had been a pleasant one, and thank the good Lord, there were no rail strikes this month—so far.

Vincenzo used his priestly "uniform" to skip the water taxi line. It wasn't that he tried to jump the line but that the handful of local Italians ushered him to the front with a gracious "Buongiorno, Padre," and the tourists were simply happy to observe the spectacle.

His meeting with the Americans was arranged for the next morning. *No harm in enjoying a light dinner with Bruno tonight*, Vincenzo thought. He had met an Italian chef called Bruno in Capri the day before his meeting with the Russian, and they had agreed to see each other again as soon as possible. They had not slept together—nothing so ungodly—or even kissed. But there *was* a mutual attraction. Vincenzo and Bruno had hit it off during Vincenzo's visit to one of Capri's most celebrated restaurants, La Capannina Capri. It was one of Capri's culinary hotspots, a two-generation affair—one day, probably three or even four—of fine dining, good cheer, and hospitality second to none, not to mention the exquisite cuisine and the chef—Bruno—who came to every table to makes sure guests old and new were satisfied and made to feel welcome and special. Bruno had chatted with

154

Vincenzo for so long at his table by the open window that looked onto one of Capri's enchanting passageways that the owner had come to remind Bruno that orders were running behind in the kitchen.

The next day, Bruno had been sitting on the terrace of the five-star Grand Hotel Quisisana and spotted Vincenzo walking by. Bruno had run after Vincenzo and persuaded him to join him for a lunchtime drink—his treat—which was probably a good thing given that the cocktails were twice the average price of any upscale European bar, but worth every lira. Vincenzo had passed on the cocktail and ordered freshly squeezed lemon-orange juice. They had spent several hours talking and, among other things, discovered that they came from the same part of Italy, just one town apart. They also both loved Italian cuisine.

Now, as the water taxi plowed through the opaque emerald waters of the Venice lagoon and canals, and the wind caressed Vincenzo's face and thinning hair, he was happier than he had ever been. *Can there be anywhere more beautiful on God's earth than Capri and Venice? I am blessed to be an Italian.* Vincenzo was also blessed to be doing God's work as directed by the Holy Father himself, and today, there was even a chance of romance to boot. *What exciting times I live in.* He inhaled deeply to appreciate the salty and pungent smell of Venice waters.

Bruno had taken two days off from La Capannina to travel to Venice to meet Vincenzo. It was better they did not meet in Rome for obvious reasons—Vatican spies would not approve. Vincenzo was even tempted to wear civilian attire this evening—he wanted to put Bruno at ease—but he decided against it. Had he not worn his usual priestly garb, this night might have been his last.

Vincenzo checked in at the much-celebrated Gritti Palace Hotel, where a special rate was given to clergy with a Vatican connection. The two men met as arranged at 6:00 pm and began their reunion by circling Piazza San Marco, listening to a few minutes of a string quartet playing some Vivaldi, and then they walked two blocks to the Red Lion Gallery, where they enjoyed a Venice Biennale temporary Monet exhibit on loan from the Musée de l'Orangerie, Paris. They had dinner on the terrace of the Gritti Palace ristorante—melon, prosciutto, linguini vongole, and veal Milanese with the most delicious sauce Vincenzo had ever tasted—all the while overlooking the serene Grand Canal and the smooth gray dome of Basilica di Santa Maria della Salute.

Vincenzo was looking forward to liaising with the Americans to discuss and execute Pope Karl's peace plan. *But that's all in the future,* he thought. *Tomorrow's another day, and the night is young.* Normally on business trips, he would have spent the evening alone in his hotel room after prayer at a local church, of which, of course, there were always plenty to choose from in Italy. But Bruno had made a special effort to meet up in Venice, and Vincenzo felt compelled to make an exception to his usual routine. *Love* was too strong a word, but Vincenzo was certainly intrigued by this chiseled-jaw chef from Capri with grey sideburns and a killer smile. Nothing could or would ever come of it, he told himself, but he couldn't help entertaining the idea of a romantic liaison. If Bruno pressed him, he would be honest about the possibilities and his intentions or lack thereof. But for now, this was a pleasant meeting of two intelligent minds, both of whom appreciated the arts, Italian literature, and Italian cuisine. They also both showed interest and even mutual respect for each other's profession.

As Vincenzo sat at their table, he could hear the turquoise-green Grand Canal water lapping at the rounded stone balustrade. In the near distance, crammed together like cattle, tourists chugged to-and-fro on the vaporetti, and Vincenzo was grateful to be part of the Italian establishment. There was a certain civility to his lot. He felt a sense of belonging in his beautiful country of Italy, and he sensed, for that matter, Bruno did too. What could be more Italian than church and cuisine? As Bruno talked about his family, his favorite Italian dishes, and his restaurant plans and dreams that might involve Paris or London, Vincenzo listened intently. Boats cruised by, and their wakes made a slapping sound on the moorings beside them. Basilica di Santa Maria della Salute really was looking its best as the setting sun lit up its dome from the west.

After dinner, Vincenzo and Bruno took the hotel boat launch across the Grand Canal to the Fondamenta Salute. They sat on the steps of the Basilica for a few minutes looking back at the Gritti Palace Hotel. They watched tourists coming and going on the vaporetti and taxis, and they tried to guess people's country of origin from either their appearance or by eavesdropping on their conversations they could make out—English, American, Danish, French, German, and Swedish among others.

As they ambled east along the Fondamenta Salute, they passed the gondola stop—Traghetto Dogana—and made a spur-of-the-moment decision to hire the gondola back across the Grand Canal to Piazza San Marco. As they settled into the short journey bobbing and weaving across the water, the priest and the chef held hands. Neither knew where this journey would end, but they were truly in the moment and loving every minute.

It was dark now. The gentle and distant hum of tourists walking along the embankment next to the Doge's Palace wafted across the water like a companion to the comforting *slap-slap-slap* of the gondolier's oar.

"Please take us along the canal to see the Piazza San Marco lights."

"Of course, gentlemen," the gondolier replied. "As you wish. No problem."

Vincenzo and Bruno settled back into the red velvet cushioned seat. Vincenzo draped his hand over the side of the gondola and felt the splash of water as their vessel bounced along.

Bruno took off his glasses and looked even more handsome in the low light than Vincenzo had imagined. "Why *did* you become a priest?" he asked.

"Why did you become a chef?"

Bruno smiled. "I asked first."

"But I'm a priest."

Bruno smiled again. "Okay, you win. Like many other Italian chefs, my grandmother was responsible. My earliest childhood memories are of summer visits to Sorrento, to stay with my nonnina. My grandfather had died many years earlier—I never knew him—so to me, it seemed as though cooking and baking were like her husband, my grandfather. All the different aromas that came from my nonnina's kitchen ... I can smell them now. The first recipe I ever made was sfogliatella. I remember all the steps as my grandmother guided me. Those layers of parchment-thin pastry. It took us many hours. Truly a work of art. I still remember the taste of the dough.

"Signore," said the gondolier. He pointed to Piazza San Marco in the distance. "Please, enjoy," he said proudly as if he had created the scene just for them.

"It never fails," said Vincenzo as he surveyed one of the most famous squares in the world by night. "*That's* why I became a priest. The wonder of God's work, my devout love of Italian churches, monasteries, and cathedrals. It is truly a miracle that even the simplest Italian church can be the most beautiful piece of architecture God has ever created with a little help from mankind. But I always knew there was more to life."

"More than what?"

"More than what we see and hear, and touch and feel. It's as if God's earthly creations make me wonder how much more there can be."

"The good Lord? A higher power?"

"If you like. I prefer to use the word *spirituality* than power. Power suggests effort or something physical to me. But God's grace is more magical."

"Like you."

"Thank you, kind sir." If it had been daylight, Vincenzo believed Bruno might have caught him blushing.

Vincenzo's gentle heartbeat was rudely disturbed by the ugly sound of a motor launch—a patrol boat, perhaps? It approached their gondola, traveling faster than all the other boats they had observed that evening. It was heading straight for them.

The gondolier muttered, "Mama Mia ..."

"Signore, does he see us? Is the lantern sufficient?" Vincenzo pointed to the light hanging from the post behind the gondolier.

"Sì, sì, signore. No problem. Tranquillo. You can relax. We keep going."

Still the motor launch came toward them, and still it seemed to Vincenzo that it was heading straight at them. It was particularly odd and somewhat mysterious because there was such a massive expanse of water around them.

The launch made a pass so close that the gondolier had to stop and steady himself from the turbulent wake and choppy water. "Hey!" he shouted in the darkness as the launch distanced itself. "Are you blind? Are you crazy?!" The gondolier shook his head. "I am sorry for this donkey's anus."

"No problem," Vincenzo said playfully. "That was the most exciting thing that happened to me this week."

Bruno said sotto voce, "Apart from meeting me, of course."

Vincenzo raised his eyebrows to flirt but was distracted again by the motor launch circling and heading back again in their direction.

"Holy Madonna," said the gondolier, starting to sound exasperated.

This time, the motorboat slowed as it approached them. It was dark, and the faces of the man or men aboard were not visible. *At least they didn't smash into us,* thought Vincenzo. For a moment, it crossed his mind that the motor launch had something to do with tomorrow's meeting with the Americans, or even something to do with Pope Karl. It was just a feeling.

The motor launch revved as it slowed down and came alongside. The gondolier frowned and peered at the boat, trying to understand what was behind this unprecedented harassment.

Then things became clearer.

This was an unmarked carabinieri motor launch. The men aboard were wearing carabinieri uniforms, but their faces were covered.

Stranger still.

The boat came to a floating stop, and Carabiniere #1 used a long pole with a hook on the end to draw their vessel to the gondola. "Come with us, gentlemen."

"This is an outrage," said the gondolier. "I have never experienced such a thing on the canal. What business do you have with my passengers?"

Carabiniere #1 took out a pistol and pointed it at the gondolier. "Signore, it is not you we have business with. But if you prefer, we can take you with us too." He switched his pistol toward Vincenzo. "You are the priest."

Vincenzo raised his hand, although it was obvious from his cassock.

"Come with us now. And bring your friend."

Bruno and Vincenzo got up, trying to keep their balance on the choppy water. Vincenzo said, "I am from the Vatican. I work for the Holy Father. This must be a mistake."

Bruno said, "What's happening?"

Vincenzo continued, "Leave this to me." He turned to the two men on the motor launch, one of whom was still pointing his pistol at Vincenzo. "Please, there must be some mistake."

Carabiniere #1 replied, "Father Alfonso, there is no mistake. Think of it as God's plan."

Then Vincenzo noticed something even more strange. As they stepped onto the motor launch, he saw that there was a silencer attached to the end of Carabiniere #1's pistol.

CHAPTER TWENTY-SIX

Gulf of Finland

Steele took a shower in the boat's tiny water closet and was grateful to lose the smell of stale milk. He was equally grateful for the change of clothes provided, including a thick, gray seaman's turtleneck. He kept the black boots from the wardrobe truck as the yellow fisherman's Wellies in the cabin were utterly ridiculous if he wanted to blend in when they reached land.

Several hours after they had set sail, Oksana, the somewhat masculine skipper of the small fishing boat, leaned down inside the cabin and said in near-perfect English, "There's plenty of tea in the pot. Or have some fish soup—it's ready now. Don't burn yourself on the stove."

From inside the cabin, Steele replied, "Thank you, Oksana. Soup smells wonderful."

Masha said to Steele, "And thank *you* for everything."

"No need to thank me. I have no idea what happened, and I was just following orders. But I'm glad you're okay."

"Me too."

"And I'm sorry about your parents."

"I'm still shaking." Masha held out both hands, which were trembling involuntarily.

"I'm not surprised. The last twenty-four hours—"

"I didn't know they would execute my parents. You must believe me."

"I believe you. I don't blame you, Masha."

"They are pigs. They are animals."

"Who's *they*?"

"I don't know exactly, but my guess is KGB—they have no conscience. My father was working on a top-secret and politically sensitive mission, and I think there are people in my government who were not supposed to know about it, but they found out anyway."

"What kind of mission?"

"Submarines."

"*Submarines?*"

"Yes."

"But why would they kill both your parents because your father was doing his job?"

"We only have one political party in my country, but it is never simple. There are factions within factions. Everyone has 'interests.' Life is complicated. Even our *glasnost* leader is not popular, except to the rest of the world."

"So, your parents have nothing to do with your defection … your escape. Did they know about your plan?"

Masha's eyes watered. She continued, "Maybe this was my mistake. Maybe I am crazy. All I ever wanted to do was to leave my stupid country, but I didn't think my parents would die for this."

"I'm sorry." Steele reached forward and squeezed Masha's hand to comfort her. But the sensual reaction he received was more than he bargained for. Masha gave him that unmistakable look, and he felt a subtle surge of desire. *Not now,* he thought.

Steele pulled his hand away. "Masha, how are we going to clear these waters without getting thrown into the Lubyanka?"

"Your people have arranged this. No one cares about a fishing boat. The submarines are much more important." Masha stood up, used a metal ladle to serve them soup, and sat back down to eat.

"And now they want to blame *me* for your parents?"

"Standard operating procedure for KGB. Blame the foreigners. Never take responsibility if you can help it."

Steele said, "*Crime and Punishment,* the sequel."

Masha smiled. "You begin to understand strana chu-*des.*"

Steele recalled the *Alice in Wonderland* reference Russians loved to equate with their complicated character and national identity.

"It certainly is a weird kind of Wonderland."

Masha shrugged in resignation and tucked into her fish soup.

"So, the submarines—"

"Yes, the reason I am here is because of submarines ..." Masha paused and did not continue.

"Are you going to make me guess?"

"It began with my friend, Astrid. She is my pen pal from Sweden. Astrid Aronsson."

"Any relation to the Swedish prime—?"

"Yes, she is the daughter of the prime minister."

"And you know her because—"

"I told you. She is my pen pal."

Steele nodded slowly. He patiently stirred his fish broth. "You're losing me. How does the daughter of a Russian admiral become friends with the Swedish prime minister's daughter?"

"Through my school. It began when I was in high school. We corresponded only. No telephone calls."

"You were just pen pals."

"Yes. A few months ago, when I returned to Leningrad, I told Astrid that my father is—was—a high-ranking Russian admiral. She explained to me in a letter that she listens to her father's private conversations and gave me the idea to listen to my father's telephone conversations. She said it was interesting. She said I would learn things about my father and his politics. Astrid is a very political young woman."

"And so are you."

"Yes, we are similar."

"You're telling me you eavesdropped on your father and used this information to help you defect?"

"I didn't plan this, of course. But yes, this is what happened."

Steele's eyes narrowed. "I wish I was a journalist—this would make phenomenal news."

"You can tell it. I don't mind. If I am free in Stockholm."

Steele shook his head. "I have other plans right now."

It really was quite an extraordinary story. He didn't show it, but Steele wasn't sure if he believed a single word Masha was telling him. He continued, "So, how did you get involved with my people? Patterson?"

"Every piece of information is important and has a price. Astrid taught me this. One tiny piece of useless information to *me* might be worth a lot to *you*. That's how spies work. You know this."

"I'm learning fast." Steele peered through the porthole and saw land in the distance. It was still daylight in this part of the world. "Where is that? I thought we left Russia."

"That is Estonia. But it will take us one more day to reach Stockholm."

Steele continued, "So how did you get the information to us?"

"Astrid. It was her idea. She said she knows people in her country who can help me escape."

"Escape?"

"I told her my dream is to leave Russia and live in the West."

"Astrid arranged this?"

"Not exactly. But she made me promise not to tell any Russians and that someone British would make contact."

"Patterson?"

"Yes."

"How?"

"He made reportage on educational ties between Russia and Sweden. He interviewed me at the institute, and that's how we make contact."

"So how does that get you out of Russia? Did you steal the czar's crown jewels from the Hermitage too?"

Masha smiled. "Much simpler. My father was working on this propaganda exercise against Sweden. I don't know every detail, but what I heard from my father was worth much to your people. I took mental notes for many weeks. I never wrote anything down, of course."

"You gave everything to Patterson?"

"Yes, but I am not stupid. I keep some secrets for myself. Understand?"

"Insurance."

"Yes. They promise me I can stay in Sweden or go wherever I want—even change my identity."

"How much information do you have? Did you steal documents?"

"Of course not. I listened to my father in his home office. I have an excellent memory; as I told you, I never wrote anything down."

"How did they find you originally? Before the interview."

"I met Mr. Bird from the British embassy. When I was in Moscow. Through your friend, Katya."

"That's why they wanted *me* to come back," said Steele rhetorically.

"I learn that every connection and relationship is important."

"You're damn right … so what are you going to do in Stockholm?"

"What are *you* going to do?"

"I certainly won't be going back to Russia anytime soon. I'll take one step at a time—probably spend some time in Germany first."

"You speak German?"

"*Jawohl, gnädige Fräulein.*"

"*Alles klar.* But you don't want to use your Russian in Russia?"

"One day, perhaps. When they let me back in."

"Perhaps you can work for Russians?"

Steele raised an eyebrow. "Good one, Masha. I don't think so."

"Everyone has 'interests.' I am doing what's best for me. I don't believe in our system."

"Right. I get that." Steele took a few more mouthfuls and finished his fish soup. "What's the big secret with the submarines?"

"This is a propaganda exercise to play with the Americans. Put pressure on Swedish navy to react. We like to push buttons. See how much Americans will allow … cat and mouse."

"But Sweden's neutral."

"Not really. They say they are neutral—my father told me this—but really, they are slaves to America."

"Interesting."

"Astrid's father wants to change this."

"How?"

"He wants to make distance—make problems—between Sweden and USA. Astrid told me. He calls this his geopolitical philosophy."

"Did she say why?"

"He hates Americans."

"Why?"

"I have no idea."

"Are you going to see Astrid when you get to Stockholm?"

"Yes, of course. I am going to stay with her."

"What?"

"She is my friend."

"But—"

"Sweden is neutral. And Anders Aronsson hates Americans. I will be the perfect guest."

Steele was no seasoned spy, but if instincts had alarm bells, they would be clanging loudly. *Something is off here.* For now, he would keep his thoughts and suspicions to himself, but whatever Patterson, Bird, Rhodes Stampa, and whoever else was involved had concocted, Steele was on the ground, and his so-called mission was far from over. As the Sandhurst instructors used to warn the cadets before every military exercise: *Anything could happen in the next twenty-four hours, gentlemen … and it probably will.*

Venice, Italy

Were it not for the dire circumstances, Vincenzo would have enjoyed bumping across the Grand Canal in a motor launch heading out to sea at breakneck speed. But his godly instincts told him loud and clear that even his prayers would be futile at this point.

He had tried to speak to the two men dressed as carabinieri—tried to reason with them. But Carabiniere #1 had placed his finger to his lips, pointed his gun at Vincenzo's head, and Vincenzo got the message loud and clear. For some reason, they had put Bruno inside the cabin, and Vincenzo couldn't see him. He thought about shouting out to Bruno to make sure he was okay but decided that might escalate the situation. Whatever these men—these impostors—wanted, they were making a terrible mistake.

The launch sped southeast, keeping its distance from the Chiesa di San Giorgio Maggiore Island. Suddenly, the boat slowed and came to a stop in the middle of the lagoon before reaching the Adriatic Sea proper. Vincenzo could still see land, but there was no doubt that anything that was or was not about to happen out here was completely untraceable. *Is this connected to my meeting tomorrow?* he thought. *Or is there something about Bruno I don't know?*

It was true, they were effectively strangers. Vincenzo and Bruno had met briefly in Capri—albeit in one of the finest restaurants—and Bruno had spent much of this evening talking about his *nonnina*—his granny—her cooking, and his childhood hopes and dreams. *But perhaps Bruno's every word was a lie?* Whatever Bruno's true colors, Vincenzo knew one thing here and now. The men who had abducted them were no angels, and it didn't feel as though there were any angels looking over him right now.

Carabiniere #1 switched off the engine. The lights of Venice flickered like distant stars.

Vincenzo nonchalantly wiped his brow and was now sweating profusely. "Bruno," he said loudly—consequences be damned.

He felt a painful blow to the side of his head that nearly knocked him to the floor. Again, Carabiniere #1 raised his finger to his lips. Again, Vincenzo got the message.

The door to the cabin opened, and Bruno was manhandled to the deck by Carabiniere #2. Vincenzo would recall the look in Bruno's eyes for the rest of his life. It was a look of sheer terror but with a calm resignation that only God himself could bestow. It was as if Bruno knew what was about to happen and was somehow at peace with it. And it was as if Bruno also knew that Vincenzo could do absolutely nothing about it.

Carabiniere #1 raised his pistol and shot Bruno in the forehead. He slumped to the floor, and before the blood had time to flow, both men quickly tied a rope that was already attached to an anchor in a small crate to Bruno's leg.

They tossed him overboard.

Vincenzo froze. His eyes had never been so wide open and looked so terrified.

He tried to move—a hand, a foot, turn his head. But Vincenzo was rooted to the spot, physically incapacitated for what seemed like an eternity.

"Sorry about your friend," said Carabiniere #1 in Italian but with a slightly strange accent. "But it's not like you knew each other well? Am I correct, Father Romeo?"

Vincenzo remained silent.

"This is a different world, Father," the man continued. "My mother was a godly woman, but for my father and me, God never paid the bills."

Vincenzo opened his mouth to speak, but nothing came out. He was literally speechless.

"There's nothing to say, Father. Don't trouble yourself."

Vincenzo's eyes watered, and he began to shake. *Help me, God. Please help me.*

Carabiniere #1 said, "This is a simple message, Father. But we wanted to make it very clear. Think of it like a Caravaggio— in one of your churches. The slaying followed by a message from the heavenly host."

Vincenzo decided not to inform the killer that Caravaggio had never painted a fresco in his life.

Carabiniere #2 raised his pistol and pointed it directly at Vincenzo's face. "Are you ready to die, Father?"

Vincenzo was praying hard, eyes closed. With every cell in his body, he was trying not to give in to evil. He was trying to keep faith in his Lord. But hope was fading fast. Slowly, Vincenzo shook his head.

Carabiniere #2 rocked his head from side to side as if he was weighing what to do next.

"Okay, Father. I like you. And it's a good thing you wore your uniform, or we might have killed both of you." The man looked deep into Vincenzo's eyes as if he was still weighing his next move. Then he said, "I will not kill you today, Father. But please remember something. There are people, friends of mine, who do not want you to talk to the Americans. Understand?"

So, this was about the Americans.

Vincenzo nodded. *They are going to spare me. Thank you, God.*

Carabiniere #2 shrugged as if his work was finished. "That's all."

Carabiniere #1 turned the key, and the engine burst into life. He shifted into gear.

The patrol launch surged away from Bruno's burial at sea. Vincenzo felt the gentle spray of water on his face and was grateful to be alive. But his life would never be the same again.

CHAPTER TWENTY-SEVEN

Kremlin presidential apartments, Moscow

"Please," said Irina Borisovich Leontev. "Drink your tea while it's hot, Oleg. You want sugar or honey?"

"Thank you, Irina Borisovich," said Oleg with a smile. "I will have honey."

Mikhail Pavlovich Leontev, president of the USSR—but, Oleg sensed, perhaps not for much longer—uncrossed his legs and leaned toward Oleg. "These are difficult times, Oleg Stepanovich. You have an exceptional record, but I am very disappointed."

"I apologize, Mr. President. I am not a magician. These were not *my* orders. Our people acted without authority."

"How can this happen? We cannot execute Italian nationals on their own soil, especially in their most treasured city of Venice. This will be an international scandal as I try to make peace and bring our country into the twenty-first century."

"I understand, Mr. President."

"You told me you can bring the Americans to a peace summit—détente—these are political, not security matters, but I trusted you and believed you are up to the task."

"I stand by my promise."

"You told us the Italians can help. Explain why the Vatican is involved?"

"Mikhail Pavlovich, I understand your concerns, but I can't control Old Guard KGB—Admiral Pushkin and General

Urmancheva, for example. I will clean up their mess, but I need your help."

"I will not allow you to *execute* all your problems away."

"*Our* problems, Mr. President." Oleg sat up straight and sipped his sweetened tea. "I am not responsible for Admiral Pushkin and his wife, nor the Italian."

"Then who?"

"I can only assume that certain Old Guard 'friends' who are not really your 'friends' suspect you are trying to make peace with the Americans. They will not stand for it."

The Russian president frowned, shaking his head.

Oleg continued, "No one knows about our plan, Mr. President—except you, me, and your dear wife."

"It doesn't make sense. Why was it necessary to kill this Italian? I thought we wanted the Vatican on board with our plan."

"We do. And they will be. I met with this Vatican contact personally. He will facilitate the necessary seal of approval from the Americans. I will find out who killed the priest's friend. It will not stop us."

"Why do we need this Vatican priest?"

"Insurance. I don't trust Americans."

"Why should the Vatican help us?"

"The Holy Father has, shall we say, a vested interest. Especially with this clown—this cowboy—in the White House. They don't trust him either."

The president raised an index finger. "This 'cowboy' is much more cunning and intelligent than you give him credit for—ruthless even. If we are not careful, he will bring us down *and* humiliate us on the world stage. Our mighty hammer and sickle are melting." He gave Oleg an intense stare. "I need you to understand something—we *need* the Americans."

"I understand, Mr. President. But not everyone in our country is your friend. I warn you that General Urmancheva is working against you—us. He doesn't want your peace plan to succeed."

"*Our* plan."

"Of course, Mr. President.

"I gave *you* full control of this mission."

"I will not disappoint you."

"Irinichka, please leave us for a moment."

"Of course, my dear." Irina pointed to the tray of tea. "You have everything you need, gentlemen." She walked across the room, her perilously high heels clicking with every step. She opened the ten-foot double doors of the presidential apartment and left the men to their secrets.

"We can speak freely," continued Mikhail Pavlovich. "As you know, this is the only room in the Kremlin without listening devices."

Oleg squirmed in his seat. He hated this man—this weak man and so-called "leader" of the great Union of Soviet Socialist Republics. But Oleg was in this for the long haul—he would do whatever it took, for however long it might take, to make Russia invincible again. He would continue to placate President Mikhail Pavlovich Leontev, the farmer's son, and his tea-connoisseur wife. They were, in fact, the easy part of the equation to resolve—to liquidate. The Americans would be more difficult.

Oleg said, "I will bring you détente on a silver tray with caviar, Mr. President. I promise you that the Italian is a minor setback. Don't give him a second thought. And I promise this assassination will remain between us and our misguided 'friends' of General Urmancheeva."

"*Minor setback?* Listen to yourself, Oleg Stepanovich. I agreed to your outlandish idea to involve the Vatican, and look what happened. One of our own men—the cultural attaché's rotting corpse—is discovered in a vineyard on the island of Capri next to a child. *How does our cultural attaché wind up dead on the island of Capri?*" Leontev's face flushed red with anger and exasperation. "This is unacceptable!"

"There was no other way, Mr. President. I take responsibility."

"Oleg Stepanovich, I am losing patience with your methods.

This is not medieval Mongolia. Joseph Stalin is dead. We must have standards. We must play the game—the fine art of international diplomacy." Then he looked at Oleg for a moment before he said, "We are losing the game, and we are running out of time."

"I promise I will deliver the summit. But you must allow me to operate freely. There will be setbacks, but it is my duty to be your loyal servant. We must try to control the Old Guard. They will ruin everything."

The president exhaled and said slowly, "I have little influence over the Old Guard. The only way to control them is to implement new ways—*glasnost*."

"That is why I wanted the Vatican to give us their blessing. The Americans can play games, but if the Vatican is on board with our peace plan, this will help us execute our mission. I call it 'sacred icing' on the cake."

Leontev nodded. "I agree. The sooner we organize this summit, the sooner we save our country."

Oleg took another sip of tea and cleared his throat. "Mr. President, do you plan to dissolve the Soviet Union? There are rumors you plan to allow the reunification of Germany."

"I will do what is best for our people. There will be civil war, famine, devastation if we do not allow the republics their autonomy."

He did not show it, but Oleg could not believe what he was hearing. This maniac wanted to seal the fate of the Soviet Union. He was about to decimate everything the Bolsheviks had fought for. Oleg had even heard rumors that Leningrad was to be renamed. "Mr. President," Oleg continued calmly, "you are a popular man. Our country is lucky to have you."

"Thank you."

"But you are naïve, Mr. President. If you help me, I can deal with the Old Guard."

"Help me, Oleg Stepanovich. Who executed Admiral Pushkin and his wife?"

"A British spy was responsible. This man was helping Admiral Pushkin's daughter to defect. This is unacceptable. Admiral Pushkin allowed his own daughter to spy on him."

Leontev threw up his hands in frustration. "What are you saying?"

"I am saying, Mr. President, that Admiral Pushkin was working *against us* with this submarine intimidation—and he was foolish enough to be caught by his own daughter."

"Submarines?"

"They used our naval assets—submarines—to intimidate Sweden."

"Intimidate?"

"The goal was to intimidate them, so they went running to the Americans for help."

"Why?"

"To set the Americans against us."

"And stop the peace initiative?"

"Correct."

"I will order them to cease."

"I gave the order. They have already ceased operations."

"We agree at last."

"There is one submarine left in the area ... one last task."

"What task? I want our vessels out of Swedish waters—neutral waters. They must return to Severomorsk immediately."

Oleg said, "I wasn't going to tell you—"

"Tell me what?"

"It is better you don't know."

"What are you plotting?"

"Masha Pushkin ..."

"The Admiral's daughter? What about her?"

"She knows everything."

"Everything?"

"If she gives information to the Swedes, or the Americans or British—whoever is meeting her in Stockholm, this will ruin everything."

"You have lost me."

"Admiral Pushkin's daughter has taken flight."

"When? How?"

"She wants to defect to Sweden. She is sailing there in a fishing boat as we speak."

"Impossible. If what you say is true—"

"Yes, she knows too much, of course. She will tell them everything once she gets to Sweden."

"Then you must stop her."

"We will stop her before she gets there."

"How?"

"Let's just say, Mr. President, I have one last mission for *Golden Fish II* before she comes home." *Golden Fish II* was one of the submarines Admiral Pushkin had ordered to probe the Swedish shoreline.

"Very well. You have my blessing. The future of Russia is at stake."

"My feeling precisely."

Oleg needed to clear his head. He walked down the grand staircase from the Kremlin apartments and exited the building and the Kremlin walls, past the ceremonial honor guard of the Internal Security Service wearing their great coats and fur hats. He walked to the embankment and glanced up at the golden domes of the Kremlin cathedral. He would never allow the Soviet Union to die. He was disgusted with his president, who already seemed to have accepted the fate and demise of the Soviet Union. Damn him, there were even rumors and blasphemous talk about the Berlin Wall being dismantled.

I will never allow the Berlin Wall to fall. Over my dead body. I will never allow the USSR to disintegrate. I will do whatever every it takes to keep us united.

Oleg spent the next thirty minutes walking along the Moscow River, meticulously thinking through and planning his next moves. He stopped at a public telephone and dialed a Leningrad number.

"Claudia?"

"I serve you, Oleg Stepanovich," Claudia answered in Russian.

"I am glad I caught you. There has been a change of plan."

"I am listening."

"The British spy—"

"It would be an insult to spies to call Jack Steele a spy."

"Call him what you want. Do you know where he is?"

"As I reported to you already. He is on the boat with Admiral Pushkin's daughter."

"Perfect."

"Why?"

"We can 'kill' two birds with one stone."

"I don't understand. I am on my way to Stockholm—to observe and prepare the mission."

"I have other plans for Masha and Jack Steele. I just had a very important meeting with our industrious leader. Steele and little Masha have reached their expiry date. Continue as planned but stand by for changes."

"Changes?"

"Yes, you have a green light for Stockholm."

Claudia replied in German, "Alles klar, Genosse." *Understood, Comrade.*

Oleg hung up, stretched, and started walking back to the office … to KGB headquarters on Lubyanka Square. *It's a pity,* he thought, *Lieutenant Jack Steele will never serve his Queen and country.*

CHAPTER TWENTY-EIGHT

Santa Maria del Giglio Church, Venice

Earlier that morning, Vincenzo woke up from the nightmare that he immediately understood was not a nightmare—it was his new reality. The carabinieri impostors had allowed him to leave the boat at a deserted landing to the south of Basilica di Santa Maria della Salute. He walked back to the north side of this small island in the middle of the night and took the Gritti Palace shuttle boat back across the Grand Canal to his hotel, where he finally collapsed into bed at 2:10 am.

He was exhausted and terrified, and his head was spinning from the nightmare that had changed his world forever. Emotionally and physically paralyzed, he had lain awake for an hour, perhaps less, and finally fallen into a turbulent three- or four-hour sleep.

When Vincenzo opened his eyes at 6:05 am, he did not feel rested. His first instinct the night before had been, of course, to go to the police—but on reflection, he wasn't up to it. He was afraid that ending up at the carabinieri's regional headquarters on Campo San Zaccaria in the middle of the night, claiming to have witnessed a murder drowning without any kind of proof or witnesses, might ruin everything—as selfish as that seemed—both from Pope Karl's perspective and from the perspective of the American he was scheduled to meet in less than two hours. In short, he was in spiritual diplomat mode, and a voice inside told him to act for the greater good.

Vincenzo also needed to pray. *Only God has the answers,* he reminded himself.

He left the hotel and walked toward the Santa Maria del Giglio Church, also known as St. Mary of the Lily, which referred to the flower classically depicted in one of the paintings inside. He passed a gondola winding its way peacefully to its first fare of the day, but unfortunately, Vincenzo would never look at a gondola or gondolier in the same way. *Did the gondolier from last night go to the police?* For now, it was anyone's guess.

Reaching the church, Vincenzo took a moment to appreciate the stunning Venetian baroque façade, probably the finest in Venice. It was time to sit and pray inside—meditate, even.

Vincenzo promised himself that he would catch these men— these *murderers*—but, he reasoned, it must be on his terms. His head was telling him to go to the police *now,* but part of him doubted their ability to solve a murder committed by the Italian Mafia or whomever these people were. Local police, he reasoned, were more used to solving crimes of fake paintings and objets d'art thefts. He couldn't recall the last time he had heard or read about a murder in Venice.

"Buongiorno," he said to the old lady sitting at the entrance to the church, who kept a watchful eye on visitors. *If this was Russia,* he thought, *she would be the church's very own babushka.* Then he thought about the Russian diplomat, Oleg Pugachev, who had started this whole "world peace" initiative in Capri. *Is it conceivable Oleg had something to do with Bruno's murder?*

Before he had time to answer his own thought, the Venetian babushka replied, "Buongiorno, Padre." She crossed herself, presumably happy that a holy man had crossed her path so early in the day—a sign of good things to come.

Vincenzo settled in one of the ornate yet deeply spiritual— for him—side chapels. There was something about a chapel within a chapel that made it even holier. It was early for tourists, so he could make the most of his space, his priestly office, so to speak. On this early morning occasion, there was no need to cool off inside one of the confessionals.

Vincenzo knelt and said his prayers, but then he sat back up onto the chair and settled into a more meditative posture—straight back, feet one foot apart, toes pointing forward, hands resting uppermost on his thighs. Again, his head was telling him to run to the police, even though the criminals had threatened him and told him not to talk to the Americans.

He exhaled slowly and steadied his breath. He closed his eyes and looked at the "third eye" on the dark movie screen of his mind and waited to see … it … him … God.

God was a powerful and mighty force. Prayer and meditation had worked for him his entire life, even when he was a boy and teenager. It had brought him clarity and answers in times of trouble and strife, like when his father had died of cancer. Such a terrible disease—such a painful and slow death. He recalled the stench of his father's bad breath after it got to the point when the nurses stopped brushing his teeth because he was close to the end. It was his meditation in those hospice gardens in Ravenna that got him through his father's death. Prayer was one thing, but meditation was even more powerful. Indeed, Vincenzo often pitied people who had never discovered the experience and art of meditation. He had met many people who had finally made the effort, but often only on their deathbeds. His father had been one of those poor souls. *Better late than never.*

Now, ensconced in the early morning tranquility of Santa Maria del Giglio's east chapel, Vincenzo spoke softly, even though there was no one around. He thought of all the people still sleeping or waking up now or having breakfast. *Why do people miss the best part of the day?*

"Please, God, reveal thyself. I love you; guide me, reveal thyself," he repeated over and over. This was, in fact, his mantra.

Then he allowed himself some questions. *How is this possible?* One day ago, he had been on top of the world—the pontiff's assistant planning for world peace. He was part of something good, something beyond good. *Is this a punishment? Is this God's plan? Was my liaison with Bruno a sin? Surely not. Surely God is more reasonable.*

No answers came to him. Nothing to help him decide his next steps.

He adjusted his position and exhaled again. He concentrated on the point between his eyebrows and focused deep into the darkness, searching for the proverbial light. He knew it would work. He knew God would guide him. Bruno was dead—murdered—and deserved to be avenged. His life meant something—and not just to Vincenzo. The owner of La Capannina Capri would be frantically searching for him. All the affluent travelers, minor celebrities, and tourists would not get the chance to taste and appreciate Bruno's culinary art.

Life isn't fair. But Vincenzo had a job to do—that much he knew.

I love you; guide me, reveal thyself. Call it a prayer, a mantra, whatever. This was how it was done. God would guide him and help him honor Bruno's memory.

Suddenly, Vincenzo experienced the white light shining from his third eye. It was an awesome sight even though his eyes were closed. There was no sense of smell, touch, taste, or sound—it was pure stillness, and the message came loud and clear.

Continue your journey. The Americans will help.

The thought, guidance, and this sign were as clear as the marble statue of Jesus Christ right in front of him in this secluded side chapel. Vincenzo had learned from his prayer over the years that a message or guidance from God was not always clearly understandable at first. Sometimes the "guidance" or "message" did not make sense. But he had also learned to allow the message to sink in to gain a true sense of it.

Vincenzo looked up at the stained-glass window above Christ's statue. The morning sun was streaming through. It was clear to him now. He *must* continue the journey. The beauty of the stained-glass rural scene with farmers and bales of hay reminded him of Tuscan rolling hills, one of his favorite places in Italy. Vincenzo would meet the Americans as arranged, and he would ask *them* for help to find Bruno's killers. *That*, he realized now, was God's plan too. Involving Italian police and all the red tape that would bring would ruin everything. Who better than the Americans and their CIA resources to avenge Bruno's death? *Yes, they might laugh at me.* He wondered who would be sent to meet him. *Which fortunate soul is worthy of this papal plan?*

Vincenzo stood up, shook the folds of his cassock, and tightened his belt one notch. He fished out a 10,000 Italian Lira note for the candle collection box. He chose the tallest, thickest candle on offer, lit it, and placed it in the iron holder. He loved the smell and the sound of burning candles. He said a prayer for Bruno, and for his father, who had taught him many years ago to light a candle for the departed in church. *Our parents never really leave us*, he mused, smiling to himself.

The air was still fresh and light as Vincenzo exited the exquisite church that in any other country would be a landmark tourist destination. In Venice, as in most Italian towns, an exquisite church was commonplace, and he was proud of his heritage. He skipped down the steps and was surprised to feel a bolt of fear rush through him; his life would never be the same again. He hadn't bargained for this lethal adventure, but God had been clear. He was to continue the journey—dig deep, and find courage.

The fear subsided as quickly as it came. The only thing he had to do now was get the Americans on board, and there was no time for any more prayers.

CHAPTER TWENTY-NINE

Campo Santo Stefano, Venice

Vincenzo stopped at the Bacaro e Trattoria da Fiore for a glass of prosecco. "Venetian courage," he would call it. But then he changed his mind. He rarely drank—usually, only when he was very nervous. This wasn't the time to start.

Instead, he walked across the cobbled square that was Campo Santo Stefano and marveled at the centuries-old stone buildings—aesthetically pleasing exteriors and chilled interiors. He glanced from the shimmering reflection of canal water at the bottom of one of the buildings upward to the open windows of another and wondered who might live behind each one. *People live here,* he thought. *Wonder of wonders ...*

He sat down in the early morning shade of Café Lucia and ordered a freshly squeezed orange and lemon juice and a *ristretto*—super strong Italian espresso. It was 7:00 am, and there was still an hour to go before his meeting with "an American"— no one had given him a name, just a location. He was wearing his priestly garb; *they* would find *him*.

Vincenzo sat and observed the sun creeping up the side of the ancient dwellings; pigeons swooping in for their first scavenge of the day; businessmen and women elegantly dressed, some with soft black or brown leather attaché cases, heading for work; and the odd street cleaner diligently sweeping. There would be few tourists for another hour or two.

More residents opened windows and shutters over the next

hour, and on the far side of the campo, he could hear a violinist warming up and playing monotonous scales—but even those were pleasing to the ear before his or her morning practice transitioned into the sweet sound of an unaccompanied Bach partita. Perhaps the violinist was one of the string quartet musicians from Piazza San Marco he and Bruno had enjoyed the night before on their walk? *What a difference a day makes.* He knew the expression well—but *never,* he thought, had it been so pertinent to his circumstances.

Two ristrettos later, a voice from behind said, "Father Alfonso?"

A silhouetted man stood between Vincenzo and the morning sun and stirred him from his reveries. But there was no mistake about the voice. The American's deep, sultry tone—like one from the many Hollywood movies he had watched over the years—snapped him back to reality.

"Yes," replied Vincenzo in English, "Father Vincenzo Alfonso, papal assistant, at your service."

The man said, "Kolby Webster, deputy director of the CIA, also ready to serve." He smiled. "Pleasure to meet you, Father. I'm early."

Webster, a slender man with thinning dark hair and unusually large hands, sat down as they shook hands. Webster's grasp was, as Vincenzo might have imagined, as firm as they come. It was as if this one man, Webster, contained the power of America in one hand.

Webster glanced at the menu and ordered as soon as the waiter arrived a moment later. "Double espresso, milk on the side, orange juice, and"—he looked at Vincenzo as if his request might need translation—"a ham and cheese omelet made only with egg whites, Worcestershire sauce on the side if you have it."

Vincenzo was about to translate, but one look at the waiter told him there was no need. This waiter was au fait with Americans ordering in English without any attempt to speak Italian. The omelet variation was no problem.

"So," Webster began, whipping off his Ray-Bans, "how can we help you, Father?"

"Please," Vincenzo replied in English, "you call me Vincenzo." Now that Webster's sunglasses were off, Vincenzo saw the eyes of an Asian American.

"Gotcha, Vincenzo. I won't argue with a man of God."

Vincenzo smiled. He wasn't sure how to begin, so he said, "Thank you for coming."

"Thank you for inviting me. Sounds interesting."

"I ... I was curious to see who they would send. You must work closely with your president."

"I was with him yesterday—hot off the press before I jumped on the plane."

"I can't imagine you came to Europe just for me. But we appreciate the window of opportunity."

"I like you already." Webster smiled again. The espresso con latte arrived, and Webster heaped three dainty teaspoonfuls of brown sugar crystals into the tiny cup. "I'm en route to Sweden, actually—Stockholm. I've never been, but I hear the food's interesting."

Vincenzo nodded. "Your world is very different from mine, I'm sure."

"You might be right there. A lot of moving parts these days ... peace initiatives, the Soviet Union falling apart, and even talk of the Berlin Wall about to fall. *World's a-changing* would be an understatement."

Vincenzo nodded. "Forgive me ... I should be better informed on my current affairs. Why is Sweden so important?"

"My business there is confidential—secret, in fact—but there's an election next week, and we—President Madison, I should say—is taking a personal interest. Let's say we want to make sure everything runs smoothly."

"But Sweden is a neutral country. Why is it any of your business?"

"Straight shooter. I like it, Vincenzo. You're correct. It's not really any of our business, which is why my visit is ... it's 'unofficial.'"

"They can't run their own elections?" asked Vincenzo.

International politics, particularly in northern Europe, was not his strong point, nor did he have much cultural or political interest in Scandinavia. But he knew from Vatican chitchat and unscientific gossip that although Sweden was a neutral country, it was much polarized by extreme politics on the left and right. On the one hand, Swedes were very conservative—they even boasted a royal family. Although it could not be compared to, say, the British royal family, it was nevertheless well respected and played an important role in Swedish society. On the other hand, Sweden's socialist, left-wing players were not afraid to rock the boat and show their disdain for things anachronistic, old-fashioned, and, as they saw it, unprogressive. Anders Aronsson, Vincenzo had read, espoused these views.

"They sure can," said Webster. "But I don't need to remind a man of your intellect that the world doesn't always work that way."

"So, they need a little help from their friends?"

"Let's say we know our Russian friends also like to take an interest and/or rock the boat depending on *their* interests. We want to make sure it's a fair fight. We don't want the Sovs to tip the scale."

Vincenzo wanted to ask if the Americans had thoughts on who might win the election, but he decided to get to the point of the meeting. "As far as the American-Soviet peace initiative is concerned, the Vatican would like to offer more than prayer and blessings."

"That's an unusual offer, Vincenzo—direct from the pontiff's lips, I assume?"

"Correct. Pope Karl is eager to help your peace initiative in every possible way."

"Your team's getting political?"

"I suppose, technically. But the Holy Father believes there is an overall good that will come of this."

"Whose idea?" Webster's eyes narrowed.

"You might be surprised."

"I'm sure I would ... that's why I'm asking." Webster glanced around the square as if he had all the time in the world and wasn't particularly interested in the answer.

"The Russians came to *us*."

Webster pulled down the corners of his mouth. "Really?"

"Yes, I met with them personally."

"I'm more curious now."

"They think we can smooth out any rough edges in your plans."

"Why would there be rough edges?"

"Politics."

"Still doesn't make sense, Vincenzo."

"Why not?"

"Why do we need you? We were already working on a peace initiative—a summit. Hasn't been a US-Soviet tête-à-tête for a while."

"I understand."

"Do you?" Webster studied Vincenzo intently.

"Yes, I think I do. But the way *I* understand it is that the Russians don't trust *you*—"

"And you—or the Russians?—think a little papal intervention will smooth things over?"

"It's as simple as that, yes," replied Vincenzo.

"The Russians feel that Pope Karl watching over this international fellowship will even the playing field?"

"I believe so. As I said, it comes down to trust."

"Insurance?"

"Precisely."

Webster cocked his head to one side. "Just in case ..."

"Just in case what?"

"That's what I'd like to know. Just in case what?"

"I don't follow."

"What are they afraid of?"

"I think—"

"It's a goddamn summit, Vincenzo. I mean, it's not like POTUS is going to pull out a gun and shoot President Leontev."

"I'm not sure that I—"

"All I'm saying, Vincenzo, is that we like your idea—we *love* it, in fact—but we like to understand the thinking behind an offer like this. Just so we're all on the same page."

The violinist somewhere in the opposite corner of the square stopped playing.

"Thank heaven for small mercies," said Webster.

Vincenzo raised an eyebrow. "You don't like classical music, Mr. Webster?"

"I love Vivaldi—"

"I think it's Bach—"

"I love Bach as much as the next man—just not at eight in the morning."

Vincenzo continued but decided not to tell Webster the truth about Pope Karl's ties and history with the Soviet Union. After all, his role was a papal diplomat right now. "As you know, Pope Karl hails from East Germany. He has spent much of his life under the Communist iron fist."

"Poor bastard—no offense."

"Pope Karl has seen much suffering and persecution on *his* side of the Iron Curtain."

"So, he wants to make things right?"

"Make things better. Isn't that what most of us want?"

Webster nodded, clasped his hands together, and leaned back in his chair. "Well, that all makes perfect sense, Vincenzo. Pretty much as I suspected. But we needed to meet in person to make sure."

"I agree." Vincenzo cleared his throat. "Pope Karl also agrees."

"Well, then, we accept your proposal—your offer to help facilitate the peace process—and please accept our thanks and gratitude from President Madison."

Vincenzo felt an overwhelming sense of relief. He exhaled more forcefully than he intended and looked away with a frown as the waiter arrived with the egg-white omelet.

"What's the matter?" asked Webster. "You didn't think we'd see eye to eye?"

"Not at all, Mr. Webster."

"Call me Kolby."

"Thank you, Kolby. But you see, there's one other matter … a more personal matter."

"Fire away, Vincenzo. Anything you need."

"I have a friend called Bruno. He's a chef."

"Fine profession. I wish I—"

"I should say, *was* a chef."

"What happened?"

Vincenzo paused, not for effect, but because he was paranoid that what he was about to say might unravel everything he had accomplished in the meeting so far. "He …"

Webster smiled sympathetically as Vincenzo found the words.

"He was murdered. Drowned."

"That's terrible. I'm sorry for your loss."

"Thank you."

"When was this?" Webster was genuinely concerned.

"Last night."

"*What?*" The CIA veneer of cool, calm collection faded for a moment. "*What do you mean? How?*"

"We were abducted. On a boat. My friend Bruno was shot in the head and pushed overboard. I have no idea why."

Webster collected himself. He asked slowly, "Did they threaten you?"

"Well …"

"They threatened you, didn't they?"

"I know it's a lot to ask," continued Vincenzo. "But I'd like you to find out who's responsible."

"I already know, my friend."

"You know?"

"I can make an educated guess based on twenty-five years in the business of murder, deceit, and deception."

Vincenzo waited with bated breath. *How does he know these things?*

"I'm guessing they threatened you and told you not to come today."

"Yes, that's what they said."

"First off, you're a brave man. I admire your courage. Second off, that's how they operate."

"Mafia?"

"Of course not. This was a Russian hit, Vincenzo. That's what they do. That's how they work. *That's who they are.* Understand?"

"Not exactly."

"They play both sides. They cover themselves."

Thinking about it, it seemed obvious to Vincenzo who the killers were. He had not wanted to connect the murder to his meeting with the Americans. But now he realized that to conclude otherwise would be foolish and naïve.

Webster continued, "The Russians don't play by our rules, my friend … Moscow rules, Vincenzo. Moscow rules."

"Can you catch the men who did this?"

"I'd prefer to kill them."

"I'm sorry?"

"Bad joke. You said, catch?"

"Have them arrested?"

Webster flashed an ironic smile. "Apart from our other small errand to save the world?"

"I feel responsible for his death."

"Don't be. But sure, Vincenzo, I'll add catching Bruno's murderer to the shopping list. Like I said, I'm ready to serve."

CHAPTER THIRTY

Baltic Sea

Masha was an excellent kisser—that much he could remember. When he woke up, they were both under the patchwork quilt, the *same* patchwork quilt. But infinitely more jarring was that they were both naked.

Did we, or didn't we? Steele was embarrassed he couldn't recall what had happened the night before. Accompanied by the gentle *chug-chug-chug* of the engine, they had polished off the fish broth as night fell, and Oksana had opened a bottle of red wine for them—surprisingly good red wine. On reflection, Oksana's ruddy face and the twinkle in her eye suggested she might know a thing or two about wine. As his mind began to clear, he also recalled Masha's electric touch; her stroking his forearm, then his cheek; and he also remembered her placing both hands on each side of his face and swooping in for a wine-laced passionate embrace.

Steele had enjoyed wild romantic thoughts of falling madly in love in Stockholm and running away with Masha on their own boat—to hell with the British army. But then he realized he would need a few hundred thousand Euros to cover his exotic dreams.

But he honestly couldn't remember if they had slept together. He felt lethargic, even though, looking at the bed cover and how Masha was neatly carved into the sheets, they had been asleep for some hours, and he should have felt rested.

Masha's hair was silky and blonde. He had never thought of

Russians being blonde—*wasn't that more Ukrainians?* But Masha *was* a beautiful blonde, and it was only now, after the debacle in Leningrad, that he grasped how stunning she really was. *If a woman looks this good first thing in the morning, she might be a keeper.* The other thing he noticed was Masha's body scent. It was wonderful. He asked himself when dating—or sleeping—with a prospective partner if he would be content to spend the rest of his life with this woman's body scent. On this occasion, it was a resounding *yes.*

Then he thought about the bloody image of Masha's parents murdered on their bed and felt guilty for allowing things—pure lust, or was it something more?—to spiral out of control last night. *The last thing Masha needs is a fling with an amateur spy.*

Steele glanced out of the porthole next to the bed and saw the expanse of deep blue infinity beckoning. Yes, he needed fresh air. Through the window of the cabin door, he could see Oksana's lower legs. She was still at the helm. *Does the woman ever sleep?* The boat was still moving, so by all accounts, she must have been standing there all night.

Masha stirred and said, "Good morning, Mr. Jack."

Steele glanced down and smiled. He still didn't feel awake, and he was on the verge of feeling woozy, even nauseous. "Good morning, Mashinka," he said in Russian, using the diminutive form of her name. Trying to ignore his stomach growling, he added, "Goodness gracious, little fir trees and sticks." It was his favorite Russian expression, and it made most Russians smile to hear a foreigner use it.

Masha propped herself up on one elbow and smiled. "You are quite the Casanova."

"Really?"

"I was surprised."

"*Really?*" He couldn't be sure if she was serious—and he was too embarrassed to ask because his question would imply that he had forgotten everything about anything that might or might not have happened last night.

Masha flopped back down on the sheets and stared at the ceiling. For a moment, Steele thought he saw sadness in her eyes.

"You okay?" he asked. "Perhaps we can get Oksana to show us where the eggs are."

"Coffee. I need coffee."

"Me, too." Steele got up, slipped on his boxers, and began to make coffee with all the paraphernalia in plain sight on the countertop.

"I am adopted, Jack."

Steele turned. "What?"

Masha wasn't even looking at him when she spoke. "Admiral Pushkin and Tatyana are not my parents."

"Oh ... my god. So—"

"So, I lied to you, yes."

"That's ... okay."

"But don't feel bad."

"I don't. It's fine."

"I lie about this to everyone, not just you."

"I'm sorry. I mean, I'm not sorry. I'm not quite sure what to say."

"You don't have to say anything."

"Is that why you want to defect?"

"Not really." She sat up and gestured for him to continue making the coffee. "I don't know, perhaps."

"That's very difficult."

"It's not your problem."

Steele smiled. "I wonder how that will change things for you when you get to Sweden." *How does that change things for* my *mission when we get to Sweden?* was Steele's actual thought. *Do* my *people know about this? Why did they keep me in the dark?*

Steele reeled back through all that had happened, starting with Nigel Rhodes Stampa in the Lamb and Flag pub in Camberley. *It would have been helpful to know my target was living with her adoptive parents.*

"Jack, it makes things easier. I have no attachment to Russia."

Steele poured water from a plastic container into the coffee machine and hit the toggle switch. "Do you know who your real parents are?"

"I have names. But I never met or tried to meet them."

"Why not?"

"As the Admiral used to say, *best to let sleeping dogs lie.*"

"I can respect that. Makes sense."

"Maybe it does, maybe it doesn't."

"Do you know where they are?"

"Where they *were* ... Apparently, my real parents were Ukrainian. From Odessa. My real father was a merchant sailor, and my mother worked at the best hotel in Odessa. When I was ten years old, my father told me that my real parents died in a fire."

"I'm sorry."

"But I don't believe him. He also told me I might have a brother."

Steele searched for something reassuring to say as the coffee percolated next to him. "At least you know *something* about them. I mean, some people don't know anything."

"And now I am free."

Steele smiled flirtatiously but with warmth and kindness. "You certainly are." He still had no idea what had happened between them, and this conversation wasn't giving him any clues.

Oksana opened the door to the cabin. "Good morning, love birds," she said in English with a slight American twang. "I'm glad you slept well. It's a beautiful day out here. About eight hours to our destination. Time to get up."

"Thank you, Oksana. Be right out." Steele poured coffee and handed a cup to Masha, still in bed. "I'll be on deck."

"Thanks, Jack." She placed both hands around the cup and sipped gratefully. "For everything."

Oh, sweet Jesus, Steele thought. *What does that mean?*

Steele threw on the rest of his clothes and grabbed a hunk of yesterday's bread from the counter and took a couple of bites. He stepped out onto the deck, coffee in hand, and placed his cup on the side rail.

The sky was blue, the air was fresh, and Steele concluded for a moment or two that what could only be described as "amateur espionage" wasn't so bad after all. He had completed his task. He had helped to "extract" Masha from Leningrad, and they were heading for the neutral safety zone of Sweden. Steele and Masha would part company. He would return to England, reenter the army machine, and become a tank commander in The Life Guards, Household Cavalry, as he had dreamed and planned for ever since he could remember.

Steele glanced at Oksana, who was peering—to be more precise, focusing, almost transfixed—on something he could not see from his seated position. She moved her head from side to side and adjusted her gaze as if she was locked on one point of focus out in the expanse of Baltic Sea halfway between Tallinn and Stockholm.

He stood up and saw it immediately. "What in God's name?"

"It looks like …" Oksana paused, and she slowly shook her head. "It can't be …"

In the middle distance was a large, gray metal monster. But it wasn't a ship—it was the wrong shape. It was almost like an upside-down ship, but with smoother edges and much more solid—there were no masts, cranes, or towers.

Steele said, "Oksana, I'm no expert, but that looks like a submarine."

By now, the vessel was looming larger by the second—but still far enough away not to be an immediate threat. It was, however, close enough to light his adrenaline on fire, and Steele's instincts told him that the spectacle before them would become a clear and present lethal danger very, very soon.

"Yes, Jack," said Oksana finally. "You are correct."

Steele spoke in a measured tone. "How bad is this?"

"Good question. I think the answer is *very* bad."

"Can they see us?"

"Of course, they can see us. They have radar and periscope."

"So that's great?"

"Not so great."

"Why not?"

"They can see us, and they are still heading straight for us. If they don't change course and we don't change course, we will become sunken treasure in less than five minutes."

"So, change course?" Steele smiled nervously.

"I already did—twice."

"And ...?"

"And as you can see, they are still heading directly for us."

As Steele turned to observe Oksana's facial expression, he accidentally knocked his coffee into the water. His heart sank—and not because he'd lost his caffeine. As the coffee disappeared into the depths of the all-powerful sea, the fragility of life struck him like a punch in the face. *If that submarine doesn't stop, it will all be over.*

CHAPTER THIRTY-ONE

Soviet Navy Submarine, Komsomolets, Baltic Sea

Captain Viktor Tolmachenko read the signal. It could not have been any clearer:

Destroy the fishing boat without firing a shot …

Leave no trace … Coordinates to follow …

The coordinates had arrived minutes later, and the K-278 Komsomolets submarine was now surfacing and ready to ram the fishing boat, thus completing its mission. It was, of course, an unfair fight. The Soviet nuclear submarine outweighed the fishing boat by a thousand to one—perhaps more. It would be like swatting a fly. Even if the occupants of the fishing boat were not killed on impact, they would drown in the freezing waters of the Baltic Sea within a few hours, probably less.

The signal from none other than General Urmancheva was crystal clear: Under no circumstances were they to use the main armament or any kind of small-arms fire—but the target vessel was to disappear off the face of the ocean by means of an "accidental" collision. Were any kind of wreckage to surface, it would be reported as a freak accident at sea.

At first, Captain Tolmachenko had been confused by these orders coming from the general. But he double-checked and was told to obey the order. He replied to the signal with a question before confirming his mission. *Are we to shoot survivors?* The answer was no, presumably because bodies with bullet holes would be considerably more suspicious than bodies without bullet holes. In other words, any survivors from the collision were to be left to drown.

The captain, of course, had no idea why they were about to execute this particular mission. *Orders are orders*, he reminded himself. The last few days had been busier than ever before and equally as puzzling in terms of their unusual locations off Scandinavian coastal waters. Yes, they were in the middle of the Cold War, but the usual cat-and-mouse games between the Americans and themselves were more intense than ever before.

Sweden was a neutral country. *Why do our superiors risk conflict with Sweden? What political advantage do we gain? If anything, this harassment works against our political goals.* Again, Captain Tolmachenko knew better than to give any more serious thought—let alone voice his concerns to his superiors or subordinates—to the matter, but he couldn't help wondering.

He swiveled the periscope, first one way, then the other. Still no visual of the target, even though coordinates had been triple-checked, and his chief navigation officer—known affectionately as "Yuri" after Yuri Alekseyevich Gagarin, the Soviet cosmonaut—had informed his captain that they were—or should be—right on top of the target.

Seated a few feet from the periscope, Yuri said, "Captain, …"

"I'm listening."

"I have him. Two minutes to target." Yuri stared intently at his smorgasbord of radar screens. "I confirm no ammunition to be loaded."

"Two minutes to target. No ammunition to be loaded."

Beads of sweat trickled down Yuri's temple. "Captain …"

"I am listening."

"I don't understand, Captain."

"That makes two of us, comrade." Captain Tolmachenko threw his subordinate a concerned glance and pressed his face back into the periscope. A moment later, he said, "Now I see them." The captain made minor adjustments to the periscope and added, "Target confirmed. Prepare to submerse once we complete the mission."

"We cannot just ram them. They will be destroyed."

The captain remained silent.

"Who are they?" asked Yuri.

"It is better not to know details."

"Nationality?"

Captain Tolmachenko shook his head. "Believe me, comrade, I prefer to engage in fair fights. This is not why I joined the Soviet navy."

"I understand, Captain."

"There are matters Mother Russia permits us to understand and matters she prefers not to share. Is that understood, comrade?"

"One hundred percent, Captain," Yuri replied, glancing at the radar. "One minute to target, Captain."

"Confirmed. One minute to target."

Baltic Sea

"What the fuck?" said Steele. He looked at Masha and said, "I'm sorry."

"Why you are sorry? I got us into this," said Masha. "Oksana, what are you doing? Change course!"

Steele's untrained nautical eye sensed they probably had less than one minute to live. The enormous vessel was nearly upon them—a direct collision course. The mechanical sea monster that had appeared out of nowhere was about to obliterate them.

By now, Oksana had turned their boat 180 degrees and was "running away" as fast as their engines allowed.

Again, Oksana sounded the horn.

Again, Oksana changed course.

Still, the renegade submarine remained in relentless pursuit.

Even though they were heading in the opposite direction, Steele knew—as he suspected did his shipmates—that this "escape-and-evasion" strategy was utterly futile. *We cannot out-run a submarine.*

Oksana opened a wooden box next to the helm. "Here—" she said, handing him a flare. "Just rip, twist, and pull."

Steele gave her a look that said, *Are you serious?* But he concluded that any attempt, effort, or action that might save them were worth a try. He ripped open the flare, pointed it toward the submarine, and ignited it. A satisfying *whoosh* immediately followed, but the results were distinctly unsatisfying.

The submarine was gaining on them by the second.

"I don't understand," said Steele, his voice thick with nervous energy. "What do they want from us?"

Oksana said, "I'm afraid they don't want anything *from* us, Jack."

"What do you mean?"

"I have changed course five times. We are moving *away* from them. They clearly see us, and the only thing they can possibly want right now is to feed us to the fish."

"*Fuck!*"

"Who are they?" asked Masha.

"Your comrades, of course," replied Oksana. "It looks like you are more important to the security services than you thought. But not in a good way."

"They want to kill Masha?" asked Steele. "Kill *us?*"

"Come on, Jack. They told me you are a military man. Why else would a Soviet nuclear submarine try to destroy my boat?"

"*Nuclear?*"

Oksana said, "Of course." Looking over her shoulder at the submarine bearing down on them, she added, "It's impossible. I am sorry for this, guys."

Steele said, "You're not responsible."

"This has nothing to do with you, Oksana," said Masha. "It's my fault."

"I am your captain. I am responsible for both of you. My apology stands."

Masha climbed up onto the railing next to the steering wheel and looked down into the water. "If I jump, maybe they will stop."

Steele grabbed Masha's arm and yanked her back down off the railing. "What are you doing?"

Oksana smiled despite the situation. "That's very heroic, Masha. But it won't change a thing. I know your people; we are *all* one target now."

Steele, Oksana, and Masha stood side by side, transfixed on the looming catastrophe approaching. It was as if, Steele thought, they were about to be swallowed up by a gigantic steel whale. *"Fuck it!"*

Masha said, "Jack."

"What?"

"I hate that English word *fuck*. Can you at least swear in Russian?"

Steele eyed Masha. *Sweet bloody Jesus, she's trying to be funny. God bless Masha. And I only hope Jesus is watching.*

HSwMS Gotland, Baltic Sea

There was only one female submarine captain in the Swedish navy, and Captain Paula Wallenburg was proud to be that woman. She was of medium height, thin and toned, with an angular face and prematurely gray hair in a ponytail. None of her male subordinates had ever questioned her command capabilities because she was a woman. In fact, some said she commanded even greater discipline and respect because of her "calm and motherly" leadership.

Both American and Soviet naval fleets and strike groups were made up of thousands of personnel and dozens of vessels, including aircraft carriers, frigates, destroyers, hunting and nuclear submarines, and supply ships. But His Swedish Majesty's Submarine Gotland had a crew of thirty-five and was just sixty meters long. This one Swedish stealth-class sonar submarine—still using nineteenth-century engine technology that allowed it to stay submerged for up to two weeks—had the capability to penetrate the most sensitive enemy tracking devices and destroy key command vessels in any fleet—American, Soviet, or Chinese. Once discovered, however … if Captain Paula Wallenburg penetrated the Soviet sonar shields in a war, it would become a suicide mission. Once the stealth submarine opened fire, their position would be compromised, and the fight was on.

But Sweden was a neutral country and not at war with the Soviet Union, which made this decision even more excruciatingly difficult. It would turn out to be the most important decision of her career to date and, if she got it wrong, might catapult the Cold War into a very "hot war" within hours. The United States and NATO may or may not come to Sweden's defense. Captain Wallenburg would do everything in her power, of course, to ensure that the present situation did not escalate to that extent.

Her orders were simple. Admiral Olof Bergman had delivered them to her in person before HSwMS Gotland had left Muskö naval base after its forty-eight-hour replenishment. The mission was top secret, but had she known that not even the prime minister was privy to Admiral Bergman's orders, she might have thought twice about her actions.

HSwMS Gotland was to ensure the safe passage of a fishing boat en route from Leningrad to Stockholm. There was a VIP on board, and that was all she knew.

Captain Wallenburg and her crew continued to track the Soviet vessel. There was no doubt about it—it was heading straight for the fishing boat she was charged to protect. Until now, the Swedish submarine had remained in stealth mode. She was confident that no one on board the Soviet submarine knew her current position. The good news was that stopping the submarine would be easy—all she had to do was "show" herself. She suspected that as soon as the Soviet submarine captain became aware of her presence—and therefore, a witness to his attack or whatever was about to happen—that he would abort his mission. The bad news was that this option was out of the question.

The Americans and Swedes had spent years developing the top-secret technology that allowed them to track and follow enemy warships and even larger submarines without being detected. It was a game changer in the current arms race and, quite simply, might mean the difference between war and peace.

An immediate decision was required: Obey her orders and risk exposing one of the biggest military secrets of the century or fail her mission and allow the fishing vessel to be destroyed. Captain Wallenburg was not in the habit of failing.

All she had to do was surface. The Soviets would instantly detect her position and abort their mission. The cost of this option was incalculable, not just in terms of defense budget Swedish krona and American dollars, but also in terms of decades of maritime warfare research-and-development man-hours.

Amazingly, and contrary to what any reasonable outsider who did not know her might have expected, Captain Paula Wallenburg did not need more than a moment to decide. This third-generation Swedish naval commander—the first female in her naval family—made her decision that would never be known to those on board the fishing boat but would, however, decide the fate of one Swede, one Russian, and one Englishman.

CHAPTER THIRTY-TWO

Submarine USSR Komsomolets

"Thirty seconds to impact," said Yuri, the Russian submarine's chief navigation officer.

"Understood. Thirty seconds to impact," replied Captain Tolmachenko. This was the most unusual mission he had undertaken in thirty years. It was one thing to duel with a superpower, with NATO, to use your skills, training, and expertise to outsmart, unhinge, and defeat your opponent. *But this? Why would they allow me to pulverize a defenseless fishing boat? Then again, I can't pick a fight with General Urmancheva. It would be the end of my career.*

Captain Tolmachenko buried his face in the periscope. He could even make out the crew on board the fishing boat.

"Captain ..." said Yuri.

"Speak to me."

"You're not going to believe this."

"I am trained not to believe anything until I see it with my own eyes or hear it from you. What is it?"

Yuri spoke slowly, his eyes pinging back and forth between radar screens. "Unidentified vessel, starboard, one mile, within firing range." Yuri's eyes widened. "But ..."

"But what?"

"It appears to be surfacing."

"Who is it?"

"Not one of ours."

"Prepare fire mission."

"Prepare fire mission, Captain."

"Americans?"

"Negative, Captain."

"Then who? How is this possible?"

"I don't know, Captain. This makes no sense."

Captain Tolmachenko glanced up from his periscope to see Yuri sweating profusely and several of his officers exchanging glances with each other as the situation became more puzzling. "It's impossible—"

"For an enemy vessel to penetrate our screen. That's what I am trying to say, Captain." Yuri spoke quickly now, his exasperation on full display. The proximity of the crew meant that they were able to feel each other's fears and anxiety without a word being spoken.

"Position?"

"You can see it already." Yuri pointed to his master radar screen. "Fire mission?"

In a split second, Captain Tolmachenko reeled through all the options and possibilities—fire mission, abort his fishing boat mission, retreat, possible actions-on, consequences of opening fire, consequences of not opening fire, advantages and disadvantages, political and military fallout—thirty years of experience squeezed into a split second of command decision.

He spoke calmly. "Of course not, Yuri. Do you want to start World War Three?"

"Understood, Comrade Captain."

"Abort mission."

"Captain?"

"I said, abort."

"Sorry, Captain. Which mission?

"Abort fishing boat mission."

"Understood, Comrade Captain. Abort fishing boat mission."

There was a collective sigh of relief—inaudible exhales and invisible-to-the-naked-eye releases of shoulder and forehead tension.

"General Urmancheva will be furious."

"On the contrary, Yuri. I believe he will be ecstatic."

Yuri's furrowed brow indicated he was begging for an explanation.

"We have just exposed one of the greatest secrets of modern sea warfare."

"I don't understand, Comrade Captain."

"*That*, Comrade Chief Navigation Officer," said Captain Tolmachenko, pointing to the radar, "is a Swedish stealth submarine, sixty meters in length, with a crew of thirty-five men and one woman. It is known as the *Gotland* class."

"How do you know, Comrade Captain?"

"Process of elimination, Yuri. There is nothing else it could be."

Apostolic Palace, Vatican City

Vincenzo crossed the cobblestones of San Domaso Courtyard and entered the Apostolic Palace. It was one of those days when the aircraft high above painted a satisfying white wisp across the clear, blue canvas sky. He glanced up to thank the good Lord. Vincenzo ascended the lift to the third floor and walked along the loggia—thick bulletproof glass on one side, a Venetian fresco on the other—and turned right to the papal apartments.

He eyed yet another Pontifical Swiss Guard in full dress uniform. Vincenzo always admired the bright orange and yellow of the Renaissance-inspired uniforms—and wondered what this handsome guard looked like in civilian attire. As usual, the guard made no eye contact. What was it, Vincenzo wondered, that had inspired *this* young Swiss citizen to remain unmarried until the age of thirty and, instead, join the oldest (founded 1506) and smallest army in the world—the 135-strong Swiss Guard? Was it the honor of being part of the five-hundred-year-old tradition of protecting the pontiff, or was it the honor of protecting the holiest man on earth? *If only I could grow a few inches. If only I was Swiss.* The unmarried qualification would not have been an issue, he quipped to himself, but he missed the height minimum by an inch.

Joking aside, Vincenzo was in excellent spirits and thankful to be alive. *Such is the power of my master and Lord.*

Vincenzo walked past the guard and entered the private papal apartments, expecting to see Pope Karl sitting in his beige chair next to the solid oak wooden desk scattered with books, papers, and a rotary phone and wearing his white soutane. He was looking forward to catching up—he had missed the supreme pontiff, and they had news to exchange. He had executed an important phase of their peace initiative, and he couldn't wait to share. He also needed guidance from the Holy Father on how to cope with and process Bruno's murder. He wanted to ask his master if he had made the right decision not to make it public. In retrospect, he wondered if telling the American about it had made things better or worse. Pope Karl, he knew, would deliver wise counsel.

As Vincenzo closed the door behind him and turned, he stopped in his tracks at the sight of Monsignor Franciszek, whose presence he had not been expecting. Monsignor Fran, as he was known in the city-state, was the dean of the College of Cardinals. As such, Monsignor Fran was an important man who would preside over the next conclave whenever God himself decided it was time.

"Your Eminence ..."

Monsignor Fran looked up from Pope Karl's desk.

"Where is the Holy Father?"

"Come, come in," replied Monsignor Fran. "All in good time. How was your trip?"

Vincenzo walked slowly toward the desk.

"Please, have a seat. How was Venice?"

"Please, Your Eminence, you are worrying me. Where is the Holy Father? Is he sick?"

"Pope Karl has asked me to take care of things on his behalf. Please, sit down."

"Please tell me—is he okay?"

"Of course, Father Alfonso. Our esteemed master is in good health and in reasonable spirits under the circumstances. He is mentally and physically on retreat, you might say."

"Where?"

"He wishes his whereabouts to remain confidential—for the time being."

"Confidential? But I am his—"

"His private secretary, assistant, close friend, and confidant. Yes, I am aware—and please know that he appreciates you more than you will ever know."

Vincenzo shifted uneasily in the armchair facing the pope's desk and its unexpected occupant. "This is highly irregular. I have important news for the Holy Father. I have just returned from—"

"Venice. Yes, I understand. He explained everything to me. How were the Americans? Your reception?"

"There was only *one* American. The American was fine. He agreed to our plan. But I would rather give details to the Holy Father. You must tell me where he is—immediately." Vincenzo knew that he was well beyond his station to make demands to His Eminence Monsignor Fran, but after Bruno's death, Vincenzo's life, he felt, was unraveling fast. The meeting with Kolby Webster had gone according to plan, but now that he had returned to the city-state, he needed to share *everything* with Pope Karl. He needed to share everything before his head exploded.

"Please, Vincenzo. Calm yourself. There is no need for commotion."

"The worst thing you can say to someone who is not calm is 'calm yourself.' I find it has the opposite effect. At least with me."

Monsignor Fran raised both hands, palms facing Vincenzo.

"Father Alfonso, I can explain. I *will* explain if you allow. You *deserve* an explanation."

Vincenzo exhaled. "Thank you. I am waiting."

"Our Holy Father told you about the 'difficulties' within our church?"

"Child abuse?"

"Yes."

"Yes, he told me before I left for Venice. What about it?"

"He feels responsible ... to blame, even."

"That's not what he told me. He was very concerned, but there's no reason for him to blame himself."

"He feels he should have done more. I am not sure how much he shared with you, but he blames himself to the point he has made himself sick. It's possible he might not resume his duties."

"His duties?"

"Yes, he has asked me to investigate the possibility of him resigning—the mechanics, how this might work in practice."

"*Resignation?*—Impossible. It's forbidden."

"While he is still alive *and* mentally well."

"Of course, he is mentally well. I was with him three days ago."

"I understand, Father Alfonso. But I'm afraid there are things he did not share with you."

"Monsignor Fran, there are things I *must* share with him. Immediately. We are in the middle of an important peace initiative."

"He asked me to work with you. Whatever it is you want to tell the Holy Father, you can tell me."

"How do I know—"

"How do you know you can trust me?"

Vincenzo hesitated, shaking his head, and did not reply. He was feeling light-headed. He did not want to say it, but yes, that is exactly what he was thinking. *How do I know I can trust you? What is happening? Where is the Holy Father?*

"I know you are close with the Holy Father," continued Monsignor Fran. "As I said, he is *very* fond of you—but there is something he did not tell you—or anyone else, for that matter."

Vincenzo remained still, which helped him steady his nerves and become a little calmer. He sensed an explanation might finally be forthcoming.

"It was a shock to me too. And what I am about to tell you must remain between *us*. It must not leave this room. Do you understand?"

"I understand."

"It is a matter of life and death."

"Whose life and death?"

"Pope Karl's life, and the death of the Roman Catholic Church."

CHAPTER THIRTY-THREE

*Tserkov Spasa na Krov (Church of the Savior
on Spilled Blood), Leningrad*

Oleg sat on one of the chairs near the front of the deserted church. He was alone, that is, apart from the old babushka lying in an open casket a few feet in front of him with a peaceful expression across her embalmed face. The priest had told Oleg a few minutes earlier that she had died a natural death. *I should be so lucky*, Oleg reflected.

Then he heard footsteps behind him.

Claudia sat down on a chair a few feet in front of him. To the casual observer, two people had come to pay their last respects to the woman in the casket. It was anyone's guess if they knew each other.

Claudia said, "Sorry I'm late. The foreigners are still filming that wretched movie. They have closed all the streets again."

"Don't worry. Be happy. We have time, Claudia. It's nice to see you again. It's been a while since Berlin."

"Regretfully, Oleg Stepanovich. But I am pleased to see you again in person after all this time."

"Me too. And don't be hard on the foreigners. These movie-makers helped us uncover the most sensitive, top-secret defense program of the decade—*today*—and they are completely igno-rant of their role."

"How? What happened?"

"One of their stuntmen works for *us*. That's how we

210

pointed you in the right direction for Mr. Steele and his Russian girlfriend."

"Das freut mich sehr," replied Claudia, knowing that Oleg spoke excellent German—*I am very pleased.* She continued in Russian. "What happened in the Baltic?"

Oleg smiled his trademark, weasel-like smile—the corners of his mouth turned up—but his eyes remained devoid of emotion. "Comrade Claudia, you know better than to ask such things. I could have you imprisoned for 'excessive curiosity.'"

Claudia froze, her gaze fixed on the gold iconostases in front of her. "I apologize, Oleg Stepanovich, I—"

"It's a joke, Comrade Claudia. Come on now, Fraülein, where's your sense of humor? You are supposed to dispel your East German reputation that your people lack a sense of humor."

Claudia smiled subserviantly.

Oleg said, "We had to abort the mission. Your Englishman will live to eat more pork sausages—for the time being."

"I can't say I am disappointed."

"Why not?"

"We have invested a lot of time—"

"Why didn't you argue your case when we spoke yesterday?"

Claudia laughed nervously. "It is not my place—"

"You are a good soldier. You follow orders."

"Correct, Oleg Stepanovich."

"Please don't look so serious. Things could be worse—you could be lying in that casket." Oleg leaned forward and tapped Claudia on the shoulder. She turned to face her superior. He said, "Of course, I am happy to share. After all, you were instrumental in this magnificent naval coup d'état."

"I was?"

"If it were not for you, we could not have known their destination. The fishing boat was easy to track. We don't know why yet, but someone—by all accounts, Westerners—did not want Masha or Jack Steele to die."

"How did they—"

"Games, Claudia. We are all playing games. But no one likes to play by our Moscow rules—so they cheat. And sometimes we win, and sometimes they lose." He playfully raised an eyebrow.

"As I said, Steele could be useful. Your people gave him to us after all."

"I am aware. But why are you so sure?"

"Something about his expression."

"His expression? Tell me."

"When I saw him in London, my instincts told me his heart is not in it. He was different from our meeting in Berlin."

"You spoke to him in London also?"

"No. It's just …"

"Just a feeling?"

"Yes, a feeling. Besides, you and my superiors ordered me to follow him for several weeks. It would be a waste—"

"No waste, Claudia. Seeds, my dear comrade, seeds." Oleg leaned back slightly and crossed his legs at the ankles. We are like our iconic Ukrainian farmer—scattering seeds to feed the world. But not every seed takes root."

"I understand, Oleg Stepanovich. I agree."

Oleg nodded. He eyed the old babushka in her casket. "Do you know why I wanted to meet here?"

Claudia shook her head.

"From time to time, I like to see a corpse at close quarters."

"Why?"

Oleg continued, "The priest told me she died of old age. God rest her soul."

"But why a corpse?"

"Why? Why does death have to be joyless? Look at her,"—he extended both hands toward the casket as if he was welcoming an old friend—"look at that peaceful face. She had a great inning, as the British say—you know cricket?"

Claudia nodded.

Oleg said, "She is ninety-one years old."

"And you see *joy* in this?"

"It gives me a sense of urgency, excitement—it makes me want to *live*. But I see you don't appreciate my warped sensibilities, am I right?"

"Not at all, Comrade Oleg." Claudia eyed the corpse. "I just never thought of it like this."

"Your father might explain better."

"My father?"

"He is a man of God."

Claudia turned slowly toward her superior and frowned. "How did you know? No one knows this."

"Please, Claudia. You are a highly respected intelligence operative—one of the HVA's finest. But we all have secrets. ... By the way, if your wall tumbles, you are welcome to come and join *us*."

"*Tumbles?*"

"Things are not looking good. The Soviet Union is disintegrating thanks to our leader. But don't worry. We have contingencies—hopes, dreams, aspirations, plans. I have it all up here." He pointed to his temple.

Claudia started as Oleg suddenly and aggressively slapped his hands together as if he was playing the cymbals. But the expression he wore was considerably less musical. Venomous would be precise—he spoke slowly with a mixture of anger, determination, and hatred in his eyes. "Whatever happens to our union in the future, I will not rest until my people have the respect they deserve. Do you understand?"

"Of course, Oleg Stepanovich. I agree."

"I am sick of the Americans taking over this world under their NATO disguise. They are creeping toward us, leaving our Iron Curtain in tatters."

"I hope our union does not crumble, as you say. I honor and serve the Soviet Union and the Eastern bloc—and I honor the East German people."

"I would expect nothing less."

After a few moments of silence apart from the gentle hiss of candles burning around the casket, Claudia continued, "My father? How—"

"We are brothers-in-arms, Claudia. I am sure you know this. Your father is an important man, a true Patriot."

"Thank you, Comrade Oleg."

"You're welcome, Comrade Claudia."

Claudia asked, "How did they stop our ... *your* mission?"

"Mine? Yours? It's all the same. The Westerners were expecting Masha."

"How?"

"*How?* I would like to know details too. We will find out."

"She defected? The British helped?"

"Yes, of course, the Englishman. But there is a difference, wouldn't you agree, between sneaking out of our country on a fishing boat and sneaking out of our country on a fishing boat with a NATO submarine waiting to escort you to safety?"

"The Swedish navy?"

"Yes. But don't worry, we are more than delighted with the outcome."

"You were going to destroy the boat?"

"Yes. Masha knows a lot—too much—from her father, of course. And by all accounts, she has already 'shared' too much. But in this case, what we got in the Baltic Sea was a thousand times more valuable."

"I see. This is good news."

"This is great news, believe me, Claudia. It also means I have leverage with my people for the next phase of our plans—our 'international peace initiative.'"

"I am ready to serve, Oleg Stepanovich."

"Of course you are. And you would be wise to ask no further questions."

"I know my place."

"Indeed. And let's just say the Russian navy had a bonus day today."

Claudia held the prayer book she had picked up on the way in and leafed through a few pages. "I'll say a prayer."

"No need, comrade. God will not help us fulfill our destiny. I prefer to rely on loyal colleagues like you. But feel free to do what you must."

"What about the election? It might complicate things with Masha. She is friends with the prime minister's daughter."

"Remember, all good things come to those who wait. I have other business in Stockholm, so continue your mission, but be ready to alter course if necessary."

"You are going to observe the election?"

"Yes, I am curious to see how things turn out once we show the Americans what happens when they interfere."

"Maybe I should make contact with Masha?"

"Why?"

"Maybe she will have second thoughts about her actions?"

"Dear Masha is a traitor. There is only one fate for her. The only contact you will have with her is your last contact with her. But wait for my order."

"I understand, Oleg Stepanovich. But what about Steele—the two of them are close. Shall I wait for him to leave Sweden?"

"Not necessary."

Claudia hesitated before she said, "Then—"

"Correct. If Mr. Steele remains in Stockholm, he will be collateral damage when the time comes to show Masha what a paradise the West can be."

CHAPTER THIRTY-FOUR

Stortorget, Stockholm

Jack Steele and Simon Bird moved to the edge of the large crowd of Anders Aronsson supporters that filled Stortorget, the oldest square in Sweden's capital. *Not quite as large as the crowd that packed the streets to overflowing in the labor demonstrations of 1892*, Steele thought.

Masha had given him a potted history of the capital after they slept together on the boat. He had begun to see why she was so enthralled with the place. Now Steele recounted to Bird—in whimsical fashion—that he hoped there would be no repetition of the Stockholm Bloodbath of 1520 when, for three days, the Danish-Swedish king Christian II had beheaded and hanged ninety people.

"Aronsson's impressive," said Steele as he watched him on the podium.

"If you like that sort of thing," replied Bird, who had arrived three hours earlier from the British embassy in Moscow. "Bit too sure of himself for my liking. But then again, he's the prime minister, and I'm a civil servant."

About five hundred Anders Aronsson supporters, who were becoming more excited, animated, and passionate by the minute, applauded spontaneously. They listened intently to their prime minister and leader of the Social Democrats. He had been speaking for ten minutes, but he was only getting started.

It was Sunday, therefore less vehicle traffic. This made

Aronsson's amplified voice carry even farther across the square and around the streets of central Stockholm. It was as if the entire city—not to mention the country, when you considered those at home glued to their televisions—was watching, getting ready to make up their minds and cast their votes the following Wednesday.

"So, whose side are *we* on?" asked Steele.

"The Royal we?"

"Yes, HM government?"

"Who do we want to win this election?"

"Yes. Is it a secret?" Steele pulled up his collar as the wind picked up and it began to drizzle. "Aronsson seems pretty far left?"

"He is. But that helps with Russia. At least, that's the theory. Sweden's supposed to be neutral, but Aronsson wants to make friends with the Ruskies. He's a commie bastard in the guise of a liberal leftie, his enemies would have you believe."

"That far gone?"

"By all accounts. And Aronsson hates Madison even though the Russian navy has been yapping at his heels recently. They say he's too scared to do anything about it—won't even think about firing any kind of warning shot across their bows."

"Literally fire a warning shot?"

"Yes, and we can't get involved because it's not technically a NATO problem."

"Even though we'd probably end up supporting Sweden if the shit hit the fan."

"Correct."

"He certainly stepped up for *me*. Or one of his admirals did."

"Maybe. We don't know why your Russian submarine scarpered. Still too early to know if the Swedes had anything to do with it."

"Who else?"

"We'll find out soon enough."

"I owe someone a bottle of schnapps. Big time."

"Sounds like you do if they were as close as you say."

"They were."

In their middle distance, Aronsson continued his oration, his eloquent and measured tone reverberating around the square and beyond.

Bird said, "That man is driving his top brass barmy. He won't let them retaliate."

"Would they engage a Russian nuclear submarine?"

"Probably not, but they would like to play more than cat and mouse when the Soviet navy encroaches on Swedish waters. And some of the sightings were not even confirmed as Russian navy."

"What does that mean? NATO?"

"Not necessarily. That's the point. They appeared and then disappeared in a flash before they could be identified by the Swedes as NATO vessels."

"Sounds complicated."

"It is. But it's also a bit odd."

"Isn't it up to commanders on the ground—or at sea—to engage, send a warning shot?"

"To an extent. But they still need the proverbial green light to open fire, even a warning shot."

"So, they're just a lean, mean, fighting machine with no teeth?" Steele exhaled.

"Pretty much."

"Isn't that what we—the Royal we—all want? Peace in our time?"

"That's all well and good until the shit hits the fan and some Soviet fanatic gains power and decides to invade."

"Masha says Mikhail Leontev is the best hope they've had for a long time—to bring Russia into the twenty-first century when it arrives. To compete with the West."

"I agree. *If* he allows the Eastern bloc to do its thing. But if Leontev isn't careful, some of them will probably join NATO."

"Switch sides? Surely not."

"You'd be surprised. That's why we continue to monitor like hawks. Espionage is more crucial now than ever before. *Trust but verify,* as Madison says wisely. I say, trust but spy the shit out of them."

Steele eyed Masha standing next to Astrid Aronsson on the podium. "She says there's in-fighting."

"Masha?"

"Yes, Russia's falling apart."

"So, the country's falling apart, and your young spy is saying Leontev's the best chance they have." Bird feigned a chuckle. "See what I mean?"

"I do. It's complicated."

"The next decade will be a very bumpy ride. But I'm looking forward to debriefing Masha. I'm sure she has a lot to share."

"Let me know if I can help. She trusts me."

Bird shot Steele a knowing glance. "I'm sure she does."

Steele smiled in spite of himself.

Their conversation was interrupted by more cheers, roars, and a round of applause from the crowd. A piercing technical whine from the loudspeakers followed, after which Arsonsson continued his anti-American rhetoric.

Bird said. "The good thing about the Cold War was that it was *cold.* Frozen. There wasn't much movement or conflict—apart from the spy game, of course. Two sides, black-and-white-ish, Iron Curtain—and that *was* a good way to keep the peace."

"But not sustainable?"

"If you ask me, we should aim to keep it that way for as long as possible."

"You think perestroika and glasnost put a spanner in the works?"

"Yes, progress too quick."

"Why do you think it's out of control?"

"People, my young friend. Perestroika and glasnost are all well and good, but we never control the minds of others.

Obscene egos, megalomaniacs, and narcissists—nearly always men, I might add—and the international brotherhood and unity of arseholes who get sucked in. Even Madison wants to bolster his legacy."

"Can't blame him. I would, too."

"Meaning?"

"He's trying to ditch the goofy cowboy image. I suspect he feels people don't take him seriously because he was a famous actor. Maybe he's got something to prove."

"Oh, believe me, he's taken seriously."

Steele glanced at Bird. "What do you mean?"

"It's top secret. Come and work for us one day—when you've finished playing tin soldiers. I'll buy you a drink and tell you the whole story. But for now—"

"Fair enough. I know my place." Steele held up both hands to surrender his line of questioning.

"You did an excellent job, by the way."

"Thanks, I didn't really do much."

"Modesty will get you nowhere. Don't sell yourself short—you were calm under pressure, Jack. And you got *her* out." Bird gestured to Masha.

Among the small entourage of friends, political aids, and helpers, Masha was smiling and whispering to Astrid. They were clearly enjoying themselves in the semi-limelight.

Steele caught Masha's eye. He nodded and smiled. "*Fuck,*" he whispered under his breath, but Bird heard anyway.

"Did you?"

"Did I what?"

"Did you sleep with her? She's a pretty girl. I'm not sure I could refuse. If, for example, we were stuck on a boat in the middle of the Baltic Sea."

"Come on, Simon. You're a bloody spook. You're trained to control yourself at the drop of a hat."

"Something like that." Bird looked at Steele, waiting for a reply.

"I'm not going to answer." *That's two women I've slept with I am not telling them about.*

"Fair enough. Wise chap. You know I'd have to put it in my report. Always remember, in our world, if it's in the report, you're fine. When it's *not* in the report, and you get caught lying, then it's a big problem."

Steele pretended to be engrossed in Aronsson's speech, but he was thinking about Claudia and his night in Berlin. *If the shit hits the fan, I'm screwed. I lied to the security services, and it's too late now to tell them.* Steele mumbled quietly, "No use crying over spilt milk."

"What did you say?"

"Nothing."

"You should think about joining our merry band of brothers. My guess is you'll be bored stiff when you become a fully fledged donkey walloper." Bird was using the playful but disparaging nickname bestowed on all rank and file of the Household Cavalry by the rest of the British army.

"I'll give it some thought, Simon. But for now, I'm quite looking forward to the gunnery range in boring old BAOR."

Steele lied. Bird was right. Steele was starting to loathe the idea of being a tank commander, stuck in an old barracks in the middle of nowhere in Germany—British Army of the Rhine. Espionage was infinitely more interesting—but probably more dangerous if this first assignment was anything to go by.

Aronsson gesticulated with both fists—not aggressively tight fists, but more of a thumb-uppermost "offering" gesture, as if he was about to hand someone a piece of paper. He used his entire body—bending his knees slightly, turning to the left and right to make eye contact with his supporters as he made his points. Anyone watching in person or on television would be utterly convinced of the passion of his convictions and might even switch allegiances, swayed by his powers of persuasion.

He spoke in English to make the most of the international media presence. Most Swedes were used to this.

"And I challenge our partner, President Brad Madison, to think outside the box. Do not be a coward, Mr. President"—the crowd cheered and jeered at the same time, not quite sure which emotion would best show support for Aronsson's dig—"I say again, President Madison, do *not* be a coward. Hang up your holster and gun"—Aronsson made a swift cowboy gesture by pretending to draw a revolver from his hip and fire into the crowd, much to their amusement and delight—"and put your thinking cap on. Yes, Mr. President, we know you have a brain under that ten-gallon hat." Again, the left-leaning, progressive crowd erupted as their leader poked fun at the American president like no other leader in recent Swedish history.

Aronsson smiled and nodded as if he was sharing an inside joke with his audience. He held up both hands to settle the crowd. He turned to Astrid and observed her giving her Russian friend a look that said, *Welcome to my world.*

Masha smiled at the prime minister and shouted above the noise. "Amazing," she said, clapping in his direction. "Hurrah!"

Aronsson turned to face the crowd and continued, "Extend an olive branch, Mr. President. Yes, tear down the Berlin Wall if you can—show our fellow citizens of the world what awaits them on *this* side of the Iron Curtain. Make the first move, Mr. President. Extend the hand of peace!" More cheers erupted from the crowd. "Why should our Soviet brothers and sisters trust *you*, Mr. President, if your own people—and certainly *our* people—cannot trust you? Show the world we can trust you!"

Knowing the low regard his supporters had for the American president, he waited for the applause he knew would follow. The crowd cheered on cue. Even Astrid, who did not support her father's political philosophy, was smiling and clapping as if she was suddenly his biggest fan.

Aronsson knew he was treading an exceptionally fine line, given his classified knowledge of the American president's top-secret Deception Committee vendetta against the Russians. Madison was up to something—something big—and Aronsson was determined to flush it out in the open.

"Make no mistake, Mr. President. I demand that *you*"—he paused for effect—"end the Cold War!"

Aronsson waited for his proverbial gauntlet to hit the proverbial ground—his left-leaning supporters' psyche. But a deafening bang pierced the quiet before the deathly storm. His "gauntlet" never touched the ground.

CHAPTER THIRTY-FIVE

Certosa di San Giacomo Monastery, Capri

The view was even more exquisite than Castle Gandolfo's lake view. In the distance, Pope Karl stared at the picture-postcard sea and the Faraglioni—the famous three towering rock formations just off the island's coast. Locals, tourists, the rich, and the super-rich took turns enjoying the playful ritual of boating under the center rock's archway, which had been carved out by the wind and sea spray over millions of years. The pontiff had yet to experience the ritual, but one thing he knew for certain was that he would never "kiss his sweetheart" under the arch for good luck as the superstition held.

Certosa di San Giacomo Carthusian monastery, established in 1371, was open to the public during tourist hours—museum and art gallery wing, monastery grounds, and the old chapel—but no one knew about or had access to the secluded wing on the west side of the monastery. Apart from the monks who tended to Pope Karl's basic needs—food, water, reading material if requested, and a generous supply of Mediterraneo room diffuser liquid perfume donated with pride and pleasure by Carthusia I Profumi di Capri, none of the visitors had any idea that the holiest man in the world was a short walk from their guided audio tour. Furthermore, the Capri monks, who were spiritually blessed but bereft of mental health training, could not know that Pope Karl II, formerly the East German Roman Catholic priest by the name of Joseph Rohweder, was hanging by a thread both mentally and, he would also admit, morally. He felt tormented to be in such an idyllic location feeling so utterly demoralized and depressed.

There was, of course, nothing he could do to change the past—the litany of sexual abuse scandals that had plagued his church. He could not shake the feeling that if he had acted sooner—years earlier, in fact, even as a lowly priest when he had suspected such things were taking place—that he might have been able to stem the tide of suffering that a tiny minority of priests had inflicted on their unwitting congregations.

But as terrible as this was, it was not his most pressing problem. For the third time that morning, he walked away from his window and out into the small courtyard filled with shrubs and flowers surrounded by centuries-old stone walls that seemed as though they might talk to him.

He sat on the lone bench to wait for his visitor. This simple wooden bench was not quite as grand as the Castello Gandolfo bench he was so fond of, but it served its purpose when he debated whether to throw himself out of his bedroom window and plummet to a near-certain death two hundred feet below. At least the view of the sea and the Faraglioni would be magnificent as he entered the kingdom of heaven, he mused semi-earnestly.

At that moment, a different inner voice had beckoned him away from the window and into the courtyard. Yellow roses had been planted by the monks—they did their own gardening—but there were also blue and red wildflowers scattered around the courtyard and around the stone well in the center.

Again, he thought about taking his own life. *I can simply jump down the well. A broken neck would suffice.*

He began to pray:
Dear Father, I love you, guide me, reveal thyself ...
I have sinned in thought, word, and deed
and I need your help, dear God ...
Please rid me of these thoughts of self-harm.

*Please help me to make the right decision for me, my people, and
my daughter, Claudia.*

Yes, he thought, it *was* rather shocking that the holiest man on
earth had a daughter virtually no one knew about who worked
for the Hauptvervaltung Aufklärung—HVA—or Main Directorate for Reconnaissance that was East Germany's foreign intelligence service. He had also lied about his previous marriage and
his parental status when he entered the priesthood—although,
to be fair, it was several years later that his ex-wife had told him
about their daughter. By then, of course, it was too late to come
clean and tell the church about his past. Truth *and* lies always
catch up with you in the end.

And *that* was what that cunning fiend of a man—the Russian
KGB officer by the name of Oleg Stepanovich Pugachev—had
so despicably yet cleverly used against him. It was the worst
kind of blackmail, a trap constructed with both truth and lies
inextricably linked. "She works for us now," Oleg Stepanovich
had warned. "There is no turning back. If you do not follow
my orders, we will liquidate Claudia and, of course, your godly
reputation along with her."

That was all, of course, *before* he became Pope Karl II. Before,
during, and after the conclave, when everything had happened
so fast, it seemed too late to do anything about it—the lure and
magnificence of the Almighty and holy power were too much to
refuse. If he had told anyone about the blackmail, the heinous
threat to his only daughter—his own flesh and blood—his entire
world and the reputation of the Roman Catholic Church would
have come crashing down.

He had repented. But what good would that do in the eyes
of the world? God was forgiving, but the world was not. People
were not. He had allowed himself to be blackmailed by the Russian security services and their legendary unforgiving and evil
methods, and then he had accepted the most important holy job
on the planet—supreme pontiff of the Roman Catholic Church.

A gentle breeze swept into the courtyard—a welcome relief to his maze of tortuous thoughts. Perhaps there was still time to change, to do something. He could make amends. He could follow Oleg's orders to facilitate the peace summit, but it was now time to admit (to himself and those he trusted) the real reason why Oleg wanted the peace summit. Pope Karl had suspected all along that Oleg planned to assassinate the American president.

> *Please, God, guide me toward the truth.*
> *Please, God, reveal thyself and the truth.*
> *Please, God, guide me.*
> *Please, God, reveal thyself.*

A white and yellow butterfly—the colors of the Vatican flag—landed on his forearm.

> *Thank you, Lord.*

This is a sign to act. Pope Karl stared at the butterfly and smiled for the first time since he had arrived in Capri. *God does indeed work in mysterious ways. Yes, my Lord, I understand.*

He got up and walked to the center of the courtyard and picked up the small wooden bucket on a piece of thin rope. He threw the bucket down the well and heard a *plop*. As he pulled up hand over hand the bucket now full of water, his entire life played fast forward on the movie screen of his mind—his East German childhood, his teenage love affair with Claudia's mother, his unexpected—to himself and all those who knew him—decision to join the priesthood, and his equally unexpected rise to the very top.

Then it came to him, and it felt as though he had known what to do all along. That was usually the way prayers were answered.

He grappled with the bucket and placed it on the side of the well. He used the metal cup sitting on the top of the well to drink. The water was cool and refreshing. Then he carefully re-coiled the rope and placed it on the ground, ready for the next time.

> *It is not about me, my Lord.*
> *It is not about them.*
> *I will do as you command.*
> *I will keep going.*
> *I will not harm myself.*

Pope Karl sat down on the bench and looked around. He noticed more details now: the wheelbarrow in the corner; the crumbling, rusty, iron grid covering one of the windows that was probably once a prison cell; an old water pump handle that was overgrown with weeds; thick wooden shutters behind the windows; a triangular stone arch that was probably once some kind of fountain or perhaps a doorway that now led nowhere. He noticed the meticulous way someone had laid paving stone to the well from four directions and the smooth, rounded top of the garden wall.

Time stood still.

He loved his daughter, Claudia, whom he had once met in secret many years ago when she was a little girl. She was beautiful, clever, and resourceful, and although he had not had contact with her since that one and only meeting, his HVA contacts had sent periodic updates full of praise for Claudia, her work, and her talent as a field operative—or spy. *She was doing God's work, they had said. Not quite,* he had thought at the time, *but I know what you mean.*

Monsignor Fran entered the courtyard. "Excellency … How are you?"

"Welcome, young man." Pope Karl smiled. He and

Monsignor Fran were the same age, but he always called him "young man" when they were spending informal time together.

"Have you made a decision?" asked Monsignor Fran. "I know it is not easy."

"I have. I will make amends."

"But it must be your decision."

"We will facilitate the peace process—but from this moment, I refuse to be blackmailed."

Monsignor Fran frowned. "I understand. But your daughter—"

"Claudia's fate is in God's hands now."

"Very well, Excellency. I understand this is a difficult—"

"An excruciating decision."

"What shall I tell the Russian?"

"Have Vincenzo proceed as planned. Do not mention our conversation."

"Of course, Excellency." Monsignor Fran moved toward the well and helped himself to a cup of water. "If you don't mind me asking, how did you reach this decision?"

Again, a yellow and white butterfly landed on the edge of the wooded bucket, and both men smiled and appreciated God's beauty.

Pope Karl eyed the butterfly. "A friend gave me a helping hand."

Stortorget, Stockholm

Anders Aronsson did not know what had hit him—literally. And neither did anyone else, for that matter. As the crowd scattered, Astrid and the rest of her entourage hit the deck. She crawled across the podium to her father, but it was too late. It was a professional job. Someone had assassinated her father, and the bullet—a single bullet—had pierced his heart.

Even so, Astrid looked around for help and met Masha's eye.

For a split second—perhaps less—Astrid saw a void in Masha's expression, or perhaps—when she reflected days later—she had imagined it. Then Masha frowned, her eyes watering and expressing sympathy for Astrid's pain and suffering.

No more shots were fired.

Masha reached Astrid, knelt, and placed a hand around her shoulder.

"I am so sorry."

Astrid said nothing. She pressed her hands into the chest wound, blood seeping through her fingers, but her father's lifeless body told her it was futile. There was nothing anyone could do as the bodyguards attempted their same futile lifesaving steps. Seconds later, emergency service personnel were on their knees next to the prime minister, trying to resuscitate him.

Then it hit her. Astrid's father had simply been too progressive. All his speeches, all their conversations suddenly slapped her in the face as he lay next to her. *Of course, they were going to kill him*, she thought. *It was only a matter of time.*

Astrid had always assumed that because Anders Aronsson was her father, he was also invincible, no matter his political agenda and ideology. She had thought naïvely that peace between East and West was a good thing, something people should want. She had thought his reaching out to the Soviet Union and thumbing his nose at the Americans would bring East and West closer together. He was kind of a political and diplomatic fulcrum, so to speak.

How could I be so naïve?

The emergency responder sighed, shook her head, and sat back on her haunches. Her eyes watered, and she gave Astrid her best look of sympathy. "I'm sorry, Miss, there's nothing more we can do."

Astrid sobbed, and Masha rocked her back and forth to help console her friend. She, too, had been in the same situation—mourning close family—just days before.

Masha said, "I don't understand what is happening. It's not possible."

Astrid looked at Masha, tears streaming down her face. Astrid nodded in agreement. "Me neither."

They squeezed each other tighter, but once again, Astrid thought about the empty look in Masha's eyes the moment Anders Aronsson had been shot.

CHAPTER THIRTY-SIX

Stortorget, Stockholm

"Wait, there's nothing you can do," said Bird. His grip was tight, but not tight enough.

Steele pulled away and ran toward the podium against the crowd of frantic—many of them hysterical—Aronsson supporters. He pushed and shoved and, in turn, was pushed and shoved right back as men, women, and children of all shapes, sizes, and ages fled Stockholm's main square. In the distance, Steele observed that the only people *not* moving were the small huddle around what was presumably Aronsson's injured—or worse, dead—body.

Bird caught up with Steele. "Listen to me, Jack." This time his grip was stronger, and Steele relented and slowed to a walking pace.

"What? They need help, for Christ's sake."

"It's too late, Jack. We must leave now."

"What are you talking about—I need to help Masha and Astrid. The guy's bleeding to death."

"Aronsson's dead."

"You don't know that."

"It looks bad."

"What's happening?" Steele's voice was strained now, and he could feel his heart pounding against his chest. A familiar refrain from his Sandhurst instructor a few weeks before came to mind—*Anything could happen in the next twenty-four hours, gentlemen ... and it probably will.*

"Masha is not your friend, Jack. She's a Russian." Bird paused—his eyes locked with Steele.

Steele looked away and kept moving, using his elbows to fend off the hoards. "I don't understand. Tell me what the fuck is going on."

"I will. I promise. But we need to get you away from here—and I should probably come too."

Steele craned his neck above the crowd to see the podium. Bird was probably right. From the passive body language of Astrid and Masha and the first responders, he could tell that Aronsson's body was lifeless. "Fuck. What the *fuck?*" Steele shook off Bird's grip. "I'm okay. Leave me alone."

"This way, Jack. Forget about them. It's over."

Reluctantly, Steele halted, turned, and began to walk in the opposite direction, away from the carnage. "Who did that? Do you know who did that?"

"I don't. Not yet. But I have a pretty good idea."

"I need to see Masha." Steele turned again.

Bird placed his hand on Steele's forearm. "No, Jack. She's the last person you need to see right now. Trust me."

"Frankly, I don't trust you. I helped Masha defect. Astrid Aronsson was helping her too, and now her father's dead. Forgive me if I don't trust you, Simon. What have you people got me into?"

"Believe me, this is not how we expected things to go."

"You think Masha had something to do with this?" He glanced at the podium as the first responders were manhandling Aronsson's body onto a stretcher. The ambulance driver killed his rotating red lights.

"I have no bloody clue right now. But I know that you don't need to be here. As you point out so astutely, you helped Masha Pushkin defect from the Union of Soviet Socialist Republics. And now she's standing next to a dead prime minister who's just been assassinated. Not a good look."

Steele could hear the proverbial alarm bells going off inside his head. "When you say, 'you helped,' you mean '*we* helped'?"

"No, Jack, I mean, '*you* helped.' As far as we're concerned, no one else from our side was involved. That should have been made clear to you in London."

They reached the edge of the square, and Bird made a right turn down Slottsbacken toward the British embassy. *At least*, thought Steele, *we're not in Russia. At least I'm with my own people.* "But we had nothing to do with the poor bastard back there."

"Right, Jack. But nothing is black-and-white in our world, and a whole load of gray just rained on our parade. Don't you see, Jack? You can be directly implicated."

"That's ridiculous, I—*we*—had nothing to do with this. You know that."

"It doesn't matter what I think or know. The point is, how will others use what they know or don't know to their advantage? You slept with Masha, for God's sake. We didn't tell you to do that."

Steele shook his head, wiping the rain off his face, and raised his voice. "You can vouch for me, right? We're on the same side. I don't understand what the bejesus you are trying to tell me."

"There's a reason we sent for you, Jack. Don't you get it?"

"No, I don't—forgive me for being thick."

"There's no trace, you see," Bird continued in a cold, emotionless tone. "If the proverbial hits the fan, which it has now done, you're just a British soldier who went rogue—no connection with the security services."

Steele gave a sarcastic chuckle. "Okay. Now I get it."

"We didn't know this was going to happen. You need to disappear off the face of the planet—or at least the continent."

"You want me to disappear?"

"Yes."

"For how long?"

"As long as necessary."

"What does that mean?"

"Look, sometimes things happen we can't control. You're an easy fall guy, that's all. The Russians will say you flipped Masha and conspired with her and the assassin to make the Russians look bad. Classic Moscow rules."

"Why would anyone believe that?"

"Attack is the best form of defense. Whoever was responsible for Aronsson's murder will be looking to deflect blame. Right now, you are the perfect man for the job."

Steele exhaled and said, "What if it wasn't the Russians? What if it was the CIA? They hate Aronsson more than the Russians. Did you hear his speech today?"

"You're right. And yes, if it *was* them, they will be looking for a scapegoat the same as the Russians."

"But we're on the same side."

"We're on the same side until we're not," continued Bird. "Look at it from their side. *If* the Yanks really are responsible for this, who better to blame than a British army rookie ensnared in a Russian honey trap." Bird stopped, looked up at the adjacent house number, and shook out his umbrella. "We're here."

"Where?"

"Our safe house."

"I thought we were going to the embassy?"

"Too obvious."

"But—"

"We need to isolate you immediately—just in case."

"Just in case what?"

"Just in case the Russians try to kill you for helping Masha. Just in case the Americans really are responsible and want to use you as a convenient foil because you slept with Masha. Just in case the press finds you and blows what little cover you have … shall I go on?"

"I get it, I get it."

"You're a hot potato, Jack. We don't want you baked to a crisp."

Oval Office, the White House, Washington, DC

"Goddamn that man!" said POTUS.

Kolby Webster, deputy director of the CIA, replied, "He's dead, sir."

"I know he's dead. He screwed everything up, goddamn him!"

"He probably didn't mean to—"

"Aronsson was trying to be a smart ass. He just couldn't help himself."

"He was certainly more left of center than we'd have preferred."

"Left of center? He was a commie bastard, for God's sake. Did you hear what he said in that speech?"

"But he's dead, sir."

"No shit, Sherlock. He's dead, but he threw down the gauntlet. He made me—and you, and every goddamn American—look bad. He made out that *we* are the bad guys. Can you believe that?"

"I mean, he was thumbing his nose for sure—"

"Hit the nail on *that* head, Deputy Director." Madison sat down so hard in his chair behind the Oval Office desk that he nearly tipped backward. "You know what they're going to do now?"

"The Russians?"

"Yes, the goddamn Ruskies."

"Blame us?"

"Of course, they will. They'll blame us. Damn right, they will."

"But they have no proof?"

"They don't need proof—they have a propaganda machine that covers ten time zones and half the goddamn globe."

"Not quite, Mr. President."

"Shut up, Kolby." Brad Madison picked up the phone and

slammed it back down. "Goddamnit, I can't remember who I was about to call."

"Sir, we have this under control."

"Do we?"

"Yes, sir. It's unfortunate that this happened—and there *will* be consequences. But there's no way we can be linked to this."

"Don't you get it, Kolby?"

Webster frowned. "I just—"

"This is how they play. Moscow rules."

"Right."

"They don't need proof. They make shit up—any old bull-shit—feed it into their propaganda machine, and bingo, they've changed the course of history. That's how they play."

"I'm losing you, sir. Regardless of Aronsson's assassination, what is it we want?"

"I want to bring those commie bastards to their knees. *That's* what I want."

"What about glasnost and perestroika? Isn't that progress? I thought we wanted a peace summit, sir? That's why I went to Venice."

"Of course, I want the peace summit. It'll make me look good. It'll help my legacy and ensure our re-election next year. But what I *really* want is to tear down that son-of-a-bitch Iron Curtain and knock down that BS Berlin Wall."

"But that's happening—as we speak. The Deception Committee is working, Mr. President. It's doing its job."

"Sure, it's working. It *was* working until this asshole went too far and got himself shot."

"Sir, it wasn't his fault. He didn't order his own assassination."

"You don't understand, Kolby. Sweden was right where we wanted them. They were serving a purpose—*our* purpose."

"Making nice with Russia."

"Right, it was a peaceful distraction. We pissed them off with our submarine cat-and-mouse bullshit, and they fell for it."

"The Russians?"

"Yes, the Russians."

"So, that's good?"

"No! It's not good. It *was* good until the goddamn Brits screwed up with this Masha Pushkin thing. I don't know what the Brits are up to, but they just ruined our entire plan. We had the Ruskies on the run at sea. They had no idea where we were."

"The Gotland class sub was unfortunate."

"Do not utter that name, Deputy Director."

"We're in the Oval Office."

"Precisely."

"My apologies." Webster cleared his throat. "Sir, I realize the assassination changes things. But we can correct course—concentrate on solutions. I think that would be in everyone's best interests."

Madison placed both hands over his face and rubbed his eyelids. "I might have to meet Mikhail Leontev after all. That's the bottom line."

"Understood. Is that so bad?"

"I'm not happy about it."

"I thought that was the plan. The Vatican?"

"It was *one* of the plans."

"I understand Mr. President."

"We had them by the balls, goddamnit."

"The Deception Committee still has legs."

"Sure, it does, Kolby. It's just that I'm going to have to do the deceiving in person as well now."

Webster nodded slowly. "What does that look like, Mr. President?"

"It looks like I'm going to have to go back to my roots."

"Sir?"

"I'm an actor, remember, Webster. Did you forget?"

"No, sir, I hadn't forgotten. But—"

"It's gonna be the performance of a lifetime. We will destroy those commie sons of bitches if it's the last thing I do. Iron

Curtain? Berlin Wall? It's horseshit, do you understand me, Kolby? It's fuckin' horseshit and bullshit all rolled into one big pile of shit. Do you copy, Webster?"

"Yes, sir. I copy. Shall I call our Italian friends?"

"I don't care if you call God himself, but I want them to fulfill their 'heavenly' offer."

"No problem, sir. They're already on board."

"If that priest guy—what's his name?"

"From the Vatican? Vincenzo …"

"Right. If he gives you any trouble, tell him we'll take his mother on a boat ride, courtesy of the local carabinieri."

"Va bene, Signor Presidente!" *You got it, Mr. President.*

CHAPTER THIRTY-SEVEN

Certosa di San Giacomo Monastery, Capri

At 6:05 am, one day after Monsignor Fran had arrived in Capri, the two holy men sat one pew apart from each other in the monastery chapel.

"It's time," said Monsignor Fran.

Pope Karl replied, "The Americans?"

"Yes, they have already extended the hand of 'friendship' to the Russians, but they want to accelerate the process."

"Vincenzo?"

"He's on his way. We will facilitate as planned."

"Are they expecting my presence?"

"No need, Excellency. I will be your representative. You can remain here in the monastery. No one needs to know where you are until you are ready."

"I agree. I will wait patiently in Capri's celestial wings. But we must warn Claudia. She doesn't know about me."

"I understand, Excellency. Perhaps Vincenzo can help. He is doing his job well—a reliable go-between."

"He is a loyal servant."

"Excellency, do you know where Claudia is? We can get word to her. Perhaps she will come here to meet with you?"

"Impossible. She is an HVA operative working for the Soviets. That is a ridiculous suggestion."

"Of course, Excellency. I wasn't thinking."

"It must be done with extreme caution if she has any chance

of surviving this. She must know the truth. Then she can decide what to do."

"Perhaps she will not wish to respond. Perhaps she enjoys her work?"

"Of course, that is possible. But blood is thicker than water. Once she knows her father's identity … I will pray for her to make the right decision."

Monsignor Fran looked up at the wooden cross—Jesus Christ straddling its width—bathed in a rainbow light from the nearby stained-glass window. "If … when she finds out the truth about her father, perhaps she will not want to put you in harm's way either. Blood is thicker than—"

"I understand, Monsignor Fran. There are no guarantees either way." Pope Karl closed his eyes for a moment. Then he said, "In the meantime, we will fulfill our duty to God and world peace."

"But one thing I am still not clear about … why do the Americans and Russians need us? They have their own channels?"

"Why does anyone need the church? Yes, it can be done without us." Pope Karl turned to his trusted Monsignor with a hint of resignation in his eye. "But it's better *with* us."

"Now I see—both spiritually and strategically."

"Correct. At least, that is my understanding."

"There is another problem."

"You are in charge now, Monsignor Fran. I am the senile one. It will be your job to deal with problems."

"I understand, Excellency. But the Soviet Union is crumbling much quicker than anyone expected."

"Berlin?"

"The wall itself looks set to fall. To be knocked down, literally."

"By whom?"

"Germans—East and West. Crowds are massing in the streets. They want to be reunified."

"And the Soviets?"

"They have made no comment and taken no action to quell the unrest."

"Troops? Tanks?"

"No, Excellency. That's the strange thing—they seem to be allowing this to happen."

"Never trust a Russian or pretend to know what they are thinking." Pope Karl made the sign of the cross and said, "Forgive me, Father."

"Never trust an American. They are just as crooked as Russians but even more dangerous."

"Why?"

"Because they have the money to pay for it."

Pope Karl smiled. "Then we will just have to keep an eye on both of them."

"Perhaps this is why they asked us for help in the first place?"

"Because they don't trust each other."

Monsignor Fran nodded. "There is one more problem."

"I thought I was supposed to be retiring."

Monsignor Fran smiled. "Touché, Excellency. But the problem is real. We were planning to hold the summit in Berlin. Both sides agreed. But it is too dangerous now. The security situation is—"

"Uncertain. I agree. If what you say about the wall is true—about the turmoil."

"We need a location for the peace summit. Neutral, safe, secure … peaceful."

Pope Karl stood up and shuffled slowly toward the entrance of the chapel with the cardinal close behind. They exited into the bright sunshine and sweet-smelling fresh air blowing in from the sea. Pope Karl looked up to the sky. "What's wrong with this?"

"The monastery? Capri?"

Pope Karl nodded.

"But Excellency, this is a sacred place. This is *your* sacred place."

"I didn't say I wanted to be involved. But as I said, there's no harm in being nearby in case you need me—waiting in the celestial wings."

"But Excellency—"

"You said it yourself. 'Neutral, safe, secure ... peaceful.'"

Monsignor Fran paused, seeming to warm to the idea. A slight trace of a smile appeared on his face. "Now that I think about it. ..."

"Less thinking, more praying, young man."

Monsignor Fran nodded. "Very well, Excellency. I will make the arrangements."

"And besides," said Pope Karl. "Who wouldn't prefer Italian linguini over Berlin sausage?"

Soviet Embassy, East Berlin

One week later, Oleg Stepanovich Pugachev had already accepted the fact that the Soviet Union was disintegrating before his very eyes. But he wasn't going to allow it to happen without a fight. And even if it did happen, he vowed to spend the rest of his life fighting the injustice and, as he saw it, the biggest geopolitical disaster of the twentieth century.

And this vow started now.

For the fifteenth time in an hour, he picked up the telephone and dialed every number he could think of at his Moscow KGB headquarters. For the fifteenth time, no one answered—a scenario that would have been utterly inconceivable one week ago.

President Leontev was allowing—no, he was actively supporting—the Soviet Union to fall apart. Originally, it had been Oleg's idea to hold a summit, but not for the same "peace" strategy the Americans proffered.

There was only one reason for a summit—and that was to

assassinate the Russian president. Who knows? He might even give the order for the American president to be liquidated too. That would really set the world on fire. Perhaps the ensuing chaos might prevent the fall of his beloved motherland and her Communist union—the Union of Soviet Socialist Republics.

Claudia entered the room. "I have tried every military unit in the city. No one cares. No one is replying. Where is everyone?"

"Thank you again for coming. I appreciate your loyalty."

Claudia said, "Of course, Oleg Stepanovich. It is my duty. I am ashamed of the East German people. They have no idea what they are doing. How could it come to this?"

The steady hum of crowds amassing outside the building grew louder. Oleg stood patiently at the window surveying the scene, looking for any sign of Soviet or East German security units.

But there were none.

"If they enter this building, our secrets will be lost. Our operations will be set back fifty years."

Claudia said, "I understand, Oleg Stepanovich. But we can't fight all of them. How many guards do we have?"

"We have two armed guards at the main entrance. There is an old wooden door at the rear of the building that can be breached in ten seconds."

"I tried every HVA unit in the city. No one wants to help. They say they are awaiting orders from superiors."

"You spoke to your superiors?"

"Yes, of course. I told them the Soviet embassy is about to fall."

"And?"

"And … nothing. Silence. It is as if they did not care."

"Believe me, comrade Claudia, the only people that care now are standing in this room."

A quick burst of small-arms fire clattered outside.

Oleg bit the inside of his cheek so hard he tasted blood. "How do I know you are not with them?"

"I am with *you*, Oleg Stepanovich. You are the only person who gave me a chance to succeed in this miserable business. I trust you, and I hope you trust me."

"Thank you again for your work in Stockholm. Things did not turn out as we expected."

"The nature of our profession, Oleg Stepanovich. Isn't that so?"

"But we achieved our aim. At least the circumstances have been created for our 'peace summit.'" Oleg smiled, but his eyes remained as emotionless as ever. "We achieved a great victory in Sweden—the Gotland class. A secret we tried to uncover for many years."

"But it all means nothing if our great Soviet Union falls."

"Not true. Every battle is important. I was expecting the assassination."

"It wasn't us?"

"I didn't say that. Let's turn our attention to the present."

"Of course, Oleg Stepanovich. What do you suggest? I am prepared … to die if necessary."

"That will not be necessary. I will make you a promise."

Claudia waited.

Oleg said, "If anyone is going to die, it will be me. These are your people. They will not harm you."

"My loyalty is to the union."

"Noble and honorable indeed. Again, I am grateful."

Claudia touched the grubby net curtain and stared at the sea of angry East Germans outside the building. "I heard that the wall has been breached."

"You heard correctly."

"They could storm this building at any moment."

"Again, you are correct. But I have an idea that will save this building, our secrets, and the lives of many of our comrades."

"Please," said Claudia. "I am listening."

CHAPTER THIRTY-EIGHT

Cavalry and Guards Club, Piccadilly

Steele alighted the #74 bus at Hyde Park Corner. He negotiated the slow-moving flow of traffic to walk across Hyde Park Corner and underneath Wellington Arch itself. The arch was established in 1883 and so called because it had originally supported a colossal equestrian statue of the 1st Duke of Wellington. The Quadriga of War statue replaced the duke's statue atop the arch in 1912 because the duke's statue was deemed too unsightly. Number 1 London, as the Iron Duke's home, Apsley House, became affectionately known, sat just across the road, and Steele always felt a sense of optimism and pride when passing these historic central London haunts. It made him proud to be British.

The Wellington Arch housed the smallest police station in London from the 1830s to the 1950s. Many years earlier, Steele's mother, April, had always pointed out the arch and its police station whenever they circled Hyde Park Corner on the upper deck of a red London bus on their way to Harrods or Changing the Guard at Horse Guards or Buckingham Palace. Never would he have dreamed that joining The Life Guards, Household Cavalry, would lead to the epic adventure behind the Iron Curtain over the past few weeks that was not, he sensed, yet over.

Steele crossed several lanes of traffic again to reach Green Park and worked his way through the park to his destination on Piccadilly.

Why did I agree to this insane mission?

Steele had been in London for one day and managed to visit his mother for only an hour. He wasn't exactly under house arrest, but they had told him to "keep a low profile." He had planned to meet his mother at The Queen's, a pub on St. George's Terrace in Primrose Hill, but, on second thought, he deemed it too risky and not "low profile" enough, and instead, they went for a walk to the top of Primrose Hill to take in the panoramic London view. The last thing he wanted to do was put his mother in danger.

"When I die," April said, "You can scatter my ashes over there." She pointed to the second park bench in from Primrose Hill Road, where she often sat after her walk around London Zoo. "Too many dogs use the first bench for their business," she observed, and Steele chuckled.

Then April had told him the latest saga about the two red telephone boxes next to the pub that Camden Council had tried to remove several times over the years. They wanted to replace them with modern "open kiosks." The eclectic mix of bohemian, professional, intellectual, and gentrified residents of Primrose Hill had finally won the battle to keep the red telephone boxes "for the sake of tradition." April concluded, "We finally beat the buggers. The boxes are here to stay."

"Won't be long before telephone boxes are obsolete, Mum," Steele continued. "It's going to be all mobile phones and email soon."

April raised an eyebrow and gave him a look that needed no explanation. Then she said, "I don't want to know."

Now, as arranged, Nigel Rhodes Stampa, MI6, met Steele outside the tall neoclassical building opposite Green Park—127 Piccadilly, London W1. Devoid of vulgar accoutrements such as brass name plaques or signs, the majestic house number was all that was needed for those who needed to know that this was, in fact, the elite—gentlemen members only—Cavalry and Guards Club. There was even a separate "ladies' dining room" on the third floor, set apart two floors above the majestic, dark-wood paneled gentlemen's dining and smoking or anteroom room on the first floor (that in the United Kingdom was the American second floor).

An elegantly dressed woman in a red dress stood at the porter's desk. "Ladies' entrance is outside and to the left, Madam. You need to reenter the building at the side entrance and take the lift to the third floor."

"Thank you," she replied, appearing not too troubled by the inconvenience. Steele heard the hint of a foreign accent. The woman exited with a click of her high heels.

Steele and Rhodes Stampa approached the porter's desk.

"Good morning, gentlemen," said the porter, who sported round spectacles and gray hair.

"We're here for lunch," said Nigel.

"Fine choice, sir. Guest of ...?"

"Wing Commander Jenkins."

The porter nodded and peered through his glasses at today's luncheon guest list. In a second, he had found the reservation. "Thank you, sir. Wing Commander Jenkins is expecting you." He gestured for them to enter the inner sanctum of the Cavalry and Guards Club, the décor an ornate mixture of old master paintings, marble floor and statues, discreet lamps and wall chandeliers, and a scarlet carpeted staircase. There were also several large nets of burgundy and navy-blue inflated balloons covering the stairwell floor as waiters and catering staff prepared for some kind of celebration. They set out champagne, wine glasses, and all manner of plates, cutlery, and three-tiered hors d'oeuvres stands on white linen-covered tables.

"Forgive me, gentlemen," said the porter. "I nearly forgot. The Grenadier Guards are having a wives' and girlfriends' regimental bash tonight. Lunch is served in the ladies' dining room today. You can take the stairs or the gentlemen's lift.

"They have separate ladies' and gents' lifts," Steele commented under his breath. "Good old Blighty."

"It won't last for much longer. Women's lib is gaining ground fast. It's all the rage." Nigel waved and thanked the porter. "Tradition, dear boy. It's why everyone loves us so."

"Whatever you say, Nigel," Steele scoffed. "I say we take the stairs and burn a few calories."

Thirty seconds later, slightly out of breath, they passed the members' smoking room on the first floor, and Steele coughed.

"Don't worry," Nigel said. "You'll get used to it."

"Cigar smoke? Jesus," said Steele as he slid his hand along the highly polished wooden banister. "Lunch *and* lung cancer?"

"They don't charge for the smoke."

"I'm glad I'm not paying."

They reached the third floor and entered the ladies' dining room. Wing Commander Nick Jenkins was already seated and beckoned them over to a secluded table in the corner by the window overlooking a magnificent autumnal view of Green Park. As Steele sat down, he could also see the back of the Ritz Hotel from an angle he had never seen before. From where they sat, Green Park and its lavish shrubs and flowerbeds looked like a sprawling garden extension of the Ritz, which, of course, it wasn't.

Nigel slid his napkin from a silver ring and placed it on his lap. "How did *you* become a member here, sir? You're RAF."

"My father's a member, so they let me join."

"Cheeky one, sir."

"He was heartbroken when I chose the RAF over the army. But he still wanted me to be a member here."

"Bully for you," replied Nigel. "The club, I mean. It's not cheap."

"You're right. Bloody expensive. He still pays most of the bills, thank God."

Nigel and Jenkins chortled; Steele remained neutral but smiled anyway.

After drinks were ordered and menus perused, Jenkins said, "So … you've had quite an adventure, Jack."

Steele frowned and leaned forward, elbows on the table as if he was worried about being overheard.

"Don't worry, Jack," said Jenkins. "This is the Cav and Guards Club. No microphones."

Nigel added, "It's probably safer than the Queen's bedroom."

"More top brass here than the band of the Grenadier Guards," added Jenkins.

"Great," Steele replied. He sat up and told himself to enjoy the moment. After all, he was still alive, back home in London, and no one had harmed or assassinated *him* … yet. "What's the plan?"

Jenkins sipped the large gin and tonic that had just arrived. "The plan for you, Jack?"

Steele nodded.

"Plan is that there is no plan for the moment."

Nigel added, "Actually, sir, that's not quite correct. There's been a development."

"I'm all ears."

"Me too," added Steele.

Nigel turned to Steele. "I was waiting for lunch before I told you. Wing Commander needs to hear this too. Technically, he's still in charge of you."

"How long will I be in London?"

Nigel said, "That's just it. The plan was to leave you in the officers' mess at Hyde Park Barracks until all this blows over. But the commanding officer doesn't want you there."

"Why not?" Steele and Jenkins said in unison.

"Apparently, he doesn't like you."

"What?" said Jenkins.

"I risked my life and probably put myself in more danger than he'll ever know," countered Steele. "What did I do wrong?"

Nigel said, "You did nothing wrong."

"Does he know about Masha? Does he know about the mission?"

"No, that's just it. We can't tell him. If we could have, he might have warmed to you."

Steele asked, "What's the 'development?'" He leaned back and clasped his hands. He did not like where this conversation was going. He already had a bad taste in his mouth, and it wasn't just from the overly tart olive juice in his vodka martini—shaken and stirred but far too "dirty."

"Thing is, Jack, we have new intel ... the Sovs are looking for a scapegoat. They know you helped get Masha out of the country, and they want blood."

Steele tried to find comfort in a sip of martini. "My blood?"

"That's the way they are, I'm afraid. They want revenge."

"Do we know yet who *was* responsible for the assassination?" asked Steele.

"It's complicated."

"Sounds like it," added Jenkins. "I'm not happy about this."

Steele said, "Makes two of us."

"By the way," Jenkins continued, raising his voice. "Why wasn't I informed about what happened in Stockholm? Damn it, I thought Steele was in Russia, for God's sake. I looked like a bloody fool when we found out about the assassination, and *my* man, Jack Steele, was standing in the front row watching the damn thing."

"Yes, sorry about that, sir. *We*—in fact, those above me at Vauxhall—like to keep things close to their chest."

Steele raised both hands as if to pause the conversation. In a low but animated tone, he said, "Nigel, who the bloody hell shot Aronsson?"

"Fair question. I can't tell you who shot Aronsson. I don't know—even if I did, I couldn't tell you. But more importantly, we think *you* are in danger. That's why you can't stay in London. And your commanding officer doesn't want to put men and horses at risk."

"What?" Then Steele glanced at Jenkins, who appeared equally perplexed.

"As I said, we have reason to believe that your life is in danger."

"From whom?"

"The Russians. Who else?"

Steele said, "Why? Aronsson was Swedish."

"That's not the point. You made the Russians look foolish. The daughter of a Soviet navy admiral was standing next to Aronsson when he died. She was laughing and smiling with *his* daughter. *You* helped her escape."

Sirloin steak with roast potatoes, peas, carrots, and gravy arrived, but Steele suddenly lost his appetite. "*We* helped her escape." Steele looked at Jenkins. "*You* sent me there, remember?"

"Don't worry, Jack. This will all blow over. I promise."

"You know something, Nigel? I hate it when people promise me things. Especially people in your line of work. Excuse me, gentlemen."

Steele placed his napkin on his chair, left the table, and exited the dining room. Reaching the landing, he said to a passing waiter, "Where's the gents, please?"

"The gentleman's cloakroom is just across the landing, sir. Second door on the right after the Battle of Waterloo," he said, gesturing to a huge military painting that hung floor to ceiling.

As Steele crossed the landing, taking in the oil painting featuring the Duke of Wellington on horseback brandishing a saber, he sensed that someone was watching him. He glanced up and saw the woman in the red dress exiting the door next to the gents, presumably the ladies' room. She avoided eye contact, which was odd, Steele thought, because most members and guests seemed to be overly polite and friendly.

Steele's heart skipped a beat. *Claudia? Impossible.*

He looked again, but the woman was not Claudia, though she did seem to have a foreign air about her. She had black hair and wore heavy makeup, especially the rouge on her cheeks. French? Russian, perhaps?

Two minutes later, Steele exited the gentleman's cloakroom

and glanced over the banister at the preparations three floors below. He could hear the gentle thump-thump of a base drum and a distant clash of cymbals as the band began setting up in the dining room on the first floor.

I want answers, he said to himself as he rounded the corner near the ladies' dining room.

Then he saw her again. The woman nodded to someone stepping out of the lift. Before Steele had time to turn, he felt a powerful hand on his back. It wasn't just a hand, Steele recalled later, it was more like a human piston.

Next, he felt himself flying—except that he wasn't flying, he was falling like a block of concrete toward the black-and-white marble mosaic three floors below.

It's over, he thought. The bastards got me.

Then everything went black.

PART 3

CHAPTER THIRTY-NINE

Soviet Embassy, East Berlin

Oleg and Claudia reached the ground floor of the Soviet embassy. The noise of the crowd was getting louder, and several bottles smashed on impact as they hit the front door that was currently locked.

Oleg looked around and asked the babushka sitting at the front desk, "Where are they?"

"Who, Oleg Stepanovich?"

"The guards? Where are the guards?"

"I'm sorry, Oleg Stepanovich. Internal Security left their post an hour ago."

"Are they still in the building?"

"I'm sorry, Oleg Stepanovich. I don't know. No one has told me anything."

Oleg turned to Claudia. "Wait over there." He pointed to an alcove next to the front entrance. "Whatever you do, do not come out."

Claudia nodded. "But—" Then she obeyed the order.

Oleg turned back to the babushka. "Elena Mikhailovich, you can go now."

"Thank you, Comrade Oleg. But I have nowhere to go."

"Elena Mikhailovich," Oleg raised his voice. "Go and find a safe place—*now.*"

The babushka nodded and scuttled away toward the basement.

Oleg opened the door and stepped outside to confront the crowd single-handedly. The masses surged forward but stopped short of making physical contact. A Molotov cocktail landed a few feet to his right, but he nonchalantly took two steps and kicked it away like a child's football.

"Comrades," he began in perfect German. "I understand your frustration. I, too, am frustrated."

A large bearlike man shouted, "Who are you?"

"My name is Arkady Gregorovich. I am the head of the cultural section here in Berlin."

"We are coming in!" shouted a young woman.

"Yes, we are coming in!" shouted a middle-aged man. "Move aside, or you'll regret it."

Oleg stared at the men and women at the front of the crowd—*peasants and children*, he thought—and moved one step closer to them. "Comrades. I am on your side. I came out to warn you." Oleg's German was flawless, and his words seemed to settle the crowd.

"He's lying," someone shouted. Oleg could not see if it was a man or a woman. "He's Kah-Geh-Bey!"—the German pronunciation equivalent of "KGB."

"Yeah!" the masses crowed in agreement. "Kah-Geh-Bey! Kah-Geh-Bey!"

Oleg didn't often smile, but now he did. It was one of his best smiles—even his eyes showed emotion. He was a good actor. "Comrades. You can do whatever you want. It doesn't matter to me. I am a simple bureaucrat—Soviet style—like a thousand bureaucrats among your own family and friends. I am a simple, gray bureaucrat."

"Step aside!" someone shouted again.

"I can step aside," Oleg continued. "But the first dozen comrades to enter the building will be shot dead in five seconds. The next dozen might make it to the staircase while the Internal Security Service guards reload. But they will die from automatic fire within thirty seconds of you entering the building. I am just the messenger—this is what will happen if you enter the building."

"He's lying!" shouted the first bearlike man. "Where are the soldiers? Show us the soldiers!"

"Show us! Show us! Show us!" the crowd began to chant.

Oleg held up both hands and countered, "I cannot show you the soldiers. They have their orders."

A woman stepped forward. "The only person we trust in your government is President Leontev. He is on our side. He wants the best for us and for Ost bloc."

Now it was Oleg's turn to take a step. The crowd recoiled ever so slightly. Oleg felt as though he was gaining their confidence. *I will not allow them to maraud my embassy.*

Oleg said, "You are correct. I honor and revere Mikhail Pavlovich, president of our Union of Soviet Socialist Republics, and I want the best for you all. I don't want you and these young people to die. You are free already. The wall is down. Why waste your lives entering this building to be executed en masse— your young, healthy bodies will be riddled with bullets for no reason."

Oleg allowed his words to ruminate among the crowd.

Then he continued, "Look at one another. Please. Look at your comrades standing next to you." Oleg raised his arms, encouraging them to converse and decide whether their plan was worth risking life and limb for. "The mayor's office is two blocks away. Please, go and help yourselves. Your German brothers and sisters will not stop you. But if you enter *this* building, many of you will die."

"He's lying," an old man shouted. "He's Kah-Geh-Bey. I see it in his eyes."

This made the crowd bubble up again—the collective body unable to decide whether to stay or go. Men and women took a step, then two steps up the embassy steps toward Oleg. He stood still—unflinching, unmoving, the expression on his face giving nothing away.

A young man with glasses and long hair stepped forward on one side. "I'm going in!" he shouted.

The crowd cheered. "Me too!" shouted a young woman next to him.

The door opened, and everyone's focus shifted.

Claudia exited.

Oleg said quietly, "I told you to stay inside."

"I know," she replied. Claudia walked forward to the top of the embassy steps and stood next to Oleg. "Comrades," she began. "My name is Claudia. This man is my boyfriend. He wants the best for you."

"Are you German?"

"Yes," she smiled. "I am a Berliner … like you!" Claudia smiled and pointed at the embassy as she began her next speech. "I am telling you—one Berliner to another. If you enter this building, you will die. Do you understand me, comrades? I have no reason to lie."

Claudia locked arms with Oleg as if they were standing at the altar about to be married—one unified couple.

Another shift in the crowd—this time, Oleg sensed apathy. It was as if, thought Oleg, they were tired of the back and forth, and their adrenaline was dissipating. His ruse, with Claudia's help—the icing on the blini, so to speak—was working.

The first few rows of people began to look at one another, asking each other's opinion, and then, slowly, one by one, starting to turn away—starting to walk away. The rear of the crowd moved first, then the middle section, followed by the front section as they lost interest and support—moral and physical—of the crowd leaders.

"We'll be back later," someone shouted but with little conviction.

"Yeah, we'll be back," voiced another.

"Leon, Leon, Leon!" A woman began to shout Mikhail Leontev's short-form nickname. The crowd imitated as they departed, and it wasn't long before everyone was shouting the Soviet president's name in unison—*Leon … Leon … Leon.*

Oleg released Claudia's arm. Then he said, "I told you to stay inside. Why don't you follow orders? Give me one good reason why I shouldn't report you?"

"Oleg Stepanovich …" Claudia hesitated, then she said, "Because the crowd was becoming aggressive. I thought—"

"I am joking," said Oleg. "Thank you for your help. It was an excellent move. Perfectly executed. We achieved our goal."

"You're welcome. I thought things were—"

"You did well, Fräulein. I like courageous women."

They watched the crowd dissipate and then turned to go back into the deserted embassy. Oleg felt empowered and knew that once his superiors found out what he had achieved, promotion would be assured. He had single-handedly prevented the most important embassy in Europe from being overrun by traitors to the motherland. The Berlin Wall had fallen, but he had saved the embassy from being pillaged, not to mention the humiliation that would have inevitably followed. He would not mention Claudia's part in events, and Elena Mikhailovich would be happy with a small bribe to stick to his version. He could just order her what to say without the bribe, but the poor old hag deserved something for her years of service sitting at the entrance of the embassy. Everyone had fled the building, and she had remained at her post.

Once inside, Oleg closed the door and bolted it shut. He turned to Claudia and said, "I made a good decision many years ago."

"I don't understand."

"I recommended to your highly respected HVA that we recruit you."

"I didn't know."

"Tell me something, Comrade Claudia."

"Of course, Oleg Stepanovich. Anything you ask."

"Who is your father?"

"My father?"

"Yes, do you know the real identity of your father?"

"He lives in West Berlin. But I lost contact with him many years ago. I don't think I would even recognize him now."

Oleg said, "Would you like to meet him?"

"I … I am not sure. I have not thought about this possibility for many years. I was resigned to the fact that we might never meet."

"But I would like to thank you for your service today."

"I don't understand."

"It's not complicated. Let me know if you would like to meet your father, and I can arrange this."

"I don't know what to say."

"You don't have to say anything. Let's find Elena Mikhailovich and ask her to bring us some food. I have quite an appetite after today's performance."

"Thank you, Oleg Stepanovich."

"And I have another question."

"Of course, Comrade. I honor and serve you."

"How would you feel about a trip to Italy?"

"Are you joking again?"

"No, I am not joking. In fact, I am godly serious, and I am not even a spiritual man."

Claudia frowned. She was confused but nodded anyway.

"But first, I need you to find our British friend. I think your instincts were correct, and I believe he can be of service to us."

"Service?"

"Yes, every man has a weak point. I think you already know Mr. Steele's."

CHAPTER FORTY

BAOR, Sennelager, Germany

Two days later, Steele woke up but did not immediately open his eyes. *Where the bloody hell am I?* From the medicinal smell, he guessed he was in some kind of hospital or sickbay.

Then he remembered. Shit! I thought I was dead. He recalled imagining what his skull might look like once it hit the marble floor in the Cavalry and Guards Club. It was true what they said about your life flashing before you. The two or three seconds it took after being pushed from the third floor until he hit the ground was like an entire lifetime. He had somehow managed to replay the most significant events of his life as he hurtled toward the floor.

Then it hit him—a crushing pain in his head, arms, and legs. *But there's no pain in my back*—that much he was grateful for.

"Hello, Mr. Steele," said a female voice. The tone was soft, with a quality of compassion and efficiency. The nurse spoke with a Worcestershire accent. "You've had a fall. You suffered a concussion, but you are very fortunate—no broken bones."

"Where am I?"

"You're in the sick bay of Athlone Barracks in Sennelager. You're in Germany, Mr. Steele."

"You can call me Jack," he replied before the pain pummeled his head.

The nurse smiled and said, "I'm sorry, sir. I can't do that. You're an officer, and I'm a lowly corporal."

Steele opened his eyes. "Where am I?" he repeated, forgetting the nurse had already told him.

"Germany, sir. BAOR, Sennelager. Your regiment is based here."

"Germany? How?"

"You had a nasty fall, and you were flown out to Germany under sedation. You must be a very important officer, sir."

"What? Why?" Steele struggled with the wooziness that came over him. "I don't—"

"You need to rest for me, sir. That's all I need you to do for the time being."

"How did I get here?"

"They flew you out from RAF Northolt, sir. My understanding is that they thought you would be safer here. But that's all I know."

Steele shook his head. "I don't understand ... ."

"But the good news is that you're going to be just fine, sir."

"I fell..."

"Yes, sir. You fell three floors. Who do you think you are, Superman?"

Then he remembered. "Someone pushed me."

"I don't know the details, but as I say, sir, you're going to be fine. You already had your X-rays and a CAT scan. Doctor thinks you'll be up and about in no time."

"How ...?"

"How did you survive?"

"Yes. I fell..."

"Apparently, you fell into a pile of balloons, sir. Lucky for you, there was a party that night."

"Sorry?"

"The balloons broke your fall, sir. Saved your life."

A man wearing a suit appeared behind the nurse. "I'll take it from here, nurse. Thank you."

Steele squinted, focusing to see who it was.

"Hello, Jack. It's me, Nigel Rhodes Stampa. How are you feeling?"

Steele thought for a moment and said finally, "I feel like shit."

"Right you are. Silly question. It's good to see you awake, Jack."

"Thanks."

"But as that very pretty nurse said, you are going to be just fine. I escorted you here at the Wing Commander's request. Least I could do under the circumstances, of course."

Steele's head started to clear. He felt as though he was gaining clarity of mind by the second. "What happened again?"

"Well, Jack. It's like I was saying at lunch before we were so rudely interrupted." He paused for effect, but no one was laughing. "Sorry, not funny. Bad timing."

"What happened?"

"Right, Jack. Yes, well, it's like I said … your life was—probably still is, I'm afraid—in danger."

"Russians?"

"We think so."

"Masha?"

"That's right, Jack. Perhaps Masha. But don't worry about her now."

"Aronsson?"

"Yes, it's good you're starting to remember. That's a relief, I must say. I feel responsible, Jack. We didn't take good enough care of you. We were a bit blasé if you want my honest opinion. I take full responsibility."

"What the fuck?" Steele winced in pain. His head was throbbing.

"Take it easy, Jack. Just rest up, will you? There's a good fellow."

"Why Germany?"

"Safest spot for you, old boy. No one will ever find you here, I guarantee it."

"Barracks?"

"Yes, you're safe and sound in your regimental sickbay—Athlone Barracks. They brought you here from the garrison hospital in Paderborn. Like I say, you're going to be just fine."

"I don't want to stay here."

"I understand, Jack. I'm afraid you don't have much choice. Orders are orders. We think they might still want to get to you, Jack."

"Why?"

"They tried to kill you, Jack. If it wasn't for the balloons, it would have been lights out."

"What happened?"

"Cavalry and Guards Club, remember? We were having lunch?"

Steele closed his eyes, and it all came back to him. He shook his head as he relived the fall.

"The Wooden Tops saved your life, Jack."

"What?" Steele mumbled.

"If the Grenadier Guards hadn't had their bash—complete with regimental balloons—you'd have hit that marble floor like a ton of bricks."

"Okay." Steele was still having trouble remembering everything.

"The balloons, Jack. You hit the balloons, and they broke your fall."

Steele nodded. "Who …?" He felt a surge of fear and adrenaline as he remembered the moment that someone had pushed him over the banister.

"I must go now, Jack. London's calling. They'll take good care of you here. If they need anything, the garrison hospital's nice and close. But you're here for your own safety, okay?"

Steele nodded.

"One more thing, Jack, before I go."

Steele nodded again, trying to be helpful—an honorable soldier—in his semi-confused state.

"Don't worry about it for now, but they want you to try again."

"Try again? What are you talking about?"

"Our people want to turn the tables on them, Jack. If the Russians are after you—we want to make the most of it."

Steele spoke softly. "I'm a pawn? Cannon fodder." Then he smiled to himself. "You *people* don't give a damn about me."

"Not true, Jack. You're not a pawn or cannon fodder. But there's a lot going on. Berlin Wall just fell. Looks like Germany will unify—Soviet Union might not be a union for much longer. We need every advantage we can muster. I'll be in touch once you're feeling better. Follow your instincts. If there's any unusual contact, be careful, try to find out what they want, and report back. It's a cat-and-mouse game. Just make sure you're not the mouse. Nurse has my details."

Nigel left the room, and Steele felt more confused than ever.

★   ★   ★

Less than half a mile from Steele's location at Athlone Barracks, Claudia sat in a BMW SUV in a clearing in a secluded wood. The autumn leaves were turning, and she cracked the window to listen to the sounds of a creek's gentle hiss nearby.

A random thought came over her ... *I wonder if I will ever have children.* It was so far off her usual radar of strategic and operational thoughts about her work that it caught her off guard, and she physically shook her head for a moment.

Then Claudia smacked her cheek a couple of times to bring herself back to reality. She thought about the summer evening she had spent with Jack Steele in Berlin. If she was honest, she had enjoyed herself with him—the young man was cultured, well-informed, and quite amusing. The sex wasn't bad, either. Not that this was anyone's business except her own. *She* had decided to "groom" Jack Steele, a future British army officer and perhaps a future spy—it was *her* instincts that began this operation. And now, as summer turned to autumn—and after the Old Guard KGB screw-up in Leningrad—she was acutely aware of the need to make progress with Jack Steele.

She had even caught the attention of none other than Oleg Stepanovich Pugachev, one of the KGB's rising stars. *The man is a ruthless weasel, but just the kind of weasel who might become head of the KGB or even Russia's president one day. And I saved his hide in Berlin. He owes me.*

The local German cleaning staff were Claudia's eyes and ears inside the British army barracks for the time being. Her subject, Jack Steele, was apparently alive and well—not that she had wanted him dead in the first place. Neither she nor Oleg had wanted any harm to come to Jack Steele, but during such times of Soviet existential turmoil and the fall of the Berlin Wall, factions within factions were created, wires were crossed, and "accidents" happened.

The Soviet Old Guard, Oleg had explained, had deemed it necessary to exact revenge on Jack Steele for his part in Masha Pushkin's defection. In the spy world, the Soviets had become a laughingstock for allowing a rookie British spy to escort Masha out of the country under their noses on a fishing boat, of all things. The Old Guard KGB had taken care of Admiral Pushkin for his submarine mission incompetency and for being ignorant of his daughter's plans to defect. But the one thing they had not foreseen was Jack Steele. They had had eyes on various British operatives in Russia—the cultural attaché in Moscow and a dubious British journalist they also suspected had ties to the British security services—but Steele they had missed. And Masha's links to the Swedish prime minister's family also had somehow—unfathomably, in Claudia's opinion—been overlooked.

Masha had been standing next to Anders Aronsson when he was assassinated. Oleg had refused to tell Claudia who was responsible, but if it wasn't the KGB, then only the Americans could have done it. But that didn't make sense, either. Claudia still had no idea *why* the Americans or the Russians would want to assassinate the Swedish prime minister.

But hers was not to reason why, and she would forge ahead nevertheless.

Oleg was a shrewd, highly successful, and ruthless operator. She would remain loyal to the HVA and their KGB brethren. Oleg had given Claudia meticulous orders. She had been on her way to London to locate Jack Steele, but after the "accidental" fall, HVA intelligence had flagged a change of plan regarding her target, and Steele was now at his regimental barracks five minutes from her current location.

It would be impossible to reach him without causing an international diplomatic incident at worst or, at best, provoking the ire of local West German police. As an undercover HVA operative in West Germany, local police contact was the last thing she needed. The barracks were well guarded and protected, and scaling a barbed wire fence was not one of her strong points.

But as of five minutes ago, none of that mattered now. Her intelligence source—probably the highest-paid cleaner in BAOR—had left her a message in this tree dead drop in the woods that said it wouldn't be long before 2Lt. Jack Steele was on military duty again.

Claudia would make her move.

CHAPTER FORTY-ONE

Three days later, Steele entered the officers' mess dining room at Athlone Barracks at 8:00 pm. He had borrowed an absent officer's black tie, as this order of dress was de rigueur for dinner each and every night in The Life Guards. Regimental tradition dictated the dress code. The only exception was the duty officer, who wore regimental mess kit complete with a scarlet tunic, shiny black boots, and spurs.

"Come on in, Jackie," said a young subaltern, beckoning Steele into a dining room full of other young officers. "Good to have you. I'm Peter Gabriel." They shook hands and sat down at a long, highly polished dining table laid with dinner plates, candles, and regimental silver.

"Feeling better, Jackie?" another officer chimed in; a titter of amusement followed. It appeared that Steele had already been christened with a female nickname, which he would try not to take personally. "Thank you," Steele said. "Great to be here."

"Here," said Captain James Montague-Smith, the regimental adjutant, who, Steele could not help noticing, had remarkably large ears. "Have a seat next to me."

Another officer had informed Steele earlier in the evening that the adjutant's family owned half of Monmouthshire, but he had refused to join the Welsh Guards—an infantry regiment—because, by his own admission, he was "too lazy to walk everywhere and preferred to ride in a tank."

The adjutant said, "Corporal Jones is going to take care of you, aren't you, Corporal Jones?"

"Yes, sir. Leave it with me, sir." Cpl. Jones, the duty mess waiter for the evening, approached holding two bottles of wine. "Red or white, sir."

"Red, please."

The bass tone of young men's banter filled the room once again.

Steele grew even hungrier as the smell of beef burgundy wafted from the kitchen, the swing doors of which were discreetly hidden behind a large, framed set of screens displaying original regimental battle colours dating back to the Battle of Waterloo.

They had taken good care of him in the regimental sickbay, and, thankfully, there had been no further complications—not a single broken bone or fracture. After the regimental doctor had given him a clean bill of health, he was given a room in the officers' mess but was under strict instructions not to leave the barracks. Technically, he *was* a commissioned officer because he had passed out of Sandhurst. But he was not yet a tank troop commander. The adjutant had told him that morning that he would return to Bovington for his Royal Armoured Corps training course "as soon as all the fuss had died down." (*Died*, Steele mused, *being the operative word*.) For the time being, tank commander and gunnery training would have to wait.

In the meantime, the regimental quartermaster had issued Steele with all the necessary kit for a five-day regimental exercise on the Sennelager training area that would start the next morning. Although he wasn't qualified to command a tank yet, he would, at least, get some experience inside a tank—in the loader's position. He was thankful not to be sitting in the gunner's seat, as this would mean sitting between a C Squadron tank call-sign commander's legs with very little room to move and not much to do for five days. At least as the (ammunition) loader, you could move around inside the tank and—by tradition and necessity—were the de facto cook and drinks maker using the boiling vessel—known as the "BV"—to prepare tins of army rations, hot drinks, and soups for the crew.

As Steele made himself comfortable, he glanced up at the regimental paintings that reminded him of the Cavalry and Guards Club and felt sick at the thought of being pushed over the railing. *Whose arm had felt like a human piston? Why had they tried to kill me? Surely the KGB must have more important spies to liquidate.*

In front of him, atop the fifty-foot dining room table, was the silver statuette of a Life Guard's officer on his charger with front legs kicking out and the officer brandishing a saber. A small plaque on the base of the ornament told Steele that this piece of silver alone had been around since 1817, just two years after the Battle of Waterloo. Steele was indeed joining a historic band of brothers. These officers were in good spirits, about to enjoy a hearty dinner before their week-long exercise, where they would be on army rations for the most part.

"How long you in for?" asked 2nd Lt. Gabriel. He made the length of army service sound like a prison sentence.

"Regular commission."

"Good for you, Jackie," said another subaltern. "Me too."

"That's great. Sorry, I …?"

"Sebastian. Sebastian James. Boys call me 'Bastard.'"

"Good for you, you bastard," said Steele, trying to be funny with a quip that crashed and burned.

The adjutant said, "I hope you're ready to freeze your bollocks off. It's going to be a cold one."

"Take your hip flask," said 2nd Lt. Gabriel. "Corporal Jones will take care of you if you don't have any of the hard stuff with you, won't you, Corporal Jones?"

"No problem, sir," confirmed Cpl. Jones, moving to Steele from Captain James Johnson to pour the red wine.

"Thank you, Corporal Jones."

Then Lt. Gabriel said, "So, give us your story, Jackie. How did you get here? We heard you were in some kind of accident?"

"Yes, that's right. But I'm afraid I can't talk about it."

"What? Of course, you can, Jackie. We're all ears, aren't

we, boys? You're one of us now, Jackie. No secrets from your brothers-in-arms."

"No, really, I'm sorry. I'm not allowed to talk about it. Orders are orders, as they say."

"Leave it," said the adjutant. "He'll give us the scoop when he's ready. Besides, he's already onto *you*, Peter. You're the worst secret keeper in the entire bloody regiment."

A group seal of amused approval filled the room as one more young officer entered the dining room. "Sorry I'm late, chaps. Trouble on the tank park. Someone found a hole in the fence." He looked at Steele. "You must be Jack Steele. I'm Harry Winters."

Steele turned to shake hands.

"There's a call for you."

Steele said, "Sorry?"

"You have a call. You can take it in the telephone booth."

"Right. Thank you. Where *is* the telephone booth?"

"Outside the door to the right." Harry gestured with a flourish.

Steele got up and followed directions.

The adjutant turned to Winters and said, "Did you inform the RP and file an incident report about the hole?"

"Yes, James. That's why I was late."

As Steele reached the door, 2nd Lt. Gabriel raised his glass and shouted to Steele, "If she's pretty, tell her I'm available."

The band of brothers laughed, and as Steele exited, he heard 2nd Lt. Winters saying, "Ignore him, Jack. He hasn't had any for six months. And the last one he had to pay for."

Another burst of laughter.

Steele exited the dining room and entered the small telephone booth with a comfortable chair and a single beige telephone on a mahogany writing desk. He picked up the receiver.

"Hello?"

The female garrison operator said, "Second Lt. Steele?"

"Speaking."

"Good evening, sir. I have a call from an external domestic line. Will you accept?"

Steele's heart skipped a beat. A local call? *No one's supposed to know I'm here.* "Err, yes, thank you, operator. I will," he said slowly.

After a series of *clicks,* a woman's voice said: "Jack?"

Steele detected a trace of German. It certainly wasn't anyone from the army or security services. "Yes, who is this?"

"Jack, this is Claudia Rohweder, we met in Berlin."

Silence.

Steele held the receiver away from his ear and looked at it in disbelief for a moment. *What the bloody hell?* "Yes," he said hesitantly. "I … I remember you." Then he decided to sound more confident. "Of course, I remember you. How—"

"How did I find you?"

"No, how are you?" Steele smiled. It felt comforting to hear a somewhat familiar voice after all he had been through.

"I am fine, Jack. This is probably a shock for you."

"A little. Yes, how *did* you find me?"

"If you think about it, Jack, it was *you* who found me." Her tone was flirtatious. "I am just returning the favor."

"I suppose that's true," Steele recalled the memorable night they had spent together—including the sex. But that was then, and this was now. *I should hang up.*

"Jack, I really enjoyed meeting you. I have some important information I think you might be interested in."

Steele did a double take. The implication of this sentence transformed the entire encounter in Berlin—the one that he had not told anyone about, including the army or the security services—into something much more serious. He had always suspected that Claudia might be more than she seemed, but he had deftly managed to reject the idea in his own mind and move on. *It was just a fun one-night stand,* he had told himself dozens of times. *Nothing happened, and no one needs to know.*

But all that had just changed with one sentence. *I have some important information.* Evidently, Claudia wasn't calling to rekindle an old flame.

"What kind of information?" He picked up a pencil and slid The Life Guards regimental notepad toward him.

"Secret information. Information your people will be interested in."

"I see. Sounds interesting."

Damn it, she must be a bloody spook. What other explanation is there?

"It's *very* interesting, Jack. And so are you, by the way. I propose we meet as soon as possible."

"That's not possible, I'm afraid. I'm tied up for the next few days. Perhaps when I get back?"

Yes, this was the right move. Nigel had said someone might try to contact him, but he had assumed that "someone" would be Russian. This bizarre call was a bolt from the blue but felt like something he should pursue—this time, he would report all the details to Nigel and risk the consequences. He would have to tell him everything.

"I will call you," said Claudia. "No problem."

Claudia hung up, and Steele sat back in his chair. "What the hell was that?" he said to himself, scraping his hand through his hair and exhaling.

He wished he could have met Claudia immediately. He was intrigued. *What on earth does she want? And how the hell did she find me?* He cursed the fact that he had to get up at 4:00 am for breakfast and the start of the five-day tank exercise.

It was time to tell Nigel everything about that night in Berlin—whether or not it meant the end of his career in the army and any aspirations he had of working again for the security services one day. Then another thought occurred to him. *Perhaps Nigel knows about Berlin. Is that why they chose* me *for Russia?*

Steele picked up the receiver and dialed "0."

"Operator?"

"Yes, sir. How may I direct your call?"

"London district operator, please."

Steele heard a loud guffaw coming from the dining room next door. It was time to play soldiers—tomorrow was his first adventure inside a main battle tank—but first, he had some explaining to do to his MI6 minder in London.

CHAPTER FORTY-TWO

Grand Hotel Quisisana, Capri

ather Vincenzo Alfonso alighted the SNAV Naples–Capri ferry. As he stepped down the gangplank onto the wharf, he recognized the same hotel porters from his last visit to Capri. They waited in their pristine white uniforms with scrambled egg-peaked caps to meet ferry passengers, their wizened faces burned to a crisp from standing in the sun all day with little to no shade.

Vincenzo carried a small suitcase, which meant he did not need to take an expensive open-top taxi ride to the Piazzetta di Capri. Cheapest of all—he did not like to squander his Vatican expense account—would be the bus, but there was already a long line of tourists, domestic and international, waiting for the next shuttle. No, he would take the middle option and ride the funicular to get to his 4:00 pm meeting at the hotel. Astonishingly, Monsignor Fran's office had booked Vincenzo into the luxury Grand Hotel Quisisana, where he had enjoyed a cocktail on the terrace with Bruno on his last visit to meet the Russian.

What happened to Bruno? Why have the police not made progress in their investigation?

As he ascended in the funicular, admiring the view back to Naples and Mount Vesuvius to the east, he vowed that once this peace summit was over, he would spend as much time and energy necessary to get to the bottom of what happened to his … friend? Boyfriend? Lover? He wasn't even sure how to describe their relationship.

God rest Bruno's soul.

Vincenzo exited the funicular and allowed himself to be jostled by the throng of happy tourists, all of them delighted to finally arrive at their very own Shangri-La. He had never smelled such fresh, warm—even in autumn—island air anywhere else in his beloved Italia. Punctual as always, Vincenzo had time to order a single espresso from the funicular café and stop for a few minutes to savor the panorama. It really did feel like you were on top of the world. No wonder Capri had been the destination of the rich and famous global family for decades.

Then Vincenzo made the short five-minute walk down Capri's narrow streets. It was extraordinary, he thought, that one of the great jewels of Italy was maintained using little unique-to-Capri electric carts that carried deliveries, baggage, and even the well-heeled elderly and frail to their destinations.

As he walked down the hill toward the Grand Hotel Quisisana, he glanced at sumptuous and inviting—even to a man of God—boutiques and shops—high fashion, shoes, jewelers, art galleries, interior décor, and, of course, ice cream. He thanked God that the only thing he could afford was the ice cream. As he passed *Buonocore Gelateria,* the most famous homemade ice cream vendor in Capri, where there was a queue day and night, a small boy looked up at Vincenzo as the boy relished and devoured his large double cone using what could only be described as "tongue acrobatics."

The Grand Hotel Quisisana terrace—with its cream-colored walls, wicker furniture, terracotta floor, and white linen tablecloths—was as inviting as Vincenzo remembered. It was no wonder that so many of the guests were rumored to vacation here, not just year after year but decade after decade.

Vincenzo found a table against the wall of the hotel in a nook that was still in the shade; he settled into the comfortable cushions on a long seat flush with the hotel. He looked around and marveled at his good fortune to be there. It was 4:15 pm on one of the most expensive drinks terraces in Europe, if not the world. If a hotel could merit more than five stars, the Quisisana would deserve ten.

A waiter with a thin face and prematurely gray hair arrived in seconds. "What can I get you, Father?"

"I will wait for my friend, thank you."

"Who is your friend? Perhaps I know him?"

"Monsignor Fran. He's a guest."

"Yes, Father. I know him. He drinks mineral water, still, with a piece of orange, not lemon."

"Bellissimo," replied Vincenzo. *Wonderful.* "And freshly squeezed orange and lemon juice for me. What's your name?"

"My name is Raffaele. Pleasure to meet you, Father."

"It's my pleasure also. How long have you worked here?"

"Twenty-seven years, Father. And *my* father also works here before me."

"God bless you, Raffaele. That is certainly a calling."

"Yes, sir. I am very 'appy here."

"You like people."

"Not all people, Father. But yes, I like people. I like to *watch* people."

"Does your father still work here?"

"Yes, Father. His name is Paulo. He is the head waiter."

Vincenzo smiled, leaned back against the wall, and surveyed the beautiful people, immaculately dressed, even in their to-and-from-the-private-beach gear, ambling up and down from the Piazzetta.

No sooner did Raffaele depart than Monsignor Fran skipped down the steps of the hotel entrance and approached Vincenzo.

"Welcome to Italy's jewel," said Monsignor Fran as he sat down.

"Buongiorno, Your Eminence. It is a pleasure to see you again. I am fortunate to be in Capri again so soon. But I am confused."

"Confused?"

"Yes, why did you invite me here? And why am I staying at the hotel and not the monastery?"

"I will explain."

Monsignor Fran dipped into a small dish of large green olives. "You won't find any better in the whole of Italy."

Vincenzo smiled, waiting patiently for the explanation, and also helping himself to an olive.

"You have performed your duties magnificently."

"Thank you, Excellency. But with the greatest respect, why are we here? And what is the 'matter of life and death' you spoke about in Rome?"

"Yes, yes. You are right to be *agitato.*"

Vincenzo exhaled calmly. Then he continued, "Excellency, I sense you are playing games with me. Sacred games. Holy games. This is not what I do. This is not why I am here. I am here to serve His Holiness."

"Yes, and Pope Karl is very much looking forward to seeing you. You will be with him soon. But to answer your first question—the reason we are not staying at the monastery is that it is safer for His Holiness if *we* stay here at the hotel."

"Safe? Pope Karl is here—on the island?"

"Yes, you see. I am explaining everything to you as I promised."

"Is he …?" Vincenzo frowned. "Is he all right? Is he sick? Physically? Mentally?"

"He is a little jaded. But he needed to take a step back—to achieve his mission. *Our* mission."

"I am as confused as ever."

"The peace summit is arranged. You helped to achieve this. Thank you."

"Where? Berlin?"

"Berlin is too dangerous—too unstable. The American and Russian presidents have agreed to accept our Italian hospitality."

Vincenzo frowned again. "On Capri?"

"Yes, here on Capri."

"But it's not safe—"

"Why not? There could be no place safer. We are surrounded by water—we have the perfect setting of the monastery to make peace. It can be easily guarded."

"But who will protect them?"

"American Secret Service, carabinieri, Russian KGB, and, of course, Italian navy—the usual army of protectors. But it will all be done very discreetly. It will be a secret meeting. No media."

"Why is it a secret? Isn't that the point of the summit—to make peace and tell the world?"

"There will be a communiqué once the meeting has finished. Once they have achieved something concrete."

Vincenzo nodded. "And Pope Karl? Is it safe for him to be here at this time?"

"Of course. Why not?"

"I am no security expert, but it seems unwise to have such important men all in one location."

"His Holiness has his reasons."

"What reasons? I hope you have not invited me here to taunt me with secrets."

"Secrets, secrets. His Holiness has shared a secret with me. And I think he will share it with you also. But he also has an interest. An agenda."

"Please, continue."

Raffaele, the waiter, arrived carrying a silver tray bedecked with drinks with one hand and fresh bowls of mixed nuts and more olives in the other.

Monsignor Fran and Vincenzo said in unison, "Thank you."

Monsignor Fran continued, "For many years, Pope Karl was holding a secret." He studied Vincenzo for a moment. "He has a daughter. But no one knows about her."

Vincenzo froze as he raised his glass of freshly squeezed orange and lemon juice to take a sip. Then he said, "You are correct, Excellency. I, for one, had no idea."

"Do not take this personally, Vincenzo. I, too, was not privy."

"Somehow, I do not find that comforting."

"Our pontiff wanted to do many things as pope. But his hands were tied because of this daughter."

"Why? Who is she?"

"The problem is not who the daughter *is*. But where she is and what she does."

"She is probably in East Germany?"

"Yes, or possibly Russia. His Holiness doesn't know precisely."

"Why is it so hard to find her? Her job?"

"Let's just say, others do not want her to be found. She works for their security services."

"Does she know who her father is?"

"No. That is another part of the puzzle and, as you can appreciate, complicates matters considerably. That is why Pope Karl has protected her all these years. He was worried for her safety, for her future."

"But what is wrong with having a father who is the pontiff? Surely, this is an almighty blessing?"

"You are naïve, Vincenzo. Think about it. Think about the consequences for the Holy Father, the church, and his daughter if the truth came out."

"Why so terrible? The Berlin Wall has fallen—this is the perfect time to reunite." Vincenzo shifted in his seat, leaning closer to Monsignor Fran. "Is this why our master has been behaving so … so strangely? He has cut himself off from us."

"This situation has been playing on his mind for many years."

"I understand. It must have been difficult."

"Yes, Vincenzo. I have known the pontiff for many years. One thing you must understand is that Pope Karl never planned to be a priest, much less pope."

Vincenzo nodded. "This is—"

"Let me finish—"

"Wait ... Pope Karl's daughter works for the security services," Vincenzo said slowly. His eyes widened, and he stopped
savoring the olive he had bitten into. He glanced around him, as
though he suddenly realized that anyone of these hotel guests
could be a spy or secret agent.

Monsignor Fran allowed the bombshell to settle.

Vincenzo said, "That cannot be."

Vincenzo's thoughts came thick and fast, as though he were
suddenly riding inside a pinball machine and he was the ball.
He sat up straight and observed the scene in front of him—an
international set drinking, laughing, posing for photographs
for the roaming photographer. A couple of fat, bald men—self-
ishly, thought Vincenzo—were smoking huge cigars as big as
bratwursts.

Then the news sank in. Who *is* Pope Karl? *I have no idea who
this man is.*

It was true. Vincenzo had firmly believed he had a special
bond with his master—that the man who was king of the holy
world would share his innermost secrets with him. After all,
they had agreed together that something extraordinary was
needed to maintain peace and world order while the Soviet
Union was breaking apart before them. It was, potentially, an
extremely dangerous and volatile situation. The fall of the Soviet
Union might lead to World War III or even nuclear war—they
had agreed. Vincenzo and his master had made a pact—they
had agreed to cajole, facilitate, pray, and do whatever it took to
organize the peace summit. *Was the pontiff involved in Bruno's
murder? Please, God, no.* Now, three weeks after the murder, there
had been no news from the American. Vincenzo began to think
that it must somehow be connected. His calling, his job, and his
assignment in Venice. *It feels as though this peace summit is more
than just a peace summit.*

"Who murdered my friend, Bruno?"

The split-second pause and darting of Monsignor Fran's
eyes told Vincenzo that the next sentence was a lie.

"I don't know," said Monsignor Fran. "Who is Bruno?"

"Bruno is my friend who was murdered in front of me. I was on an assignment for His Holiness."

"I'm afraid—"

"Until now, I did not think it was connected."

Monsignor Fran shook his head. "Vincenzo. I swear to you. I have no idea what happened to your friend."

"I don't believe you, Excellency. Frankly, I am not sure what I believe anymore."

"You are confused, Vincenzo. You feel betrayed."

"Yes, I do."

"I haven't finished."

Vincenzo eyed Monsignor Fran. "There's more?"

"Yes, there's more. The reason Pope Karl has shared this secret about his daughter"—Monsignor Fran smiled faintly—"is because he refuses to be blackmailed any longer."

"Blackmailed?"

"By Soviet authorities—secret service."

"KGB?"

"Yes. They threatened to kill his daughter if he stepped out of line. He is an East German native. Ost bloc."

"I understand."

"Pope Karl has a mission. Until now, this secret was preventing him from achieving a goal. Pope Karl wants our Catholic Church to find a new home in Russia. He believes he can persuade the two most important world leaders to help him."

"How?"

"It's very simple. He will share his secret with the world."

"But you said he wants to protect his daughter."

"Correct. But now that the Berlin Wall has fallen, he believes it is time to put the situation in God's hands. Now he is prepared to sacrifice himself and even his daughter for the sake of the greatest church in history."

Vincenzo shook his head in disbelief and confusion. But his

next utterance contradicted his gesture. "Yes," he said. "The greatest church in history. That much we agree upon."

At that moment, three tall, thin, beautiful models—one male, two females—all dressed in white linen dresses and hats, paused their slow saunter through the narrow streets of Capri to flaunt themselves and their fashion to the affluent spectators on the terrace, including the two Vatican guests.

Father, Son, and Holy Ghost," thought Vincenzo. *Bless me, Father, for I need your help.*

CHAPTER FORTY-THREE

Sennelager Training Area, West Germany

The first day's tank exercises went smoothly. The weather was cold but not freezing. Apart from the evergreens, of which there were many in these parts, the trees were transitioning through their shades of yellow, amber, orange, and red.

Steele tried not to mess up any of his simple tasks in front of the men he would one day command. C Squadron made a dozen practice assaults on fake positions at the squadron level of fourteen tanks. After two days of training at squadron level, the entire regiment would come together and join forces for assaults at battlegroup level, with artillery and infantry taking part. As tank crew loader, Steele performed physical actions of loading the ammunition—armor-piercing fin-stabilized (FIN), or high explosive squash head (HESH)—as he steadied himself across the bumpy terrain and executed the vehicle commander's orders. At one point, Steele dropped one of the dummy rounds onto his thumb, winced in pain, and kept going without anyone seeing.

At night, they were supposed to "bivvy up"—set up a canvas tent contraption on the side of the tank for protection from the weather while they slept. But in practice, Steele's crew took the shortcut on the first night. At dusk, after they had eaten and set up a perimeter guard and latrine in the woods around their troop "hide," the tank commander—a large, blond-haired corporal of horse with a ruddy complexion that made him look perpetually healthy—swiveled the tank housing 90 degrees so the barrel pointed outward and sideways. This left the tank's warm engine deck exposed for the four-man crew to lay down their sleeping bags and, in theory, enjoy a more comfortable night than sleeping on the soggy ground next to their MBT. The only problem with this "workaround," Steele discovered during the night, was that the engine deck eventually cooled down, and it was like laying on a cold metal freezer shelf. His sleeping bag literally froze to the metal engine deck. He decided he would try the damp, frosty ground the next night.

Steele yawned. Reveille had been 4:30 am on this second day of five, and he already felt exhausted from lack of sleep, sentry duty in the middle of the night, and the relentless attacks, firing drills, map-reading, maneuvering, orders, and counterorders, loading and unloading of dead-weight dummy ammunition, and making tea, coffee, and boiling army Compo-rations all day long. Being inside a tank wasn't as easy or as fun as he had imagined it.

The troop of three tanks headed for the metal road that was also open to the public and headed west to the next meeting point on this vast expanse of barren terrain. Other tanks in the squadron slotted in behind them. They would travel in convoy to the next section of the training area. The soldiers were euphoric to have completed two days of exercise—two down, three to go. *This* is why they had joined the army—to command, ride, fire, and drive main battle tanks. And some, but by no means all, were genuinely hoping for a real war to practice their skills. Steele was not one of them—he hoped his feelings about that would change.

There were now nearly fifteen tanks in convoy. When tanks moved in convoy on a road day or night, procedure dictated that each vehicle must stop and ensure its lights were free from mud and dirt. But 2nd Lt. Peter Gabriel forgot to carry out this simple order.

Suddenly, the entire column of tanks came to a halt.

"Hello, all call signs … STOP, STOP, STOP. NO DUFF. I

REPEAT, NO DUFF." There was no ambiguity about the squadron leader's order. "No duff" meant the information was genuine and not part of any kind of exercise.

Apart from the low rumble of tank engines in the cold night air, it was as if nature itself had gone silent.

Five minutes later, the C Squadron leader gave an update over the radio. "Hello, all call signs, remain in position. RTA in progress. NO DUFF ... NO DUFF."

Steele thought that perhaps a vehicle's tank track had come loose, or a tank had run out of petrol or smashed into a road sign. "Any ideas?" Steele asked Corporal of Horse Bunting.

"Not an igloo, sir," replied Corporal of Horse Bunting in a London drawl. He stood upright in position and peered into the darkness. "No, sir. I can't see a thing out there."

"Does this happen often?"

Trooper Fry, the tank's driver, said, "I was on an exercise once, sir. One of the tanks ran over a command vehicle—nearly crushed one of the DS."

Steele replied, "Sounds nasty."

"It was like this, sir. Nighttime. No one could see a bloody thing."

The conversation was interrupted by another message from the C Squadron leader. "Hello, three zero, ask Second Lieutenant Steele if he speaks German."

Corporal Bunting said, "Did you hear that, sir?"

Steele replied, "Yes, I speak German."

"Hello, Zero Charlie Alpha, that's an affirmative. Yes, my Two Lima Tango speaks German. Affirmative."

"Roger that. Send him to the back of the column. Immediately. Require linguist for RTA."

"Three zero, roger that. He's on his way."

Corporal of Horse Bunting nodded to Steele. "On your way, sir. You're needed ASAP."

"You might get a night in a warm bed," said Tpr. Fry as Steele climbed out of the tank.

Steele said, "I'll be back soon, boys. In time for your bedtime story."

Using his army-issued torch, he jogged toward the back of the column. An RTA, he thought—road traffic accident. It seemed odd that there might be an accident, as there was only one road around the perimeter of the training area, and, as far as he knew, they were the only ones using it.

Working his way through dense woodland on both sides of the road, Steele rounded the first bend and saw that the rear of the column was only half a dozen tanks away. There was a bright light mixed with the universal blue flashing lights in the distance—emergency vehicles were already on the scene. Steele hoped he could help. As he got closer, he saw a kind of mist or fog surrounding the crash site. But then he realized, it wasn't fog; it was smoke from the crash itself.

Something didn't feel right. There was an odd smell in the air, even though it was a cool night. Given the apparent serious-ness of the situation—flashing lights, two German VW Polizei vehicles, two ambulances, and the British army liaison officer's patrol vehicle—there was no hustle and bustle or even audible conversation. No orders were being shouted—a distinct lack of urgency.

Then Steele saw why.

As he reached the last tank in the column, the emergency vehicle floodlights lit up a civilian-sized vehicle, now a mangled ball of metal. The ball of metal had once been a civilian estate car, perhaps a VW Passat or BMW. Amid the cloud of smoke and wreckage, there was a smell that Steele did not recognize. A moment later, he learned that it was the smell of death.

Inside the vehicle were five people of different genders and ages, including a child. Steele concluded it was probably a family—an entire family. The driver's head was smashed into the steering wheel, and Steele saw that the skull was split open and the brain visible. Stunned and sickened by the sight of five corpses tragically killed outright in whatever incident had taken place, Steele felt lightheaded. He felt as though he might faint. Then he turned to the side of the road, bent over, and threw up the army bacon burger Compo-rations he had happily devoured earlier that evening.

"Mr. Steele," said the squadron leader—officer ranks below captain were addressed as "Mister" in the British army—"It's okay. We don't need you after all."

Steele stood upright. "What happened?"

"Tragic accident, I'm afraid. Looks like they were taking a shortcut across the training area—driving at speed—came around this corner and smashed into the back of four zero."

Steele glanced at the back of callsign 4-0. The rear lights were caked with mud. From what the squadron leader had said, if the car was driving fast, it would have been like smashing into a solid metal wall at 60 or 70 mph. The driver and passengers hadn't stood a chance. The tank, on the other hand, was unscathed.

"Can I do anything?" asked Steele.

"I'm afraid there's nothing anyone can do here. We thought we might need your German. But they're all dead."

Steele nodded, turned, and walked slowly back to his tank.

So, this was it, he thought. This was death in all its glory. It was pretty much how he had pictured a horrific car accident would be, but he had not prepared himself for that nauseating, unexpected metallic smell of death. He turned to his right and threw up again as he made his way back through the autumn leaves toward his tank.

"Jack," said a woman's voice.

Steele turned and peered toward the source, his eyes getting used to the dark after the bright emergency vehicle flood lights.

"Who's there?" he asked.

"It's me, Claudia."

I must be dreaming, thought Steele. *What is going on?* "I don't understand," he said. "Claudia? What on earth are you doing here?"

This was no hallucination. Claudia, the beautiful woman he had slept with in Berlin, was standing in front of him.

"I've been keeping an eye on you, Jack."

"Me?"

"Yes, it's been difficult to get a chance to talk."

"Claudia, I already told you on the phone, I can't talk now. I'm on an army exercise, in case you can't see." He pointed behind him. "These are called tanks."

"It's nice to see you too, Jack."

"I'm serious. I don't understand what you are doing here. Five civilians just died. Do you understand?"

"This was an accident. It wasn't supposed to happen like this."

"You had something to do with this?"

"This family was supposed to break down in the middle of the road—stop your vehicles so I can talk to you. I don't know how this happened."

Steele shook his head in disbelief. "This is insane. Now you're saying I'm the reason those people are dead."

"I'm sorry, Jack. But this is very important. I promise this was not supposed to happen."

"And whatever you think is going to happen with me is *not* going to happen."

"I was waiting for a chance to speak to you."

"You're insane. You should leave before I alert German police. They're thirty seconds in that direction."

"Come with me, Jack. We can help each other. You don't want to risk your people knowing about us."

"*Knowing* about us? I don't know you."

"Jack." Claudia cocked her head in a bizarrely flirtatious way. "You know me *very* well, remember?"

"You want to blackmail me now? Is that what you want?"

"No, Jack. I want to help you, and I think you can help me too."

"How?" asked Steele.

His mind was racing. Nigel had told him "they" might make contact. He had told Steele to be vigilant, ready, and report anything unusual. So, was this the contact he had talked about? Did Nigel know "they" would contact him? And who the bloody hell is "they" anyway? Russians? Germans?

Claudia continued, "We want to thank you."

"Thank me?"

"Yes, without you, we would never have discovered the submarine."

"Which submarine?" *How does she know about the submarine?* His head was pounding.

"It is known as the Gottland class submarine. We were searching for it for many months, even years. You helped us find it."

Steele smiled, feigning ignorance. "I've no idea what you are talking about."

"The Swedish navy saved you. You *and* Masha, of course. It was a very expensive rescue."

"Why?"

"The Americans are furious. I don't blame them."

Steele shook his head. He couldn't believe what he was hearing. A few moments ago, he was shivering from the cold and the shock of seeing five mangled bodies. Now the adrenaline had kicked in, and Claudia, this spy or whatever she was, was recounting the details of his mission to Russia. *I must find out who she is and what she wants. Nigel would approve.*

"Claudia, if that's your real name—"

"It is, Jack. It *is* my real name."

"I had nothing to do with any submarine. You're mistaken."

"Are you saying you don't know Masha?"

Steele hesitated. "No, I am not saying that."

"Masha is in danger."

"What do you mean?"

"Masha is thankful you helped her with her 'dramatic' escape from Mother Russia."

"How do you know this?"

"It's time, Jack. I will explain everything, but you must come with me."

"I don't understand—where to?"

"I promise, Jack. I will explain everything. I don't want to hurt you."

"Hurt me?"

Claudia pulled out her Makarov 9mm from the pocket of her leather jacket.

Steele glanced at the pistol. Claudia's finger was comfortably nestled around the trigger.

If Steele had to guess, she was serious about her "invitation," but he doubted she would shoot him here and now. Too risky. On the other hand, she knew a lot about everything that had happened, and he might be able to use this encounter to find out who killed Aronsson.

Steele said, "I'll go with you on one condition."

"Forgive me, Jack, but in case you hadn't noticed, you are not in any position to negotiate."

"I'll come with you if you tell me who killed Aronsson."

Claudia smiled. "We think alike, Jack. I asked my superior the same question a few days ago."

"So you don't mind sharing."

"Of course not. A gesture of good faith, shall we say."

As far as he knew, no one in British intelligence knew the identity of Aronsson's assassin. Suspicions but no proof. He—rookie Jack Steele—was about to score one of the biggest pieces of international political and criminal intelligence of the year.

Claudia said, "It's not exciting, I'm afraid. In fact, it's obvious."

Steele said, "KGB?"

"Jawohl. The KGB assassinated Anders Aronsson."

"Why? He was trying to build bridges with you. He was pro-Russia."

"Or anti-American? Doesn't matter either way."

"Then why?"

"KGB wanted to send a message."

"To whom?"

"Masha and the Americans."

Steele's heart skipped a beat. Masha? He knew Masha. He had slept with Masha. "I don't understand. She defected. You want her back?"

"Not me, Jack. I work for HVA—East German security—not KGB."

"But you work *with* your Russian friends?"

"Yes, we cooperate. Of course. You see, that is the beauty of Russia. You never know if the great bear is going to feed you or eat you."

"I still don't get it. Why do you need me?"

"Enough, Jack. Let's go." Claudia raised her pistol with a look that said, *Don't fuck with me—I've run out of patience.*

"You're kidnapping me?"

"Let's just say we're going on some top-secret R&R, as your British army friends like to say."

CHAPTER FORTY-FOUR

Sundbergs Konditori, Stockholm

Astrid spooned the cream from the top of her cappuccino, savoring both the cream and the chocolate flakes that came with it. It didn't seem right to be "enjoying" this kafé without her father, but she concluded that he would want her to be happy as she tried to pick up life after his death. Astrid and her new best friend, Masha Pushkin, had settled into one of the more secluded back rooms for privacy from paparazzi, spies, and nosey old women who seemed to have a habit of trying to comfort Astrid over her father's death whenever they saw her in public. Perhaps it's a cultural thing, she thought, that old Swedish women felt comfortable starting a conversation in this Konditori that was more than two hundred years old. So far, no one had noticed the daughter of the assassinated prime minister this morning.

"What are you going to do?" asked Masha in English.

"I don't know. But I must do something."

Masha touched Astrid's blond hair like a big sister trying to comfort her sibling. "There's something I must tell you."

Astrid looked deep into Masha's eyes. "Before you tell me anything, I need to know if I can trust you."

"Of course, you can trust me. That's why I am here. We are friends. Pen pals, remember! You helped me escape from the Soviet gulag."

"Not really. But I can't help thinking that ever since I've known you—"

"I ruined your life?"

"No—well, yes. That is what I am thinking. But I know you had nothing to do with my father's murder."

Masha placed her hand on Astrid's forearm. "I was about to apologize."

"Apologize?"

"I was selfish. When we conceived this idea—of escaping … defecting—I was only thinking about myself. I was only thinking about 'poor me,' how terrible my life was in Russia, and how I would do anything to escape. To get away from those imbeciles—military, the party, KGB."

"It was my idea too. I wanted to help you."

"But I did not think about the consequences for you and your family."

Astrid sipped her cappuccino. By her own estimation, she had matured beyond belief, almost overnight, since the death of her father, and one of her new ways of behaving was to voice precisely what was on her mind. "I must say that I think it is strange that my father was assassinated within days of your arrival here. My father warned me—"

"He warned you?"

"Yes, he said he wanted to help Russians but that they are dangerous people. 'You can't trust a Russian,' he said."

"I understand. I agree with you, Astrid." Masha sighed. "What I wanted to tell you was that I think your father's death *is* my fault. It would not have happened if we had not been friends. I am so sorry."

"Why is it your fault?"

"No one ever leaves the Soviet Union. Bad things happen to people who betray Mother Russia. People commit suicide, fall out of windows, and die in car crashes. I was naïve—"

"Did you pull the trigger?"

"No, of course not."

"Then you are not to blame."

"Not directly. But I think I know who is to blame."

Astrid stopped mid-sip and looked up.

Masha said, "I think they were sending me a message."

"Who?"

"We have a new era of KGBshnicks."

"*KGBshnicks?*"

"Those people in the KGB who support the new era of peace and détente. They support Mikhail Leontev and his peace initiative. But my father was old-school ... he was old-school Soviet, but even though he was not my real father, he explained many things to me. He told me never to repeat it—my life would be in danger if I did."

"Old versus new KGB?"

"Yes, he knew Mikhail Leontev would cause a rift in our country. This starts with KGB."

"What does the Old Guard want?"

"They don't want change. They don't want people to defect. They don't want a new system—perestroika, glasnost—in my country. It's too dangerous for their old ways—nepotism, old cronies, the Communist Party is all that matters to them. It is their religion."

Astrid frowned. "I'm confused. What's wrong with friendship and peace?"

Masha smiled. "You sound like me asking my father the same question."

"What did he say?"

"He said it's complicated."

"That's what parents say when they don't want to explain their opinions."

Masha smiled. "It is easier to keep a nation like mine under control under the old system, not the new one. They fear we will end up like Ukrainians."

"What's wrong with Ukrainians?"

"Nothing at all. They are forward-thinking, clever people. They are sick and tired of being held back from the future. They want a future with Western Europe, not Siberia—especially the young people. One day, I think they will rebel."

"What about *your* young people in Russia? Why do they allow this to happen?"

"They are not stupid. They support Leontev's efforts. But if he fails, they will leave the country—like me—but it will be easier for them. They know they cannot fight our system from within. They will not risk spending ten years in a Russian gulag."

"And Ukrainians?" asked Astrid.

"I don't know. Perhaps they will join the European Community one day."

Masha and Astrid laughed. Then Astrid said, "Politics. I hate politics."

"That's not surprising—your father was a politician, and now he's dead."

"Both our fathers are dead because of politics." Astrid slowly shook her head. "But I don't understand why they want to harm you, a young woman. A beautiful young Russian girl."

Masha smiled in spite of herself. "Don't be naïve."

"Do you know why … or who?

"Both. From conversations I overheard with my father, I have a good idea."

"Tell me. I want to know."

"The KGB's job is to stop defections. They failed. My father told me about one man whom he thought was trying to kill him. In fact, he told me that if anything happened to him, it was likely this man would be responsible. I believe this same man was responsible for assassinating your father. The shame and humiliation of my defection were too much, and he wanted to send *me* a personal message disguised as a political assassination."

"But that would mean—"

"Yes, this man knows about us."

"Smoke and mirrors."

"Yes, smoke and mirrors. Nothing in my country is ever what it seems. Westerners don't realize how fragile your democracy is."

"But it was pointless to kill my father. What did it achieve?"

"Of course, you are right. But in my country, the 'message' is more important than the lives of others."

"Who is this man? *Where* is he?"

"His name is Oleg Pugachev. He pretends to be a progressive KGB man, but really, he is diehard old-school KGB. My father was very suspicious of him."

"I hate this man."

"There is a rumor that he might be president one day."

"Let's make sure that never happens."

Masha smiled. "I wish."

"I'm serious."

"What are you talking about?"

"If this man is responsible for my father's death, and you say he is threatening you, then we have no choice."

"No choice?"

"We will make sure he never succeeds."

Masha pointed at Astrid and said, "You are crazy, my dear Astrid. No one gets close to this man. No one knows where he is. He is KGB. Do you understand? He is *Komitet Gosudarstvennoy Bezopasnosti.*"

Astrid smiled. "You said yourself the Soviet Union will fall apart if Leontev fails."

"Yes."

"You said there is going to be a summit—a peace summit."

"So?"

"I would bet my life that this man 'Oleg' will be there."

Masha nodded. "It's possible. So?"

"He will have no idea that we are coming for him."

"*We?*"

"Two young girls. No one will even notice us."

"You are crazy. Did Herr Sundberg put something in your cappuccino?"

"No, I am not crazy. If this man is responsible for executing my father, I want revenge, plain and simple. Is that too much to ask?"

"How will we find him? It's impossible."

"If *I* find him, will you help me?"

"I don't understand."

"What don't you understand? If I find this man, will you help me avenge our fathers—*both* our fathers? It's a simple proposition. My father used to say, *Simplicity serves success.*"

"Tell me how."

"Björn will help me."

"Who is Björn?"

"My ex-boyfriend. We are still good friends. He owes me. His father is a Swedish admiral—Admiral Olof Bergman."

"How does this help?"

"He listens to his father's private conversations—like us. Where do you think I got the idea?" Astrid cocked her head in a gesture of supreme confidence.

"You are crazy. We can't assassinate a KGB man at a world peace summit."

"I didn't say I wanted to kill him. But it will be the end of his career in espionage. That much, I owe my father."

Masha's eyes widened, even more confused. "I still don't understand how?"

Astrid pointed to their reflection in the antique mirror across the room. "Look in the mirror," she said. "Who could resist us?"

"He will recognize me."

"Fear not, comrade Maria. We will transform you into a Russian spy after all."

CHAPTER FORTY-FIVE

A7 Autobahn, near Stuttgart, Germany

"Nice countryside," said Steele in German.

"It's even better once we get to Innsbruck. Unfortunately, it will be dark by then."

"I'll try to manage my disappointment."

"Slow down, Jack." Claudia shifted uneasily in her seat even though she was pointing her pistol at Steele.

Steele eased off the accelerator of the black BMW E30 estate car.

"Danke sehr." *Thank you.*

"Don't mention it," said Steele, switching to English.

"I appreciate your cooperation. You won't regret it."

"Famous last words."

"I mean it."

"You can put the gun away."

Claudia remained silent for a moment, then holstered her Makarov 9mm.

"How are you planning to get across the border? If I'm not mistaken, this takes us to Austria."

"Everything is under control, Jack. My BMW has diplomatic plates—didn't you notice?"

"Nice touch. You're very organized."

"I'm a professional."

"And thanks for bringing a change of clothes. Very thoughtful ... so, what's so special that you had to abduct me from my army training?"

"Honestly, it wasn't as difficult as I thought it would be. You seem eager to cooperate."

"After that carnage, I was happy to take a break. Besides, as you said, we're old friends."

It wasn't quite true, Steele thought. They weren't exactly old friends—they had met for one night a couple of months ago—but the fact they knew each other *was* one of the reasons Steele had acquiesced and gone with Claudia.

Claudia became more relaxed now that she had holstered her weapon. "You seemed more than happy to leave that place."

"Let's just say I'm curious," he said. "You don't seem very upset about five innocent people dying on your watch."

"It's business. Of course, I am sorry, but I don't know what happened. I hired them to do a job, and they failed. Right now, there are more important considerations."

"Cold comfort, I must say."

Steele thought about the last thing Nigel had said to him. *If there's any foreign contact, find out what they want.* Nigel had not sanctioned him taking off on a wild goose chase. But Steele was convinced this was a matter of national and international security, and he wanted to make his mark.

Claudia smiled and changed the subject. "You want to know why we chose you? Why *I* chose you, in fact."

"Perhaps I'm not who you think I am."

"You served us well in Leningrad."

"It wasn't intentional, I can assure you."

One of the things Steele admired about Germany was the clean, well-made roads—particularly the autobahns. Furthermore, the adventurous side of him loved the fact that there was no speed limit on German autobahns. He was used to the pedestrian 70 mph on UK motorways. Steele recalled his first cultural exchange visit when he was seventeen to a German family in Cologne. The father had driven his Mercedes 220 at 140 mph for a few moments on the autobahn—just for fun. Then the father pulled over and allowed Steele—with his newly acquired British driver's license—to take the wheel and do the same. Ecstasy to a teenage boy.

All of which brought Steele back to the present, and he accelerated.

"Slow down, Jack." Claudia gripped the handrail above her. "You want to kill us?"

"Honestly, I have a fatalistic attitude about these things."

Time for my mini-command performance. I need answers—now— before this goes any further.

Steele accelerated some more. The two-lane autobahn was nearly deserted on this stretch, but it probably wouldn't be for much longer as they got nearer to the border.

The speedometer's needle touched 95 mph.

"Enough, Jack."

"I thought you liked danger, Fräulein Claudia. Who did you say you worked for?"

Steele pressed the accelerator again—the needle reached 100 mph. The BMW's steering wheel began to judder. Steele gripped it harder.

Claudia drew her weapon. "I said, enough, Jack Steele!"

Steele ignored the command, looked ahead, and switched the headlights to a high beam. "Just in case."

He adopted a maniacal look in his eyes—all for Claudia's benefit.

The BMW hit 110 mph.

"Pull over. NOW!" screamed Claudia, her forehead shiny with sweat.

Still all clear ahead. Steele pressed yet more on the accelerator.

The speedometer read 120 mph.

"Apparently, BMWs can reach 150 mph, no problem. I've always admired German craftsmanship." Steele had to raise his voice over the sound of the engine, and he smiled as though he was enjoying himself. Underneath, he was terrified, and his brow, too, was sweating.

Steele gripped the steering wheel even tighter. *This better work. One wrong move and we end up like the family who drove into the back of the tank.*

"Tell me what the bloody hell is going on!" Steele screamed. The aim was simple—to scare the shit out of Claudia—and his performance was working. Claudia had laid the Makarov in her lap and was holding on with both hands.

"You are going to kill us!"

Steele raised his voice over the turbo engine that was now propelling the BMW along the autobahn at 140 mph. "Maybe, maybe not! But there's nothing I hate more than being kept in the dark. Now tell me, who the hell are you, and what do you want?"

Steele made a right incline onto a services slip road. *Time for the final act.*

Up ahead was a petrol station, and beyond that, the pictur-esque German countryside with a fence and a red barn in the distance. Steele decided he would crash the fence and end up in the barn that was hopefully full of hay if Claudia did not start talking. But then again, he had no idea whether he had the guts to go through with it.

"I'll try not to hit the petrol pump!" He was surprised at his level of bravado—or perhaps insanity. *Must be the adrenaline,* he thought. *I hope to God it works.*

"Um Gottes, Willen! Enough!" Claudia braced for impact. "I will tell you everything, I promise!"

Steele slammed on the brakes.

Rote Stube Gasthof, near Innsbruck, Austria

Three hours later, Steele and Claudia, both with more color in their cheeks than during Steele's stunt, sat in a typical, pictur-esque Gasthof just over the Austrian border.

"You are a fucking crazy Englishman," said Claudia.

"Yes, you might be right. Honestly, I surprised myself. I'm not really trained for this sort of thing."

"Very funny."

"I'm completely serious."

Claudia shook her head. Three hours after Steele had scared the living daylights out of her with his rocket-man stunt, she was still on edge and wondering if she had bitten off more than she could handle. But it was too late now. Oleg had ordered her to bring Steele to the summit—and she planned to deliver, whatever it took. She had changed course—from necessity—and that meant revealing part of the plan to Steele. It didn't really matter, she thought, Steele wouldn't survive the summit anyway—if Oleg stuck to the plan. Her British asset was just another pawn in Oleg's master plan.

"Tell me one more thing," said Steele as he cut into one of the biggest Wiener schnitzels he had ever laid eyes on. "I understand that you need a rookie like me. Dispensable—a no-one-gives-a-shit-whether-I-live-or-die type of thing, but do you really believe everything your Russian boss is telling you?"

It was an interesting question—one that Claudia had asked herself many times.

"I have no reason not to," she replied. "He is my superior. We are the same."

"Really? East Germans are the same as Russians?"

"Yes, of course. We are Socialists."

"Or Communists?"

"Virtually the same thing. Old people call it communism, and young people prefer socialism."

"That's a simplified version."

"I like to keep things simple. It makes life easier. Think of it like this—we are all for one and one for all."

"Not like the 'greed' that plagues us in the West."

"Correct. One day, your country and perhaps even United States will be crying out for socialism."

Steele raised an eyebrow. "Hard to believe, but anything's possible, I suppose."

"It might not be *our* socialism. But your people will become sick of the greed, I promise you."

"The greed I can't deny, but why would President Madison want to destroy the Soviet initiative? He wants peace. He wants Leontev to succeed."

"You are a brave man; I give you this. But you are also foolish—unable to see what is in front of your face."

"Help me clear my London fog."

"The Americans are not content with East–West 'la-la' land."

Steele smiled. "What do you mean?"

"American president is like a magician. You know what is sleight of hand?

"I understand."

"He makes sleight of hand. He shows us one thing, but really, he is performing another trick."

"How so?"

"What I am about to tell you is top secret. If you meet Oleg, you can't tell him I told you this. He will kill me. But you deserve an explanation."

Again, Claudia thought back to Oleg's meticulous instructions. *Truth is the best form of trust. Make him trust you.*

Steele placed his hand on the large glass of Weizenbier and leaned forward, pretending not to take Claudia's tone seriously. "You have my word," he whispered.

"Have you heard of the Deception Committee?"

"No. It sounds like a Frederick Forsythe novel."

"Believe me. It is not a novel."

"I believe you." Steele took a gulp of his Weizenbier, which had come highly recommended by the waitress.

"Jack, you must understand me. I am not doing this job because I hate the West."

"Are you sure?"

"I am doing this because I want to protect my people—our way of life."

"Okay. Fair enough. How does the American president fit in? And this 'Deception Committee?'"

"There is a summit arranged. American and Russian presidents will meet. Their hope is to build détente. New relationship. End of Cold War and old Soviet regime."

"And ...?"

"And it is all bullshit."

"How do you know?"

"Politics—domestic or international—is about interests."

"Agreed ..."

"Madison only pretends he wants peace, that he is working for this new era of peace. But he does everything behind the scenes to create the opposite. The Deception Committee is a secret mission to make everyone think Russia is the bad guy. This is the simplified version."

"Make it more complex, Claudia. I can handle it."

"The plan is to destroy Russia and make peace with every Eastern bloc state and invite them to join NATO."

"Come on, Claudia. That's a fairy tale. I studied Russian, and I lived in Russia. That will *never* happen."

"It is not a debate."

"I just spent six months at Sandhurst. None of the instructors mentioned that scenario as the remotest possibility."

"I will prove it to you." Oleg, Claudia thought, was right. *A little bit of truth goes a long way to make trust.*

"Okay."

"Madison's mission is to destroy Russia. For example, you know what happened in Sweden."

"Yes, I was there."

"Swedish prime minister was becoming too friendly with Russia. Madison hated this. It would destroy his plans. They wanted to protect this secret submarine class."

Steele's expression became more serious. "The Gottland class?"

"Correct. Without you, we would never have found this Gottland class submarine."

"Without me?"

"Technically, it wasn't your fault."

"So how—?"

"The Swedish submarine captain—a woman, I might add—decided your lives were more important than a national security secret they shared with the Americans."

"I had no idea."

"Neither did the Swedish prime minister. His own military kept this a secret. They were afraid Aronsson would nix it."

"Jesus Christ." Steele raised both hands in a gesture of surrender. He wasn't expecting this bombshell.

"Now you understand why your plan to help Masha Pushkin was—how do you say?—a blessing in disguise for us."

"*Shit.*"

"You see, Jack. Everything is not as you think. Your people are not as rosy as you think. Especially your big brother Americans."

"But why did the KGB assassinate Aronsson?"

"You are not listening, Mr. Steele."

Steele cocked his head. "You're losing me."

Claudia continued, "We had nothing to do with Aronsson's death even though your people want to blame us."

"Then who *was* responsible for crying out loud?"

"The Deception Committee was responsible for Aronsson's assassination."

"That's absurd." Steele scoffed. "CIA?"

"Not CIA. Pay attention." Claudia leaned toward Steele. "Deception Committee," she hissed.

"I don't get it. I've never heard of the Deception Committee."

"Precisely. Officially, it doesn't exist."

"But why would they assassinate Aronsson?"

"You hear what you want to hear. It was in their interest to remove him. If you like Forsythe, surely you know that truth is stranger than fiction?"

Steele sat still for a few moments letting this treasure trove of information wash over him. "One more question," he said slowly.

"Bitte."—*Please.*

"Now that you have my full attention, where are we going?"

Claudia smiled. "Don't worry, Jack. Somewhere warm, where at least you won't need your umbrella."

Steele smiled, excused himself, and went to find the bathroom.

CHAPTER FORTY-SIX

Soviet Embassy, Berlin

"I understand, Mikhail Pavlovich," said Oleg, pressing the receiver to his ear. "But there's nothing more we can do here."

The Russian president, seated in his Kremlin apartment, replied, "What happened?"

"The Berlin Wall has fallen. There was a miscommunication from local authorities, and one thing led to another."

"Which 'thing' led to 'another' thing? Explain."

"East German authorities gave a press conference with inaccurate information, and the next thing we know ... East and West Germans are tearing down the wall to be reunited."

"Inaccurate information or misinformation? Was this a deliberate act of sabotage? Treason?"

"We don't believe so. It was a bureaucratic error. As you know, Mr. President, our people are very good at those."

"I see." Leontev sighed and said quietly, "Not good."

"Please repeat."

"I was talking to my wife. She's standing next to me. I just told her that things do not look good."

"We must deal with the situation."

Leontev said, "It wasn't supposed to happen this fast."

Correct, Mr. President, thought Oleg. *You weren't supposed to throw the entire Soviet Union away so easily.*

"I understand, Mr. President. But I think it is even more

crucial that you meet with the American president. We must stick to the plan."

"In Berlin?"

"No, Mikhail Pavlovich. The venue has changed. Berlin is too unstable and unpredictable. We cannot protect you and the American leader here."

"Then where?"

"The Vatican has arranged a secret location for the summit."

"The Vatican is still involved?"

"Yes, they are offering to host the summit."

"Will I meet Pope Karl?"

"I am not sure about his location, but it might be possible."

"I have a proposal for him that I will share with you—I think it will help ease tensions and show the West we are willing to turn the page—a new era of détente."

"Are you certain that you want to turn the page?" Oleg's face flushed an angry red, but fortunately for him, there was no one around to see his reaction.

"It is time to make progress."

"Of course, Mr. President, please tell me."

"Oleg Stepanovich, you surprise me. This is unlike you to break telephone security protocols."

"I don't understand."

"My proposal is too sensitive to share over the telephone, even on this secure line. Isn't that what you have taught me?"

What is this madman going to do? thought Oleg. *Perhaps I need to liquidate him before he meets the American president.*

Oleg continued, "I trust your judgment, Mikhail Pavlovich. It is time for a new era—however you plan to do this will be music to my ears. I will meet you tomorrow as soon as you arrive in Capri."

"Capri?"

"Rest assured, the necessary security measures and logistics are in place. You might even enjoy it more than your dacha on the Black Sea."

Leontev chuckled. "I was always very curious about Capri. It looks like paradise. I loved the old Hollywood movie, *It Started in Naples*. Very romantic. It was made in Capri, you know."

Oleg frowned, then winced as though he had just sucked a slice of lemon. "No, I have not heard of this movie."

"Never mind."

"I will see you tomorrow, Mikhail Pavlovich."

Oleg replaced the receiver and poured himself a shot of vodka. The Soviet embassy was still virtually deserted inside and out, apart from a small detachment of Russian army Internal Security Service guards who had finally arrived to prevent the embassy from being ransacked.

The outside world was changing before his very eyes. He could see and hear East and West Germans thronging the streets with cries and shouts of jubilation.

Comrade Lenin is turning in his mausoleum. The end of the Soviet Union? he thought. *I will never let this happen, even if I must become president myself.*

MOD, Whitehall, London

Unusually, it was a bright, sunny day in London. Wing Commander Nick Jenkins looked out of his window and admired the eclectic beauty of London's South Bank across the Thames. He had heard rumors afoot that some kind of large Ferris "with people pods" wheel was being planned to add some "excitement" and a new tourist attraction to the London skyline. *Absurd idea,* he thought. *It will never happen.*

There was a knock on the door, and Nigel Rhodes Stampa entered.

"Sorry, Wing Commander," Nigel began.

"Come in, Nigel. How are you?"

"I wanted to tell you in person."

"Sounds ominous."

"It's about Steele."

"Thought it might be. I am beginning to regret the entire Jack Steele debacle. More trouble than he's worth."

"We got Masha out."

Jenkins cleared his throat. "We got her out, but at what cost."

"We couldn't have foreseen—"

"Couldn't, shouldn't, didn't … doesn't really make any difference. It happened."

"Any word from the Pentagon?"

"What kind of word do you expect? Yanks are livid. I don't blame them."

"Perhaps if they'd told us about the submarine?"

"It was their secret to share or not share as they deemed necessary."

"Ambitious project."

"Apparently, there was a woman in charge."

"Of the sub?"

"Yes, things might have turned out differently otherwise."

"Steele would probably be dead, and our efforts to help Masha defect assigned to the annals of Vauxhall Bridge."

"Precisely." Jenkins sighed. "No use crying over spilled defections. So tell me, what's the update? Put me out of my misery."

Nigel sat down in the compact leather armchair opposite Jenkins. "Steele's done a runner."

"What?"

"Literally."

"What are you talking about, man?"

"I received a message on my answer phone—we traced it to a motorway service station in Austria. He's on his way to Capri—in Italy."

"I know where Capri is, Nigel."

"He said it was a matter of national and international security. Wants me to meet him there."

"Madison and Leontev are—"

"Yes, sir. The peace summit will take place the day after tomorrow. They were scheduled to meet in Berlin, but due to recent events—"

"Back up, Nigel. The last thing I knew, Steele was safely ensconced at his barracks in Germany to prevent something like this from happening."

"Correct. He was."

"So what happened?"

"Apparently, he was on exercise, and there was some kind of RTA. Next thing he knew, an old 'friend' turned up and forced him to take a ride. He also said, 'She works for the other side.'"

"What does that mean?"

"I'm not one hundred percent, but I think it means someone from Soviet or East German security."

"What exactly did he say?"

"He said it was a 'friend' from Berlin who turned out not to be so friendly.'"

"When was he in Berlin?"

"Over the summer—but he didn't report any unusual contact."

"So, we're in the dark on this one?"

"I'm afraid so."

"Bloody mess."

"I'm taking the first flight to Naples. Ferry to Capri. I might even arrive before him … or them."

"No, you will not. Don't even think about it."

"With respect, sir—"

"With respect, Nigel, I'll call the prime minister myself if you or any of your people so much as pick up a pair of sunglasses."

"We can't leave Steele without backup."

Jenkins feigned a smile and frowned immediately after. "That's *precisely* what we are going to do."

"Sir?"

"If Jack Steele did have some kind of contact from an enemy security service, we have no idea what he might be involved in.

How do we know we can even still trust him? He's a fucking Sandhurst cadet, for Christ's sake."

"But he got Masha Pushkin out of Russia. He's one of us."

"We can't be sure. And this loose cannon caused a massive rift with the Yanks in the process. There's no telling what else he might screw up if he's heading to that summit."

"So why wouldn't we reel him in? Send a team?"

"Do you recall why we chose him in the first place?"

Nigel shifted in his chair, causing the leather to squeak. "Because he's dispensable and has no ties to our security service."

"Precisely."

"He'll be a sitting duck if anything goes wrong."

"Tough titties, as the Americans say. I am not taking any more chances with him, and I am certainly not risking any of our people."

"But what if the American president is in danger? This summit might be a trap."

"Not our problem. Madison decided to keep secrets from us. Let him figure it out."

"And Steele?"

"Ditto. If something happened because he did not inform us about contact with the enemy in Berlin, let him figure it out."

"I don't like it."

"You don't have to like it, Nigel. I'm in charge of Steele, thanks to you people, so I'm afraid you'll have to lump it."

CHAPTER FORTY-SEVEN

Air Force One, Naples Airport

"How are we getting there?" asked Madison on touchdown at Naples Airport.

"Italian navy will provide transport," replied Kolby Webster, deputy director of the CIA.

"Where's Marine One?"

"Logistics. We switched venues on short notice, Mr. President. Marine One had engine problems in Berlin. The Italian navy has helicopters too."

"I hope it's safe."

"As reliable as Neapolitans making pizza."

"And where are we staying?"

"Five-star–plus accommodation. Grand Hotel Quisisana has reserved an entire floor for us. It's in the center of Capri town."

"And where's the summit?"

"At the monastery. A five-minute walk from the hotel."

"How fitting. A peace summit inside a monastery."

"I thought so too, sir."

"You said 'walk'?"

"Yes, sir. The streets are more like alleys, or passageways—no room for vehicles."

"Got it."

"You'll love the place."

The heat enveloped them as they walked down the steps of Air Force One onto the shimmering Naples Airport tarmac.

"Just so we're clear," continued Madison, "I want to be in and out of there like shit off a shovel, understood? No niceties, no lunches, dinners, or breakfasts. Let's just concentrate on the optics and be done with it."

"Roger that, Mr. President."

The small entourage of American power and might walked toward the waiting Italian navy helicopter.

"One more thing," said Madison. "The Deception Committee. Did you tidy up things in Stockholm? Wouldn't be a good look if they found out about Aronsson."

"I have no idea what you're talking about, Mr. President," replied Webster. The faintest smile played on his lips.

"Very good, Kolby. We might have lost the Gottland class, but we sure as hell don't want to jeopardize the DC. Let's not so much as think about it until we're back on Air Force One."

"Understood."

Madison raised his voice above the sound of helicopter rotor blades. "Now let's hope the commie bastards brought some beluga, at least."

President Madison, Kolby Webster, and a small, hand-picked entourage scrambled aboard the less-than-salubrious confines of the Italian navy helicopter. Madison looked around and said, "And these guys are NATO members."

None of his team replied, and they settled in for the fifteen-minute ride to Capri hospital, where they would land on the roof helipad. From there, it was a five-minute trip to the Grand Hotel Quisisana, where the next security perimeter would be set up.

Marina Grande, Capri

The SNAV ferry reversed engines as it slowly made its way into Capri island's main port and marina. The rich denim water sparkled as only the Mediterranean knows how, and, for a moment, Claudia wished she had a normal past (complete with mother *and* father), a normal profession, and—glancing at Steele—a normal boyfriend. She had found Steele attractive in Berlin—not that it would have made any difference to her master plan even if her British asset was unattractive—for he was perfect for her brief. She would follow Oleg's orders to the letter.

"Have you been here before?" asked Steele, watching the churn and spray from the side of the vessel slowly subside.

"No, you?"

"I came with my grammar school friend for the afternoon a few years ago."

Claudia was puzzled. "For the afternoon?"

"We were determined to visit every famous tourist spot in Italy and had no idea that Capri proper—the town and jewel—is up there." He pointed to the mosaic of white villas high atop Capri island that boasted a view of Marina Grande and, in the far distance behind them, Naples and Mount Vesuvius.

"You should have read the guidebook."

"That's just it. We didn't have one. All we had was a map, and I was in charge. Shoestring tourism."

"What?"

"We were poor students. Not much money for food and accommodation—just a map, an Interrail ticket, and a backpack."

"Is that how you ended up in Berlin?"

"Yes, we made it to Berlin also that summer. I was fascinated by the wall."

"Everyone is fascinated by the wall."

The snorting ferry gently bumped the dockside, and Steele and Claudia reached for the handrail to steady themselves. The passengers began to assemble for disembarkation.

Steele moved closer to Claudia and continued, "I suppose you're right. Back then, you would have been on the other side."

"Yes, I was on the other side. You should have come to visit."

"I wanted to practice my Russian with all your friends, but my best mate wanted to visit cathedrals. There wasn't time for everything."

"I suppose cathedrals are important for some people. Who knows, maybe even for an atheist like me."

This man has no clue what it was like for my people, Claudia thought. *His naïveté is endearing but—like most Westerners—astounding. It's a pity he will never leave this island.*

★   ★   ★

They took an open-top taxi to the Piazzetta and walked down past the shops and boutiques. Twenty minutes after disembarkation, they arrived at the Grand Hotel Quisisana. Claudia directed Steele to wait on the terrace. It took all of four minutes to check in, and no questions were asked once Claudia showed her fake West German diplomatic passport.

Claudia joined Steele on the terrace. A waiter with a thin face and prematurely gray hair arrived to take their order.

Once the waiter left, Steele said, "We're staying here? I thought you would want to be low profile."

"Why, Jack? We have nothing to hide. We are tourists, remember."

"What do you want me to do?"

"I want you to follow my orders. You are here for a reason."

"You want me to witness an assassination, and you're not sure it will be successful?"

"Correct. You will be the hero, and you will give your people a full report even if it fails."

Steele, of course, had no intention of being a silent witness. Once Claudia had explained her harebrained plan, *his* plan all along was to thwart the assassination attempt, which is why he had managed to leave a frantic telephone message to Nigel at the Austrian Gasthof, and why his stomach was churning even though he was doing his best to exude confidence and calm. He had no way of knowing if Nigel had received his message, or what, if anything, Nigel or Wing Commander Jenkins or MI6 or anyone else who was supposedly on *his* side was going to do about it. For all he knew, the message might never have been received, or worse, it had been received, and they had decided to ignore it.

In other words, for all he knew here and now, he was completely on his own.

"You seriously think there will be an assassination attempt?"

"I *know* it. We work with the KGB, remember? They don't make mistakes. The Americans plan to assassinate the Russian president and blame us. You are here to tell them how things unfold."

"How about we stop the damn thing from happening in the first place? Wouldn't that be a more 'peaceful' gesture? This is a peace summit, right?"

Claudia smiled. "In an ideal world, perhaps—if we had met on your Interrail trip—we could play fairy tales. But this is international politics, plain and simple. Our interests versus your interests. I need you to follow *my* orders."

"Or what?"

Claudia reached inside her attaché case that—now that Steele thought about it—had not left her side since they'd climbed into the BMW in Sennelager. She pulled out an envelope and handed it to him.

"What's this?"

"Take a look. I think it's self-explanatory."

Steele slid his hand into the envelope and pulled out several black-and-white photographs. His eyes widened as he flipped through them. "What the fuck?"

Steele placed the photographs back in the envelope, and before he could think about what to do next, Claudia took the envelope and returned it to her attaché case.

"What are you doing, Claudia?"

"I am doing my job. As I told you, it is best to follow my orders. I promise you that you will be a hero by the time we leave this island."

The proverbial wheels were spinning even faster now inside his head. "Is that a live or dead hero?"

Claudia smiled. "What kind of person do you think I am?"

The waiter arrived with drinks and a bowl of fresh olives. "Please enjoy," he said, smiling. "It's a lovely day on Capri. Welcome to Grand Hotel Quisisana. If there is anything you need, ask for Raffaele."

Steele smiled as Raffaele walked away. *If only Raffaele had a magic wand.*

Steele continued, "You played me well. To answer your question, I have no idea who you are. But you are very good at your job. You knew I wouldn't crash the car."

"Let's just say I am a good actor also."

"Touché."

"I am glad we understand each other now, Jack. Please wait here. Do not leave the hotel. And for the record, we are sharing a room so that I can keep an eye on you—no other reason." She smiled and walked away. Once Claudia had entered the hotel, Steele exhaled long and hard. "*Fuck it,*" he said under his breath. "I'm completely and utterly screwed. Goddamn that woman."

Then he thought about the photos he had just seen—they were numbered with a thick "#" in chronological order—Steele and Claudia in bed together in Berlin; Steele and Masha climbing aboard the fishing boat in Leningrad; Steele and Masha in bed together on the boat; Steele and Masha climbing off the boat in Stockholm, and Steele standing next to Simon Bird at the rally the day Aronsson was assassinated.

He leaned back and ran his tongue along the front of his teeth to remove a piece of olive. His house of cards had just collapsed, and he had no idea what spy game he was playing, let alone how to play it.

CHAPTER FORTY-EIGHT

Grand Hotel Quisisana

Steele got up and picked his way through a sea of wicker chairs to reach the hotel entrance. He asked Raffaele where he could make an international call and was directed to a small telephone booth near the inside bar.

Steele quickly made a connection with Headquarters London District, which was the most secure way of getting through to Nigel at MI6's Vauxhall Cross Building on the south bank of the river Thames.

"I'm sorry, sir," said the male operator at Vauxhall Cross. "There's no one listed under that name."

"What?" replied Steele. "Please try again—Nigel ... Rhodes ... Stampa." He spelled out the surname.

"One moment, sir."

Steele heard a steady flow of computer taps as the operator re-entered the information.

"Sorry, sir. Still nothing coming up under that name. Would you like me to try another name, sir?"

Steele shook his head in disbelief. "Yes, please try, Wing Commander Nick Jenkins, at MOD."

"I'm sorry, sir. You'll have to go back to the London District operator for MOD. Transferring now."

Steele heard a series of clicks, but a voice inside him told him to terminate the call. He couldn't explain everything to Jenkins without sounding like a completely mad rogue soldier. He wasn't sure how much Nigel had told Jenkins, so he decided to wait and see if there was another way to connect with Nigel. Perhaps one of the officers at his regiment could help him.

Sweating and frustrated, Steele exited the telephone booth and walked across the shiny marble-floored vestibule back to the terrace, which was abuzz with conversation and downtime gaiety. He made his way back to the table that he had asked Raffaele to hold for him.

He sat down and looked up at the two women who had followed him to his table.

"Hello, Jack," Masha said in Russian. "What are you doing here?"

Steele froze, assuming he was seeing things. Standing in front of him in semi-silhouette because of the sun behind them were—no, it couldn't possibly be—Masha and Astrid."

"Masha?" Steele moved his head to see them from a clearer angle.

Bloody hell. It really is Masha and Astrid.

Steele snatched the white linen table napkin and wiped his forehead. Switching to English for Astrid's sake, he said, "Masha, Astrid, um, have a seat." He looked at them intently as though they were ghosts, still not quite believing what he saw. "What is going on?"

Masha said, "What are you doing here? You remember Astrid—"

"Of course I do." Steele frowned. "Masha, you can't be here."

"What are you talking about? I can be anywhere I want. I defected from my country, remember? I'm free."

"That's not what I meant. How did you even get here? You're a Russian national—"

"Astrid has government connections in Stockholm. I already have an alternative passport and identity."

"This is insane. You should *not* be here. You *cannot* be here."

Astrid said, "Why not?"

"There are things about to happen ..." Steele was at a loss for words. He swallowed. "There are things that might happen here that you do not want to be involved with. Dangerous things."

Masha said, "Believe me, Jack. There's nothing more that can happen to Astrid and me that did not already happen. Her father was shot in front of her, remember."

Steele looked at Astrid and then back to Masha. "Look, I'm very sorry about what happened. But there's a peace summit about to take place here, and you must trust me when I tell you that you don't want to be here. Especially you, Masha. You're putting your life in danger."

"Jack, you must understand two things: One, we are not leaving—there's a reason we are here. And two, when I explain to you why we are here and what we know, trust me when I tell *you* that you will be glad we are here."

"Your *people* are here, Masha. You know who I mean. The people who killed your father. Do you understand what I'm saying?"

"Of course, I understand. But this is Europe, not Soviet Union. There is Italian security, American and Russian security, and an international press pool here for this summit."

"It's supposed to be a secret."

"It's not." Masha glanced at Astrid as if she was seeking Astrid's agreement to voice her next thought.

But Astrid said, "Jack, we know who killed my father. That's why we are here."

Steele said, "You have my full attention."

"Have you heard something about 'Deception Committee?'" asked Masha.

Steele froze. Then he said slowly, "As a matter of fact, I have."

American Nomad, Marina Piccolo, Capri

It was, Oleg thought, a nice touch of tradecraft that the Russian president would be staying aboard a lavish yacht called *American Nomad*.

Claudia climbed out of the open-top taxi, and they greeted each other in front of the small, white Chiesa di Sant'Andrea— Saint Andrew's Church. They made their way down stone steps to the beachfront. Oleg recalled all the scantily clad girls amassed on the public beach the last time he was here. Pity, he thought. Where did they all go?

Although it was October, a tiny armada of luxury yachts still dotted the bay of Marina Piccola. Even in the autumn, yacht owners traveled halfway around the world to drop anchor within sight of the awesome Faraglioni Rocks, Capri's most famous landmark.

Five minutes later, the yacht's Russian captain greeted his compatriots, and Oleg and Claudia climbed aboard the vessel that was so large it had its own helipad.

Apart from the yacht's captain, who helped Claudia onto the boat, no one else was around.

"Thank you, again, for coming," said Oleg. "Welcome aboard."

"I am at your service."

"The president will arrive in Capri today. Would you like to meet him?"

"Of course, that would be a great honor." Claudia followed Oleg's lead and sat down on the white cushioned seats that ringed the stern area of the yacht.

"Good, you will meet him later."

"And the American president?"

"He is also arriving today, but his security detail decided it would be safer to stay at the Quisisana. But there is a change of plan."

"You still need me?"

"Of course, why else would I invite you here?"

"Same plan as we talked about?"

"I will get you through the security ring inside the monastery, and you will do the rest."

"And Steele?"

"Make sure he is close by."

"At the monastery?"

"Yes."

"You want him to witness my mission?"

"Not necessary. He just needs to be 'on location,' so to speak."

"I don't follow."

"The plan is very simple, comrade. I will 'manage' Steele's fall from grace once you have finished your task. I will implicate him in the assassination."

"How?"

"After the assassination, I will make public all the photographs and other evidence we have gathered—this will raise enough questions to implicate him *and* British security services."

"I can't make him stay there. He is already suspicious."

"Tell him to wait in the garden cloister—the one with the old, medieval iron gate. There are only three ways out. Two are with the person who has the key to the gates, and the third is down the well in the middle of the cloister."

"Very good, comrade. I understand."

"I appreciate your—how shall we say—bilateral cooperation. The motherland will be deeply indebted once this despicable business with the DDR has subsided. We will find a way back for your country."

"Even though the wall has fallen?"

"We can rebuild a wall. I will make sure of it. We already did it once after World War Two."

"So, it's tomorrow."

"Our president will go to the monastery for a meeting with the pope. You will complete the task once they have spoken. I will make sure Pope Karl is nowhere near you. We have Vatican helpers."

"I'm confused, Oleg Stepanovich. I am here to liquidate the American president. Steele will take the blame."

"Nearly."

"Nearly?"

"Russia's domestic politics are very complex. My updated plan is to assassinate *my* president."

Claudia set down her drink and sat bolt upright. "But—"

"I know. It is a little confusing."

"This is madness. I cannot be involved—"

"This is business. And you are already involved. Deeply involved. This is the future of the motherland. Remember why you joined the Soviet security services in the first place."

"Comrade Oleg, I remember very well. But I assumed all along it was the Americans—"

"Never assume, dearest Claudia. You must always be ready to change direction or navigate a new course, I should say, given our beautiful location." Oleg gestured to the paradise scenery around them—sparking blue sea, stunning rock formations along the shoreline, and millions of dollars' worth of luxury yachts dotted around.

"I am a trained assassin. I will do my job. But I don't understand—"

"Perhaps now you can see why I recruited you. Russian security cannot be implicated for obvious reasons."

"What about HVA? *My* people."

"My team will extract you immediately after the mission and make you disappear."

"How?"

"Do not worry about details—we are surrounded by sea."

Claudia frowned nervously. "My job is to worry about details."

"I will have you on a boat and back to Berlin via Dubrovnik and Belgrade. No one will ever know you were in Italy."

"Why do you want to assassinate your president?"

"This is a fair question. But it is better for you if you don't know the details. Let me just say that Mikhail Leontev is responsible for the end of the motherland as we know it."

Claudia exhaled. She knew better than to debate this ruthless KGB leader. "As you wish, Oleg Stepanovich."

"You were with me in Berlin. You saw with your own eyes what the West has planned for the German Democratic Republic."

"Yes, I saw."

"Think about this as you carry out your mission."

"Why did you ask if I want to meet your president before tomorrow?"

"I am a curious animal. I thought you might find it useful to assess your target."

"I don't need to meet him."

"As you wish. But think about it."

CHAPTER FORTY-NINE

Grand Hotel Quisisana

The next morning, Masha and Astrid found a table on the terrace for breakfast. There was a cooler breeze in the air now, but it was still pleasant enough to sit outside and—if so inclined— for tourists to spend a few hours on the beach. But the beach was not on their agenda.

"I told you this was a foolish idea," said Masha. "And crazy."

"It's not foolish or crazy. They are both here—American and Russian presidents—arriving today in the name of peace. Meanwhile, my father was murdered by one of them."

"We don't know this."

"Björn told me the truth."

"Tell me exactly what he said."

Masha recalled that Björn was the Swedish admiral's son whom Astrid had dated for a short while and to whom Astrid had given highly sensitive logistics information about her father's general election campaign in Stockholm. If Masha had to guess, Björn might even be one of the reasons—even if not directly responsible—for Aronsson's demise. The Swedish conservative elite hated Aronsson and his liberal vision for nonaligned Sweden. The Swedish military had been cooperating with NATO since 1960, but Aronsson had wanted to make friends with Moscow. In fact, he had been due to fly there for a meeting just weeks after the assassination. It was all too much of a coincidence.

Perhaps Astrid's boyfriend did share more than he realized or was supposed to.

"His father is the top Swedish admiral. He told me details about the Americans no one outside Swedish intelligence could know."

"He's just a boy."

"He's a young man."

"Even if you are right about this information, I still don't understand what you can accomplish here."

"I don't know precisely, but we are here now." Astrid leaned forward and clasped her hands. "Masha, let me ask *you* a question. Why did you come here?"

"I came because you are my friend."

"Sometimes it doesn't seem like it."

Raffaele arrived to take their breakfast order. "Buongiorno, signore. The usual? Two orange juice, two croissants—with honey for one and peanut butter for the other—and one eggs Benedict."

They had only been at the hotel for a day, so Masha was surprised and impressed that Raffaele had remembered their breakfast order.

Astrid nodded. "I'm honored you remembered, and that you have peanut butter."

Raffaele shrugged—both corners of his mouth turned down. "We have many Americans here on Capri."

"What is your name?" asked Masha.

"Raffaele. I am the head waiter here at Quisisana."

"Pleased to meet you, Raffaele."

"Grazie mille. I will return with your breakfast before you can say 'Grand Hotel Quisisana.'"

"Nice man." Masha watched him leave and then turned to Astrid. "I just don't understand what you plan to accomplish here. No one will believe your story."

"I have to try."

"To give top-secret information to America's enemy and live to tell the tale?"

"I am doing it for my father. You, of all people, know what it's like to lose your father."

Masha spoke for a moment without looking at Astrid, "That's true. But I left the Soviet Union to get away from this craziness."

"I understand. And thank you for coming with me even if you don't agree with my intentions."

Masha eyed Astrid. "The truth is that I would not be here without you."

"What do you mean?"

"If we hadn't started writing to each other. If you hadn't encouraged me to leave my country. If you hadn't shared the stories about your father—about freedom and democracy."

"It doesn't seem so wonderful anymore," Astrid reflected.

"I'm glad I came."

"I don't understand why more people don't defect from your country—and from Eastern Europe. I don't even know why my father wanted to visit Moscow and make a new relationship with Leontev. Russians are not our friends."

"It's a good question, but it's complicated."

"Your country sounds like hell. The only reason I would ever want to visit is for the ballet and the caviar."

"It's easy for you to say—Western freedom and democracy are in your blood thanks to your father and people like him."

Astrid leaned her chin on both hands, elbows on the table. "It wasn't worth it."

"What do you mean?"

"I lost my father—the person who meant the most to me. I have never loved anyone so much in my life."

"I'm sorry, Astrid." Masha squeezed Astrid's slender hand. "You never finished telling me what happened to your mother. How did she die?"

"She died when I was young. Cancer."

"Terrible. I'm sorry."

"It's okay, thank you. It was a long time ago. My father meant everything to me, even if I didn't always agree with his politics." Astrid placed her hand on Masha's forearm. "You see why this is important to me. If the Americans were in any way responsible for my father's death—my father's murder—they must pay."

"I understand. But you can't assassinate the American president—and we don't have enough evidence to accuse the American government."

"Maybe we can find a journalist?"

"This summit is supposed to be secret. There is no press. Who are you going to ask? That tourist photographer over there?"

Masha pointed to a roaming photographer with gray hair and thick-rimmed glasses with equally thick lenses. He was politely soliciting hotel guests and passersby to take an impromptu holiday portrait that could be viewed and purchased at his photo booth shop the next day.

"I don't think he will be much help." Astrid smiled. "He's not a reporter anyway. But maybe there's another way."

As she finished her sentence, the gentle buzz of a helicopter high in the air caught their attention. Astrid gestured toward the sky. "You see. Someone important has arrived, and still no press. It doesn't make any sense."

"It's an off-the-record summit, perhaps?"

"And why does *that* make any sense?"

"You're right. It doesn't."

"And neither does the Deception Committee. And both these things together make even less sense. Why would the American president agree to meet the Russian president and not want to tell the world?"

"They have a pool reporter. There's someone from the White House press pool with them always."

"Americans love to be 'open and transparent.' Unless ..."

"Unless what?"

"Unless they decide not to be."

Masha frowned, confused.

"It's bullshit," Astrid continued. "Someone here needs to know the truth. Why don't we tell the Russians? They might listen to you."

"I don't think they will believe a Russian defector and a grieving Swedish politician's daughter. And anyway, you would probably never see me again."

Raffaele arrived with the breakfast tray and placed the continental breakfasts—complete with American condiments—on the table.

Astrid said, "Raffaele, did you know that there is a very important meeting here today? VIPs?"

"On Capri? No, I didn't know this." The waiter avoided their gaze as he spoke.

Masha sensed that Raffaele knew more than he was letting on. "Signor Raffaele, do you know who this woman is?"

"No, signora, I don't. I heard you say, 'Astrid' when you arrived."

"This is Astrid Aronsson. Her father is—was—Anders Aronsson, the Swedish prime minister who was assassinated a month ago."

Raffaele looked at both guests. "I am very sorry to hear this. Please accept my condolences."

Astrid said, "Thank you."

Masha continued, "More than your condolences, Astrid would appreciate your help."

"Of course," said Raffaele. "Whatever I can do. I cannot imagine—"

"We do not need your imagination, Raffaele, we need information."

"I will try."

"Astrid must speak with someone in the Russian delegation. We believe President Leontev's life is in danger."

Raffaele smiled nervously. "I'm sorry, signorine. But I don't know how I can help—"

"We know the Russian president is staying here—here at the hotel," Masha pressed.

"You are mistaken, signora." Raffaele scanned the tables around them before he leaned toward them and said, "I wish I could help you. But the Russian delegation is staying on a private yacht."

"Please, Raffaele," Masha continued. "We must talk to someone in their security detail. We see the helicopter up there, and the number of carabinieri has doubled since we've been sitting here this morning. He must be nearby. His people must be close."

Raffaele cleared his throat. "Signorine, it is true there is a meeting on the island. I don't know where. It might be on a private yacht. There is a VIP staying here at the hotel, but I can confirm it is not the Russian president."

"Then who?"

"I can't say anymore. But if you are certain your information is important—"

"It's a matter of life and death, Raffaele. Please ..." Masha sensed that she was making progress with this hotel observer-in-chief—

Raffaele pointed to a man with a widow's peak seated three tables away from them dressed in a long black cassock—a priest, perhaps. "I believe the church is helping to facilitate this meeting. Perhaps you can talk to this priest if you are worried about a security matter."

"Do you know his name?"

Raffaele leaned toward them. "His name is Vincenzo. He works for the Holy Father."

Masha and Astrid glanced at each other—genuinely surprised and somewhat amused.

Raffaele's voice fell to a whisper. "By God's grace, the Vatican is here to bring peace."

Masha said, "How do you know this?"

Raffaele raised his eyebrows in preparation for the 'intelligence' he was, begrudgingly, about to share. "I oversee the food delivery for this 'unofficial' meeting." He raised his index finger to his mouth.

Masha said, "Thank you, Raffaele. Perhaps we will ask Vincenzo what's on the holy menu."

CHAPTER FIFTY

Certosa di San Giacomo Monastery, Capri

After hearing the news about this so-called "Deception Committee," Vincenzo felt sick. As he walked to the monastery, he began sweating beneath his cassock. What these two foreign women had told him made sense. After all, he was a good judge of character, and the daughter of Anders Aronsson had no reason to lie. She had lost her father under unquestionably tragic circumstances.

He had to warn the Holy Father. *His* Holy Father.

Ever since he had met the Russian here in Capri, he had believed it was the Russians who had instigated this peace summit. All along, any doubts he possessed were *against* the Russians. Why did everyone—including himself—always assume the Americans were above suspicion? He had trusted the Americans' motives for this meeting—the deputy director of the CIA had explained everything in Venice—but now alarm bells were clanging. He still wasn't sure who or what was a potential threat, but an overwhelming sense of danger and imminent threat enveloped him.

He entered the monastery's cypress-tree–lined driveway and passed through a series of checkpoints—first the monastery docents, then members of the Vatican Swiss Guard security— that would lead to the pontiff. Vincenzo was already a familiar figure at the monastery, as he had been helping to prepare for the imminent peace summit.

The pope's presence on the island was supposed to be

a secret. It was odd to be in such close proximity to the Holy Father without seeing the bright orange-red-blue uniforms of the Swiss Guard. But the plain-clothed young men—attempting to be incognito but instead standing out like burned calamari because of their Swiss features, blond hair, and too much sun—were stationed along the tall-ceilinged corridors that led to much narrower passageways inside the fourteenth-century monastery. The sound of his leather shoes echoed around the white-plastered archways as he clipped along at God's speed.

Vincenzo reached a large iron gate that opened onto an exterior courtyard. A senior monk had given Vincenzo his own set of keys, which he now used to open and lock the gate. On the other side of the courtyard was another heavy iron gate that led to the temporary and secret papal apartment location. At the end of this west-wing corridor, Monsignor Fran was seated at a desk. He stood up and raised both arms—he had become the pope's gatekeeper, it seemed. "One moment, Father Alfonso … Vincenzo. His Holy Father is resting."

Ignoring Monsignor Fran point-blank, Vincenzo kept moving. He knocked on the door and entered in one movement. Inside, as expected, Pope Karl was seated behind a small wooden table next to an open window that overlooked the scenic turquoise-emerald sea and the Faraglioni Rocks in the distance.

Vincenzo said, "Your Holiness, I must speak with you urgently." Vincenzo glanced over his shoulder to see Monsignor Fran in the doorway. "Forgive me, but I must speak with the Holy Father in private." Vincenzo stepped back to the door and gently closed it in Monsignor Fran's face.

Monsignor Fran placed his sandal in the door well, but before he could object further, the pope gestured to Monsignor Fran for them to be left alone.

"I am very happy to see you, Vincenzo. Thank you for the work you have done."

"Your Holiness, I have grave news. I fear we are being deceived."

"Please take a seat." Pope Karl gestured to the chair opposite. "Explain."

"Can I ask—?" Vincenzo shifted uneasily on the rickety chair. "Do you trust Monsignor Fran?"

Pope Karl made a fleeting glance toward the closed door. "Of course, I trust him with my life."

"Very good, Your Holiness." Vincenzo took a deep breath. *Steady yourself,* he thought. *God help me if I am wrong.*

"Why do you ask?"

"I was suspicious of the Russians all along. It was just a feeling. But I had no proof to offer you."

"And now?"

"The Russians came to us asking for the summit. I thought it was strange and unusual, but we both agreed it would be a good thing for the world—for world peace—and even for our church."

"We did. You are correct."

"But it seems that the Americans may not have the best intentions. In fact, President Madison himself is the one I am talking about." Vincenzo took a deep breath.

"I don't follow."

"There is something called the 'Deception Committee.'"

Pope Karl looked intently at Vincenzo. The look in his eye seemed to transition from surprise to sadness and finally to a sharp sense of resignation. Vincenzo got his answer without a word leaving the pope's lips.

Vincenzo said slowly, "You know about this, Holy Father?"

Pope Karl stared at the perfect view from his window that was in deep contrast to the not-so-perfect confession he was about to make. "I have not been honest with you, Vincenzo."

Grand Hotel Quisisana

Steele had waited two hours for Claudia to return. She had promised him "something big" was about to happen. There were now two helicopters circling above bijoux Capri, and three times the number of carabinieri were either stationed on street corners or passing by the Grand Hotel Quisisana in small groups as Steele waited for Claudia's return.

Screw it, he thought. *It's now or never.*

From what Masha and Astrid had told him, the VIPs—the presidents? the pope?—were meeting today at the monastery or on a yacht down at Marina Piccolo. Given that the monastery was close by, he would start there and hopefully find this priest, "Vincenzo," or someone from the Vatican to warn—that they were being duped, taken for a holy ride. The so-called peace summit was not what it appeared to be.

Within minutes, Steele had broken a sweat as he forged down the twists and turns of cobblestone pathways and stone steps to the monastery. He had no clue how he would gain entry or if he would gain access to Vatican staff—but he had to try.

What choice do I have? Wait for Claudia? She's an East German spy, for God's sake. God only knows what she's up to and why she brought me here.

Astrid had given him solid evidence that the so-called Deception Committee existed, and despite President Madison's public persona and agenda, it was entirely conceivable—and indeed probably—that his delegation was using this peace summit as a smoke screen for something considerably more nefarious.

Steele slowed his pace as he reached the first monastery attendant. So far, so good—the tourist part of the monastery was still open to the public. Yes, there were helicopters and an increased security presence, but he found it hard to believe that Pope Karl himself was here. He scanned the tourist booklet handed to him by the attendant that would guide him from room to room around the monastery. Given the vast expanse of this landmark tourist gem, he suspected that his chances of finding the Vatican priest were slim to none.

Steele walked down a long, arched-ceiling corridor, made a left, then a right turn, and tried to escape the tourist trail—away from where the guidebook was telling him to go. He reached a large courtyard with what the guidebook said was a working water tower in the far corner that dated back two centuries.

But there was no sign of a security detail, let alone Vatican staff or the pope himself.

Then the painfully obvious occurred to him—if the pope's presence was a secret, simply asking about the pope or anyone from the Vatican might be the worst thing he could do. He didn't have any form of genuine ID; he'd decided it would be a mistake to carry the fake East German diplomatic passport Claudia had used to get him across the Austrian and Italian borders. In other words, he couldn't even prove who he was, even if he located the priest he was searching for.

Steele debated whether to abort and return to the hotel. Perhaps *my best option is with Claudia after all?*

Then he turned a corner and was confronted by a group of Japanese tourists, complete with guidebooks, cameras, and backpacks. Beyond them, a man with blond hair in a gray suit stood at the end of a stone colonnade. He certainly wasn't Japanese and didn't look Italian. He looked more like a … German? Or Swiss?

Then Steele realized … from the height, stature, and hair color, the man at the end of the passageway might be a member of the elite Vatican Swiss Guard.

Finally.

"Hello," Steele said as he approached the man, "Guten Tag." Perhaps the man would respond more positively to German. "Wie geht es Ihnen?" *How are you?*

The young man who looked like an Aryan warrior replied in German. "How can I help you, sir?"

Steele smiled and continued in German. "I need to speak to a priest called Vincenzo. He works for the pope."

"Last name?"

"I'm afraid I don't know."

"Your last name?" The man shot Steele an irritated glance.

"My name's Jack Steele."

"The priest's last name—the one you are looking for?"

"I don't know."

The gray-suited Adonis clicked his radio Pressel box three times but said nothing.

Strange. Perhaps he doesn't understand me? Perhaps I should switch to English?

Before Steele could explain further, two more gray-suited strapping young men appeared from nowhere and firmly grasped both his arms. The first Adonis stepped forward and punched Steele in the stomach.

"What the bloody hell?!" Steele bent double and—winded—struggled for a moment to breathe. He realized that he had made a terrible mistake. These security people were not taking any chances, and his unwanted questions had set off some kind of one-strike-and-you're-out alarm.

Adonis said, "Who are you?"

After exhaling a few times to catch his breath, Steele finally managed: "My name is Jack Steele. I'm a British soldier. I—"

"ID."

"Umm ... ID. It's a long story ... I can explain."

But he couldn't.

Steele reeled through possible explanations—a British soldier kidnapped by an East German spy; a friend of the slain Swedish prime minister's daughter; the British spy responsible for the defection of a Russian admiral's daughter. None of it sounded remotely plausible. It was laughable and absurd.

"I ... I need to speak to Vincenzo. That's all I can tell you. It's a matter of papal security. The pope is in danger."

He blurted out this sensitive piece of information without thinking. Telling these guards he knew the pope was here was probably the worst and last thing he should have said—the nail in his cross.

The Adonis and his two colleagues dragged Steele down several flights of a nearby staircase. The temperature dropped, and daylight disappeared. They were heading down into the bowels of this medieval monastery. A minute later, they reached a corridor lit by very weak, bare electric light bulbs. "Where are you taking me?" Steele asked.

No reply.

But Steele knew the answer. They were in what could only be described as a dungeon passageway. No one except a prisoner would find himself here, whether it was the fourteenth or the twentieth century.

Adonis opened an old wooden door, and the security detail threw Steele into the dungeon onto a wet, slimy floor. "Wait," said Steele. "Please, I need to speak to Vincenzo."

The door slammed shut.

"You don't understand!"

On the other side of the door, the Adonis replied in English, "We understand perfectly, Mr. Steele."

As their footsteps disappeared, Steele turned over on his back. He was lying in a shallow puddle of water. High above him was a small circular window—crisscrossed with bars—that allowed him to make out the cold, wet cobblestones around him that were already making him shiver. "Nice work, Watson," he said to himself, trying to maintain a smidgeon of humor and therefore hope.

CHAPTER FIFTY-ONE

Two hundred feet above Jack Steele on the west side of the monastery in the secret papal apartment, Vincenzo said, "But what is this 'Deception Committee'?"

"Let me finish."

"I'm sorry, Your Holiness."

"You are a loyal servant, and I value your service and friendship."

"Thank you, Your Holiness."

"You are correct about the Deception Committee. I have been in contact with the Americans as we prepared for the summit."

Vincenzo frowned, shaking his head as he spoke. "I don't understand."

"I have a daughter, Vincenzo. Her name is Claudia. Fortunately, she has no idea of my identity, as I left her mother many years ago before I became a priest."

Vincenzo sat still and silent, transfixed on the pope's mouth that seemed—in his mind—to be moving in slow motion as Vincenzo tried to make sense of the shocking revelation.

"The Russians have been blackmailing me for many years. I have had, you might say, one foot in both camps. I have betrayed the church I love and serve."

"Blackmail?"

"Yes, the Russian security services threatened to kill Claudia and her mother if I did not cooperate."

"How did you help them?" Vincenzo probed. He thought about all the planning and steps—meetings, research, letters, calls, faxes—he had taken to arrange this peace summit, and which of Pope Karl's thoughts and sentiments, if any, had been genuine and which had been part of this apparent charade.

"I ignored crucial matters—matters I should not have turned my back on."

"Child abuse?"

"Yes, that was one of them."

"What does it have to do with the Russians?"

Pope Karl sighed. Then he said, "Before Mikhail Leontev rose to his position, by God's grace, I was told to ignore the child abuse scandals in America—on Oleg Stepanovich's order."

"Who is this man?"

"You already know him. You met here."

"The Russian I met here was called Arkady Gregorovich."

"A false name, to be sure."

"And his plan is to—"

"To cover the Americans in a veil of evil."

"I see … I am shocked … I don't know what to say. Perhaps I should not be surprised."

Vincenzo felt as though he was having an out-of-body experience. It was as if he was hovering like a bird outside the open window of this room and looking at himself seated opposite the pontiff. It was as if black was now white, and white was black. His entire world had suffered a seismic shift. Everything he had thought, said, and done in recent months took on a completely new meaning. It was as if someone had turned his sense of good and evil on its head.

"The Russians told you to ignore the sins of our clergy?"

"Yes, above all in America. This was their goal."

"Why America?"

"Whatever happens between America and Russia on the outside, both sides need an enemy. It suits their interests. The worst sexual abuse indiscretions within our brotherhood were in America—within the church. It was a simple but devious goal—"

"Make their adversary the embodiment of evil."

"Yes."

"And you allowed them to do this?"

"If I wanted to save my daughter's life, I had no choice."

"Where is she? Why not tell her? We could have protected her."

"Not so easy. She works for the HVA."

"East German security?"

The pontiff nodded. "She is a wasp within the hive, so to speak."

Out of the corner of his eye, Vincenzo saw the blue sky and sea and nature's gray-textured creation that were the Faraglioni Rocks. He saw the luxury yachts dotted close by and imagined the fun and frivolity, not to mention the obscene and unnecessary money being wasted, as they wined, dined, took drugs, and engaged in whatever else the super-rich do on their private yachts. For a second, Vincenzo felt like running to the window and jumping, knowing that he would plunge to his death two hundred feet below.

But a voice inside him said, *You must act now. I am expecting great things. I am counting on you.*

Vincenzo metaphorically shook himself to his senses. He said, "With respect, Your Holiness, why am I here? Why are *you* here?"

"Everything on God's earth comes down to interests. I have decided I no longer want to be blackmailed. I have decided that perhaps the Americans—my enemy on my side of the Iron Curtain for most of my life—that perhaps the Americans can help me. After all, I am pope."

"But you sold your soul to the Communists. Surely, with respect, it is too late for anyone to help." Vincenzo was verging on blasphemous insubordination.

"I understand you are upset. Angry. You have a right to feel like this."

"What did you do?"

"President Madison wanted a ... favor."

"What kind of favor?"

"He wants to win the Cold War—destroy the Soviet Union as we know it."

"So why have a peace summit?"

Pope Karl smiled. "This peace summit is a façade. The American president's goal is to bring the Soviet Union to its knees."

"But why?"

"Because he can. The biggest secret of the Cold War is not the missiles, warships, submarines, or nuclear weapons. The biggest secret is that the Soviet Union is—and has been for some time—on the verge of economic collapse."

"But they are a superpower. How is this possible?"

"Do you recall the massive explosion of the Yamal pipeline in 1982?"

"Yes, of course. It was the biggest non-nuclear explosion ever recorded."

"It was a three-kiloton burst. And do you know who was responsible?"

"I thought it was an accident."

"The CIA was responsible—the Vatican has proof. I have read certain documents."

"To weaken the Soviet economy?"

"It was just the beginning."

"So the Russians fight back by attacking the Catholic Church?"

"Like President Madison, the famous Hollywood actor, the Russians are good at theater. They make the most of their actors—the talent available."

"They made you one of their 'actors'?"

Pope Karl smiled with sad eyes.

"Why are you telling me this?" asked Vincenzo.

The door opened, and Monsignor Fran appeared. He raised his brow as if time had run out.

Pope Karl said, "Give us a moment."

Monsignor Fran closed the door.

Pope Karl continued, "To answer your original question, dear Vincenzo. The Cowboy-in-Chief is a clever man—charismatic, intelligent … but ruthless. He created a secret committee."

"The Deception Committee."

"Smoke and mirrors to capture the Russian bear."

"I can't imagine the Russian bear will ever surrender."

"Perhaps you are right."

"I thought we were not to be involved in politics."

"A godly sentiment—but in reality, this, I think you understand by now, is impossible."

"Unfortunately, I am starting to understand."

"This much I owe you."

"Thank you, Your Holiness."

"Two years ago, President Madison asked me to host a peace summit."

"Two years ago? That's when I started working for you."

"Correct."

"Why the Vatican?"

"A rich tapestry of conspiracy. It would be more convincing if *we* arranged it."

"If *I* arranged this?"

"Yes. I confess to you that I lied. An evil force at work."

"You are not an evil man."

"Even the Holy Father must confess his sins. Even the Holy Father can fail."

"Is this why you came to Capri? Incognito?"

"I came to escape myself. But events in Berlin have changed everything."

"You gave me this job to work with the Russians, knowing that this is an American aggression all along?"

"I needed someone I could trust. A godly man who would not question me."

"I was wrong to be suspicious of the Russians."

"No, you were right. The Russians are not saints."

"How so, after everything you have told me?"

"The Soviet security services have no conscience, no scruples. They kill, maim, torture, blackmail, and bribe to achieve their goals. I grew up in East Germany. The Stasi are no better. I fell into the trap. A simple East German priest becoming pope was not entirely an act of God."

"The Russians made you pope? I don't believe it."

"Not exactly—but I am saying nothing is ever what it appears to be. Perhaps where you are going, I hope and pray it will be different."

"I will pray for you on my return to Rome. But how will you atone, Holy Father?"

"It is too late for atonement."

"What do you mean?" Vincenzo felt a shiver run down his spine.

This doesn't feel right.

Vincenzo continued, "I propose we hold the peace summit regardless of the circumstances."

Then Father Vincenzo Alfonso heard a metallic click behind him. Had he been a soldier, he would have known that it was the click of a semiautomatic pistol.

But it didn't matter. The *click* was followed by a piercing but muted *bang*. These were the last sounds Vincenzo heard on God's earth.

CHAPTER FIFTY-TWO

American Nomad, *Marina Piccola*

As the helicopter swooped in from Naples Airport, the downwash from the rotor blades lashed at the water surrounding *American Nomad*. Oleg and Claudia sheltered from the air blast in the yacht's bridge area. Oleg also observed the human ants on the beach in the distance—many stood up and came to the water's edge to gawp at the somewhat cinematic action of a helicopter landing on one of the luxury yachts in the distance. Perhaps they thought they would see the VIP passengers from the helicopter or yacht—which, of course, they wouldn't unless they happened to have an astronomer's telescope in their beach bag.

American Nomad's captain greeted his VIPs and escorted them down to the bridge where Oleg and Claudia were waiting, surrounded by a sumptuous repast—Russian style—including vodka, blini, and caviar, but also other Mediterranean seafood hors d'oeuvres. Oleg had helped himself to several morsels of caviar and other delicacies, but the speed at which he ate gave him indigestion.

"Quisisana Hotel has done us proud," he said. "I like this Swedish delicacy they suggested. I never tasted it before. Try it."

As Claudia declined the offer, they turned to see the Russian president and his wife arrive on the rear deck.

"Hello, Comrade," said President Leontev. "I don't think you have met my wife."

Oleg bowed obsequiously. "It is my honor and pleasure to meet you, Irina Borisovich." *This woman is a bitch,* he thought. *No doubt she is complicit in the glasnost and perestroika that are destroying the motherland.*

Irina Borisovich Leontev, the Soviet president's wife, acknowledged Oleg with a deadpan expression. "I have heard much about you, Oleg Stepanovich."

"I hope you approve," Oleg replied. He gestured toward the table, but then he remembered Claudia. "Forgive me, I nearly forgot. Allow me to introduce my colleague from HVA."

Nods and more obsequious and disingenuous smiles were exchanged, and Oleg felt an undercurrent of friction and distrust directed toward him, mainly from Irina. Thinking on his feet, he decided he needed to separate the president from his wife as soon as possible. Oleg gestured to the table. "Please tell our steward what you would like to eat—or drink."

Leontev, it seemed, wasn't hungry. He sat down and said, "So tell me, Fraülein ...?"

"Please, Comrade President, I would be honored if you call me Claudia."

Oleg was impressed. Nothing like charming the target you have orders to assassinate.

Leontev continued, "Very well. Where are you from, Claudia?"

"Berlin, Comrade President."

"I studied in Berlin, many years ago. Wie geht es ihnen heute, Fraülein Claudia?"—*How are you today, Miss Claudia?*—Leontev chuckled and eyed Oleg. "So, I wasn't informed this had become a Russo-American-German affair." He looked at Claudia suspiciously.

"Nothing to worry about, Comrade President," Oleg added. "After recent events in Berlin, Claudia and her talents have become indispensable. As you can understand, the geo-political situation has become considerably more complex overnight.

Our HVA colleague has become invaluable as we navigate this new era."

Leontev said, "I think I am hungry after all. Irinichka, please eat something, my dear."

Oleg and Claudia remained standing as a steward served the VIP guests.

"So, we meet with Madison today?" asked Leontev.

"That's correct, comrade president. At two pm."

"Are they coming here? The yacht is a perfect setting."

"No, sir. The Americans requested we meet at the monastery. For security reasons."

"And the pope? I was looking forward to meeting the Holy Father."

"But sir, that's not—"

"I, too, have my spies, Oleg Stepanovich." He smiled.

"The Holy Father is happy to accommodate us, but I'm afraid a face-to-face meeting will not be—"

"Nonsense, Oleg Stepanovich. I insist." He turned to Irina. "Would you like to meet Pope Karl?"

Irina pulled a face that made it clear she was ambivalent on the matter.

How do they know about the pope? thought Oleg. *I don't like surprises, and I don't like politicians going behind my back.*

Oleg quickly revised his plan. There was no way Oleg himself could be a part of the entourage—it would spoil everything. There was only one possibility: Claudia would accompany his loyal KGB officers to the monastery *with* Mikhail Leontev. But Oleg would have to deal with Steele and make sure he was in the best location inside the monastery to be implicated in the assassination. A meeting with the pope was the last thing he needed to add to the agenda—he couldn't imagine who had leaked the pope's location to Leontev—but whatever the new circumstances, he would adapt to the situation, his end goal uppermost in his mind. This was how, at the young age of thirty-two, he had reached the position he had reached within the KGB. *Nothing is going to stop me. Leontev cannot be allowed to remain in power—it will be the end of the motherland.*

Everyone paused to watch the helicopter taking off.

"Where is he going?" asked Leontev. "Don't we need him to get to the monastery?"

"It is easier by private motor launch, Mr. President," reassured Oleg. "Much safer and less conspicuous."

"Understood." Leontev nodded and leaned forward to help himself to more caviar and blini. "If we are meeting Madison at two pm, we will need to leave soon. Please have your contact request I meet with Pope Karl at one-thirty."

"Very good, Comrade President," replied Oleg. "Everything will be arranged as you wish."

"Please, help yourself," continued Leontev, "there is plenty here." He pointed to the spread of hors d'oeuvres. "Fraülein Claudia, I am sure Comrade Oleg has taught you how to enjoy caviar when you were in Berlin together. Bitte sehr, nicht Scheu sein." *Help yourself, and don't be shy.*

Oleg stepped forward. "Forgive me, Comrade President … if you don't mind me asking. Who told you about Pope Karl's presence on the island? Why do you want to speak with him?"

Leontev frowned. "None of your business, Oleg Stepanovich."

Oleg bristled, stopping just short of blushing red with anger. He did not enjoy being reprimanded in front of two women. Nevertheless, he said, "Forgive me, Comrade President—"

"I was joking with you, Oleg Stepanovich. Come, now. Try not to be so serious. This is a day of great progress and celebration."

"Sir …?"

Leontev continued, "You have done a great thing here, Oleg Stepanovich. This summit will bring value and great progress to the future of the motherland. We finally have the Americans coming to meet us halfway."

Oleg replied, "I don't understand, Comrade President."

"Glasnost. Perestroika. Our efforts to be transparent and progressive are reaping rewards already. And as for the pope, it is my idea to talk to him." Leontev looked at Claudia. "He hails from Berlin too, you know?"

"Yes, Comrade President, I am aware."

"I think it would make sense to offer the Catholic Church some incentives in our country in the future—a sign of the times. An apolitical and spiritual act of goodwill."

It was all Oleg could do to stop himself from choking on his blini and caviar. *What is this buffoon planning?* "I … I think we should talk—"

"Think about it, Oleg Stepanovich," Irina interrupted. "This is the perfect opportunity to do something beyond politics. The world is watching."

"With respect, Irina Borisovich, it is not a good idea to mix politics and religion."

Precisely what Leontev had in mind was anyone's guess. But Oleg knew—as he always knew and had learned over the years—that he must adapt to the situation in real time. The last thing he needed was the Roman Catholic Church having any kind of influence or even power over the precarious, existential balancing act that was now the Soviet Union. Oleg was desperately trying to mastermind the rebuilding of an unraveling empire, the instigator-in-chief of which was sitting right in front of him. He thought about drawing his pistol and shooting Leontev in the head right then and there. But that wasn't part of the plan, and he would also have to shoot Irina and the yacht captain too. Someone might be watching from another yacht or the beach, especially after the helicopter had attracted so much attention to the yacht. Carabinieri—and almost certainly Secret Service or CIA or both, doing their due diligence—were also probably observing from a safe distance. His idea was unsound.

He would allow the meeting between the pope and Leontev to go ahead. Afterward, Claudia would complete her task in the secrecy of the monastery that was currently—intentionally so—now controlled by the Vatican Swiss Guard. He was confident the pope would stick to his side of the bargain.

Oleg stepped down inside the cabin next to the bridge and motioned for Claudia to follow.

Oleg spoke in a hushed tone. "Allow the meeting between the pope and Leontev to go ahead as he wishes."

"And Irina Borisovich?"

"I will ensure she stays on the yacht."

"I understand. And Steele?"

"Where is he?"

"At the hotel—safe and sound. Ready for his task."

"I'll send one of my men to get him and bring him to the monastery. Are you sure he is at the hotel?"

Claudia nodded and said, "Of course, where else would he be?"

"Proceed as planned with Steele."

"I will not fail you."

Oleg's eyes narrowed. "I respect your work and your talent, but I find these operations work better if my team has an incentive ..."

"Of course, I understand. What is my incentive, Oleg Stepanovich?"

"If you fail this mission, it will be your last."

CHAPTER FIFTY-THREE

Certosa di San Giacomo Monastery, Capri

S teele walked slowly around the cell, trying to see where the floor was dry. At some point, he would have to sit down. He ran his hands over the wall space in case there was a way to climb up and reach the window high above him. But even if there was some fortuitous, magic rock wall that led to the window, breaking the damned thing at ceiling height would be a physical impossibility.

His only way out was to hope that Claudia would somehow find him. *The godly irony*, he thought. *I am praying for and counting on an East German agent to rescue me from the Vatican Swiss Guard inside a Catholic monastery.*

After what seemed like an eternity sitting in the dark, colder-by-the-minute dungeon, Steele still had no plan. It was futile even to brainstorm—to formulate your "actions-on," as he learned at Sandhurst. The only "action" he could muster was to bang on the door a few times and shout. No one replied, and all he could hear was water trickling down or through the stones in his cell.

Another fifteen minutes went by, and then he heard footsteps. Moments later, the door opened, and two tall men walked in carrying something large and heavy, which they placed unceremoniously on the ground near Steele.

He said, "There's been a misunderstanding. I need to speak to Vincenzo. Please."

The men in suits backed up as though they couldn't get away fast enough. They were about to close the door, so Steele tried in German. "Please, you must find Vincenzo for me. I am a British army officer."

The taller of the two men—Steele could see that it was the "Adonis" from earlier—said, "You are a long way from home. My suggestion is that you keep quiet unless you want to end up like him."

Steele looked down at the disheveled shape on the ground and realized it was a human body. "What are you doing?" he asked incredulously. "Who is that?"

"Your wish is our command, Mr. Steele. Meet your friend, Vincenzo. Sorry, he won't be able to answer your questions." The door slammed shut, and the dungeon went black. Steele took a few steps back from the body and waited for his eyes to become accustomed to the dark. The light from the tiny window finally allowed him to see the body. He walked forward and extended his foot. He poked at the body, and his worst fears were confirmed. If this *was* the priest called Vincenzo, it was a very deceased Vincenzo.

Steele felt light-headed. He stumbled backward until he hit the wall and sank down on his haunches. He placed his hands on his head and clawed his scalp.

"Fuck!" he said. *"What the fuck am I doing here?"*

Seeing the corpses from the car crash at the Sennelager training area was terrible. *But this,* he thought, *is the darkest moment in my life.*

True to his word, Oleg had insisted Irina remained on the yacht for "security" reasons. Now the plan was to allow Leontev to have his meeting with the pope and then escort him to another part of the monastery on the pretext that he was about to meet the American president.

Claudia would lead him to a secluded part of the monastery she had scouted. But even if everything went according to plan, Oleg had been clear that Steele *must* be implicated in the assassination by his physical presence at or near the execution.

As they entered the monastery, Claudia walked a few steps behind President Leontev. She was accompanied by two KGB officers who were under her command as per Oleg's orders.

A third KGB officer met them as they reached the first cloister and approached Claudia. He whispered, "I can't find the British asset."

Claudia replied, "He's at the hotel. He knows the summit is about to take place. I told him I would send for him."

"I understand. He wasn't in his room. I looked everywhere."

"That's not possible."

"I'm sorry."

"The head waiter told me Steele was asking about the monastery."

"That makes no sense."

"I understand."

"Find him. You *must* find him. I will join you."

The KGB officer peeled off as two members of the Vatican Swiss Guard led the Russian entourage down exterior stone passageways, across cloisters, and past great works of art by Karl Wilhelm Diefenbach hanging on interior walls. As soon as the president was safely in the papal apartment, Claudia would help her KGB colleagues find Steele. Time was running out. If she didn't find Steele, their plan to assassinate the Soviet president would fail.

At this moment, she had no idea of Oleg's whereabouts. His men had intermittent radio contact, but even if she had the capability to send a message, Claudia did not want to sew any seed of doubt in Oleg's mind about her ability to execute the mission. She specifically ordered the KGB officer not to tell Oleg that Steele was missing.

Up ahead, just within earshot, the group arrived at a desk

situated outside the door to the papal apartment. A Vatican Monsignor introduced himself as "Monsignor Franciszek."

The Monsignor welcomed the president, they shook hands, and Monsignor Francizek opened the door to Pope Karl's office. The two men shook hands, Leontev entered, and the KGB minders hovered outside. Claudia approached one of the pope's security men.

"My name is Claudia Rohweder. I am with President Leontev's security detail."

"Captain Bernsteiner—Klaus. Welcome to Capri. How can I help you?"

"We believe there is a foreigner on the monastery grounds posing as British army personnel. If he is here, or your men find him, I need to take custody of him immediately."

"Who is he?"

"His name is Hans Birkner." Claudia pulled the fake East German passport from her back pocket. She hesitated for a moment as she formulated her next sentence carefully. "We believe he might pose a threat to the peace summit. He has been under a great deal of stress recently. He had a bad fall on an assignment in London and has not fully recovered."

The Swiss Guard said, "I know this man."

"You know him?" Claudia snapped.

"Yes, we already have him in custody."

"What?" Claudia smiled nervously, barely able to hide her relief. "How?"

"I wondered why his German is so good. Now it makes sense."

"This is very important. Please explain."

"As you know, we have a detailed list of all security personnel, officials, and VIPs allowed in the monastery today. You are on the list." He held up his clipboard and flipped to a page with Claudia's name and photograph. "The British subject—East German, I mean—is not on the list. I personally memorized all the headshots we received."

"Where ... did you find him?"

"He was in close proximity to the Holy Father's apartment."

"Where is he now?"

"He is safely away from the area—this afternoon's events."

"I need to speak to him immediately."

"Of course. I can take you to him. Or we can bring him to the cloister courtyard—there are gates on both sides—if you prefer to stay close to President Leontev. The Americans will be arriving shortly. We don't have much time."

Claudia couldn't believe her luck. "Yes, thank you, Captain Bernsteiner—Klaus." She smiled flirtatiously and touched his forearm. "That would be helpful. Unfortunately, this man is deluded about his role here today. I will have one of my men escort him from the monastery."

Steele slowly walked toward the corpse. If this *was* Father Vincenzo, as the Adonis who had locked him up had suggested, it made no sense whatsoever. Why would a priest who was staying at the Quisisana Hotel—by all accounts directly connected to the pope—be lying here dead?

Steele scanned the lifeless body, trying to see how the man had died. He crouched down close to the body and shook the man's arm for signs of life. Then he lifted the man's limp wrist to check for a pulse. *This man is dead.*

Then, as he looked at the cassock the man was wearing, he noticed a moist area around the dead man's heart. Steele was no expert, but it looked like Vincenzo had been shot in the back because the exit wound was clearly visible on the front of his body.

Almost as if Steele was trying to lay Vincenzo to rest, he carefully rolled the corpse from a crumpled heap onto his back. As Steele placed Vincenzo's arms onto his front, he heard the faintest sound of keys in one of the pockets. Steele patted the body. He felt a bundle of keys inside the man's cassock pocket.

Perhaps this dead priest is carrying a key that might get me out of here? God works in mysterious ways.

Steele retrieved the keys, stood up, and walked toward the door. He felt for the lock in the near darkness and tried to match the size of the keyhole to one of the keys in the bunch. He attempted to insert the first key, then a second, then a third— without success. Steele made a mental note of which keys he had tried as he worked his way around the bunch, trying each key. It was like a perverse Russian key roulette, he thought, with escape instead of death as the outcome.

Still no divine intervention—still no magic key that would open this door and get him out.

Then he heard footsteps. Seconds later, the door opened, but unfortunately for Steele, it was unlocked from the outside.

Now what? he thought. *Where is Claudia, and what the bloody hell is going on?*

He placed the keys in his pocket and sank down on the floor.

CHAPTER FIFTY-FOUR

"You have done well," said Monsignor Fran. "It's time. Leontev will arrive any minute."

"I know why you are doing this," said Pope Karl.

"We are spreading the word of God."

"I know you plan to kill me, too."

"Nonsense, Excellency. You have read too many conspiracy thrillers. You will remain in Capri and live out your days in blissful ignorance, as we agreed."

"Was it necessary to kill Vincenzo? I did not agree to this travesty."

"Vincenzo knew too much, Excellency. I warned you about your need to share—to be too honest. Even God must master discretion."

"He was a good man."

"So are you."

"I am not a good man. I deserve what you have planned for me."

Monsignor Fran smiled. "You are making this too easy, Most Holy Father. But you are wrong. There are no plans to kill you. You flatter yourself, Your Holiness."

"I deserve my penance. Please keep your word when you become pope. We must cleanse the church of hypocrites."

"Let us see if the Russian president can help our plan come to fruition."

There was a knock on the door.

"Enter," said Monsignor Fran, raising his voice slightly.

A Swiss Guard opened the door and nodded. Monsignor

Fran acknowledged the heads-up and walked toward the door to welcome the Russian president.

President Leontev was a much smaller man than Monsignor Fran had imagined. "Please, Mr. President. Pope Karl is honored to receive you." With a two-handed handshake followed by a flourish of his right arm, he ushered Leontev into the pope's office-cum-sitting room.

Pope Karl stood up to welcome his visitor and made the sign of the cross.

Monsignor Fran said, "You have much to discuss. I will leave and give you privacy."

Pope Karl thanked his papal assistant—Monsignor Fran, who, like the Russians, had used Claudia's very existence to black-mail him. Nevertheless, the pontiff blamed himself for allowing the situation to spiral out of control once the Russians had set the wheels in motion many years earlier. He also blamed himself for not having the strength to stand up to Monsignor Fran.

Pope Karl beckoned his guest toward his desk and asked, "English or German? I'm afraid my Russian is mediocre at best."

"I always enjoy practicing my English. But I wish my wife was here—she would enjoy teaching you some Russian."

"Please take a seat. I have been looking forward to meeting you."

President Leontev said, "It is my pleasure. I thank you and your Vatican colleagues for your cooperation on the summit." He glanced out of the open window. "I envy your view. It is much more pleasant than mine in the Kremlin. If you look carefully, you can see our floating hotel. She's called *American Nomad*—ironic, don't you agree?"

"Very." Pope Karl chuckled. "The envy, however, is all mine. I wish I could spend a day on the water. I can't recall the last time I shed these holy vestments during the day."

"We are both slaves to duty. There are worse fates."

Pope Karl clasped his hands. "In fact, this meeting—this peace summit—is not what it seems to be."

"Really, Excellency? And how is that?"

"The reason we arranged this meeting is for you to meet the American president in these troubled times."

"The Eastern bloc? Of course, I understand your concern. But I can assure you, we have everything under control."

"Do you?"

"Berlin is a fait accompli. But Germany is a special case. I have known for many years it would come to this. I think it is impossible to keep a country divided forever. But the rest of the Eastern bloc is safe in our hands."

"And what do you know about the Americans?"

Leontev frowned. "I don't understand. Is there something I *should* know?"

"Yes, there are two things I would like to bring your attention to before you meet President Madison. Once you know these things, you might wish to 'adjust' your plans. That, of course, is your decision."

"You have my full attention."

As he began to speak, Pope Karl unclasped his hands and placed one on each knee. "We thank God, and we are very impressed with the work you have done to bring your country to—shall we say—more modern times. We are sure there are many who do not want you to succeed both inside and outside your country."

"I do not disagree." Leontev nervously smoothed back his virtually nonexistent hair.

"We would like to request a new initiative to bring our churches closer—Russian Orthodox and Roman Catholic— brothers-in-bibles, so to speak."

"Interesting idea. I am not sure—"

"Please, Mr. President, let me finish. We are looking for new horizons. We have not always felt welcome in the Soviet Union."

"Don't tell me—you want to open a seminary in Moscow?" Leontev smiled.

"That would be welcome in the future. For now, we simply wish to send many more Catholic priests to Russia, build more churches in your country, and be free to offer our 'perspective' as we do in other parts of Europe."

"But there are already many Catholic churches in my country."

"In fairness, 'many' would be an exaggeration. The number of Catholics in Russia and the Soviet Union is a tiny segment of your majestic population."

Leontev considered the proposition. "Your Holiness, you understand we have much going on. I am doing my best to bring peace and progress to my country. Why is this so important to you on this auspicious day?"

"Quid pro quo, Mr. President—a concept as old as time. I am going to share a secret that might end the Soviet Union as you know it."

President Leontev leaned forward and spoke in a whisper. "Your Holiness, that is precisely my goal. I have not uttered this sentiment to another living soul—apart from my beloved Irina. But, as you can imagine, I must be very, *very* careful about my intentions and every decision I make. *Even,* as you point out, in my own country."

"You misunderstand, Mr. President. What I am saying is that your enemies want to crush you *and* your country. The end of the Soviet Union is not enough for them. They are conspiring to terminate your 'superpower' status forever. Your Russian economy and global standing will be reduced to that of third-world status."

"'Enemies?' Who are you referring to?"

"When you came to us with your proposal for a peace summit, we embraced the idea. But like all important and consequential matters, nothing is ever what it seems."

"I agree. We are dealing with extremely complex matters—I plan to be measured in my actions. But I still don't understand—who are you talking about? The Americans?"

"Of course, the Americans. You don't need me to tell you this."

"Why am I here today if what you say is true?"

"Deception, dear Mr. President. Please listen carefully to what I am about to tell you. You are being *deceived*."

Grand Hotel Quisisana

"Sons of bitches!" he muttered venomously. "I will kill both of them."

Oleg Stepanovich had heard enough. He ripped off his headphones and threw them on the bed of his temporary "operations center" in room 753. The listening device had done its job, but the words coming from Pope Karl's mouth filled him with a rage he had not felt in a long time.

Not only had his president acquiesced and sanctioned the end of the Soviet Union, but now Leontev was considering and even agreeing to a new wave of Roman Catholic propaganda in Russia. Not only were the Americans intent on bringing the Soviet Union to its knees, but from what he could fathom, the motherfucking Vatican was now adding to the unfolding disaster.

Oleg hated his own Russian Orthodox Church and all the sanctimonious preaching and nonsense—that infernal incense was intolerable and had always made him cough uncontrollably as a boy. He had endured his own church over the years, but to have the Roman Catholic Church and a new wave of its pedophile priests among the Russian people was anathema to his very core. The last thing he needed was for *his* president to be hailed a hero on the international stage and for the Vatican to become Leontev's geopolitical guardian angel.

Mikhail Pavlovich Leontev must fail in his attempt to make peace. Only then will his assassination be acceptable to the Russian people.

At that moment, Oleg made the decision—contrary to all the espionage training he had ever learned—to go to the monastery. He needed to change the plan and get physically closer to the assassination he had ordered for the simple reason that if his plan failed, it would mean the end of the Soviet Union and probably Russia as he knew and loved it. It occurred to him that he might even be forced to take over the mission if Claudia failed.

As he gathered up his tools of the trade—knife, two pistols with silencers, ammunition, garotte—Oleg chastised himself for allowing the meeting between Leontev and the pope to take place. But Leontev had been suspicious about Oleg's motives and allegiances. Forbidding his president to meet the pope would have raised further doubts in Leontev's mind, and the last thing he wanted on this day was for his target to be suspicious of anyone.

It was clear what had to be done. If the Vatican was allowed to make a pact with Leontev, it would be impossible to keep communism alive and save his motherland from the west. *And,* he pondered, *how does the pope know about the Deception Committee? Is the damned Deception Committee a false flag operation after all?*

"Nothing makes bitching sense," he muttered under his breath to no one in particular. "I *hate* unanswered questions." Oleg discharged a string of expletives as he strapped the first pistol to his lower leg and placed the second inside the waistband of his trousers at the small of his back.

I will kill this pope if he thinks he can work with the Americans against my country, he thought.

It would take Oleg five minutes to reach the monastery on foot.

CHAPTER FIFTY-FIVE

Certosa di San Giacomo Monastery, Capri

After a brief struggle and a punch to his abdomen, Steele spent the next few minutes taking deep breaths as the Swiss Guard Adonis escorted him up to the courtyard near the papal apartments, where Claudia was waiting.

"Bitte sehr, Fräulein Claudia. Here is your colleague." He turned to Steele. "Apologies for the misunderstanding, sir."

Steele said, "Apology not accepted. But thanks for the punch."

The man did not reply and left the serene courtyard, closing the gate behind him.

Claudia gripped Steele's forearm and led him to the wooden bench where they sat down.

"What is going on?" asked Steele. "There's a dead priest in the dungeon below. I'm going to the police."

"Why did you leave the hotel?"

"I wanted to find out what the bloody hell is going on. Where's this summit you promised?"

"I don't know anything about the priest, but I have my orders. If you want to stay out of the dungeon, wait here."

"Just sit here and meditate? For how long?"

"You cannot leave the monastery without my permission. We are locked down for the summit, and I cannot guarantee your safety—or freedom—if you refuse to follow orders. I still have the photographs, and they will arrest you in one second if I tell the Italian authorities who you are."

Steele shook his head in frustration. "I hope this is worth it."

"Is your freedom, your career, and your life worth it? My superior is not a patient man."

Steele's head was pounding as he struggled mentally to accept his situation. He took a deep breath.

"Jack, you only have one life."

Steele eyed Claudia. "What does that mean?"

"You decide. You can tell your people everything about the Deception Committee when we have finished here."

"What if I tell the press instead? I saw a BBC journalist at the hotel. He's here for the not-so-secret summit, but I'm sure he'd be interested in an unexpected blockbuster headline."

"It's up to you. I don't care. All this will come out sooner or later. You are here to witness the most important bilateral meeting of the new era of glasnost and perestroika."

Steele leaned forward, his hands clasped. He caught sight of a centipede crawling through blades of grass between the stone slabs. "Why me, Claudia? Why did you choose me?"

She placed her hand on his back, and he recalled the night they slept together in Berlin and wished he hadn't.

"Jack—we already discussed this. You found *me*."

"Fate, right?"

Claudia did not reply. She stood up and walked toward the west gate of the courtyard. "I will be back soon. Be ready to practice your Russian. You are going to meet the Soviet president."

The corners of Steele's mouth turned upward, but he wasn't smiling.

Claudia closed the gate. "I have the key. Unless you want to jump down the well, stay here this time."

Steele leaned back. He wasn't sure whether to laugh or cry. He was running on adrenaline, but part of him wondered why death and destruction had followed him ever since he met Claudia in Berlin. He had no doubt that she had not told him the truth—yet here he was. *She's an East German spy, for God's sake; why did I think she would tell me the truth?* But parts of her story *did* make sense, and he wanted to get to the bottom of this international web of lies, secrets, murder, and deception.

He closed his eyes and dropped his hands beside him.

Then he heard them. The keys. He still had the keys he had taken from the priest.

Think, he told himself. *Just* think *before you act.*

Claudia marched toward the papal office. The holy meeting would be finished at any moment, and she would escort Leontev back through the cloister to the courtyard. The gunshot might be heard, but she would wipe her weapon clean and throw it into the courtyard as per Oleg's orders. Her KGB colleague would shoot Steele—in self-defense, and no one would care much about the demise of the Russian president's assassin. It was—she had to admit—an ingeniously simple plan. Once Steele's identity had been confirmed—that he was not, in fact, an East German diplomat—Claudia would disappear, but not before she passed the photographs of Steele's movements over the last few months to the Italian authorities. Any suspicion that this was an "inside job" by Russian or Eastern bloc actors would be averted. The chances of British intelligence services stepping forward at this stage to save their man were slim to none, she assessed.

As she reached the papal apartment, Monsignor Fran stood at the open door. Leontev was exiting, seemingly upbeat, and ready for his meeting with the American president.

"We very much appreciate your cooperation," Monsignor Fran said in English. "God bless the citizens of the Soviet Union. You will excuse me. I must go and welcome President Madison."

Leontev walked toward Claudia when he saw her waiting for him.

"How was the meeting, Mr. President?" she asked. "I hope it went well."

"It was a most enlightening encounter. Where are we going now?"

"This way, Mr. President. The Vatican people suggested you meet with President Madison in the west cloister. It is peaceful there, and secure."

Claudia steadied her breathing. She had killed before, but her target had been a low-level mafioso type from Russia who was trying to set up a drug ring in Berlin. Until this moment, it had not crossed her mind that assassinating this man might be difficult. Now, as she led Leontev to his death, she could not help asking the question, *Can I do it?*

The clicking of Leontev's leather shoes on the stone cobble-stones brought her back to the task at hand. The KGB detail had surreptitiously disappeared as per Oleg's orders, and the Vatican had also issued orders to the Swiss Guard to make themselves scarce. The only other person around when she assassinated the president would be Jack Steele.

"I had a very interesting conversation with the pontiff," Leontev offered as they closed a heavy wooden door that led to an exterior passageway where they could see the sun and blue sky once again.

"I am pleased, Mr. President." They turned another corner as Claudia continued, "This way, sir."

"Your father is a flawed but worthy opponent."

Claudia immediately slowed down.

"What did you say?"

"Your father has many flaws, but I think his heart is in the right place."

Claudia stopped dead. "I don't understand," she said hesitantly.

"Pope Karl is your father."

"Mr. President, please explain. Is this a joke? What are you talking about?"

"I realize this is a shock. But you don't need to kill me. In fact, I suggest you go and talk to your father. If you shoot me, you will never meet your father—I'm sure you understand."

"But I—" Claudia stepped backward, almost stumbling. Then she caught herself and drew her pistol. *It's now or never,* she thought. "Very clever, Mr. President. Nice try." *How does he know?*

"No trick, Claudia. Do you know where your father is?"

"No ... no, I don't. What are you saying?"

"Your father's name was Joseph Rohweder before he became a priest and before he was blackmailed by our ruthlessly efficient security services."

"Blackmailed?"

"I had no idea—until recently. Your father loves you very much. He did all this for you."

"All what?" Claudia's face flushed red, and she took short, quick breaths. "All what?" she repeated. "What are you saying? My name is Claudia Rohweder. I am an East German operative working with Oleg Stepanovich—" Then she stopped, realizing how ridiculous she sounded. "Who told you about my father?" She raised the pistol and pointed it at Leontev's head.

"I am the leader of the Soviet Union—I know everything there is to know. Thanks to your father, I even know about Madison's Deception Committee."

The feeling in her gut told her that this man—*her target*—was telling the truth. "Tell me what is going on, or I will shoot you."

"As you already planned so meticulously."

"How do you—"

"Oleg Stepanovich is not the only one with his finger on the pulse."

"Explain," Claudia demanded. In a matter of seconds, she could feel her sweating palms loosening the grip on her weapon.

"Oleg is a very clever operative. But he is not the only cunning and competent agent in the KGB. My wife, Irina, is a retired KGB officer. I am fully aware of his plan to use *you* to assassinate *me*."

Claudia's hand began to tremble.

"Please, my dear Claudia ... I don't blame you. In fact, I commend you. I commend your loyalty and your service to our cause. You are a *loyal* Communist."

"My orders are to shoot you."

"Yes, but if you do, you will *never* meet your father. Oleg Stepanovich is a clever man—unscrupulous but clever. He has been planning this, planning to use *you* for several years. He was waiting for the right opportunity. Of course, his KGB loyalists are deluded. I will deal with them in due course."

Now things began to make sense. Her relatively easy and painless ride to a senior position in the HVA; her occasional double take at newspaper photographs over the years when Pope Karl looked strangely familiar; and finally, the seemingly coincidental encounter with Oleg Stepanovich in Berlin that had led to her undercover mission to seduce a British military asset. It all led to this moment—the assassination of the USSR's president.

"I ... I don't believe you." *But I* do *believe him*, Claudia thought as she lowered her weapon.

Something inside her snapped—or "released" was a more accurate description.

"It's your choice, Claudia. You can kill me now, or you can meet your father. But you can't do both."

Claudia swallowed and began to move away from Leontev—slow, measured steps.

"One question."

"Please, Claudia."

"How did you know I wouldn't shoot you?"

"I didn't. But my wife is a good judge of character. She likes you."

Claudia turned and ran. More than anything else in the world, she wanted to meet her father.

CHAPTER FIFTY-SIX

Grand Hotel Quisisana

"**R**emind me to have someone buy a gift for Barbara," said President Madison. "I'll never hear the end of it if I don't bring my wife something from Italy's island jewel."

Webster replied, "Will do, sir. Apparently, Carthusia Parfumeria Capri is the place."

"Great. Do it. Don't spend less than $500."

"I forgot to tell you, sir. Frank Sinatra stayed in this very suite more than fifty years ago."

"And it looks like the décor hasn't changed. Can't these Europeans spruce it up a bit? It's a five-star hotel, for God's sake."

"I think that's the point—why it's so popular. Sense of familiarity, even a Hollywood hangout back in the day."

Madison grunted and straightened his tie in the mirror. "When are we leaving?"

At that moment, the telephone rang.

The president's CIA deputy director picked up. "Webster."

"Sir, there's a young lady at the front desk asking to speak to the president."

"And your point is?"

"It's Astrid Aronsson," replied the somewhat flustered Secret Service agent speaking from the Grand Hotel Quisisana lobby.

"What?"

"Yes, sir. The daughter of—"

"I know who she is, Leiniger. What does she want?"

"She … she wants to speak to the president—in person."

Webster frowned and placed his hand over the speaker. "Mr. President, it's one of our men downstairs. Apparently, Astrid Aronsson is here. She wants to speak to you—in person."

Madison twisted his face in surprise and frustration. "I don't like surprises. Find out what she wants."

Webster said, "Leininger, is she still there?"

"Yes, sir. She's standing next to me. I only called because … well, she's Aronsson's daughter—"

"Ask her what she wants?"

Webster heard his question being repeated. Then, "Sir?"

"Yes, I'm listening. You're on speaker with POTUS."

"She says she has some questions about the 'Deception Committee.' Says POTUS will understand."

Madison's eyes widened, and his face became two shades redder than his piping-hot shower had already made him. "What the fuck?!" he mouthed.

Webster said, "I'll call you back. We are about to leave for the summit."

"Yes, sir. We are all set here. It's just that—"

"We'll be down in five."

"And sir …"

"What is it?"

"The press seems to have gotten wind of us after all. Mostly Italian, but some international."

"Understood. Stick to protocol, and just be polite for now." Webster hung up and turned to POTUS. "I don't understand, sir."

"Goddamn it, man. You better figure it out—and fucking fast."

"It's not possible."

"As I have told you many times, Kolby, anything's possible, probable, *and* preventable in the world of politics. Here's what we're going to do about Astrid Aronsson."

"Yes, sir?"

"Absolutely fucking nothing."

"Loud and clear, Mr. President."

Certosa di San Giacomo Monastery, Capri

As Claudia approached the pope's Certosa di San Giacomo Monastery apartment, the door stood ajar. Monsignor Fran was not at his gatekeeper's desk outside.

She reached the door and heard a familiar voice—a Russian voice and one other, presumably that of the pope.

Claudia could feel her heart pounding. She considered drawing her pistol but changed her mind. *If I am about to meet my father, I would rather not shoot him by mistake.*

As expected, Pope Karl was still seated behind his desk. But what she had not expected was to see Oleg standing behind the door.

"I expected greater things, Claudia," Oleg began.

"Oleg Stepanovich? What are you doing here?" Claudia's eyes darted from the Russian to the pontiff and back to the Russian.

"I came to tie up loose ends I could not trust you with. It seems that my suspicions were founded."

"Mikhail Pavlovich told me everything."

"How convenient and enlightening for you."

Claudia wanted to draw her pistol now, but it was too late. Oleg had the upper hand. *What's his next move?*

"You deceived me. This was your plan all along?"

"Not exactly, Comrade Claudia. There are—as we say— many moving parts. In fact, you are *both* a disappointment to me." Oleg eyed Pope Karl.

Pope Karl said, "Claudia, my dearest. You should leave now. You don't have to be here."

Claudia stared at the pope—at *her* father. "So ..." she continued, "it's true."

Pope Karl stared intently at Claudia with a sense of defeat in his eyes and said, "Yes, it's true. This is not how I wanted us to meet. I am sorry."

"All these years?"

"Yes, Claudia. I would like to explain, but"—he gestured to Oleg, whose pistol was pointing at him—"now is not the time. Please leave us."

Oleg took two steps backward and said playfully, "Who is Claudia Rohweder? HVA agent extraordinaire and hero of the hour? Or Papa's little girl who tries to save the man who deserted her for God? I confess I do not know the answer, but I have always wondered what would happen at this moment." Oleg briefly switched his aim toward Claudia before settling back on the pontiff. "Oh, look, we are finally at this moment. More suspense than the Bond movie in Leningrad."

Claudia ignored the taunting and asked, "Why are you here?"

"Change of plan. As I said, it turns out you are *both* a huge disappointment. I will take care of Leontev and his bitch spy wife later. But first, I must say, your esteemed father has gone way beyond his godly station. He thinks he is the leader of the free and not-so-free world."

"You are insane, Oleg Stepanovich. The pope is trying—"

"The pope—your dear father—is meddling where he should not be meddling. The last thing our country needs is a Vatican guardian angel."

Claudia raised her hands but simultaneously moved slowly toward the desk and between the pope and Oleg.

"You think I would think twice about shooting you too, my dear comrade?"

"Please, dearest Claudia," Pope Karl began, "you should not be here. You do not *need* to be here. I—"

"Oleg Stepanovich, I am begging you. Pope Karl has nothing to do with our mission—"

"You don't understand, Claudia—my beloved daughter. This man will stop at nothing."

Oleg said, "Last chance, Comrade. I am on tenterhooks. Listen to your father—"

The door suddenly seemed to fly off its hinges and catapulted Oleg into the bookcase behind him.

"Run!" a voice shouted.

The momentum of bursting through the door caused Steele to lose his balance and end up on the floor. As he looked up, he saw that Claudia had not run but had instead drawn her weapon and pointed it at Oleg.

But she didn't stand a chance. Oleg, too, had re-aimed his weapon. He fired.

At first, Steele could not tell from his position who had been hit. Then Claudia dropped to the floor in front of him. As she lay next to him, they locked eyes. Even though she was clearly about to expire, her eyes smiled, and Steele recalled the night of passion they had shared in Berlin.

Steele looked up. Oleg now had his pistol trained on Pope Karl, his finger against the trigger about to shoot.

In a split second, Steele felt a rush of adrenaline and power he had never felt before. Without thinking about the consequences, he launched himself at Oleg in a flying rugby tackle. The gun fell to the floor, and Steele caught sight of Pope Karl rooted to the spot, eyes closed, hands clasped—the pontiff was praying.

With a twist and a turn, Steele wrestled Oleg to the floor, but not for long. In a swift judo move, Oleg spun Steele on his back and sat on top of him, punching Steele in the face so that he saw stars and tasted blood. Oleg reached for his pistol just a few feet away, but Pope Karl had beaten him to it and kicked the weapon to the other side of the room.

Steele had no doubt that Oleg would kill him and the pope if Steele released his grip. With a two-pronged attack to Oleg's eyes and a knee to his crotch, Steele created the space he needed to stand up. Again, Oleg lunged for the weapon, but Steele launched another bear-hug-cum-rugby tackle. The momentum of this adrenaline-filled attack propelled both men toward the window.

Steele, now on top, wrestled Oleg to the open window ledge—the Russian was now suspended half in, half out. If Steele could free himself, Oleg would plummet—headfirst—to an unsavory end. Again, Steele poked Oleg in an already blood-ied eye and managed an upward blow to the bottom of Oleg's nose—the most painful blow he knew.

Locked in battle, both men teetered on the edge of the window. Steele could feel Pope Karl behind them, but there was nothing the old man could do to help Steele without sending both warriors to their death.

Then everything changed. Oleg managed to release a knee to Steele's crotch, causing an unimaginable spasm of pain to his entire body. Steele felt the balance shift—but not in his favor. Both men toppled out of the window headfirst. Even as they fell, Steele and Oleg locked eyes for a split second. Steele couldn't be sure, but it looked as though Oleg was smiling.

CHAPTER FIFTY-SEVEN

Grand Hotel Quisisana

Three lifts descended almost simultaneously from the presidential suite on the third floor.

The president's group and his entourage exited in quick succession on the ground floor. Once the delegation had regrouped, they moved toward the main entrance—a veritable whirlwind of suits, expensive cologne, testosterone, American self-confidence, and global power.

Hotel guests did a double take. As they casually walked to and from the swimming pool and cocktail terrace, they suddenly found themselves just feet from the president of the United States of America. Hotel staff continued their work nonchalantly and acted as though the VIP and his diplomatic apparatus were regular fixtures.

Kolby Webster said, "Wait up, people. Mr. President, we are getting reports of 'shots fired.'"

"Where?"

"Monastery."

"What's the source?"

"Working on it."

"We're late," said Madison looking at his watch.

"Our people are talking to the Swiss Guard. We have carabinieri, Secret Service, and Swiss Guard along the route. And the chopper's ours, too. Monsignor Fran is meeting us here—the pope's right-hand man is going to escort us."

"I know Monsignor Fran. We've met."

"We should wait until we get the all clear."

"How are we getting there?"

"On foot. It's less than five minutes ... unless you want to ride the baggage carts—not a good 'look.'"

"Damn right."

Natalie Price, an attractive woman with long dark hair and even longer legs who was Madison's press secretary approached and said, "Mr. President, the press is asking if you'll take questions."

"I thought this was a secret."

"It was. But you can never be sure with Russians, or Italians for that matter."

Madison shrugged and said, "Sure, why not?"

As President Madison and his team exited the building, Secret Service agents fanned out left and right to cover any likely threat.

The gaggle of mainly local journalists surged forward—photographers clicked away. The sound of their camera motor drives engaging filled the piazza with a maniacal intensity.

President Madison walked across the hotel terrace and met them in front of the hotel. The scene behind the journalists was like a Hollywood backlot, he thought. It was the perfect Mediterranean scene. Capri tourists—bronzed men and women, old and young, exuded confidence and satisfaction with life. Every person seemed to be making a fashion statement in their plain white or brightly colored outfits and hats, the finest array of designer merchandise available on the planet, and their expensive jewelry beaming as they strolled past pastel-colored boutiques.

Back to business ...

Webster followed his boss close behind and within earshot. "We have the area secured, Mr. President. All set."

"Let's make this quick," Madison replied.

"Understood, sir. Monsignor Franciszek is ready once we have the all clear."

A British journalist shouted, "What do you hope to achieve today, Mr. President?"

Madison whipped off his aviator shades and declared, "Building bridges, that's why we're here."

Then it was Madison's turn to do a double take. Astrid Aronsson was standing next to the BBC reporter with a microphone in her hand.

"Do you see her?" Madison whispered, turning to Webster keeping his eyes on Astrid.

"Yes, I see her."

"I told you to get rid of her."

"I thought we had. Don't worry, sir. I'll sort it."

Webster pressed the SEND button on his radio, but it was too late.

Astrid shouted, "Mr. President, what do you know about my father's murder?"

Madison froze for a second but managed to regain his composure. "Miss Aronsson, it's nice to see you again."

"We have never met, Mr. President."

Madison was thrown off guard. "I mean, it's nice to meet you. I am very sorry for your loss, Miss Aronsson. Your father was a great man."

"But why did you never agree to meet my father, Mr. President?"

The collective hum of journalists and photographers jostling for position suddenly fell silent. The look on Madison's face told them he didn't want to answer this one.

Madison frowned but feigned an air of calm. If he retreated into the hotel, the vultures would suspect weakness—he needed to answer.

"Miss Aronsson. Umm … that's not accurate. I was looking forward to meeting the Swedish prime minister. It was a scheduling matter. Your father was very busy during the election."

Astrid turned toward the tourist photographer with gray hair and thick-rimmed glasses—now armed with a video camera—whom she had hired to film this encounter. She gave him the signal and tapped his arm to make sure he was recording. The BBC journalist fired a question, but Astrid spoke over him. "Is the 'Deception Committee' also a scheduling matter? Is that why it's a secret?"

"I'm not sure what you are referring to, Miss Aronsson."

"Really? That surprises me, Mr. President, because the Deception Committee was your idea."

"I'm afraid you're confused, Miss Aronsson. I'll have Natalie, here, clear up any misunderstanding." He turned his attention to the other journalists. "Please. Are there any more questions about the peace summit?"

Video camera rolling and microphone extended toward Madison, Astrid continued, "I am also confused about the destruction of the Yamal pipeline in 1982. It caused great economic harm and suffering to the Soviet people. Is it true that the CIA is responsible?"

The sabotage of the Yamal pipeline was the largest non-nuclear explosion ever. There was no doubt in Madison's mind who was responsible. *Probably not the best time to reveal that the Yamal pipeline operation was actually my prime motivation to create the Deception Committee,* he thought.

"I'm truly sorry for your loss, Miss Aronsson, but you are way off base. And if you were a real journalist like the rest of these professionals, you would know that as president of the United States, I never comment on matters of national and international security, especially where the CIA is concerned."

"Isn't it true, Mr. President, that my father discovered the truth about the Yamal pipeline—the largest non-nuclear explosion ever—and your obsession to win the Cold War? He did not approve of your 'Deception Committee'—Isn't that why you murdered him?"

Webster stepped closer to Madison and whispered, "Sir, we should—"

"I'll handle it, Kolby. It's too late now." He turned back to the presser. "Ladies and gentlemen, we must leave for our meeting with the Russian president, but I will say this to the young lady ..." Madison held out both hands as though he was about to deliver a sermon. "Prime Minister Aronsson was a greatly respected and admired politician in the prime of his political career. We are doing everything we can to help Swedish authorities find the perpetrator. Today, however, we are invited by the Vatican to enjoy the wonderful hospitality of the Italian people, and we are here in the name of peace. President Leontev has made enormous progress—glasnost, perestroika—these initiatives were unthinkable just five years ago. Our hope is that we can continue to work together to help him achieve his goals and his much-deserved status on the international stage. That's all I have for you."

Madison's entourage turned to walk back inside the hotel, but Astrid continued, "Mr. President, can you tell us why you claim to be promoting peace with Russia while developing and maintaining a secret class of stealth submarines with the Swedish navy to combat the Russian navy? Was this part of your Deception Committee?"

Madison could not hide his anger as his face flushed red. It was all he could do to stop himself from screaming out loud. He turned to Webster and gripped his arm as though he were trying to drain blood. "That girl just destroyed ten years of work."

Webster loosened the president's grip to monitor his earpiece. "I'm sorry, sir. But there's an update."

"Now what?"

"It's confirmed. There was an attempt on Pope Karl's life. The shots fired were genuine."

"I don't know what the fuck is happening on this paradise island, but I've had enough."

"I understand, sir."

Madison stopped dead. "If I ask you to do something, can you promise me not to screw it up?"

"Of course, Mr. President."

Madison leaned in toward Webster. "Get me the *fuck* out of here."

"What about the summit? We can secure another location."

"No, Kolby. We cannot and will not find a secure location. Are we clear?"

"I'll prepare the helicopter and have Air Force One standing by."

"Correct answer. And one more thing, Mr. Deputy Director."

"Sir?"

"The second we are back on Air Force One, you're fucking fired."

CHAPTER FIFTY-EIGHT

Marina Piccolo

Steele came to when he felt a blow to his ribs followed by a shooting pain throughout his entire body. Someone kicked him a second time.

Oleg?

He opened his eyes and looked at the sky. At least I'm still alive. Steele had been knocked unconscious upon landing from the papal apartment. The trees had somehow broken their fall, and the drop was not as far as it had seemed hanging out the window moments before. Now, from his position lying on the ground—Oleg standing over him—Steele understood that they were both at the bottom of a steep bank of trees and rocks that led to the sea.

"Let's go, Mr. MI6."

Steele winced at the pain he felt all over—his ribs, back, arms, and legs. "Fuck it."

"Don't worry, Mr. MI6," said Oleg. "I have vodka on my yacht. It will cure everything."

Steele slowly got himself up off the ground. "Where are we going?"

"Thanks to your girlfriend, I have much work to do."

"If Claudia was my girlfriend, she had a funny way of showing it. Why did you kill her?"

"Let's go." In one continuous motion, Oleg removed the spare pistol he had strapped to his leg and gestured for Steele to start walking.

"I'll stay here, thanks. I'd prefer to catch some rays."

"'Rays?'"

"Sunbathe."

Oleg smiled. "Sorry, Jack, but I need your help." Oleg stepped toward Steele as if he was about to whisper something, but instead unleashed a vicious blow with his knee to Steele's groin.

"Ahhhh! *Jesus!*" Steele bent double.

"Just so we understand each other."

"Okay, okay—you made your point."

Oleg escorted his prisoner through an old vineyard down to a deserted private beach. Oleg, it appeared, had made contingency plans for a quick getaway from the monastery. They climbed into a dingy equipped with an outboard motor, which bobbed gently on the sea as it waited patiently for its passengers.

Oleg started the engine and said, "We take a little trip. Very scenic."

As they headed out to sea, Oleg steered with one hand and kept the pistol trained on Steele with the other.

"You don't need me," began Steele. "I'm not as valuable as you think."

No reply.

"Why did you shoot Claudia? I thought she was one of yours."

"She *was* a talented operative. But unfortunately, she had 'family' issues."

"Your people will find out. The KGB—"

"Jack, please don't make a fool of yourself. You know nothing about my country and how we operate. We have different values from the West. You should know this by now."

"Claudia was right—you're crazy."

"I am flattered." Oleg pushed the throttle lever forward, and the boat picked up speed.

"Where are we going?"

"You will see."

"Why kill the pope?" Steele asked, genuinely perplexed. "Were you trying to frame the Americans?"

"Too many questions, Jack. It is not polite for guests to ask so many questions."

Steele steadied himself as they met a rolling wake from a nearby yacht that was cruising east toward the Faraglioni Rocks.

Oleg gestured toward the iconic natural formation. "You know that lovers are supposed to kiss when they pass through the arch."

"I read that too."

"Too bad you and Claudia won't make it. Maybe you could invite Masha instead?"

"You know about Masha?" Oleg really was an omniscient spy, Steele thought.

"Of course, Jack. I am KGB, remember? Your romantic voyage from Leningrad turned out to be a bonus for my country. For this, I must thank you."

"What do you want from me? The carabinieri will find you."

"You are my 'insurance' for now. Maybe I shoot you later."

Steele tried again. "Why kill the pope? He was trying to make peace, for God's sake."

"Pope Karl is a weak man. He is a Vatican puppet and is meddling in our affairs. He will be the first pope to resign in six hundred years."

"Is that why you wanted to shoot him?"

"It was very heroic of you to save him, but his days are numbered anyway—you can ask Monsignor Franciszek about that if you live."

Steele stayed silent and gave some thought to an escape plan. He glanced at the rock formation in the distance and the boats and luxury yachts dotted around them, but nothing came to mind.

Two minutes later, they arrived at an anchored yacht and climbed aboard.

Steele said, "Five-star accommodation for your president?"

"No, Jack"—Oleg pointed to a much bigger yacht a short distance away—"the president has his own private accommodation." Then Oleg approached Steele and said, "Turn around."

Steele obeyed, and Oleg used a pair of zip ties to secure Steele's hands behind his back. Oleg shoved Steele onto the seating area at the rear of the boat deck. "Make yourself comfortable. The show will start any moment now."

Oleg fetched a pair of binoculars from the bridge and surveyed the sky above the monastery and Capri town above it.

"Ornithology?" asked Steele sarcastically.

"What?"

"Are you looking for rare birds?"

"You could say that." Oleg smirked and adjusted his binoculars as he switched back and forth between the airspace and yet another yacht a few hundred yards to the west of their position. "The American bird. The president is about to leave the island by helicopter. But unfortunately, he won't get far."

"What are you going to do?"

"*I* am not going to do anything. But as soon as we see the helicopter, my men will shoot him down, and phase one is complete."

Steele laughed skeptically, trying to provoke Oleg. "In your dreams, Oleg."

"President Madison deserves this fate. He is not an honorable man."

"And you are."

"I honor my country. President Madison does not deserve his. But we will settle the matter here and now."

"And how are your men going to do that?"

"You will see."

"You'll never get away with it."

"I already did, Jack. There is nothing to connect me to this attack. We will enjoy the spectacle and set sail"—he looked at his watch—"which should happen at any moment."

Steele's heart sank. It was true that he had saved the pope's life, but now he was utterly powerless in the face of Oleg's maniacal plan. *There's nothing I can do to save the American president.*

"And phase two?" Steele asked. "You want to feed me to the fish?" He realized he would prefer a bullet to the head than an anchor tethered to his ankle. He also realized that he would probably have no say in the matter.

Oleg continued to study the scene with his binoculars. "Negative, Jack. I have more important targets. Let me just say that the Communist Party will be looking for a new president—someone who cares about my country and does not sell us to the West. You understand, Jack—"

The sound of a helicopter—POTUS's helicopter—high above Capri town interrupted their adversarial exchange. Steele stood up, but Oleg pounced and struck him in the side of his head with the binoculars. "I told you," Oleg insisted. "There's nothing you can do to save him. Sit down and enjoy the show."

One minute from Oleg's yacht, two waiters wearing pristine cream-colored tunics aboard the Grand Hotel Quisisana's motor launch also looked up to observe the helicopter in the distance. At any moment, they would arrive at their destination—a navy-blue luxury yacht by the name of *American Gnome.*

Like his father before him, Raffaele Sorrentino, head waiter of the Grand Hotel Quisisana, knew when to apologize to a guest in person to resolve a customer service error. Today was such an occasion. There had been a mix-up at the hotel—or so he had been informed—and the wrong buffet spread had been delivered to the wrong client. He was on a mission to resolve the matter.

"How could this happen?" asked Sergio, the young waiter-in-training accompanying Raffaele.

"Because, Sergio, people do not pay attention. We have two presidents and a pope on the island. They all need to eat, and frankly, I am not surprised something like this happened. The order with the Swedish pitepalt was delivered this morning to *American Gnome* instead of *American Nomad.*" Raffaele pointed to the helicopter. "There goes President Madison."

Sergio squinted at the dot in the sky and began to sing, "'Tu vuò fa l'Americano, Mmericano!'"

"Please, Sergio. We have work to do."

"I'm sorry, sir."

"Like I always tell you, 'attention to detail' is the most important thing in our profession. My father told me this for thirty years."

Sergio nodded earnestly. "So, who ordered the Swedish pitepalt? It's an unusual dish."

"You are correct, Sergio. Our chef had to call his friend in Stockholm to get the recipe. It turns out that this is Irina Leontev's favorite hors d'oeuvre."

"So, we are going to exchange the orders delivered to *American Nomad* and *American Gnome?*"

"Certainly not, young man. We have fresh orders free of charge, and we bring these new orders to each yacht." He pointed to the trays behind him on the deck.

As they approached *American Gnome*, Raffaele reduced speed, ready to pull alongside and hand-deliver the correct order. He would have Sergio issue the apology—for practice— and he would add a charming sentence or two to complete the matter.

Sergio used the pole with a hook on the end to pull closer to the yacht. He tethered the two boats together with a simple slip knot.

Tray in one hand, Raffaele climbed the ladder aboard *American Gnome*. Once he had negotiated the side of the boat and was aboard the vessel, he looked up. What he saw made him drop the tray. There was a loud clatter of plates, silverware, and glasses as the seafood and other delicacies smashed on the boat deck. He saw two men—clearly deceased—lying spread-eagle on deck next to the original Quisisana trays of food. One of the men's eyes was open staring at the sky and both men had what looked like vomit running down the sides of their faces. The color of their skin was angry red from the piercing mid-day sun.

"What happened, Signor Raffaele?" Sergio shouted. "Are you okay, Signore?"

Raffaele turned back to Sergio. He looked as if he had seen a ghost. "Radio for help immediately. Tell the hotel to call the carabinieri—urgent. Tell them we have discovered two dead bodies on board *American Gnome*."

As Sergio contacted the hotel, Raffaele surveyed the scene. In all his years of service for rich and famous guests, this was the most disturbing thing he had ever encountered. *If I had to guess, I'd say these men were poisoned,* he thought.

"Carabinieri are on their way," shouted Sergio replacing the radio handset. Then he climbed the ladder and surveyed the scene for himself. "What is that?"

Raffaele replied dismissively. "What does it look like? I told you already, two corpses."

"I understand, Signore. But what is *that?*" He pointed to a long, green cylindrical tube with a telescope mounted on the side, which was the most foreign object either man had ever seen on the island.

"I think ..." began Raffaele, "I think it is a weapon of some kind. A very bad weapon."

At first, the helicopter was a mere dot in the distance, but as it gained height, it flew toward them and then turned east as though following a flight path.

Oleg said, "Come on, come on ... I don't understand."

Steele squinted as he watched the chopper *chuck-chuck-chuck* toward them. "What's happening, Oleg?"

Oleg ignored the question and snatched a hand-held radio from the bridge. "Vladimir, come in … I repeat, Vlad, are you reading, over?"

No reply. The helicopter continued away from them due east.

Oleg shook his head and tried the radio again. "Vla-di-mir, do you read me? Vlad? Fire. I repeat, FIRE NOW!"

★　　★　　★

Raffaele glanced up as the helicopter flew overhead. "POTUS is leaving us. Early, I think."

Sergio replied, "POTUS?"

"President of the United States. That's what they call him for short."

"But I thought there was a summit? We prepared so much food."

"A change of plan, no doubt."

Both men looked down at the mysterious weapon and had the same thought at the same moment.

Sergio said, "Do you think …?"

"Yes, I think you are correct," Raffaele replied. "How long before the carabinieri arrive?"

The nervous young waiter did not seem to hear Raffaele's question. "You think these men were going to shoot down the president's helicopter?"

"If that is not the case, this is a very strange coincidence."

Sergio swallowed hard, looking at the corpses. "But who killed these men?"

Raffaele nodded in agreement. "Who killed these men … and how?"

CHAPTER FIFTY-NINE

"What's the matter, Oleg? Did your plan hit a snag?"

Oleg pointed his pistol at Steele, finger on the trigger. "Bitch! Fucking *bitch!*"

Steele wasn't quite sure which "bitch" Oleg was talking about, but he didn't care. He was more focused on the small black circle of the Makarov that could end his life at any moment. All it would take was for Oleg's finger to twitch half an inch. Steele could feel himself sweating all over, and his face was burning not just from the sun but from the adrenaline that made his blood flow even faster around his body. "What happened, Oleg? Maybe I can help?"

It was futile. Steele had no idea what to do or say, but asking a question in the heat of the moment, he reasoned, might elicit a response and create more time and space to survive without being shot.

"It was a Stinger." Oleg lowered his pistol and threw the handset so hard on the deck that it shattered. "They were supposed to *fire!* Bitch idiots!"

At Sandhurst, Steele had learned about the FIM-92 Stinger surface-to-air missile system—made in America. It was the weapon of choice to destroy low-level enemy aircraft, not only on the conventional battlefield but also used by mercenaries and terrorists alike to create havoc and terror on demand. Steele steadied his breath and continued his efforts to "distract" Oleg from re-aiming the pistol at Steele's head and pulling the trigger out of pure frustration.

"Maybe it wasn't their fault?" Steele offered. "Maybe the Italians got to them?"

Oleg spluttered venom. "I chose these men myself. If they failed, I am to blame." Oleg inhaled deeply, exhaled, and switched his attention away from Steele. He moved to the bridge and slid the throttle into gear. The boat surged to life, and Oleg spun the helm to turn the boat and make an escape. *The only problem is,* thought Steele, *he's taking me with him.*

Oleg seemed to read Steele's mind. "It's okay, Jack. Like I said, you are very good insurance for me. In case you are right, and the carabinieri decide to meddle in our business."

"But where can you go, Oleg?" Steele continued his strategy of asking questions so that—he prayed—Oleg would converse with him rather than shoot him. It wasn't much of a strategy, but it was all he could come up with. "Wouldn't it make more sense to go back to your president? He can protect you. Blame the Americans?"

Oleg sneered. "You like to think a lot, Jack. I like men who think. But, again, you are behind the … how Americans say? 'Behind the curve *ball.*'"

The stress was wrong—on *ball*—but Steele got the point.

"You should be with your president and his wife." Steele needed to prevent Oleg's escape. As soon as they cleared Italian waters, he would be even more vulnerable, completely at Oleg's mercy. *I'm just another witness he doesn't need.*

The yacht was fast approaching the world-famous Capri archway of the Faraglioni. There was already a queue of luxury yachts and boats on both sides waiting to pass through the formation created by erosion over thousands of years of lapping waves—it was a traditional rite of passage for Capri yacht tourists.

"I thought I had explained to you, Jack … We missed the American president this time, but I am confident my own president will not return to the motherland."

Fuck. He wants to assassinate both *presidents.*

Steele purposely changed the subject—enough with the mind games; escape from this lunatic was the new priority. "Are we going through the arch? It's good luck, you know."

"Why not? I am a romantic too, Jack. My mother was superstitious. Always leave the way you came in."

An obscenely large super yacht emerging from the Faraglioni arch headed toward them. Oleg accelerated and navigated past boats waiting in line. No one seemed to mind. Oleg shouted in Russian, "Nasha Ohcheredz!" *Our turn!* He opened the throttle further, and their yacht motored through the arch.

Now or never!

Even though Steele's hands were tied behind his back, he decided he might be able to tread water for a few moments. He would gamble that Oleg would not shoot him in front of witnesses. He needed to jump now or become a sitting duck for the next twelve hours as Oleg escaped back to Russia, presumably an easy route via Macedonia and Serbia.

Before Oleg had time to react, Steele quickly stood up, climbed onto his seat, and jumped overboard. He had no idea if it was even physically possible to tread water with his hands bound behind him, but he was about to find out.

American Nomad

Irina Leontev kissed her husband as he climbed aboard, flanked by a two-man KGB detail.

"My darling. Back so soon? Did you make world peace?"

"Not exactly. It's complicated. I still don't quite understand what happened, but it looks like we miscalculated."

"We?" She smiled. "*You* miscalculated."

"Thank you for reminding me."

"I told you this summit was a bad idea. I don't trust the Americans, and my verdict is still out on the pope."

"Wise words indeed."

"You're welcome, dearest. That is why I am here. We will get through this together."

"We heard a gunshot at the monastery. Our team evacuated us immediately, and the Americans did likewise."

"Where is Oleg Stepanovich?"

"I would love to know."

"I don't trust him, either. If something went wrong with the plan, I bet my life he had something to do with it."

Leontev shook his head. "I don't think he's to blame. He should be here any moment."

"Where else would he be?"

"I don't know. Everything was going according to plan. Pope Karl agreed to our proposal. As we were walking to the summit location—*bang!*"

"A gun?"

"Yes, the noise came from the pope's apartment."

"Then what happened?"

"Events are not clear to me. But we have reports the pope was shot."

"I don't like it." Irina nodded slowly, placed both hands on each side of her husband's head, and kissed him lovingly. "But I am thankful you are safe."

"Me too. I think we are safe here." Leontev smiled.

"Let's sit down. You should eat something. You look terrible."

"I feel guilty when I look at this food. Perhaps I should be more like Oleg Stepanovich so that my adversaries do not take advantage of me."

"No, Misha, you have a heart and a soul. Men like Oleg are born with neither. The good cream always rises to the top."

"I don't even know if the Americans are serious in their intentions. They left quickly without any communication."

"We will find out soon enough."

"Glasnost, perestroika. Perhaps it was too much change and too quick for the motherland and our people to bear."

"You care about people's lives and well-being—not just about money, wealth, and power. We both care about *our* people—what is their future? You will succeed by doing the right thing. We *are* doing the right thing. One day, our country will be a true democracy. It will take time, as we have discussed many times."

"I hope and pray."

"You know I am right, Misha." Irina looked out to sea and took in the salty air and the surprisingly warm-for-autumn breeze. "Are you hungry?"

"It so happens that I am *very* hungry. Thank you, my dearest, for calming my nerves."

The Leontevs sat down and helped themselves to gourmet hors d'oeuvres and snacks previously delivered to their boat from the Quisisana catering service.

Leontev took a bite. "Oh my god, Irinochka. Who ordered this?" He chuckled. "This food is one hundred times better than what we eat in the Kremlin."

"Oleg ordered the food. He did something right for once, except the hotel delivered the wrong order. They forgot my pitepalt."

"Do they have Swedish pitepalt in Italy?"

"Of course. You can order anything from Grand Hotel Quisisana. They are sending a fresh delivery."

"You deserve a treat, Irinochka. Thank you for loving our people and for being the love of my life."

"Thank me when we make glasnost and perestroika a permanent reality for the motherland."

Steele splayed his legs as he hit the water to create the loudest possible splash and draw attention to himself. At first, he stopped himself momentarily from sinking. But he had not considered the weight of his clothes and shoes. He kicked furiously, keeping his head above water for a few seconds. Drowning had always been his least preferred way to die, but it was now clear to him that, barring a miracle, he would drown in less than thirty seconds.

Steele tried to shout for help but instead swallowed a gulp of salty sea water that made him cough and choke. *Please, God, someone sees me.*

Steele began to sink. He wondered how long he would be able to hold his breath and how far he would plummet before he perished. Again, he managed to stall the descent by kicking frantically. But with his hands tethered behind his back, it was hopeless. He started to feel lightheaded, and his vision began to blur. On the verge of blacking out, he swallowed what seemed like a tidal wave of water that made his body convulse. The pure physics of his situation meant that it was impossible to resurface, even if he had the power and strength, which he did not. His plan had failed.

During his final coherent seconds, Steele pictured his adversary making an escape and wished Oleg had simply shot him dead in the water. He thought about his mother and brother, Masha, Aronsson, Nigel, Jenkins, Patterson the journalist and Claudia the spy—then Raffaele the waiter, Astrid, and finally the pope himself. The people and events that led to death's door blurred into one final movie that lasted a few more seconds. *What about the pope? I saved his life. Please God help me.*

★   ★   ★

Steele made a half turn and saw a torpedo of bubbles beneath the surface in front of him. A woman wearing an Italian flag bathing costume suddenly appeared. She put her finger to her lips, then wrapped her arms around him in a strong embrace. A moment later, he felt another person behind him trying to reverse his downward momentum. The woman in front and the person behind kicked hard. Like human propellers, their efforts seemed to work. For a second, Steele had hope, but then it all went black.

Moments later, he opened his eyes to find himself lying on a wooden deck with a crowd of people looking down at him. "Quickly," he said, standing up as if nothing had happened. Even his clothes were almost dry. *How long have I been out?*

He scanned the Faraglioni in the middle distance and saw Oleg's boat still visible on the far side. None of the passengers said anything as Steele ran to the helm and opened the throttle.

There's only one way to stop Oleg, he thought.

After what seemed like a few seconds, Steele had successfully covered the short distance to and maneuvered his boat alongside the navy-blue yacht Oleg had pointed out earlier. The passengers on board Steele's boat were dancing to music and seemed not to notice or care about his manic and frantic actions as he jumped across to the navy-blue yacht.

Two men wearing military fatigues were singing, dancing, and drinking vodka straight from a bottle. They smiled and welcomed him as if they were expecting him.

"Jack Steele. Welcome, Jack Steele!"

He ignored them and picked up what he was looking for—the FIM-92 Stinger missile—just as Oleg had told him. Placing it firmly on this shoulder and looking through the sights, he locked on to Oleg's boat on the other side of the Faraglioni. *Less than five seconds before Oleg disappears from view,* he estimated.

One of the men in fatigues said in Russian, "Let's go, Jack! You saved the pope! You are hero of Soviet Union."

Steele ignored him and took aim at Oleg's boat, placing his finger on the FIRE button. But just as he pressed the rubber, he felt a simultaneous slap to the middle of his back.

As soon as he felt the blow, Steele knew instantly that his aim was off target. But it was too late to correct his aim. The missile shot out of its cylindrical casing toward the Faraglioni.

Steele froze and, almost in slow motion, watched the Stinger missile rocket across the surface of the water to impact. The ancient Faraglioni rock formation and a dozen luxury yachts nearby exploded like a volcanic eruption into a massive orange-red ball of fire, rock, and boat debris—Steele heard hysterical screams of yacht passengers who were catapulted into the air or on fire. He had single-handedly destroyed thousands of years of natural beauty in one second. He turned around to see that a carabiniere had climbed aboard and was pointing his weapon at Steele. The Italian screamed, "Bastardo!" He pointed the gun at Steele's head and pulled the trigger.

CHAPTER SIXTY

Grand Hotel Quisisana

Steele let out a slight gasp as his body jolted from the nightmare. He opened his eyes and had never been more thankful to breathe, which he did for a few moments without moving any other part of his body. As he emerged from the deep sleep, he wiped the sweat from his brow and attempted to clear his foggy brain. Yes, he *had* jumped off Oleg's boat to escape, and yes, he *had* been rescued from drowning. But the rest—drunken passengers, Russian assassins dancing and offering him vodka, and Steele firing a Stinger missile at the Faraglioni—must have been a dream.

A gentle breeze danced from an open french window leading to a balcony. From the bed, he could see a view of the blue sky and the twinkling, sapphire-blue sea.

"*Jesus!*" he said to himself. Then out loud, as he put his palms together, "Thank you, God. Thank you so much."

Steele steadied his breathing as he continued to piece together exactly what had happened—fact versus fiction, fact versus dream.

Someone *had* saved him—a woman, he thought. Perhaps two? He recalled jumping from the yacht as Oleg fled. Steele's plan had worked after all. Someone on another boat must have jumped in and rescued him. He recalled his futile kicking action and then the blurred apparition of a young woman appearing in front of him. That part was real. But thankfully, the drunken

Russians, Steele firing at Oleg, and destroying the Faraglioni were part of the nightmare he had just woken from. Thankfully, the carabiniere had not shot him after all.

I'm alive. That's all that matters. I'm still here.

Steele shifted onto his elbows and glanced at the nightstand. There was a hotel card leaning against the lamp:

> **Meet us downstairs on the terrace**
> **when you wake up.**
> **Masha & Astrid xo**

Steele felt giddy with excitement. *The nightmare is over.* At least now, he was sure that he had *not* destroyed thousands of years of natural beauty with a Stinger missile or killed dozens of innocent people aboard their yachts. But it was also true that Oleg had escaped, and there was nothing he could do about it. *What does it matter?* he thought. *I'm not the police. I'm just a Sandhurst cadet who can't read a map and got very lost.*

Steele threw on a T-shirt and shorts and suddenly noticed that his British passport was also on the bedside table. He picked it up and read a note inside:

> **Thought you might need this.**
> **Take a break. You deserve it.**
> **N.R.S.**
> **P.S. Trust no one.**

Holding his passport and reading Nigel Rhodes Stampa's initials on the note, Steele told himself that he was no longer dreaming and that he had survived. He drank from a bottle of mineral water left on his bedside table and made his way downstairs.

Espresso … I need a triple espresso.

The hotel lift made its friendly ping—he turned right,

traversed the marble-floored lobby of Grand Hotel Quisisana and exited through the electric sliding glass doors. Outside, it was warm and sunny with a slight breeze. He inhaled the perfect fragrance of island air mixed with the aroma of espresso and expensive perfume worn by hotel guests enjoying Capri.

"Jack!" He heard his name and looked left. "Over here." Masha was waving from their breakfast table in the corner.

Steele nearly stumbled over the wicker chairs in anticipation as he made his way toward Astrid and Masha. Both were wearing Ray-Bans and sipping espresso; a basket of croissants sat in front of them as if they were just two BFFs enjoying the holiday of a lifetime rather than a Russian defector and the bereaved daughter of a VIP assassination target.

Steele pulled out a chair and sat down. "What happened?" he asked. "Can you please tell me what the bloody hell happened?"

Masha said, "Of course, Jack. It's okay. You can relax." She touched his hand, and he recalled their night of sensuality on the fishing boat. They locked eyes for a moment. She was as beautiful as he had remembered.

Then Steele looked away and smiled nervously at the absurdity of the situation; thoughts and questions avalanched inside his head. "Fair enough," he said. "I'm sitting down and relaxed. Good thinking."

"You are a local hero, Jack," continued Astrid. "You saved the pope's life. You are the new James Bond of Capri."

"I'm much better looking." Steele grinned. "Just joking."

Astrid laughed.

"And thanks to Astrid," Masha continued, "President Madison will find it very hard, if not impossible, to get reelected next month."

Steele asked, "Why?"

Masha said, "We told you about the Deception Committee?"

"Of course."

"Now the whole world knows about it too."

"How?"

"We crashed Madison's press conference. In fact, it was just over there." Astrid pointed to the piazza where she had called out President Madison. "I shared some secrets he never thought would be revealed in his lifetime, let alone before the election."

Masha said, "I think you could say Astrid 'spilled some beans.'"

"Congratulations." Steele nodded supportively and ordered a triple espresso from a passing waiter. "And Leontev?"

"Probably in Moscow," said Masha. "And probably very grateful that he also knows the precise details of Madison's plan."

"Do you know anything about Claudia?"

Astrid said, "I don't know Claudia. Who is Claudia?"

Steele remembered the brief message from Nigel. *Trust no one.* He wondered where they had taken her body. He wondered what the pope himself must be feeling to have met his daughter for such a short time before her violent death.

Astrid continued, "As my father used to say, 'First things first. Eat something.' Here." She offered Steele the basket full of croissants and other freshly made bread and then poured him a glass of juice.

"Thank you." But Steele had lost his appetite. He leaned back in his chair as a gaggle of day-tripping tourists followed their guide down the lane at the side of the hotel on their way to the monastery. "I suppose some things are getting back to normal here. How long was I out?"

"About thirty-six hours," replied Masha. "The doctor said you had a close call, but you just needed to rest. He gave you a sedative and told us to expect you to surface around noon today."

Astrid quipped, "You're early."

Steele smiled with relief and satisfaction that he was alive and well and no one was trying to kill him. "I nearly drowned. I—"

"You made the right decision. Jumping off the boat when you did," said Masha. "Oleg had no chance of stopping you, but if you had stayed on board, I think he would have killed you. I know his reputation."

Astrid said, "By the way, guess who saved you?"

"Who? It was a woman, I think."

Masha replied, "Two women, in fact. One of them just won the Miss Naples beauty pageant. She wants to meet you."

"I would love to meet her too—to thank her."

Masha said, "Raffaele can arrange this." She took off her sunglasses. "Now you. What happened? Before you escaped from Oleg."

Distracted by his own thoughts, Steele didn't hear the question. "Wait, I need to ask you something. Did you hear anything about a missile?"

"A missile?" Masha glanced at Astrid.

Steele clarified, "Yes, like a military weapon … an explosion?"

Astrid said, "Here comes Raffaele with your espresso. He knows everything that happens on this island. Ask him."

Steele looked up as Raffaele served the espresso. "I heard your question, Signor Steele. Yes, there was a missile, but fortunately, it was not fired."

"How do you know?"

"It was me who found it."

"Where?"

"The men who were supposed to use it became … indisposed."

"That's a relief. I think I was unconscious."

"Correct, signore. You were on your way to the bottom of the sea. But fortunately, our Italian angels, or perhaps I should say mermaids, were close by."

"Yes, I remember."

"You are correct about this missile—we found it on a boat near the Russian president's yacht—a 'Stinger,' I believe. But someone poisoned the terrorists before they could fire it."

Steele asked, "Who poisoned them?" He recalled his conversation with Oleg, who had predicted the demise of President Leontev. "They were going to kill Leontev?"

"No, Mr. Steele. These men wanted to shoot down the American president."

"You stopped them?"

"Not me. They were dead when we found them."

"Then who? Who poisoned them?"

Raffaele shrugged. "Constantius of Capri?"

"Who's Constantius?"

"Patron Saint of Capri for many centuries. Poison found its way to the bad guys. That's all I know. Carabinieri believe the poison was intended for Leontev and his wife." Raffaele clasped his hands. "Unfortunately, Constantius could not save the German woman. She was your friend?"

"Not exactly. We worked together."

"There is a rumor that she was related to the pontiff?"

"I'm not sure about that." Steele's head was pounding. He decided not to confirm or deny what he knew. *Trust no one.* How was all this possible? How was it possible that he had landed in this web of international intrigue and deception? He continued, "She was … a special person."

Masha asked, "How did you know her?"

"Like I said, we worked together." Steele sighed. "Raffaele—how's the pope?"

"Saint Constantius watches over his flock. The pope is well."

"Did you hear anything about a Vatican priest?"

"What exactly?"

"He's in the monastery—injured or dead." Steele did not elaborate.

"The monastery has many Vatican priests who come and go, and many secrets, signore. I'm afraid I have not heard anything about this priest. Some things are better left to God. You should speak to Monsignor Franciszek."

"I will. Thanks."

"But I doubt he will share secrets," Raffaele concluded.

Steele looked at his pain au chocolat and still had no appetite. Then he glanced at Masha, who seemed distracted, and he wondered if she had something to do with the poison, or the switching of the poison, or even the mysterious priest in his cell. He wondered if, in fact, Masha might be a double or triple or quadruple agent all along, and he suddenly felt the urge to interrogate her. He leaned forward and said, "Masha—" but an inner voice stopped him.

If Masha had something to do with the poison, he concluded, it was better to let sleeping "agents" lie. For now. After all, he had no proof, and the men on *American Gnome* were clearly assassins—*I'll let the carabinieri do their job.*

Instead, Steele decided to savor his return to civilization on the terrace of the Grand Hotel Quisisana.

Raffaele asked, "Can I get you anything else, ladies and gentleman? It's almost time for lunch?"

Steele exhaled. "I'll try the Quisisana Manhattan, please."

"Excellent choice." Raffaele nodded politely. "And a Bloody Mary for the ladies?"

Astrid asked playfully, "Do you remember *everyone's* orders, Raffaele, or just nice people like us?"

"It is my job and my pleasure to keep everyone 'appy," he replied. "If you are 'appy, I am 'appy."

Raffaele retreated to fetch the cocktails.

Steele raised his hand, "Raffaele, do you know how my passport got here?"

"Si, signore. It was special delivery from the British embassy in Rome."

"Makes sense. Thank you." Steele smiled, but he also wondered how Nigel knew of his whereabouts. *The ubiquitous MI6,* he thought. *Better late than never.*

A few minutes later, Raffaele returned with the cocktails and set them down.

"Let's make a toast," said Astrid. "First, to my father's memory."

Steele picked up his Manhattan and raised his glass. "God bless, Mr. Aronsson."

They clinked glasses.

"And this one is to honor a young boy," continued Astrid. "His name is Lars. Without this observant young boy, I might never have discovered who assassinated my father." Astrid sipped her Bloody Mary.

Steele said, "Explain."

"Lars was the one who observed a foreign submarine in Swedish waters. If he hadn't told his mother what he saw, I might never have been able to find out what happened to my father."

Steele said, "I have no idea what you're talking about, and right now, I don't think I want to know. But here's to young Lars."

"Me neither," added Masha. "Cheers."

Again, the three guests clinked glasses, and Steele wondered if Masha was telling the truth.

Steele said, "I am sorry about your parents too, Masha." He eyed both women. "You've both been through the wringer. You've had a rough time."

The young women nodded.

Steele asked, "What happened in Stockholm after I left? How did you both get here?"

They looked at their food in silence before Masha began to recount what had happened in Stockholm after the assassination. She explained how Astrid had convinced her to come to Capri to confront the American president. Astrid had even arranged for Masha to get a fake passport so that she could accompany her on the mission.

Steele asked, "How did you find out about the summit? It was a secret."

"After our Ministry of Defense realized they were being used by the American president and his Deception Committee. Björn Bergman—my ex-boyfriend—and his connections with the Swedish military were less protective of sensitive information and American intelligence. After my father's assassination, the Swedish military was forced to cooperate with our government once again—and not keep any more secrets, like the American operations in Swedish waters. The truth about the Deception Committee was leaking fast, and even the Swedish elites were outraged that my country's armed forces had been used for Madison's plan to ruin the Soviet economy."

Steele exhaled and shook his head. "Extraordinary ... but I'm still trying to understand exactly what happened. You're saying Madison played your government—your father—against your own Ministry of Defense?"

"Precisely," Astrid replied. "Even I admit it's very clever. But also embarrassing for Sweden."

"How was that even possible?"

Astrid replied, "Come on, Jack. You know by now. Truth is always stranger than fiction."

Steele smiled despite himself. "You're right about that."

"But we have much time to talk. I can explain everything." Catching sight of Raffaele, Astrid said, "The Bloody Mary is perfect."

"Grazzie mille, Miss Astrid," he replied.

"I have another question, Raffaele," said Steele.

"Please, signore."

"How old is the Faraglioni?"

"Many, many centuries."

"Capri wouldn't be the same without them."

"Si, signore. Without Faraglioni, Capri has no magic. It is said they will live forever and by God's grace can never be destroyed."

"Right," said Steele, "I'm glad about that." The image of

the Faraglioni exploding to smithereens caused a shiver to run down his spine. It was Steele's turn to make a toast. "Here's to Saint Constantius."

Raffaele smiled and bowed in appreciation. Astrid and Masha said in unison, "Saint Constantius!"

THE END

ACKNOWLEDGMENTS

Candace Johnson for another epic collaboration on the third book of The Deception Series; her amazing talent makes the creative process an absolute pleasure. Carol & Gary Rosenberg, The Book Couple, for endless good-humored interior book design patience, expertise, and ideas. Jae Song for his inimitable talent for map and cover designs. Steve Sklair for a fantastic book trailer. And the AR Gold list, advanced readers—Mona M., Darren B., Timothy B., Bruce B., Bruce T., Barbara W., Jackie T., Steve P., Sandy S., Mitch S., Sheila S., Marry v O., Sharon R., Manfred G., Freonie H., William H., Sharon M., Cabrina C., Lois S., Steve S., Lois W., Laura M.—and most important of all, *you*, the reader, for your support along this exciting and action-packed journey.

ABOUT THE AUTHOR

Richard Lyntton was born Richard Bramford in Highgate, London. He attended William Ellis School, Exeter University, Moscow State Linguistic University (formerly Maurice Thorez Moscow State Pedagogical Institute of Foreign Languages), and Sandhurst. Richard served as a Captain and tank commander in the British Army in the First Gulf War; European Community Task Force Humanitarian Liaison in Russia; UNHCR Liaison Officer, and United Nations Military Observer (during heavy shelling and NATO airstrikes) in Sarajevo, Bosnia; and was a United Nations Television producer in former Yugoslavia. He was called to testify at the International War Crimes Tribunal in The Hague after witnessing and filming human rights atrocities and abuses in Bosnia. His films are archived at the Imperial War Museum, London.

When he's not writing, Richard is a film & TV actor. He lives in Philadelphia with his wife, interior designer Michelle Wenitsky, and their two sons, Stefan and Blake.

Thank you for reading

LENINGRAD DECEPTION

*If you enjoyed the book, I would very much appreciate
it if you would leave a review on Amazon.
Thank you for considering.*
https://www.amazon.com/LENINGRAD-DECEPTION-
INTERNATIONAL-POLITICAL-THRILLER-ebook/dp/
B09Y2KFQ7D

★　　★　　★

*To sign up for our FREE Reader Regiment newsletter,
CLICK "subscribe now" button here:*
https://richardlynttonbooks.com/contact/

★　　★　　★

Enjoy *North Korea Deception* and *Hyde Park Deception*
available now in The Deception Series:
https://www.amazon.com/gp/product/B08LDR8RW2

Made in the USA
Coppell, TX
25 March 2024

30528436R00243